The Time Turner
by
Clare Solly

This book is a work of fiction. Any references to historical events, real people, or real places are used fictitiously. Other names, characters, places, and events are products of the author's imagination, and any resemblance to actual events or places or persons, living or dead, is entirely coincidental.

ISBN 978-1-5428-2320-3 (1st edition paperback)

ISBN 979-8-3859-8656-9 (2nd edition paperback)

ISBN 979-8-9890172-2-5 (3rd edition paperback)

ISBN 978-1-3706-1059-4 (1st edition ebook)

I dedicate this book to anyone who suffers
a broken heart:
May you also do something constructive with it.

"The choices you make day by day determine the person you will be. The one choice you can never make is love. It beguiles you. It captures *you*."

—Thomas Snow

"When forced to make the choice between two opposing forces, good or evil, black or white, turn away from either opposing choice given, and instead, choose yourself."

—Alexander Dunne

"We all start as strangers. The choices we make in terms of love are usually ones that seem inevitable anyway. We find people irrationally compelling. We find souls made of the same stuff ours are. We are all just waiting for another universe to collide with ours, to change what we can't ourselves. To fill us; to make us whole. It's interesting how afterwards, we realize that the storm returns to calm, but the stars are always changed and we don't choose whose collisions change us."

—Brianna Weist

"Thirty days hath September, April, June, and November.
All the rest have thirty-one,
Excepting February alone,
And that has twenty-eight days clear,
And twenty-nine each leap year."
—Mother Goose

Part One

I didn't believe in time travel. To me it was whimsical science fiction. The notion that time twists around itself infinitely was only a literary ruse to me. I definitely didn't believe time travel was possible. Although the idea of rewriting history is fascinating, the possibility that in a mere instant we can relive the past or perhaps change the future was absurd to me.

I wished to live in another time before. History intrigued me. I had always fancied sword fighting. And living in a moment where time or appointments were ideas not demands. Where people went to the market or the center of the town square to gain information on current events. Although I wanted to live in another time, but traveling to one was something I didn't believe.

Love is another story. I did—*I do* believe in love. It is a force that we cannot stop, cannot avoid and cannot shake. And I would give anything for love. Love seems to know no bounds. Not even time. It conquers all. It is timeless.

After hurting a love, we think, *if only I could go back in time, I would*. It's a hopeful wish to magically undo the pain. It's not actually a wish to travel through time. Or is it? Interestingly, it is *time* that is needed for forgiveness and we wish to speed forward to gain that salve.

Both love and time travel are non-linear, perplexing, and cannot be proven only experienced. It's funny that time travel and love aren't ever compared to each other. But I have started to look at their juxtaposition. I used to think both were fictional. Convinced my life was full, I thought I didn't need either.

And then, she appeared.

Chapter One

What was happening? Amelia Epoch stared into the twenty-foot-long bathroom mirror. Her wide-eyed reflection stared back at her from above the cool marble sinks in the dark bathroom. She had to get back to her cubicle in human resources before she was missed. She needed another moment. Her brain spun, but she couldn't make sense of it. What was that phone call? It must be a mistake, Amelia thought as she flattened her hands on the cool counter below. She couldn't believe it. Nothing surprising or even this astounding had ever happened for her before today. As she tucked a curl of naturally dark blond hair behind her ear, she thought about her life. For a cum laude graduate from Amherst, she was getting good at rejection. Even with her passion and savvy for design the recession slowed home buying. And even fewer were hiring interior designers with liberal arts degrees and no references. So here she worked as an entry level assistant in HR.

As she leaned on the cool sink basin in front of her, Amelia stood on her tiptoes a bit to see herself more clearly. The stretch was nice for her calves which were tight after her lunchtime run. Amelia began running in college to share a hobby with a boyfriend. The man didn't become part of her life but running did.

When she turned thirty a week ago she had told her friends she had a good feeling about this year while they celebrated at Hudson Terrace. Then a mysterious phone call at work about an inheritance? It must be a prank. The only living relative she had was her aunt Susan in Philadelphia who called yesterday to wish her a belated birthday. Three years ago she lost her mother to pancreatic cancer and shortly after her father to a broken heart.

New York was a new beginning. After moving to New York from Massachusetts after her parents' deaths, Amelia had built an urban family. This included her boyfriend Jack. Although they had only met six months ago, they were head over heels for each other. Their meet cute was one out of a romantic movie. Jack was out celebrating his acceptance into Doctors Without Borders with friends. Jack's passion captured Amelia instantly. She had never witnessed such fervent drive. Jack was perfect for her. His strong muscles, chestnut hair and light brown eyes that twinkled when he smiled or talked about saving a patient filled her with passion. They shared a love of running. He was six feet tall, a perfect height for Amelia.

Things progressed quickly. After their sixth date—a romantic French restaurant and a movie—Jack gave Amelia the best gift she had ever received. He gave her a toothbrush and asked her to be exclusive. Amelia, the pragmatist, was swept away by his romantic gesture mixed with practicality. Some might say they had a whirlwind romance. Speed didn't matter, but it was just right. They fit.

Three months after they met Jack got assigned to residency in Ecuador. Even though he was thrilled, he was willing to sacrifice it for Amelia.

"I won't stop you from following your dream," she shrugged. "Besides, it's a year working with your hero."

Still embracing her he said, "It will be sporadic but I will come home every two or three months," he looked at his feet.

"You have to go," she hid her sadness.

"You are an *amazing* woman," Jack said warmly as he swept her up in his arms.

The night before he left at his apartment. He packed before they lay in bed together, alternating between making love and lying in each other's arms, willing time to go slower. The next morning, he hailed a cab and handed her his spare keys. In the brisk January morning he held and kissed her. As the cab drove away her heart ached; it would be two months before she would see him. There was limited internet and terrible cell service in South America. He told her he would write, but she didn't plan on it as he would be too busy saving the world. She hugged herself, sending a silent prayer after her Superman to keep him safe wherever life was about to lead him.

Chapter Two

Her mind returned to the call as she continued to stare at her reflection in the bathroom mirror. Just after lunch her cell lit up with a 212 number. A New York number. She hesitated answering, preferring numbers she didn't know to roll to voicemail. In the middle of the fourth ring she remembered Jack was rerouted through a local number two days ago.

"Hello?" Amelia asked hesitantly

"Ms. Epoch?" an elderly voice questioned.

"Yes?" she confirmed skeptically.

"My name is Banks, and I'm from the law firm Albert, Banks, Banks and Smith. We represent a client who has left you an inheritance."

Immediately she thought it was a scam.

"Who was this relative you represent?" Amelia asked, buying time while searching the internet for the law firm the mysterious caller represented.

"I didn't say a relative, Ms. Epoch. It is an old client of ours. In fact, I was given very specific instructions on how to handle this case."

"Ah, and what were you supposed to do, Mr....." Amelia was still waiting for the results to pop up. Why was the Internet so slow?

"Banks."

"Right. So, Mr. Banks. What were those instructions?"

"Well, Ms. Epoch…"

"Amelia. Please, call me Amelia," she agitatedly insisted.

"Yes, well, Ms. Epoch," Amelia grimaced at the formality of the man on the line and the slow computer speed. The internet started to spit results as the man continued talking. No matches yet. "You see, it was stipulated in the will that we were to meet with you in person, preferably at our offices, to complete the legalities."

"Right. And where exactly *are* your offices?" She silently urged the computer to move faster. Finally! A weblink. She clicked. It rerouted and started to load.

"We are located on Amsterdam at Sixty-third Street," Mr. Banks said just like a New Yorker, giving the location without offering an address. "We are happy to meet you at your convenience, Ms. Epoch."

"Of course, you are," she said skeptically. The website was still loading. Her irritation made the wait more infuriating. She would have the tech guy assess the Internet speed. Finally a website popped up showcasing a picture of four men on the banner, and stoic gold lettering that read:

Law Firm of Albert, Banks, Banks and Smith, since 1873.
Wow. This was probably legitimate, Amelia thought as she
sat back in her chair.

"Alright, Mr. Banks. I think I can fit you into my
schedule. Does 12:30 tomorrow sound alright?" Amelia
asked. "I can come during my lunch break."

"Of course, Ms. Epoch." He continued giving the
building number and floor. "Just check in with the
receptionist when you arrive," he said to end the call.

Although she knew he had clicked off, she replied with
a haughty, "Tah tah!"

Questions bounced in her head and she walked to the
restroom to splash some water on her face.

"Ugh," she exclaimed to herself in the echo chamber of
the restroom. "I probably got left a cat with its own trust
fund or a musty book collection." She started to ponder.
Maybe there was a way to get out of it. Maybe if she didn't
show up, she wouldn't she wouldn't have to take care of the
cat. She sighed and went back to her desk, refusing to think
about it.

After work, Amelia had plans for dinner and was the last
to arrive. Her two best friends were happy to see her. Toni
was the self-proclaimed "Samantha" of the group, as the
Sex and the City archetype would have it, because she was
blonde, driven, and sexually ambitious. Alexia was an
opportunistic brunette who always was on a trend diet and
had a new designer purse to brag about. These two women
were a New York craft cocktail of anxiety and ambition and
a were great sounding board for anything.

Revealing her phone conversation only moments after her arrival, Amelia asked their opinions on the mystery inheritance. Alexia, having gotten three promotions and her own office in just two years said, "Amelia it wouldn't hurt to go check the place out, especially if the law firm seems legitimate."

"Mostly inheritances are a good thing, even in that Diane Keaton movie with the baby," Toni added. "I'm intrigued!"

They exhausted all possibilities. At the end of the night Amelia felt excited. Her mind whirred with hope as she ascended to the subway hollering a promise to call the both gals the moment she left the lawyer's office.

Chapter Three

F ive minutes early to her appointment, she arrived at the lawyer's office. The elevator opened to reveal a circular, floor-to-ceiling chestnut-paneled reception area. A brunette watchdog in her 50s, with a harsh bob curled at the starched collar of her skirt-suit, sat behind the oversized reception desk confirmed her 12:30 appointment and quickly picked up the receiver of the phone beside her. Amelia stepped away to wait, when she saw the wall gilded with the partner names. She started to wonder if she needed to specify which Banks.

"Mr. Banks said he will meet you in the conference room, Ms. Epoch," the receptionist motioned for Amelia to follow her through giant glass doors. They made a quick turn into a large conference room made completely of glass. In the room was an oval table surrounded by twenty chairs with water pitchers and glasses sporadically placed.

"Please have a seat," the receptionist said coolly. "Would you care for a beverage?"

"No, thank you," Amelia shivered as she sat placing her purse on the table. The receptionist left. Amelia's imagination spun. Then a little man with a slight hunch in his back, a beak of a nose and snowy white hair waddled into the room carrying a large box of papers.

"Thank you for meeting me, Ms. Epoch. I'm Albert Banks," he said.

"Nice to meet you, Mr. Banks." Starting to stand but immediately sat as he waved her back down. She watched while he pulled out several papers and placed them meticulously on the table. "Are you the first one or the second one?" Amelia asked, trying to force a joke. "On the sign? Um... I mean, the name of the law firm?"

His smile was warm and sparkled with pride. "Well, I'm actually the third, but the other partners didn't want Banks, Banks and Banks. Especially with the others having passed away." He chuckled again. Noticing Amelia's confusion, he explained, "You see, my grandfather and his brother started this firm back in the 1870's. We have been an institution for over one hundred and fifty years. I did earn my partnership here, as did my father before me. It was a tradition to keep two Banks' names..." he drifted off as he looked back up at her sitting in front of him, trying to take it all in. "Ah, but I digress. Let's talk about why you are here, shall we?" He sat and folded his hands as he looked at her. "Ms. Epoch—"

"Amelia, please."

"Yes, yes... Ms—Amelia... you are quite a lucky girl. You have just inherited a tidy amount."

She cringed. "A cat, right? I've inherited a cat, and the trust fund to keep it alive for the next sixty years."

"No, Ms. E—Amelia, you have not inherited a cat. You have inherited a brownstone in Park Slope and you have received a trust that can pay you up to $3000 a month for forty years, with a $200,000 expense account to renovate the house."

It was too much for her. "WHAT?!?" she said.

"You have inherited," Mr. Banks began to repeat in his warm baritone, "a brownstone in Park—"

"Brooklyn? I've inherited a house in Brooklyn," she said with her nose scrunched in confusion.

"I assure you Amelia, this is a good neighborhood," he explained, misreading her reaction. "This firm has been overseeing the house for a good many years."

"What do you mean, 'a good many years'?" Her eyes were filled with confusion.

"Well, it is difficult to explain," Banks continued, "The rules set out in the documents drawn up for this particular inheritance and trust state I'm not allowed to," he cleared his throat, "disclose too much about the nature of the transaction to you. This property was entrusted to this legal firm many years ago. It and the trust were not to be known to you, as specified by the notarized documents drawn up," Banks said as he gently patted the papers in front of him with his hand arched, so only his fingertips touched them, "until the specified date, which was yesterday, February 1, 2012. The firm was to act as legal guardian over the property and to rent it out to qualified and reliable renters until last month. The tenants have vacated per their lease, and the place is to be yours as soon as papers have been signed. All monies earned by the residence have been added to a previously established trust, which were put in the hands of an investor to ensure it continually grew. This was done to ensure you would receive the most money possible upon inheritance. All of it is yours, once you sign these papers here." Mr. Banks passed three sheets of paper over to her along with a pen.

All three pages were filled with legal jargon, and each had a small sticky arrow that said "sign here" and pointed to signature lines under which read "beneficiary — Amelia Epoch."

"So...no mangy cat."

"No, Ms. Epoch. No cat. Only a house and a tidy sum of money." He paused before going on. "I hope that is satisfactory. You can always purchase a cat with the inheritance money, if you so desire."

Amelia picked up the pen hesitantly, and held it poised over the first line, but stopped before signing. "And this money is free and clear? Mine?" she clarified.

"Yes, we have been keeping up with the taxes and fees, and all were covered by the trust. You shall receive a check each month in the amount of $3000, or you can specify a lesser amount if you wish for the trust to pay you out for a longer amount of time. The renovation amount will be wired to a bank of your choice, and receipts must be kept for all transactions made for the renovation for tax purposes. The first of the pages in front of you legally transfers the deed of the house to you. The second, the renovation money. The third is your trust. As you can see on the third you can specify a lesser amount, or you can contact us in the future for that."

Amelia looked up and squinted. "What's the catch?"

"No catch, I assure you," Banks stated calmly as if it was a daily occurrence to have someone inherit a house and a trust fund.

"And if I don't sign these papers, what happens to all of it?" Amelia still held the pen floating above the paper.

"Well, there is a clause here that states if not claimed the money goes to The Library Fund of New York."

"So, I can have the house and all the money, or it goes … to buy books?"

"Precisely, madam."

"Mr. Banks," Amelia said, knuckles turning white as she gripped the table with her empty hand, "is this real?"

"I assure you, it's all real. All on the up and up." he replied jovially.

"Where did it come from?" She marveled.

Banks smiled and seemed to get excited and in a conspiratorial voice said, "An author, actually. Alexander Frank was his name. I think I have an… Ah! Yes, here." Banks rifled through the papers, and passed a black and white photo to her. A handsome man with light hair and round glasses, smiled back at her. Amelia didn't recognize him, but something about his face struck her.

"Are we related?" She reached out and touched the photo with her fingertips.

"He wished his reason for being your benefactor to remain unbeknownst. I'm sorry."

"Oh." Amelia sighed trying to figure another angle for information. Her curiosity itched like an insect bite.

"Ms. Epoch, I realize that this is a lot to take in." Banks had misinterpreted her sigh. "Perhaps you'd like to consult your own lawyer and return another day?"

Suddenly clarity broke through her confusion. "This could be the stupidest thing I've ever done, but for some reason, it seems right," Amelia said, feeling an amazing wash of strength. "If I sign, will you be available to me if I have problems or questions?"

"Yes, I am the trustee and can be consulted about your inheritance."

"Great," Amelia said resolutely. And with a flourish signed all three documents stealing a glance at the photo of Alexander Frank in between each. "Is that all?"

"Yes, that is all for today," Mr. Banks replied as he collected up all of the papers on the table.

"Mr. Banks, thank you so much." Amelia stood. Then she looked at the photo and saluted. "Well, Alexander, thanks for the inheritance."

"I'm sure we'll speak again soon. Let me know where your first check should be deposited. And here," he said, reaching a hand to her, "are the keys and the address."

As soon as the metal clinked in her hand, the rest was a blur. She vaguely remembered giving Banks her bank information. The image of Alexander's photo was burned in her brain. The crinkles of his eye made her smile and she wondered what was making him laugh. It looked like he was almost blushing. He was quite handsome and looked to be in his 30s.

Mr. Banks took the photo, slid it into a folder and placed it in the box. Closing the lid quickly. He caught Amelia peering into the box.

"Nothing for you to worry about now, my dear. More things that deal with the trust. I'll walk you out," he said, as he opened the door for her. Amelia looked back curiously at the box as she walked out the door.

Banks walked her to the elevator and gave her his card. Pocketing the card, her fingers caressed the keys to her house. Her new house. In Brooklyn. Well, so much for never moving off the island of Manhattan. She owned a house. Amelia smiled as she pressed the button for the lobby. At street level, she pulled out her cell and dialed Alexia's office. She knew Toni would be waiting and a three-way shriekfest was about to happen via speakerphone.

Chapter Four

Luckily, her friends had the Saturday available after Amelia's inheritance was revealed so they went to check it out together. The entire subway trip to Brooklyn, Alexia complained about the distance and how she didn't understand how anyone could move out of Manhattan. Toni couldn't stop mentioning "this great bakery" from some cooking show and kept insisting they had to go to it even though it was nowhere near Amelia's new address in Park Slope.

They got off the F train, which only Alexia had ever ridden one drunk New Year's Eve, at Seventh Avenue and walked the few blocks to the address the lawyer had provided on Polhemus Place. As they walked up Amelia could swear she felt a pull to the building. In awe they looked up at the edifice of the stunning five-story Beaux-Arts style brownstone. The front of the house had an amazing amount of windows. The building, mostly white limestone, had stone carvings that swirled and scalloped their way along the front marking the different floors and bay windows just asking to be reading nooks. Banks had told Amelia that the lower level had been made into its own apartment, and that she could rent it out, if she so desired, but it had its own kitchen, bedroom, living room, and bathroom. There was an entrance to it from the main house as well.

"You own this?" asked Alexia in an astonished tone.

"Yes," said Amelia.

"No, but you *own* this."

"Yes."

"Wow."

"Yeah, wow," Toni finally chimed in.

"Well, we can stand out here like a pack of idiots," Amelia teased, "or we can see what wonders await us."

"You sound like Willy Wonka," Alexia laughed.

"Follow me," Amelia bounded up to the front door, keys jingling.

Putting the key in the lock she audibly sighed. She opened the door and walked over the threshold. This was hers, this brownstone. The whole house. The only other property she ever owned was a used car she had before moving to New York.

Once inside, they all took off in different directions.

"There is still furniture here," Toni said.

"Yeah, the lawyer said some was abandoned by renters and some was left for me by the mysterious benefactor." Amelia shouted out.

"This place is beautiful, 'Meel. It will need a big overhaul, but it's beautiful," Alexia said in awe, making slow circles looking everywhere and nowhere at once.

"Hey, didn't you want to be an interior designer? This would be an amazing project to show off your talents."

"Yeah," she said, as she wandered peering through each door with wonder. She stopped in front of closed, teak doors she had felt drawn to. Slowly she turned the handles, but when the doors didn't open she leaned into it with her shoulder. It was warped. She made a mental note to sand the door, and then laughed to herself. Her renovation list was started.

Inside, shelves lined two walls and there were two abandoned books laying adrift on a shelf. One wall held three large glass windows that washed the room with daylight. Metal work made it look as if once held stained glass.

A moldering sofa with a popped spring sat in front of a crumbling fireplace missing many bricks, its mantle missing large chunks. She started to walk toward it when Toni called for her from another room and so she left the crumbling study.

"You have six bathrooms, a study, two different living rooms, eight possible bedrooms, a huge kitchen, a dining room, a breakfast room, a library, a huge foyer, and sixty-six steps. And that's only in the main house." Toni reported. "And here is a list of things that already need to be fixed." Toni handed a list of at least twenty things to Amelia, who sighed.

"Come on, let's go get brunch," said Alexia as she took Amelia and Toni by the arms and the left the brownstone.

***

The renovation process started slowly. Partially because Amelia had the awful feeling that the whole inheritance was a huge prank, partially because she didn't want to give up living in Manhattan. After a month, sleeping at the Brooklyn brownstone weekends and a few weeknights, Amelia realized living in two places was senseless. After going over her personal budgets she realized she could live quite comfortably on the monthly stipend. Amelia gave in and quit her job. She hired movers to empty her tiny SoHo studio and Amelia moved to Brooklyn.

Prospect Park became the place for her daily run. It helped clear her mind and organized her thoughts. She hired a contractor for the bigger projects but wanted to do smaller renovations herself. With assistance from the man at the hardware store and an online tutorial she retiled a bathroom, repaired a loose stair, and removed sagging curtain rods and sent out draperies to be cleaned.

One day after a jog she went into the study to confront the crumbling fireplace. It made her sad. It would have to be completely redone. The contractor was coming today and she would get him to quote her a price. As she turned to walk out of the room, a protruding brick caught her eye. Amelia walked to it. When touched, the brick moved. She tried shoving it back in. It moved but wouldn't go flush. Pulling it out a bit and shoving it back in again didn't work. Amelia pulled on the brick and edged it out of its hole. There was something but she couldn't see what, even on her tiptoes. She carefully reached in quietly praying there were no bugs, and felt cloth. She pulled it out to find a small pouch. She replaced the brick, which now lay flush.

Amelia looked at the little bag. Well worn, the soft velvet bag was faded purple. She loosened the drawstrings and opened the pouch holding her hands out away from her body, to prepare for creepy crawlies. To her delight, nothing crawled out and she looked in the bag. There was a crumpled piece of old tissue paper around something. Carefully she unwrapped the precious piece. It was a white gold woman's watch with a skinny bracelet-like-band and diamonds around the face. Odd, Amelia thought, why would someone hide a watch in a fireplace? It looked antique, but not as old as the house. Amelia put the watch on and a chill ran over her. She suddenly felt she was not alone and looked around the room. No one was there. Nervously, Amelia shrugged off the feeling and left the study. She distracted herself by looking up a jewelry appraiser for the watch online.

Mid-search the contractor came and they walked to the study to discuss options for the fireplace reconstruction. Amelia, hesitant to step into the room, felt nothing this time when she entered. The feeling of someone watching her was gone. The contractor set to work, and Amelia went back to painting. She put the watch in the pouch near the kitchen sink then became engrossed with renovations.

The kitchen remodel had started, the carpenters replaced wood flooring and Amelia was continuing to repaint the front hall. Between working on and monitoring all of the action, she was exhausted.

Chapter Five

In a deep sleep, Amelia dreamt about a prince rescuing her from a high balcony. She was frustrated because she didn't remember asking the construction crew to create it.

Jarring cell phone ringing woke her. Amelia didn't know why anyone was calling her this late and was very confused. A man on the line was asking how to get up to her. Groggily she rationalized this was still her dream. Was the man on the phone was the prince who got lost on his way up. Amelia felt she was awake, but maybe this was one of those dream tricks. She was just about to ask if he was the prince. But, why was he *calling*? Amelia snapped awake with the realization. She recognized the voice. Jack! He was home!

"I wanted to surprise you," Jack's voice weary with exhaustion and confusion came through the phone. "I went directly from the airport to your SoHo apartment, only to find you didn't live there. I demanded that the doorman was wrong, but he said you moved out. So I called you."

"I have moved! I'll explain when you get here," she said and told him her new address. Hopping in a cab he would arrive in thirty minutes.

Amelia got out of bed so she wouldn't fall back asleep. She dragged the big fluffy duvet from her bed to the living room. She removed the protection tarp from a section of the sofa and sat down for a moment before hopping back up again. She was so excited to see Jack, Amelia couldn't sit still.

After making sure the porch light was illuminated, Amelia went to the kitchen and sighed when she turned on the lights. The constant state of disrepair made her feel like the kitchen would never be finished. As a distraction she filled the kettle and lit the flame on the stove. She rummaged around in the cabinets and found a box of spiced Chai and grabbed her favorite Amherst mug. The old friend had seen her through nights of test-cramming and paper writing. Amelia reminisced about her college years until the teakettle woke her from remembering the first time she colored her hair. To this day she was still baffled that she ever thought black was a good hair color for her. Thick in recollection, she tore open the tea bag, turned off the flame and poured the water. Amelia strolled to the living room and snuggled into the duvet. The steam swirled off the mug and hypnotized Amelia. Before it was cool enough to take a sip, the front door buzzed. Her heart skipped a beat. She dashed toward the front door. The duvet went flying. The tea sloshed. She glanced at herself in the mirror in the front hall. She should have brushed her hair and changed into prettier pajamas.   She was wearing a ratty Columbia University shirt she had taken from Jack's apartment and pink plaid shorts. Too late now.

She pushed the talk button and asked "Jack?" She hit the listen button and was rewarded with a tired, "Yeah, it's me."

Amelia felt her stomach flip. Only two months, but so much had changed in her life. Would Jack understand any of it? She took a deep breath and reached for the door handle.

Chapter Six

With the door no longer between them, Jack's face beamed and her worry faded. He had a suitcase in each hand and a large bag draped over one shoulder. She wrapped her arms around him.

"I've missed you so much," Amelia murmured into his neck.

Jack dropped the suitcases and wrapped his arms around her. She hugged back. His face nestled into her neck. He took a deep breath taking in her smell. Their bodies pressed together for a long time. For a moment, she feared this wasn't real. Amelia leaned away and placed her hands gently on his face. She studied him a few moments before smiling even bigger and kissing his lips. He kissed her back and she lit up inside. Jack was home.

"Darling," he said nuzzling her nose, "It's so romantic standing on your stoop kissing you," Jack breathlessly breaking the kiss, "but it's the middle of the night and I need a shower and a bed."

"Right. Yes." Amelia said and backed into the house. She tried to ignore his trite demeanor. It was the middle of the night. She pushed her bruised feelings aside, smiled at him and reached for one of the suitcases.

"Don't worry, I'll get them. Point me towards my bed," said Jack in the directness she missed.

"Well, you could take your pick of bedrooms. Do you want to be in with me, or would you like to have your own so you can spread out?"

"I have missed you. But I think it would be better to have my own room to start. I'm exhausted. I'll probably sleep for days because my circadian rhythm is off. I don't want to disturb your rest."

Amelia was disappointed, but knew it was only temporary. After sleeping with fifteen other doctors in one tent, she would want space. "Follow me," she said, bright as a sorority girl, covering her disappointment. Jack didn't notice.

Amelia led him up the stairs and to the left. Her room was to the right, with a small one right next to it. Jack might prefer space to proximity. This room had the best view, would allow him to spread out, and as it was on the opposite side of the landing he could throw a party and she wouldn't hear the noise.

As they entered the room Amelia mentioned the bedroom was a little frilly, but it hadn't been redone yet. She prattled on that she was thinking of making this room blues and dark woods. Jack set the bags down, and looked around the room.

"It looks like my great-grandmother might have lived here. So many flowers on the wallpaper." As she sighed looking at the flowers with detestation, he looked at her. "I have forgotten how beautiful you are."

Their eyes linked. Slowly he approached her like a tiger stalking prey.

"Now that I've set my bags down," he whispered in her ear, "did you want to finish what you started at the front door?"

Amelia wrapped herself around him and her mouth found his. Her heartbeat raced as he pulled her in closer. In this moment, everything seemed perfect.

After a long bout of kissing they moved to the bed, where Jack's hands found their way down the back of Amelia's shorts and up the front of her Columbia shirt. After a few minutes, Amelia pushed Jack away lightly, and suggested she let him settle in and get some rest. There would be plenty of time for all of this later. She stood up and pulled him up off the bed with her. She kissed him again, wished him sweet dreams and closed his door as she left.

Just down the hall felt miles away. Alone in her bed, Amelia dreamt about kisses. Both the ones on the front porch and the ones in Jack's room. She should have been more insistent that he sleep in her room. Amelia didn't realize how much she missed him. She hoped he would come to her room, but doubt took over. They would have time, she told herself. Plenty of time. Eventually she drifted off to sleep.

Chapter Seven

Amelia's eyes took focus on a man's chest. A sleepy, "Good morning," greeted her. Moving onto her elbows, she looked at him, "You couldn't stay away? 'Sensible' is easier in theory." She stifled a chuckle.

He pulled her on top of him and kissed her. She loved how he tasted. In addition to every perfect inch of Jack, he *never* had morning breath. As their lips reacquainted and his hands caressed her hips and legs, he pulled her on top of him.

They rolled around in bed, murmuring nothings to each other. Amelia didn't know how she was going to handle more months apart. She hadn't realized how much she missed him. Her parents' lives were so dependent, and Amelia wasn't sure she wanted that. Jack had to live his own life. If situations were reversed, she hoped he would be supportive but let her soar. She would cherish this month together.

In the midst of their canoodling, her cell phone started buzzing, becoming more insistent. First George, the contractor. Next the flooring guys. Then the tile guy. Then a guy from the hardware store. After the eighth ding, Jack became mildly incensed, and pushed her gently away from him.

"You get more pages than an on-call doctor."

"It's hard to be the popular girl." Giving a fake pout she rolled away from his cozy embrace and grabbed the phone. She started texting back. By the time she was done, he was snoozing quietly beside her. She lay there and just watched him sleeping for a few moments. Burning desire filled her to reach over and brush the hair off his forehead. He looked so peaceful and innocent. Amelia leaned over and kissed him to no response. She sighed and pulled herself out of bed. The contractor was on his way over and would be here in a few minutes. She needed to change quickly. Being in her pajamas at 3am on the front porch was cute, but in front of day laborers was not. She had to keep up appearances as "the boss." Amelia put on her daily uniform of yoga pants and a tank top, and headed downstairs to make coffee and face the day.

Jack finally emerged around 3pm, the end of the construction workday. He called her name over the banging and sawing. Exhausted, he had slept through all of the renovation noise. Instead of playing a perverse game of hide and seek, she called his cell. A few seconds later, she heard his voice in a lopsided stereo sound, "This house is so big it takes a call to find you?" he teased.

"Since I didn't give you a tour, I figured it was easier than Marco Polo,"

"Marco!" he replied cheekily.

"Polo! You're getting warmer. Head straight off the stairs. I'm in the study, third door on the left."

She started to give more directions, but a second later he entered the room. Jack found her with her hands on her hips, staring at the fireplace.

"If you're looking for Harry Potter's uncle to show his face, you have to light a fire first."

"It's tragic, this crumbling thing," she sighed. "The contractor said it will cost more to fix than to rebuild. And it would be less to just wall over the whole thing." Amelia was torn because she was drawn to the fireplace. "I have made many decisions that felt easy, but I've been thinking of this fireplace for a week with no answer."

"Why don't you step away from the fireplace. Let it rest. My opinion? You have so many other fireplaces here, so why not just cover over it and put in more bookshelves or a flat screen TV?"

Amelia smirked at him and put her hands on her hips. "Leave it to a man to put up more televisions."

Jack threw his hands up in the air, "Alright, it was just a suggestion. You don't have to take it."

She crossed to him, threw her arms around his waist and drew him in for a kiss to end the argument. His stomach rumbled in response. She leaned back and addressed his abdomen, "Everyone has to put their two cents in, don't they?" and then laughed. "Come on, let's get you some food." Taking his hand, she led him to the kitchen.

Finding the refrigerator empty, they called out for Chinese. While they waited, Amelia told Jack the details of her inheritance. When the food arrived, he told her of his trip. How it was so hot, that they would shut down the clinic midday, and instead work late into the night. And his colleagues, mostly general practitioners. Jack mentioned a groundbreaking unit was opening soon that would offer surgical care for patients. Apparently, a monkey stole their supply of gauze.

Their conversation was free and easy as always. Amelia felt the love radiating between them, and felt an addition forming to keep sharing their lives like this.

During his last anecdote he fell silent. After a few minutes of awkward silence, Amelia asked, "Is there more you want to tell me, Jack?"

Jack had been avoiding her eyes, but now looked up and met them.

He cleared his throat, "My stay may not be as long as originally promised. I know I was supposed to be here for a month, but they're short-staffed, and if I want to be on the surgical staff, to work with Dr. Elias, I have to go back in a week and a half. And you know it is my dream to work with him."

Amelia was stunned and saddened. She looked at him for a moment, searching his eyes, stalling for the correct thing to say. She loved him so much, although she had never said it out loud. She wanted to beg him to stay.

There were so many exciting things happening and she wanted to include him in all of it. But it was her recent dream to renovate and decorate. It was his lifelong dream to help others. To save lives. To study with the man who inspired him—how could she ask him to stay and play house with her when that was his choice? "If you love something, set it free…" popped into her head, and her only choice could be support.

With all the composure she could muster she said, "I hate that you have to go back so soon. If I could keep you here I would. But I want you to be happy, and I don't want to be the person that holds you in my dream, only to have us both regret it."

He reached across the table and took her hand. "How do you always know what to say that champions me, and makes me adore you?"

She feigned a smile and looked down at the remnants of General Tso's chicken on her plate.

"That is how I would want you to act if we switched places," she shrugged her shoulders. There was a giant tug at her heart, but she knew this was right.

He was leaning over her, one hand on the table and one hand gently turning her face to his. She nuzzled her face into his palm, closing her eyes. He leaned in and gave her a soft kiss. A tear trailed down her face, and he wiped it away with his thumb.

"We will spend every minute with each other. So we'll get sick of each other and it will make you want to send me back to the gauze stealing monkey," he teased.

They smiled forced smiles in tandem, but both of their eyes beamed with love. Quickly he cleaned the kitchen. Afterwards, Jack led her to her bedroom, and made love to her. They were entwined in each other's arms as she fell asleep.

The next morning, she awoke alone. Jack returned to his room for rest. Amelia got dressed and made coffee. She went to the study and stared again at the fireplace. Thoughts of making this into a man cave for Jack danced across her mind. He had mentioned a flat screen and bookshelves, and why not? Why not give him a space of his own? She could do it in dark paneling and leathers. A Humphrey-Bogart-on-African-Safari feel, just without large game heads. George, the contractor, found Amelia standing in front of the fireplace. He had followed her text message to come to the study when he arrived.

"I've decided," she sighed. "It's going to be too much work to do anything else but build a wall over it. Bye-bye fireplace."

"If dat's what you want, dat's what we'll do," George said in his thick Long Island accent. He paused, for her to say something or change her mind. She sighed again, and George started making calls as he walked out of the study.

She chased after him. "Wait," she said.

"Hold on, 'arry,"he said into the phone, "Change your mind?" he said back to Amelia.

"Yes. No, I don't know. I just…. My boyfriend is home from South America.

for the rest of this week and next. Can you have your guys

take next week off? I could use a break from all the hammering," she said with a weak smile.

"Sure, sure. 'arry, lemme call you back. Ms. Epoch," he said with a long E, "we can do whatevah you want. We are ahead a' schedule, and I have a coupla jobs I can throw my guys on. Why don't you take some time, think about the fireplace *and* the kitchen cabinets? I've got a great cabinet-maker for you. Just call when you're ready."

"Thanks, George. You're the best."

"Nah, it's no problem. We'll see ya later. And don't fugeddaboud the kitchen cabinets," he emphasized over his shoulder as he walked out of the house.

Well, Amelia thought as she locked the front door, that was easy. But—the fireplace! She still hadn't made a decision. It niggled at her brain. Something was holding her back from ripping it out. Ah well, she would figure it out eventually. Now she and Jack would have time alone and not have to worry about the hours they kept or worry about wearing clothes. Just the thought made Amelia rush upstairs. She tossed aside her yoga pants and jumped in her pajamas. She headed down the hall to Jack's room and snuggled into him. The thoughts of the fireplace had completely disappeared.

Chapter Eight

Although Jack was only home for ten days, Amelia made the most of them. They took walks around the neighborhood. They snuggled on the living room sofa. They read together in the dining room while eating any and all kinds of take out.

Amelia would sneak off to sketch or brainstorm in a room that needed work. Jack thought she did this to take space for herself, and would give her as long as he could before seeking her. Both lit up when reunited. When together, they would continually touch. Holding hands, intertwining fingers, brushing knees, nudging toes.

Jack constantly tried to make Amelia laugh or smile. Like teenagers, they made out all over the house. Amelia was continually asking Jack his opinions on colors, trim, curtains, and wall hangings as to include him. One night over dinner, she officially asked him, "Would you like to move in and share this house with me?" She regretted her awkward phrasing the moment it left her mouth.

"Share, as in split-a-meal, share? Or share as in: go to the," he held up his hands and made air-quotes, "next step in our relationship?"

"The second one?" Not meaning to make her statement a question and terrified of his answer, looked down at her plate.

"Yes," Jack said and looked at her intently.

"Yes?" she raised her head, surprised.

Jack offered a nervous chuckle, "You keep speaking in questions, do you realize that? Now you have me doing it. Yes, Amelia, I would like to live with you. Yes, I would like to renovate with you."

She jumped up and throwing her arms around his neck, dotted his cheek with kisses.

He turned toward her and with his arms drew her in. She gazed into his eyes. She had never been as sure of anything as she was at this moment. "I love you," she said and he responded by drawing her in and kissing her deeply. It was only the second time she had said that in a relationship.

Jack contacted his apartment rental office and gave notice. One day he went over to his apartment and brought back four large boxes in a cab.

"This is most of my personal stuff. I've donated the furniture." And as easy as that, Jack moved in. Amelia was happier than she could ever remember. Life had a purpose and a goal. She had the house and she had Jack. It was amazing.

All of her happiness could not delay his return to South America. Sadly, his departure came much too quickly. As his cab pulled up Amelia tried her hardest to look happy, wanting the last thing he was her most supportive face.

He leaned in to kiss her one last time. "I love you so very much. And this gift you're giving me is incredible." It was the first time he said he loved her. It wasn't as she imagined it. Nor was it perfect. But her heart swelled, and her smile was real.

She let out a big sigh, "I love you enough to let go, knowing you'll come back to me. Now, go before I start crying and chain you to my bedposts and never let you leave the house."

He chuckled, kissed her again, and hopped in the cab. She waved until his cab turned the corner.

As she turned and went back inside, she decided to start working. She thought about painting the room Jack stayed in, to get rid of those god-awful roses, but it was too soon to go in there. Instead she decided to varnish the stairway railing. It was raw wood and was the last thing the construction team sanded. Regaining drive and momentum, Amelia's spirit lifted, and she ran the last few steps to her room.

Chapter Nine

Later that evening, Amelia was washing paint brushes in the kitchen. She looked over at the counter and saw the black velvet pouch peeking out from underneath a tile sample. Drying her hands, she grabbed the pouch holding the forgotten watch.

It was beautiful and delicate with its white gold link band and nickel sized face. Instead of numbers the twelve, six and nine were skinny arrows. And instead of the three a rotating date.

Three tiny gold hands had stopped telling time. Turning the watch over, she found an engraved address. Odd to have an address as an inscription. It was a New York address. Some New York places were around for centuries. If it existed still, she could possibly unravel more of this mystery. If nothing else, she could get the battery replaced.

She took the watch upstairs. Her laptop was in her room until the front room would be finished. She was converting it into an office and formal living room. Amelia thrived designing the interior. Lately she had been dreaming of opening a design firm. As the computer booted up, she fleshed out the idea of a design business. She could take pictures of this house and use it as the beginning of her portfolio.

The computer chimed and automatically opened the Internet search page. She typed in the address from the back of the watch. The search returned a listing for Lawson's Jewelers.

Amelia called the number and got a pre-recorded, androgynous elderly voice stating the hours of operation. Tomorrow was Friday and they were open until 5pm. Amelia decided to take a trip to the city.

On the subway for the first time in weeks, Amelia remembered to text Toni and Alexia to see about meeting them for lunch.

The loud and aggressive street of the jewelry district accosted her senses and the winking diamonds that even with ten times her inheritance she couldn't afford, taunted. She walked past her destination the first time, it wasn't clearly marked and the store windows distracted her. On her second pass, she found it. It was a small window, not even two feet wide, with a glass door on one side leading to apartments or offices, and a wooden door with a buzzer next to it with a tiny label that said Lawson's Jewelers. She rang the buzzer three times before receiving an answer.

"Who is it?" asked a crackly older voice—one Amelia recognized from the recording.

"I have a watch that I need repaired," Amelia said haltingly and stumbled over her words.

"Who?"

"I need a watch battery," Amelia shouted this time, attracting looks from passersby on the street.

"We don't need any."

"But—"

The door didn't buzz, and Amelia could feel that the conversation had ended. Undeterred and curious about this watch, Amelia pressed the buzzer again.

"Who is it?" The voice was a bit angry now, and reminded Amelia a bit of the munchkin when he told Dorothy: Nobody gets to see the wizard.

"My name is Amelia Epoch. I found a watch in my fireplace and it needs its battery replaced. It—"

Before she could say anymore, the door buzzed signaling that it was unlocked. Opening the door she found a long dark staircase. She climbed, feeling like she was in a film noir, about to knock on the private detective's door.

When she reached the top of the staircase Amelia saw the door she imagined for the private investigator, but instead it read:

Lawson's Jewelers

Samuel Mercer, Jeweler

Not knowing the procedure, Amelia decided knocking was the best option. No need to poke the dragon that was inside and anger it further.

Rapping on the window twice, Amelia was rewarded with the sound of shuffling feet, and a "Come in, come in," the welcoming person on the other side of the door had been expecting her.

Tentatively, she turned the knob and pushed the door inward. When she poked her head through, she saw a hunched man, who was probably about her height if he could stand straight, coming toward her.

"Don't dawdle in the doorway, my dear. Come in, come in," he said shuffling to the high wooden counter that was just inside the door.

Amelia closed the door behind her and took the two steps forward to the counter. She took in the room. To her right, there were a few desks with papers and all kinds of tools spread all over each one, with large armed magnifying glasses standing sentinel at each. To the left on the counter was a very large brass, antique cash register, complete with the peg buttons, and the pop up prices inside the glass that ran across the top of the machine. Amelia wondered if it worked or if it was just a novelty. Next to it was a brand new credit card machine and a phone and answering machine combo with the light flashing. The countertop turned to glass showing a few scattered pieces of jewelry sitting in the case, but a lot seemed to be missing from the mannequin necks and the clear resin blocks sitting in the cases. Amelia wondered if business was that bad, or that good. She could feel his eyes on her as she took in the room, and turned her attention to him.

"Mr. Lawson, I—"

"Mr. Mercer. I won this place fair and square in a poker game many years ago. My brother-in-law never knew what hit him," he said, reminiscent as if expecting Amelia would already know the story and join in with laughter. He chuckled quietly, and then looked her directly in the eye and asked, "Did you say your last name was Epoch?"

"Yes, but—"

"Ah, so you found the watch then."

"How do you know—"

"Ah, dearie, one knows many things as an old man in the jewelry business. And watches, the time keepers, are very important."

Amelia feeling more intrigued and also mildly alarmed, smiled and reached for the pouch in her purse. "Yes, and it needs a new battery. Your address is inscribed on the back, so I thought it would be best if I came here to have it fixed."

"And you're curious about its origin and are wondering if I will tell you more about it."

"Exactly," Amelia smiled, relaxing a little.

"Well, dearie, this watch is special. As are you. I cannot tell you more about it. You'll have to just experience the joys of the watch for yourself," he said in a very authoritative way as he shuffled off to one of the worktables. "Have a seat. It won't be but a few minutes," he shouted back at her.

Amelia thought that this was a very curious situation. She wasn't going to get much out of this man. He knew more. She sighed and she pulled out her cell phone, and flipped through the different apps on the phone. She found the game she was fond of playing. It was a beat-the-clock kind of game where one moved around jewels to their matches.

Before she knew it, he was standing directly in front of her, holding out the watch. She jumped, because she didn't hear him shuffle up to her.

"Oh, you scared me!"

"Sorry, dearie. Here you go. She's working again. I checked her over quickly to make sure all of her gears were working smoothly and not in need of grease or replacement."

"Oh, thank you. How much?"

"It didn't need any grease, dearie. It was all in perfect condition."

"No," she chuckled at the misunderstanding, "I meant, how much do I owe you."

"Ah, well, you see, I was told to do whatever repairs necessary on that watch for no charge to the holder at any time."

"Oh. Who gave you those instructions? Mr. Banks?"

"Banks? No. He's in charge of the paperwork. Not the watch." He grimaced. "Now, off with you. No more questions. I can't answer them anyway. I have a lot of work to do now, dearie," he said as he put the watch in its velvet pouch, handed it to Amelia and shooed her out the door.

Turning around to say thank you, the door shut and locked, and she heard quick steps going away from the door.

"How very peculiar," she said.

Amelia was about to ponder more on the subject when her phone buzzed. She put the velvet pouch in her purse so she could read the texts. Neither one was free—Alexia was on a deadline, Toni had just returned from lunch, so Amelia left the building, grabbed a sandwich at the local deli, and walked to the F train and headed home.

Chapter Ten

Arriving at her brownstone, Amelia still felt the novelty of being a homeowner. She looked up and took a moment every time she walked to the front door. This was hers. Continuing up the steps, the wonder faded a bit. Remembering all the things still to do to get the house into livable shape, sighed as she turned the key in the lock. There was mail scattered on the floor from the mail slot. Bending over to pick up all the pieces, she was overjoyed about having her own mail slot. After she put her purse and keys on the table she thumbed through the mail. Most of it was junk. The nice thing about having a trust and owning a house was that there were very few bills. She was paying for things when she bought them, and the bills came in marked paid. Often she felt she was about to run out of money, but the bank account showed a large balance. It was somewhat of a relief. Living paycheck to paycheck was a stressful way to live.

Amelia heard her phone buzz, and she reached into her purse to retrieve it. She grabbed the velvet pouch encasing the watch as well. Alexia was asking if she was still in the city and wondering if she wanted to get drinks tonight. Amelia texted back with one hand that she was back in Brooklyn but wanted a rain check. She had fallen behind in her painting, which she had to finish before the floor installer could finish. Plopping the phone back in her purse, she took her junk mail and sandwich wrapper in one hand and the velvet pouch in the other into the kitchen. With her hands free, she unwrapped the watch. She snapped it onto her wrist. It fit perfectly.

It was an interesting watch. Not one she would choose for herself, as it was very delicate and didn't seem very practical. It was more of a bracelet with the added bonus of being able to tell the time, as long as you had strong glasses or squinted. While she examined it, Amelia wondered who the previous owner was, and how the watch came to find its last home behind the brick. Was it a secret? Mr. Mercer didn't want to reveal much. It was all very puzzling. Amelia sighed. Answers about the watch only lead to more questions. One more thing that went along with the mystery of this house.

Amelia sighed and decided to paint before she got too tired. It was a cool day for the first day of March and with the windows open, there was a nice cross breeze. She ran upstairs and changed into her comfy old yoga clothes, which were now her paint clothes.

Halfway down the stairs, Amelia realized she forgot to take the watch off. She didn't want to get paint on it, and thought she would head down to the kitchen and just put it back in its pouch. Amelia glanced down at it to check the time. She realized that the date displayed on the face was a day behind. It said 31. Removing it from her wrist while walking, Amelia was in the hall and stopped, having difficulty pulling the pin out. It was tight and tiny, and kept slipping from between her pointer finger and her thumb when she tried to pull. About to give up, Amelia finally had success when the pin gave way. She started walking again, turning the pin, and wondering why the crazy old man didn't set the date while he was checking out the watch. Amelia stopped again, only a few steps down the hall. The pin was harder to turn than it first allowed. Almost as if the watch was not wanting to change the date. Amelia laughed to herself, imagine, a watch that wanted to stay in the past. Finally, the 31 gave way to the 1 and as Amelia pushed the pin back into the watch, the lights flickered.

Chapter Eleven

Right away she knew something was different. The light was different. No, she told herself. There is *no* way the light just changed. But it had. She could *swear* it had. Goosebumps made their way from her wrists up to her shoulders, as if a ghost was caressing her. It *was* brighter a moment ago. She reasoned that a bulb must have blown. Thinking this, she looked up to the ceiling at the hall light. That was odd. It wasn't there. She hadn't been living here long, so maybe on her absentminded walk down the hall she had passed the light and kept walking. She took a few steps back the way she had come, staring up at the ceiling. Nope. No light fixtures. None at all.

And what was that scent? It was like she was visiting her grandparents—it smelled like freshly baked sugar cookies, and pipe tobacco.

Perplexed at the missing lights and the change in smell, Amelia hadn't heard the steps coming up behind her. So she literally jumped when she heard his voice.

"And who, pray tell, are you, dear?"

The voice was warm and baritone, but questioning with a strong formality.

Amelia turned around to face this sudden apparition in her house, and she was surprised to see a man with sandy brown hair, slicked to one side, with round glasses perched on his nose, guarding his soft grey eyes. His forehead crinkled, showing his puzzlement but his mouth was in a tiny smirk that threatened to turn into an amused smile. He was a bit taller than Amelia but didn't tower over her like Jack. She supposed if she were wearing heels that she and this stranger would be eye to eye.

Amelia was terrified by the presence of a man, this intruder, extremely handsome or not. She was sure she had locked all of the doors, but at the same time there was something familiar about those glasses and the squinty eyes that peered back at her.

As she had not answered his question, the stranger continued, "Are you an applicant for the upstairs maid?" He then continued to himself, "I told Mrs. Finnegan that we don't need *two* maids for only me," as he gave a frustrated sigh.

Amelia could not take this anymore and she almost shrieked, "What are you doing in my house?"

"Your house? My dear, this is my house."

"I just inherited this house this past month. I suppose I'll have to call Mr. Banks. This is ridiculous!" Amelia looked for her cell phone to give Mr. Banks a piece of her mind—the nerve! Not telling her that there were two inheritors! As she turned suddenly to follow through with this mission, she tripped over her rustling skirts. "Damn, this skirt is too—" before she could finish the thought, Amelia realized she was wearing a full-length skirt. One that went all the way to the ground. She didn't *own* any floor length skirts. She would *never own* a full-length skirt, especially not big fluffy, flouncy ones that some mother would put on her daughter if entered in a beauty pageant or for a reenactment as a southern belle.

She turned back to the stranger, who had grabbed her elbow to steady her as she started to tumble. As Amelia jerked her elbow out of his helpful hand, she looked at him and exclaimed, "What in the hell is going on here?"

"My dear lady," her helpful accoster said in a calm tone, "what a colorful vocabulary you possess. Now, may I suggest we proceed into my study and we can discuss the predicament before us?"

"How do I know I can trust you?"

"Well, uh, my dear, that is a valid point. I fear the only thing to offer you is my word as a gentleman, that the only weapon I have ever taken up is the pen."

Amelia then noticed for the first time the thick pieces of paper that the stranger was holding. Was that calligraphy? She looked back up at his smiling face. Something was so familiar about him, but she just couldn't put her finger on it.

The strange man took Amelia's changed look as an agreement. He turned and moved in the direction of the study, which Amelia knew to be in shambles. Amelia could not understand why he would want to talk things over in a dusty room with very little furniture, a crumbling fireplace that still needed renovation, and drop cloths everywhere. However, she knew there was a hammer, some large boards, and a fire poker in that room in case he tried something and she needed to protect herself.

Trust washed over Amelia the moment after she thought about the different possible weapons in the study. She looked up with her newly found trust to see that the stranger had started down the hall and was almost to the study door. Amelia caught up with him and almost ran into his back. When he stopped, he opened the door into the study for her.

Amelia walked through the door, looking back over her shoulder to say thank you. After she muttered her gratitude and turned to look where she was headed, she stopped abruptly by the sight of the room. A fire flickered in the fireplace. A fireplace that was whole. Flames danced in gas lamps above the carved white marble mantle. A tufted mustard-colored sofa with carved wooden legs and arms sat in front of the fire. To the right was a large leather wingback chair. If one were sitting in the chair, there was a direct view of the oversized mahogany desk that was the centerpiece of the room. Another large chair was behind the desk with three beautiful stained glass windows behind. A small wooden chair sat in front of the desk. And in between where Amelia now was frozen and the desk was a round, buttoned settee that was a similar color to the sofa.

It would have seemed completely out of place had it not similar upholstery.

Amelia took two steps forward into the room, as the stranger closed the door to the study, stepped around her and crossed to the desk. Placing his papers on the leather blotter that lay in the center of the mess that was on his desk, he picked up the teacup and saucer that were waiting there, and raised the cup to his lips. As he did, Amelia recognized the china pattern.

"You're drinking out of my china!" she said, pointing an accusing finger at him. It had arrived in a package from Mr. Banks last week with a note of apology that it should have been given to her when she was in his office.

The handsome stranger paused mid-sip as his forehead crinkled again.

"My dear woman, this china was my mother's. It came as a gift from the Chinese ambassador. I can absolutely assure you that you may have something similar, but this is hand painted and original."

"But I..." Amelia could not finish her thought or her path across the room. Her knees gave way and she plopped down on the oversized, firm settee that seemed placed in this very spot as if it were here just to catch her. She thought it odd for a fleeting moment that the thing was here, but too many other things were overloading her brain and senses.

When she looked up, he was standing next to her, looking concerned and proffering her a full teacup. She looked up and met his eyes, gave half a smile, and took the teacup. She lifted it to her lips without thinking and took a large sip. As she swallowed, it burned her throat with smoky warmth. She started to cough and sputter. After a few moments, she regained a normal breathing pattern, and said huskily, "That isn't tea."

"No. I thought your state and this situation called for something stronger. That, my dear, is twelve-year-old rye whiskey."

"Oh," she said, looking down into the cup. She stared at the brown liquid for a second, then brought the cup to her lips again, and downed the contents. Amelia reasoned in the moment before she upended the cup that all of this might be easier to digest if she was less sober, or maybe it would all just disappear. He made a few protestations and hesitant sounds while she swallowed, but as soon as she was done, the man sat quietly to her left side on the settee.

"Well, now," she said, feeling the warmth creep through her belly. "Why don't you start from the beginning and tell me how you got here?"

He chuckled as he removed the cup from her hands and crossed back to his desk.

"My name is Franklin Dunne. I am a novelist. I moved into this house about six months ago when I inherited it from my aunt. The last of my living relatives."

He proceeded to tell Amelia about what he wrote, about his mother dying when he was young, and how he was raised by nannies, maids, and Mrs. Finnegan, who worked for his family for as long as he could remember. His father died when he was at university, which was fortuitous, as his father wanted him to be a lawyer, a profession for which Franklin had no passion. When his father passed, he switched his focus to writing. His father left a small inheritance and a house, which Franklin didn't need, so he sold the property and rented a room in lower Manhattan for a bit. His aunt, whom he visited frequently, would always offer that he live here with her, but he loved living on the island. Eventually, she passed away leaving a huge inheritance and this large brownstone.

After they talked for a while about his past he asked her a few questions about herself. She told him where she came from, that she was from the future. She felt so discombobulated, that the truth seemed easier to tell. In a gauzy haze that made this whole situation feel unreal, Amelia told him that she had inherited this house from a wealthy benefactor and was only told about it a month previously, in her time, by Banks, her attorney. She mentioned that the year she came from was 2012 and that she was dressed in that time in stretchy pants and a tank top, not the clothes she was wearing now.

"Would you consider those undergarments?" he asked her.

"No, but they were casual clothing and are meant to not inhibit the body during exercise. I was wearing them because they were comfortable."

"Ah, well that sort of explains why you are dressed, shall we say, 'down'? It sounds like the items you were wearing could be undergarments in these times."

They continued to talk about the situation. She told Franklin about the loose brick in the fireplace, and even moved from her seat to point it out. Sure enough, it was not secure in this time either. She showed him the watch mentioning she found it behind the brick, and he examined it while it was still on her wrist. He removed the brick with some effort, as it was not quite as loose now as it was in her time. Finding nothing was behind it, he replaced the brick.

Chapter Twelve

They continued to chat as the afternoon wore on. Both felt very comfortable with this companionship. Sharing their pasts seemed easy and harmless. They both wanted to keep the conversation flowing. She sat on the loveseat in front of the fireplace, and he sat down in the great leather chair to the side. A heavy silence fell over the room before Amelia sighed. Franklin turned his head suddenly at the break in silence when she started to speak.

"How am I here?"

"That I don't know."

"Why does it feel like this is exactly where I am supposed to be, even though it is unfathomable that I am here, one hundred years before I was ever in this house?"

"That I don't know either," he said and he chuckled.

"What?" she asked.

"It is a totally ridiculous situation, one that Stevenson or Defoe might write about. Time travel. We mustn't tell anyone else about where you actually came from. They will think you daft, or worse. We must tell them that you are...," Franklin drifted off and paced. He suddenly stopped and turned to Amelia. This woman, this rather beautiful woman, just popped up in his house. It was too paradisiacal not to be real, and as an author he did have an avid imagination. She seemed to be telling the truth. Besides, his mother had once said something... But maybe she was just trying to escape the terrible marriage that she had with his father. Suddenly the memory of his parents triggered an idea. "That's it!" He shouted so loud, Amelia jumped, "We will tell everyone that you are my wife."

"What?" Amelia snapped her head toward him at this proposition thinking he must be crazy or joking, or both.

"I know it sounds preposterous. Maybe it is a terrible idea but it might work. If you are all right with playing along. Well, it works perfectly for me. Well, and for you too. You see, everyone in this part of town knows that I am the only surviving heir to my aunt's estate, including this house. They also know that I am an eligible bachelor. Yes." He started to pace again. "Actually, this suits both of us quite well, in fact. If you pretend to be my new wife, from...Manhasset, or Massachusetts, and we can make up whatever backstory we need for you and—"

"Wait. We are going to just say that I'm your wife? Wouldn't that cause issues?"

"No, actually." He replied smiling. "I was happily living as a poor bachelor, writing my stories and doing my research. Making an impoverished, but sustainable living. Then, unfortunately, I inherited this house and twenty thousand a year, making me one of the most eligible bachelors in New York City. You don't know how *exhausting* it is to be eligible. So many mothers who 'just happened to be in the neighborhood with an extra basket of baked goods, and oh, wouldn't it be lovely to have her daughter come over and help me with something?' Ugh," he shook his head. "No, having a wife is just the thing. You're perfect.

"And this will be a wonderful cover for you until we get your situation sorted out," he continued. "You can remain here, and we can try to figure out how you got here, and even more importantly, how to get you back. In the meantime, you posing as my wife—"

"But... your *wife*...I have a *life* and a ...person, a man... back in my time, presuming I can get back to my time... but even if I can't I don't know that I could... take up being your wife. Just automatically sharing your bed, and offering proper amounts of public affection—"

"My dear," he said warmly, "this is 1912. The only public affection that good society allows is your hand on mine as I escort you to and from places, and helping you in and out of a carriage. What happens behind closed doors no one knows, except the servants. And mine... well, I have only two, and need for none. In this age, men and women have separate rooms. If you never saw me for weeks, my dear, it would be a perfectly acceptable marriage according to society."

"Oh." Amelia was silent for a few minutes while she worked it out in her head. "So, by agreeing to be your wife,

I can help be a front for you, while you give me a place to stay. I don't have to sleep with you as long as I sleep in the same house. And you'll help me try to figure out how I got here?"

"You have a very vulgar way of phrasing, but yes."

"And that's it?" she asked.

"Yes."

"But..."

"Yes?"

"What if we can't figure out how I got here, or if I can't get back?" she asked, her voice full of fear, and starting to tremble, threatening tears.

"My dear," he said as he crossed toward her and put his hand on her shoulder, "then we shall resolve that issue when we get to it. But what matters is that for now you're comfortable. I'm sure this is quite a shock."

"Thank you," she said as she looked up into his eyes.

He smiled, reassuringly.

She smiled back.

"Now," he turned away from her and walked back over to his desk. "We must take care of something very important." He rummaged through his top desk drawer, pulled out a small box, brought the box back over to her, and knelt down on one knee. "I think this is the way one is supposed to do this." He said as he cracked open the box. "Will you, Amelia, marry me—for all theatrical and presentational purposes?"

She giggled a little, then composed herself, wiping the tear of fear that had crept out as he had his back turned to her off of her cheek. "Yes. Yes, I will be your wife."

"Ah, well, my dear, with all of the power vested in the invisible preacher who didn't marry us, I give you this ring with all the love and affection it should carry with it."

She looked down at her left hand, and on it was the most beautiful ring that she had ever seen. It was a large square of white gold that had so much filigree work that it looked like it was a silvery vine on her finger, and in the middle was a sapphire so dark blue and sparkly, it looked like a perfect ocean.

"And I take you to be my fake husband for all of the rest of my days. Amen." She said.

Neither made mention of how perfectly the ring fit her finger, but both noticed. They looked into each other's eyes, he was still kneeling on the floor, and she was sitting on the settee that continued to support her.

"Well, wife. I should show you around your new house."

"Wait, won't people wonder how you suddenly have a wife?"

"Well, yes. Possibly. But I just came back from traveling. I have been out of town for several months, and we can just say that the marriage happened then. In fact, we can say it was the reason I went out of town."

"Does anyone know where you went? Could we say we were in Philadelphia? My aunt Susan lives there, in the future, of course, but I think if I stick to mostly truth's — it will help me keep the story straight."

"Good idea," Franklin said. Then he turned, crossed towards the door, and started to leave the room.

"Mrs. Dunne?"

She turned her head toward him at the sound of the name. "Hmm? Oh, yes. Coming."

He had said it as a lark, but hearing her respond to his name gave him a tiny flutter in his heart. It was as if something had woken up there. He pondered the feeling as he walked down the hall. Ridiculous, he thought, and dismissed the feeling. It was more plausible to him that she had come from another time. What was impossible for him to believe was that he formed an attachment to her so quickly.

Chapter Thirteen

Overwhelmed with everything, Amelia followed him down the hallway. She had fallen through time and met a handsome stranger she immediately felt comfortable with and was very attracted to. He proposed—actually offered to pose as her husband and let her live with him—offering to take care of whatever needs she had until she could figure out how to get back to her time. All without reason or cause. Maybe he felt the same instant comfort she did? She hoped so.

She stopped and shuddered. It all was utterly ridiculous. In fact, Amelia mused this had to be a dream. Only in dreams did people immediately trust each other. Another fact to support this was a dream: her outfit. There was no way that her clothing would have magically changed to something appropriate for the time. In every movie she had seen or book she had read that dealt with time travel there was *always* a scene where all of the other characters made comments about the "strange" or "inappropriate" way that the person visiting from the alternate time was dressed. And this man—the fact that Amelia thought that she might know him—that alone made her think this was all a dream.

She looked at him. He must have asked her something because he suddenly had stopped walking down the hall and had turned back to look at her.

"Huh?" Amelia struggled to compute what was happening as she fell deeply into his eyes.

"I asked if you would like to retire. You have had a traumatic day and I'm sure you could use some rest."

"Uh, yes. Sure. Um, I mean... please."

"I shall take you to your room, then."

He led her to the stairs, but allowed her to go up first. She was sure the layout was the same, but didn't know which bedroom he intended for her use. At the top of the stairs she stepped to the side letting him lead the way.

"I don't know where we are headed now," she remarked shyly.

"Yes, well. My rooms are that way," he pointed to the hallway that led to where, in the future, Amelia's master suite was. Interesting, she thought, they must occupy the same room but in different times. His voice brought her thoughts back. "I'll put you in this wing of the house. This way I won't bother you with the odd hours I keep."

Franklin passed the first two doors, stopped at the third one and opened it. The room, decorated in burgundies and lavenders, contained a small table, a desk, a large wardrobe, a vanity and a couple of chairs all in dark woods with lavender upholstery. There was a fireplace directly opposite the door. The large sleigh bed was to the left, and although it was a gigantic bed, it seemed to take up little space in the room. There were several different woven rugs on the floor, all in burgundies and lavenders and they matched the colors in the floor-to-ceiling drapes that covered the large windows on either side of the fireplace. The room in the here and now was very similar to the one Jack occupied in her house.

As Amelia stepped into the room, she took it all in. While she was eyeing it all, Franklin crossed to the fireplace and started a fire. He was so adept, Amelia hadn't noticed his efforts, and only made notice that he was crouched on the floor, poking the fire. He stood and replaced the poker on its stand, and crossed to Amelia. "Well, that should get going in a few minutes. Take some of the chill out of the room," he said sheepishly and put his hands in his back pants pockets.

"Thank you," Amelia smiled.

"These were my aunt's rooms. Some of her clothing is still in the wardrobe there. I'm afraid it might be terribly out of date and somewhat ill-fitting to your figure, she had a much more ample waistline. But, it will be of some assistance in helping your cover story of your travels from Philadelphia. We will say your luggage was lost, and you can do your best in these until we can get you some clothing of your own," he winked at her conspiratorially.

The wallpaper came from Franklin's Victorian aunt. It made sense.

Amelia was still convinced this was all a dream and that she would wake up in her own bed the moment she fell asleep here. "Thank you," she said.

"Well," he started to take a step towards the door, hesitating as if not wanting to go, "I guess I'll take my leave of you. I'm afraid there isn't a full pitcher here for you to wash up. Do you think you can wait until morning?"

"I'm sure I can," Amelia said, already feeling her body awakening. She felt a little hazy and thought it to be her body starting to wake up, getting ready for its morning run and then a shower, back in her own time. She even thought she could smell coffee. Yup, she was sure she was waking up.

"Well then..." he started to the door. Amelia trailed politely after him a few steps before he turned around. "I..."

Amelia didn't know what came over her. The look in his eye. The smell of him. The fact that all of this would all be a juicy dream that she could tell Toni and Alexia...

She reached a tentative hand up and touched his cheek. After a moment, when Franklin offered no objection, she placed her free hand on his other cheek, leaned her weight onto her tiptoes and pulled his face down, directing his lips to hers, and she kissed him.

Chapter Fourteen

Franklin, not one to give over into romantic sensibilities, was shocked the moment Amelia's hand caressed his face. Her touch felt like a door opened within him and let in the sunlight and fresh air that he didn't realize he'd been missing. As he took in this feeling, she placed her other hand on his cheek, drawing him toward her and he gave in completely. Her soft lips on his made his stomach flip. A thousand thoughts flooded his mind. His brain panicked. However, his arms paid no attention to his brain's protests and sensibilities. They reached out, pulling this strange, intriguing, and beautiful woman toward him. His hands sat lightly on her hips like arms on a sugar bowl—delicately placed but designed to be there. As their kiss deepened, he pulled her closer into him, her arms went up and around his neck. He smiled through his kiss as she did this, and she returned the sentiment.

Franklin stopped listening to the warnings his brain was giving out, and wrapped his arms all the way around her. She felt so good pressed up against his body. A thought flashed in his mind—he hoped she didn't think he brought her up here for this reason. He started to draw back from her to say just this, but she started to suck on his bottom lip, drew her face back from his for a second, just long enough to make eye contact, and she pulled him back to her, kissing him more passionately.

His hands took on a life of their own, exploring the shape of her, and finding their way into curves, tugging at her clothing. He didn't know much about how ladies' clothing was put on the body, but his hands seemed to know how to make them come off. Brilliant, brilliant hands! He had seemed to remove her blouse, and was caressing her bare shoulders with his hands. His mouth moved from hers to her shoulders, and moved up her neck. She tilted her head back and her hands deftly removed his waistcoat, swiped off his suspenders, unbuttoned the front of his shirt, and started to unbutton his trousers. Then her hands were gone. Before he could figure out where they had disappeared because he was focused on doling out kisses to her neck and tops of her breasts, her skirts fell to the floor in a voluminous whoosh. He paused in his kissing, looked into her eyes and chuckled. She took his wrists, moved them on top of the hooks on the front of her corset and manipulated his hands to undo the first one, and snap, her breasts were a little closer to freedom. She moved his hands to the second, with the same result. By the third, he was working faster and on his own, but she kept her hands on his, with her eyes focused on his face. Finally, the thing released its grasp on her torso. He, the conquering hero, ceremoniously held the menacing beast to one side of her while leaning back from her a bit and cast it away. She gave him a wicked grin, and turned and walked over to the bed in her bloomers and chemise, which she was now lifting over her head. He stepped out of his trousers, currently around his ankles and removed his boxers, garters, and stockings as he did so. There *must* be a better way for men to wear stockings, without these clasps and braces, he thought to himself. He had it in his mind to ask her if, in the future when she came from, if there was a better solution that maybe he could adapt to his stockings here... At that moment, he looked up and saw the light from the fire flicker off her bare skin, and any thought of men's hosiery—well any sane thought, really—completely disappeared from his brain.

Franklin didn't know how he got there, but suddenly he was across the room and in front of her, wrapping his arms about her, pressing his body to hers. Then the next moment, she maneuvered them onto the bed. He felt the softness of her skin, the mounds of her breasts, and the resistance of her hip bones pressing into him. He became animalistic, and a half moan, half purr exploded from somewhere inside him. She responded back with her own hum.

He kissed her with ferocity and maneuvered her underneath him. After laying a kiss on her neck again, Franklin held back a moment. He did not want to give into his carnal need so quickly and fought with his transformation, a bit like Jekyll and Hyde, but she pulled him toward her and she wrapped her legs around his waist and moved her hands up his back and into his hair. He gave into his body's urges, his instinct, and to her. Completely. As they joined and held each other they kissed passionately. His only thoughts in this moment were of her. Through his kisses he fought himself to please her and hold her. She let out a sigh of release confirming appreciation of his passion.

They lay in a mass of tangled arms and legs, trying to regain normal breathing. She started to stroke the back of his head, and he lifted his head off her shoulder. Propping himself up, he looked down at her and smiled. She caressed his face with one hand, the way she did to start this whole interlude, and he leaned down and kissed her lips, softly but resolutely.

He rolled off her and lay on his back. She didn't move. He hoped he hadn't done anything wrong, as it had been a while for him. After a few, very long moments, she rolled over to him and sighed contented as she put her head on his shoulder and rested her hand in the middle of his chest.

"I've fallen in love with you so many times," he said in almost a whisper as he was filled with wonder and disbelief that she was really here with him.

"But you...you just met me..." she said, knowing that it was not possible, but for some reason she felt like they had known each other for a long time. This was totally a dream. It sounded just like something she read in one of those trashy bodice-ripper novels.

"I know..." he trailed off, leaving a moment of silence lingering between them.

In response, she nuzzled into him, and he held her close to his heart. They fell asleep like that.

At some point in the night, she had rolled away and was curled in a ball on the opposite side of the bed. The cool of her missing body woke him. As he gained a tiny whiff of consciousness, a few restless thoughts bubbled into his head about different things. This woke him completely. He lay there in her bed trying to fall back asleep. He even rolled over and curled up to her to coerce sleep to return, but it would not. Franklin didn't sleep well, and often couldn't get back to sleep if he woke in the middle of the night. He not only suffered from melancholia, or debilitating depression, but insomnia plagued him, too. Stories and ideas flashed in his mind at any time, in moments just before sleep, and he tried to catch them when they struck. At least that is what he blamed for both issues.

He quietly rolled out of bed, although he was unwilling to leave her. On his way out, he threw another log on the fire, and collected his discarded clothing.

On the landing, he glanced back toward the door he had closed behind him and smiled. He had no idea who this woman was, but she was his "wife" for all intents and purposes. He knew that she would alter his life from this day forward, drastically, and for good.

Chapter Fifteen

Waking in Jack's room Amelia rubbed sleep out of her eyes with confusion. She must have missed him last night, even though he had only been gone a week, and came in here to be close to him. She shook her head at herself—oh, the odd things she did when she was drunk. And that *dream*! Crazy! But she did have to admit the sex was amazing. She ached as if it had happened.

Amelia didn't want to get out of bed, but wanted coffee, and probably needed to go for a run to wear herself out so she wouldn't dream like *that* again. She rolled over and threw the covers off, but lay stiffly in bed for another minute, doing her best impression of a petulant child unwilling to go to school. Amelia made herself laugh out loud with her own behavior, and rolled out of the bed. She straightened the covers on her side of the bed and walked around to the other side—she had slept like a maniac last night. Pillows and covers strewn all about. She would have thought that she really *did* have sex last night. She removed the watch she was still wearing and placed it on the bedside table. It wouldn't be good to run with it on. Looking around the room for the pajamas she must have discarded on the floor, she instead found a pile of white lace, another pile of skirts, and—oh god—was that a corset??

No. This couldn't be... NO. Time travel *doesn't* happen. No. NO. No no no no no. She looked back down. The corset was still there. Oh shit.

Amelia sat on the edge of the bed. For a moment she had a clear head and a calm mind. She wasn't able to keep the thoughts at bay for much longer and they flooded in.

Jack. Corsets. The house repairs. A gorgeous stranger. This house. The *same* house.

How did she get here?

How would she get *back*?

Her mind spiraled through all of these things. This last thought shoved her momentary control over the edge. Tears rimmed her eyes. Sobs, just tiny waves of fear and sorrow, started in her stomach, but soon those waves became a tsunami of emotion. The tears, which at first took slow, tentative paths down her cheeks, became torrential. She lay on the bed and curled her legs up to her chest, making herself as tiny as possible. Amelia sobbed and sobbed, the thoughts running over in her mind like a frustrating playlist. She cried harder to drown them out, but it didn't work.

Amelia didn't know how long she sobbed, and would have kept sobbing if a bright-faced young woman hadn't touched her lightly on the shoulder. Amelia jumped, and her tears stopped momentarily, looking the young girl in the face.

"I did knock, missus. It's just you were crying so loud, I didn't think you could hear me, so I took it upon meself to enter, seein' if I could help." The bright faced girl with light brown, wavy hair pulled back into a bun talked with a bit of an Irish lilt.

Amelia's sobs returned, although quieter. The young lady stood unyielding, holding a tray, waiting for instruction. Receiving none, she hopped into a flurry of action picking up the mess in the room, chattering politely as she did so, hoping to distract the naked stranger on the bed from continuing to cry.

"I'm Emily, missus. Mr. Dunne says you're married recently, and that you arrived yesterday after cook and me went home for the night. He says that you were finishin' up things with your kin. He just arrived home a few days ago hisself." Emily stood and looked at her. "Mrs. Finnegan 'n me is still puzzled why he kept you to 'imself."

Amelia felt a clench of panic in her stomach.

"Course," Emily continued, "he does keep to 'imself and other than empty trays and his unmade bed, we haven't really had many clues *he* was home," she said setting the tray on the little table that had a small wooden chair on each side. Amelia relaxed a little.

Emily walked out the door to the room and returned almost immediately with a large kettle, half the size she was. "He said I was to take care o' ya until he can hire a lady's maid," she continued as she crossed to one of the walls, pulling on a handle that she had to reach on her tippy toes. She pulled, and out fell a tub. "I've not had the official position as a lady's maid, as such, but I have helped many ladies I've worked for with their toilet, and dressin' and such." She turned back quickly to the naked mass that continued to sniffle on the bed. "That's not to say, missus, that I'm assuming to present meself for the job." She turned back and started to pour water from the large kettle into the tub. "I do have higher aspirations, missus, but I guess what I'm tryin' to say is that I hope I don't fail your expectations, and I hope to do right by ya."

She had now crossed to the bed and stood in front of the lump, which had quieted. Emily whispered, "Missus, your bath is ready and your breakfast is gettin' cold. I'd suggest you partake in at least one before both is as miserable as you was soundin' before I walked in."

Amelia made a choked sound and her body heaved.

"There, there now, missus, was that a sob or a laugh?" Emily asked in earnest.

"Oh, Emily!" Amelia wailed and turned her head into the bed to muffle the sound.

Emily sat down tentatively on the bed just next to Amelia. Emily didn't know quite how to handle this completely naked stranger, but she knew what it was to have a good cry now and then. She could empathize with Amelia, and thought that if the position was switched, she would appreciate comfort. Reaching out her hand Emily stroked Amelia's hair, gently. "Now, now missus," she said in a soft voice, "it isn't as if you're being held captive by a beast of a man. Lots of women have it much worse. Mr. Dunne is very nice, and with that twinkle he's carrying around in his eye this mornin', he seems right in love you with, he does."

Amelia turned her head to look up at Emily. "He does?" she asked meekly.

Emily smiled. "See now, it's not so bad if someone loves ya."

"No," Amelia sniffled, "I guess not. And I love... I love..." but she couldn't finish and started to sob.

"Come now, missus. This behavior ain't befittin' a lady and you've got a lovely bath—"

"But I'm so far from home and I don't know if I can ever get back," Amelia bellowed through sobs.

"Ah now, is that your trouble? You are homesick, ain't ya? Aw well, Mr. Dunne will let ya go home as often as you'd like. He's very generous when me or cook need a day that 'taint ours to have off. I'm sure he'll let ya go home and visit. A very pro-gressive man, he is."

"I don't know how to go home." Amelia sat up a little and looked Emily in the eyes, hoping she would understand.

"Well missus, I don't know that either," Emily's green eyes looked at Amelia with concern for a moment, but then they changed to a hopeful look, "but I'll tell ya, a good bath will make you feel better." Emily took Amelia by the shoulders and lifted her up to sitting. Then Emily stood and held out her hand gently, as if to a child. Amelia looked at the proffered hand and then to Emily's face, which had a caring but stern look on it, as if she would take no more of this nonsense. Amelia took her hand and lifted herself off the bed. As she did, Emily's face faded into warmth as a smile crossed her lips.

They both started to cross the room and Emily looked back at her trailing patient, still clinging to her hand. "There now, not so bad, is it?"

Amelia nodded dumbly.

"In ya go," said Emily as she helped Amelia climb into the tub, letting her hand go as Amelia lowered herself in. The tub was small and Amelia had to keep her knees bent, but the tub was deep and even with bent legs, she was completely immersed in the water.

Emily returned with a tray of different things. "Now, ma'am, which soap will you be wantin'? There's lavender or there's honey."

"I don't..."

"I'd be preferrin' the lavender meself. It's soothin'."

Amelia smiled and nodded lethargically.

"Well then, good. We's in agreement," Emily said, setting a tray on the little table beside the tub Amelia just noticed. Well, she thought to herself, she hadn't really had time to explore the room yet. She was either in a state of shock and awe, or lustful passion, or this morning's bout of sadness. She wondered what other secrets this little room had.

Emily had handed Amelia the cake of soap and the sponge. While Amelia scrubbed her body, Emily lathered her hair. When they were both satisfied in their task's completion, Emily held up a large, thin and scratchy, linen towel and averted her eyes. They were not like the Egyptian cotton bath sheets Amelia had at home. Was there such a thing here, she thought?

After Amelia pondered and toweled herself off, she noticed that Emily, quick as a rabbit, had cleaned up all signs of the bath, and had stowed the tub back in the wall. She wondered where the water went.

"I'll take your towel, missus," offering a dressing gown and again averting her eyes, although she had seen Amelia completely naked both emotionally and physically. Amelia, who had watched enough episodes of *Downton Abbey,* knew how to behave, and threw her towel over Emily's shoulder and shrugged into the dressing gown. Amelia tied the robe and turned around to offer her thanks, but Emily had already hung the towel on a rack by the fire, and headed to the table with the silver tray that had two silver domes waiting. Emily removed the covers, and Amelia sat down and started to reach for the bacon that was looking up at her.

"Will that be all, missus?"

"Yes. No. Could you—would you, mind... sitting with me for a bit?"

"I'm sure I could. I'm ahead on my chores for the day, and cook's list for the market isn't that long," Emily said conspiratorially as she took the chair across the table from Amelia and pushed the tray closer to Amelia, as if encouraging her to eat.

As they sat, Amelia learned that Emily was the oldest of four and had two brothers and a sister. Her mother emigrated from England and her father was a second-generation Irishman, but Emily had been born and raised in Brooklyn. She'd been working for Mr. Dunne the last five months, "since just after he inherited," but came from another house two streets over.

Emily got up while telling Amelia the daily schedule and routine of the house, she was at the wardrobe rifling through the contents. As Emily's back was turned, Amelia took the girl in. She was younger than Amelia by a few years, and was fit. She wore a dark brown dress with a white pinafore apron that wrapped around most of her body, and it had a green sash and bow that wrapped around her waist and tied in the back. The green matched the shade of Emily's eyes. As Emily turned back towards her, Amelia appreciated the girl's soft facial features. They were calm and comforting. The two women shared a smile.

"Well, seein' that you're done eatin', why don't we get you dressed." Emily handed her bloomers, stockings, and a chemise to put on herself. She brought out a bodice—Emily informed her that it was boned and structured, so no corset was needed. It was the shade of a deep purple eggplant with a matching purple and green pinstriped blouse. It had very few frills, sleeves that went to her elbow, and a high collar. The skirt was the same purple and green.

Emily then sat Amelia down in a chair and brushed out her now dry hair, and did a sort of a twisty flip bun that looked fancy even though it took Emily less than two minutes to toss up. Emily walked to the front of Amelia with her hands on her hips.

"Well, now. That's how a lady should look," and she turned and started to leave. "There's a mirror on the vanity. Also, some powder and such are there to do your face up. Don't know how fresh it is, as it belonged to his aunt," Emily heavily hinted.

"Emily," Amelia stood and turned to the door, where she had stopped Emily, just as she was leaving, taking the remnants of breakfast away, "Thank you. You—"

"It was my pleasure, missus. Getting used to a new place is difficult. You'll be right as rain soon enough." And with a grin as big as a jack-o-lantern, Emily was gone.

Amelia watched the door shut, and then walked over to the vanity. She admired her reflection and Emily's work for a few moments. Then she started poking around in the pots and brushes that adorned the top of the vanity. She found a pot of pink cream, what she thought was rouge, rubbed a little on her cheeks and lips. Not recognizing anything else, she decided that it was enough makeup. She looked at herself in the mirror again, and sighed. It was time to face the music, or at least find Franklin and apologize for taking advantage of him and his kindness last night.

Chapter Sixteen

L eaving the safety of her bedroom, Amelia walked out on the landing feeling things were different. It was still her house. However, it was not her home. She timidly took a few more steps feeling like a child playing hide-n-seek not wanting to make a sound. It was the oddest feeling to be *in* her house but *not* her house at the same time. She took a few more steps forward toward the stairs. As she passed the doorways, she looked in. Some rooms were so familiar, and even some of the furniture looked the same. Maybe this *was* a dream. She had been having rather realistic dreams since moving into this house, but this didn't *feel* like a dream, she reasoned with herself. No. She was sure this was real.

Amelia went down the stairs, and headed for the study. It's now or never, her conscience sounded a bit like Elvis. This struck her as odd, as he wasn't even alive yet. She walked to the study door and hesitated. This was her house, but what exactly was the protocol for falling through time and landing in her house, owned by someone else, who'd made her his "wife" though she was a stranger. Amelia sighed and opted for politeness, knocking on the sturdy double doors.

"Come in," she heard a faint and distracted, masculine voice say.

She walked into the study and glanced around again, still in disbelief of its appearance. He was at his desk distractedly writing.

"What do I, oh—it's you," Franklin said the last two words as if he had lost his breath when looking up from his writing, realizing it was Amelia and not his staff. He stared at her for a long moment. Then suddenly remembered his manners, he stood, making papers on the desk rustle and flutter and the chair loudly scraped the floor, emphasizing his mistake. "How are you this morning, my dear?" he asked shyly. "Emily said you might be up and about shortly—I must say that dress looks lovely on you."

"I, uh... thank you," she stumbled over what to say. "I wanted to apologize for last night."

"What do you mean?" he asked, crossing around his desk, over to her and taking her hands in his. "It is I who should apologize. I let my passion and excitement rule me and I took advantage of you," and he looked at her as if he were begging forgiveness for a more heinous crime.

Amelia began to laugh and tilted her head to the side. "And I had come to apologize for taking advantage of you."

Their eyes met and they both laughed. He started to lean in to kiss her, but paused slightly and then retracted. "I'm sorry, my dear. After last night... I will refrain from… indulging." He stepped back. "Why don't we get to know each other better and you can explain to me how you got here, or at least the events that led up to your appearance in my hallway." He led her over to the sofa in front of the roaring fire, and motioned for her to sit first.

She sat and looked at him. Not quite knowing where to begin, she just gave him her full, unremarkable history from birth to inheriting the house and remodeling. Occasionally he would nod and "mmm" or "hmm" but he did not interrupt. He perked up and became even more interested when she mentioned she had attended college.

When she was finished, he responded. "Well, I'm sorry to hear about your parents, but at least you don't have to fret about their response to your sudden absence. You said you have a living aunt in Philadelphia. Will she be worried?"

"Probably not until a major holiday, so Thanksgiving or Christmas."

"Ah, good. Time for us to figure out our problem, uh, I mean, situation. Not that I hope it takes that long," he corrected himself as she winced. "Is there anyone else who would be concerned over your absence?"

"My two best friends, Toni and Alexia, and …" she trailed off. She felt awkward mentioning Jack after she just slept with the very real man in front of her. The man who was doing his best to help her through this fantastical situation. "I… well… there's… my boyfriend. The man in my life…I think you would say we're… courting?"

"Oh. OH. I'm … You're—"

"Yes," she hung her head. This was getting awkward. "I thought all of this was a dream and that's why I went forward with it. Not that it was bad," she jerked her head up to make sure she hadn't offended him. With pleading eyes, she continued. "Just the stranded-in-the-past thing. You were so wonderful, and you're so handsome, and I kissed you, gave in—"

"To my advances—"

"No! They were *my* advances, and..." she hung her head lower, bit her lip and continued, "they were not... unwanted."

After a silence, he reached over and took her hand in his. She sighed. They sat like this for a while. Eventually she looked up and found his eyes had been on her the entire time. Looking into his eyes, she realized she couldn't hide anything from him. Even more, she didn't want to. Amelia was about to tell him this but was stopped by a knock on the door. They leapt from each other as if they were two children caught in the act of doing something naughty. Neither gave any reply, and the knock sounded again.

"Come in."

"Sir, dinner is ready."

Amelia looked at the window and noticed light was no longer streaming in through the tinted glass. They had talked for a long time.

"Ah, yes," Franklin said, "it seems we might have missed lunch."

"Where would you like to take your dinner this evening?" said the robust woman who had entered the room. "Oh, I'm sorry missus. I've not had the opportunity to introduce meself. I'm Mrs. Finnegan but you can feel free to call me 'cook,' if you like."

"But that's not all you do around her, my love," Franklin said as he rose and rounded the sofa over to the portly lady who looked like she stepped off the set of *Mary Poppins* or *Downton Abbey*. Franklin brought Mrs. Finnegan by the hand to Amelia. As they crossed the room, Amelia took her in. Mrs. Finnegan had salt-and-pepper hair pulled back into an inverted twist. She was dressed similarly to Emily, but she was in a white blouse ruffled at the collar and sleeves, and a black skirt, with all-white apron over the front. Amelia only assumed there was an impeccably tied bow at the back of this pristine and starched woman. She was small, probably only five feet tall, but not a woman you would want to mess with. She had a warm face, but seemed to take no nonsense. "Mrs. Finnegan, this is my wife, Amelia. Amelia, this is the amazing Mrs. Finnegan. Finney has been with me since I was learning to walk."

"*Before*, ya young mite, and doncha forget it. And don't you dare call me Finney, or I'll take ya over my knee, published author or no!" After a moment of giving him a serious glare, a smile broke across her face, and Amelia knew this conversation happened often. Mrs. Finnegan turned to Amelia, clasped her hands in front of her chest, and smiled warmly, "It's lovely t' meet the girl who has stolen away Frankie's heart."

"It's nice to meet the woman who trained him and kept him well fed for me," Amelia responded warmly back to Mrs. Finnegan, turning on her charm.

"I *like* this one. Good choice, boy," Mrs. Finnegan said as she patted him on his cheek and winked at Amelia. "Now, dinner. I will not allow you to starve your new wife with chatter, no matter how in love you are," she said, teasingly. "May I suggest the dining room?"

"I think the dining room would be lovely. Is that alright with you, dear?" Franklin deferred to Amelia.

"Yes... darling," she was surprised how the endearment rolled right off of her tongue. "I'm ready for some hospitality, for a change, what with you hiding me and leaving me with an empty wash basin last night," she said, winking at Mrs. Finnegan.

"Well, then. By all means." Franklin rushed over to her, swept her off her feet into his arms, and carried her toward the dining room.

"Ah, young love," Mrs. Finnegan clucked to herself. "You get seated, and I'll bring in the first course in a moment," she hollered after them, chuckling to herself at seeing him this happy. It had been a long time, Mrs. Finnegan mused to herself, since Franklin smiled like this.

Chapter Seventeen

During dinner Emily bustled in and out a few times with different plates of food. Other than that, Franklin and Amelia were alone.

After the first course was set before them, there was a silence that Amelia wanted to break, but she wasn't sure how. Her apology had been sufficient, but she felt the need to apologize again for taking advantage and not being completely present, here in the past. Amelia started to scold herself again thinking it was a dream but then chuckled to herself. Franklin stopped eating and looked at her. Feeling his gaze, and knowing that her little laugh had increased the tension, she forced herself to meet his eyes.

"I... I was just thinking about apologizing again," she started to explain, "and had the thought that I needed to be present in the past. It's just that the two—"

"—Collide and contradict each other, although the English language offers multiple definitions for each word and allows them to work together as well as conflict with each other," he finished for her, awkwardly looking down at his plate while joining her in a chuckle. "Sorry, I tend to blurt out language usage when nervous." He looked back up at her. Amelia smiled at him and held his gaze, and then returned to staring at her plate, when he didn't say more.

They were silent for a few moments more.

"Why did you offer me marriage?" she blurted out.

He paused for a moment and looked quizzically at her before answering calmly and without condescension. "I told you that you offer me an advantageous guard against the outside world and the fortune-hunting mothers of Brooklyn."

"No, I mean, why did you offer to shield me and take me in, as you did? Why did you trust me? My story is so unbelievable," she said, not meeting his eyes. "I was convinced this was a dream."

He had lifted his fork to take a bite, but stopped and set it down. He waited a few moments before answering.

"I have been asking myself the same. I don't know. You are a complete stranger, and yet, when I first saw you in the hallway, half dressed and lost, I knew I..." he drifted off as he looked over at her, seeing her looking back at him. His face changed from clouded and searching, to a pained, misunderstood look, to resolution in the span of a few seconds. "I knew that you were a woman who..." thousands of words flooded Franklin's brain: needed help, was beautiful, was half-naked, was perfect for me... He was shocked with this last thought. It couldn't be possible. People didn't fall in love upon first glance, that only happened in sentimental novels ladies read.

"…needed help?" Amelia offered as she made a face.

"A strange woman who shouts at me, unprovoked, in my own hallway is most definitely not in need of help." He smiled at her and then they shared a laugh

"I was going to say," Franklin continued after the laughter died down, "in need of care." He gave her a gentle look through those gray eyes and impossibly long lashes that were just unfair on men. His hair, a bit softer today, fell slightly to his forehead, giving him a boyish and charming look.

"Well," Amelia heard her voice escape her more breathlessly than she anticipated, "I certainly was in need of help, so I'm glad you offered it. I hope that you don't offer marriage to all women who just show up in your hallway," she teased.

"Certainly not, Madame!" he said with mock aghast. "I reserve that for only the half-dressed ones who accuse me of stealing their china."

Amelia blushed as her heart flipped. Acknowledging this strange comfort, with his banter alleviating her fears and shame, she flicked away the shame.

"So," Amelia said, wanting to change the subject and divert her mind away from what her heart was trying to tell her, "what are my wifely duties to be? I have to learn what it is that you, and the world at this time, will require of a new wife, so that I don't give us away."

"Well, I suppose that you'd run the house. Make sure Mrs. Finnegan makes all of my favorite foods." He glanced up at her and continued sternly, "Know where my slippers and pipe are at any given moment, so when I bellow nobly for them, you will come rushing to my side." He cleared his throat and sat a little taller. "And of course you must make sure I am flush with quills and ink and paper. An author without supplies is a lonely man who makes shadow puppets to entertain himself."

Perplexed, Amelia took it in wishing she had a notepad to write out the list. She wanted to make sure that she was returning the favor of his kindness by rightly assuming the role of his wife. "Right. Where do you keep your slippers and pipe?"

Franklin laughed at the serious tone Amelia had adopted.

"Oh, you don't have either, do you?" Amelia felt herself flush from head to toe, and looked away from Franklin, hoping he wouldn't notice.

"No. I don't. And even if I did, I'm not the kind of man who would demand that of his wife." Franklin frowned. "My dear, we don't know how long you are to be here, as I'm assuming that you haven't figured out how, or why, you found yourself here. And until you do, you are simply to make yourself at home." He smiled at her before continuing. "I was just thinking about how I missed having companionship. I have male friends, but nothing is quite like a woman companion." Franklin's thoughts drifted a bit.

"But, you don't expect me to... perform like I did last night? Because I don't think I can—"

"My dear woman!" he said, truly aghast this time. "You do not have to do anything you do not want to do in this house. I will not force myself upon you. I know that I am not the kind of man whom women throw themselves. In fact, I am usually the one that shies away from women. It is understandable that you find me repulsive, and my actions repugnant, and do not wish to share a bed with me —"

"No, it's not that," Amelia said quietly. She was unsure of herself and trying to soothe this sudden self-loathing. "I do not find you repulsive, actually just the opposite. It's just that..." she sighed. "I have someone in my time. I care deeply for him. And in my time, you don't engage with others in... relations, if you are in a...commitment."

"Ah," Franklin sat down his fork and leaned back in his chair. "Yes, this Jack you mentioned. And you said you are courting, so it's serious."

"No. Well, not yet, anyway. He is traveling. He is a doctor."

"I didn't know that doctors traveled."

"They don't. Normally. Jack got it in his head that he wanted to save the world. So now he's somewhere in South America helping the starving and sick."

"Well, I can see why you don't... why you think it's a mistake—"

"It's not you. You are a handsome man, and very kind. I just... I don't want that to be part of our understanding. If you don't mind?" Amelia looked at him pleadingly.

Franklin looked back at her, not knowing what to say. This woman, this damsel-in-distress, needed him to put her needs first, which he was determined to do. "Of course.

Last night was only a dream in your head, and nothing more. Our arrangement is one of convenience and necessity, and we shall stick to that. You shall sleep in your room and I in mine. We shall be proper, and keep passion out of our arrangement."

"Thank you," she beamed and she reached out and grasped his hand, which was sitting on the table.

His heart ached a little at her touch, but he tried to show it.

Emily walked in as they were holding hands, and smiled a huge grin, misinterpreting the affection. She cleared her throat before speaking. "I'm sorry to interrupt. Would you like to take coffee in the study this evening, sir?"

"Yes, I think we shall, Emily. Tell Mrs. Finnegan another excellent meal." Franklin stood, still holding Amelia's hand, turned to her, "Shall we retire to my study, my dear?"

Amelia smiled amused with how he spoke and the idea of any man her own age referring to her as "dear." Franklin took Amelia by the arm and led her out of the room, leaving Emily to clear away the dishes.

***

A while later, Emily came to bring the coffee and desert to the study, she heard raised voices.

"I cannot believe you just said that!" Amelia said, her adamant voice carrying through the solid study doors.

Emily paused a moment before knocking.

"How could *you* possibly think that I would feel any differently?" Franklin responded argumentatively.

Emily felt three things at once: She wanted to hear more, but knew she shouldn't eavesdrop. She felt terror at hearing the newlyweds fight, and they might cease upon her entrance. And she really wanted to put the heavy tray down. The last two together won out, and she knocked hesitantly.

"Come in!" was heard in husband and wife stereo of abrupt annoyance.

"Ah, Emily. On cue as always." Franklin said more calmly than his voice had been before she opened the door. The quiet in the room was stuffy and Emily could feel the tension. This spat wasn't over. She wanted to set the coffee down, and retreat as quickly as possible.

"I'm off for the evening sir, unless you require anything else. Mrs. Finnegan is also leaving."

"No, that will be all Emily. Thank you," Franklin said with a sigh and walked over to the coffee pot to pour himself a cup.

Emily walked out of the room faster than her normal gait, glancing quickly at Amelia, stoically sitting in one of the large chairs by the fire, unmoving and unsmiling. She was just about to the door when Mr. Dunne stopped her.

"Actually Emily, wait a moment," Franklin said, turning his head to the door where she was. "You can settle the score between me and my *wife*," Emily noticed that Franklin was trying to keep himself calm, but lost his edge when he said "wife."

"I will do what I can, sir. How may I be of service?" she asked tentatively and on guard.

"You read, isn't that correct, Emily?" Franklin said pointedly.

"Yes, sir."

"And you're a woman?"

Emily laughed, then stifled it quickly, seeing that Franklin wasn't laughing. "Yes, sir."

"And have you read *Wuthering Heights*?"

"Oh, yes sir." Emily said with enthusiasm. "It is beautifully written. That poor tormented Heathcliff and—"

Amelia, who had been completely silent, barked with laughter.

"Emily," said Franklin with a resigned sigh, "you are fired."

Emily's mouth fell open and her face went white with shock.

"Emily, you are not fired," Amelia said through her laughter. "My dear *husband* would not fire *my* maid over something as silly as your opinion in literature." Emily took note of the emphasis Amelia put both on 'husband' and 'my'.

Franklin sulked, and flopped down in the chair behind his desk. "Silly women always love inane love stories with a brooding man. Doesn't mean it is literature."

"It is an absolute classic," Amelia said. "Although many men share your underwhelming sentiments for the novel. Thank you, Emily. You have proven my point, and won yourself a great deal of gratitude from me. Even if you have given my husband more reason to pout." The two women shared a moment.

"Happy to help, ma'am. Always willing to tell a man what books are good," she said with a conspiratorial wink. "If that will be all the book reviewin' you need for the evenin' I'll be takin' my leave."

Franklin started to chuckle at Emily. "Yes, go! Have yourself a good evening, and spread your terrible taste in books somewhere else." She bobbed a curtsy and left the room, shutting the door behind her.

"Poor Emily. How often do you fire her?" Emily heard Amelia say as she walked away from the study. Emily smiled to herself. This was a strong match. They would be good for each other. She rushed to share what she witnessed with Mrs. Finnegan.

Later, as Amelia fell asleep, she thought back over the events of the day. Although she felt a bit restless and distraught, she couldn't help liking it here. She was happy, and felt a twinge of guilt for happiness while being in this predicament. She dreamt of home as she fell asleep.

Chapter Eighteen

Sunlight awoke Amelia.

"Now then, what shall we dress you in today?" said the familiar female voice.

Amelia rolled over to find Emily standing at the side of the bed. "Why are you...*sleep*... not time yet..."

"Oh no, no! You're gettin' up, you are. The dressmaker is comin' today to take your measurements and to show you the best fabrics for the summer. I'm good at sewin', mistress, but I can't be makin' over all of these relics. Besides, Mr. Dunne is waitin' to have breakfast with you in the dining room."

Emily's conspiratorial whisper of the last sentence made Amelia wonder if Franklin had uncovered buried treasure in the middle of the night and was waiting to show her the haul he found. Amelia took this news to be something of great importance and hauled herself out of bed.

"Coffee. There better be coffee."

Before Amelia knew it Emily had her laced up in a dress with corset underneath. Emily also put her hair in a coif that sat neatly on her head, and then Amelia was headed downstairs to the dining room. "Off you go to the dining room, and I'm off to the market," Emily said following her downstairs but parting ways as Amelia turned to go to the dining room.

"Good morning, darling. And how is my wife today?" Amelia was greeted with a chipper voice that reached her through the sleepy haze she carried until an appropriate amount of coffee was applied.

"If you're one of those morning people, I think I might have to divorce you now. Unless you hand over the coffee, soon," Amelia grumbled, only half-sincerely.

Franklin laughed as he pulled out the chair for her to sit.

"No, I'm not much of a morning person, really," he said, seating himself, "being a writer, I keep all hours. But last night I retired when you did, got a good sleep, and was ready to see your bright shining face—" he stopped as she glared at him. "Coffee. Yes, dear."

"So you slept well, *and* you're up early."

"I take it you didn't sleep so well? You did your first night here." He looked down sheepishly. "I mean, I assume you slept well your first night here."

Amelia blushed at the reminder that he had slept next to her while she thought she was in a dream. After recovering, she replied, "No, I didn't sleep well last night. My head hit the pillow and was flooded with thoughts of Jack, and home. I tried not to be sentimental. But I cried a bit. What if I never get back?" She paused. Franklin stood, not knowing what to do for a weeping woman. He leapt to her side, and knelt awkwardly by her chair, taking her hand in his. "What can I do to help?"

The sight of Franklin kneeling, waving his napkin around, made Amelia giggle through her tears, and in a few moments she stopped crying. He handed her the napkin he was holding, and she blotted her eyes.

"It's just, I miss him so," she said trying to hold back her tears. "He has been away before, so I am used to not seeing him for a stretch of time. But what if I can't get back? What if I—" she started to cry again, but Franklin jumped in and changed the subject, distracting her.

"What do you remember about the moment you left there and arrived here? What were you doing? What were you thinking?"

"I was thinking about you, actually."

"Me? But I thought you said you didn't know who lived in this house."

"I didn't. You're right, though. I was thinking about the house's former inhabitants. I was fixing up the place and wondering about different people's tastes over the years and how they decorated it. I was refinishing the stairs, and I had gone up to change, and I had come back down and walked through the hall, and was on the way to the study — which in my time is a horrendous mess that I have yet to figure out how to remodel—"

"Have you tried recreating it?"

"The study? Well, now that I've seen how you keep it I can now—"

"No, I mean your path," said Franklin, trying to focus on Amelia's time travel. "Have you tried walking the path again, retracing the movements that brought you here?"

"Well, not exactly. I have walked the same path, but didn't recreate it, as you say. Not with the intention of traveling home."

"Well, let's try," said Franklin, jumping up from his breakfast. Amelia smiled at his enthusiasm.

"If I didn't know any better, I'd say you were in a hurry to get rid of me, *husband*."

"No. No, darling. I just..." although he knew what Amelia said was in jest, Franklin felt the conflict rise up in his chest. He wanted her to stay, to be near him, but he also didn't want to be her jailor. Franklin didn't understand this sudden need for her to stay and a need to protect her. He had been with other women, but never felt a deep attachment before. It was ridiculous, but Franklin admitted to himself that he had become attached—completely. Best to get her back to where she belonged before things got even more complicated. He had his writing to focus on. He didn't need a woman to come in and change things. "I just want to make sure we try everything we can. You don't belong here." As he said the words, he regretted them.

"Once more, you make me question if you want me as your wife," Amelia said, barbing at him.

Again, Amelia saved him from himself. Franklin's face dropped from the exuberance of his good idea, to frustration from saying the wrong thing. He didn't want Amelia to feel unwanted. In fact, he didn't want her to leave at all. But they barely knew each other, and he couldn't ask her to stay. He had to help her try every option to get her back to where she came from. He wanted to make her happy in any way possible. And achieving that would be enough to make him happy for the rest of his life. Happier than the feeling of finishing a new book and having the publisher accept it. Only when Franklin looked up into her eyes again, he knew she was teasing him. He smiled to cover his self-berating thoughts.

Amelia saw she had gone too far with her last comment. She was being a bit too familiar with this man. Although after their first night together, she shamed herself, was there such a thing as too familiar? She had only known him for a few days. It's a wonder that humans put so much importance on the first impression of another as the basis of the entire relationship. First impressions always break down. They give a false sense to everyone and no matter how true they may be—reality and time always break down what was first seen. For better or worse.

"How is it," said Amelia, snapping out of her reverie, "that you are paid to mold the English language into beautiful, amazing stories, but when words fall out of your mouth, they are thick and cumbersome like falling trees?"

Franklin smiled then looked away and rubbed the back of his neck, offering a few nervous chuckles. He looked down, hiding embarrassment and pleasure at receiving the compliment from her about his writing. He looked into her beautiful hazel eyes, always-different shades that were a bit on the teal green side this morning. A sly smile crept over his face. "Well, you see…" Franklin took a moment to compose his thoughts. "As a common man, the words habitually tumble out of my mouth at will, especially around a beautiful woman, taking my life in their hands. But as a writer I am given the allowance to write many drafts, and extensively edit."

His wry smile grew. She hoped he smiled often. He was charming when he smiled, Amelia thought. Seeing his smile released her concern that her words had hurt him. It was good to know that they shared a similar sense of humor. They laughed together briefly before he held out his hand to her.

"Shall we try to get you back?"

Amelia noticed that he never said *home* when referring to her own time. "Might as well. If we try and succeed, it will cost you a lot less with the dressmaker, who I have an appointment with this afternoon," Amelia replied weakly, failing to make a joke.

She took his proffered hand and rose from her chair. When she touched his hand, she felt a jolt of electricity run through her. She gave him a look to see if he felt it, too. He made no obvious change, if he did feel it. Maybe it was the tension of the whole situation. Possibly some residual feeling from the first night she spent in his house, *and in his arms* a voice in the back of her mind nudged her like a dog's nose. Shaking it off, she walked with him to the stairway.

"Now, why don't you show me what you did to arrive here."

Amelia thought for a moment, acknowledging he had a brilliant idea. A bit ashamed she was so taken up with everything else that she hadn't thought about retracing her steps to see if she could get the opposite effect until he suggested it. She cleared the self-deprecation and ascended the stairs to the landing. As she started down she narrated, "I had gone up to my room, changed into clean, comfortable clothes that didn't have paint on them, they happened to be a tank top and yoga pants. I was here, on the fourth step from the bottom when I started thinking about what this house was like and its past owner, and particularly the fireplace in the study. It's a complete wreck in my time. Bricks are loose, gone or broken. The mantle has huge chunks out of it. I have to make the decision if I want to tear it out and just make it into a wall, or if I want to rebuild it. The contractor needs a decision soon, because he can't start more work in that room until the fate of the fireplace is decided. So I headed to the study, wondering what kind of person lived here before, and what he did to the fireplace to ruin it." She had slowed her pace down the last few steps, but was now on the main floor and turned slightly to her right to head down the hallway to the study. Amelia took the last few steps down the hall with her eyes closed and *willed* herself to be back at home, her home. After a few moments of standing still she heard Franklin's voice, flat but with a twinge of disdain at the end confirm that she was still in the past.

"It didn't work. Do you think you did it right?"

"Is there a right way to time travel? I didn't know there was a rule book."

"Ah. Touché."

"Well," she sighed, "I did it exactly as I remembered it."

"Hmm. Maybe give it another go. This time, you don't have to narrate as you go. Maybe if you don't acknowledge I'm here, it will be as if you are alone, and that will be the key."

Amelia nodded, and headed back up the stairs with aplomb. She descended again. On the fourth stair she thought about Franklin, and the study, and the broken fireplace. She headed to the study, and stopped in the hallway. Still nothing.

"Maybe it was because you were thinking of here, my time, and that is what got you here and now. Try the same thing, but think about your time. Your fireplace and the improvements you're making there."

Amelia thought of the mess in the kitchen, the broken fireplace, Alexia, Toni, *Jack*. She tried it three times this way with no result. She tried walking backwards thinking the same thoughts. Nothing. She thought of things that might pull her back to the future: her mother's bracelet, the picture of her parents sitting on her dresser. Still nothing. She thought about the activities the day she arrived here. Varnishing the stairs, washing out the brushes in the sink, removing the watch from her wrist and putting it back on—

"The watch!" she exclaimed, remembering she was fastening it on her wrist, and was distractedly thinking of it while thinking about the past and what the fireplace once

110

was. Amelia realized that it was the key. She couldn't remember where it was. Amelia had taken it off, but didn't remember where she put it, and she remembered Emily had tidied in her room a bit and must have put it somewhere safe. But where *was* it? Emily was out running her errands for the day and wouldn't be back until much closer to dinner. Amelia couldn't wait until then. She dashed up the stairs, her skirts not making it easy. Full skirts walking at a normal pace felt like she was walking through shallow water. Running in full skirts up the stairs felt like she was waist deep in water with waves crashing against her. When she got to her room, she threw open the door and ran to the table by her bed. No watch. Frantically, she glanced around the room to see if she could see it waiting for her on any of the obvious surfaces. She hadn't realized Franklin followed her up the stairs and was now standing awkwardly in her doorway.

"Do you know where it would be?"

Amelia realized she'd had a very long inner monologue.

"I was wearing the watch the night I arrived, but the next morning at breakfast, I can't remember wearing it. In fact, I'm sure I didn't." Amelia circled the room, her brows furrowed trying to remember the details. I don't remember removing it, and I haven't seen it since that first day. Emily must have put it somewhere safe, but she's not here right now, so we will have to find it."

Still in the doorway, held by an invisible force, Franklin asked, "Would you permit me to help you find it?"

Amelia looked up at him, and realized he would not enter her room unless invited. She didn't know whether it was his classiness, the appropriate behavior of the time, or guilt over their first evening. It was probably a little of all three, and she smiled and blushed slightly. She hoped he didn't notice and tried to quickly recover by saying, "Yes, I would love the help," while looking about the room again.

He went to the opposite side of the room and looked on the surfaces of the tables and chairs. She headed to the vanity and looked in the small drawers and on top. They both examined every possible area. Having no luck, they exchanged a glance. The same idea hit them both at the same time, and they both fell to the ground and started searching on hands and knees. Although they were on opposite sides of the room, they absently bumped into each other right in front of the fireplace.

"Oh, I'm so sorry," he apologized for almost bumping her head with his.

Taking the apology for not finding the watch, Amelia sighed as she sat back on her heels. "That's ok. I guess we just wait until Emily gets back. I'm sure she'll know. And if I've waited a few days to head home, what are a few more hours?"

"Right." Franklin had stood up, and was offering her his hand. "Should we finish our breakfast then, or have a cup of coffee?" Amelia looked up, and took his hand. She started to rise, but her heel caught in one of the many ruffles in the ridiculous dress and she lost her balance, falling right into Franklin's arms.

They both froze looking into each other's eyes. He admired her hazel, as she gazed into his soft grey.

Not knowing how to make the situation less awkward, Franklin tried joking, "Well, my dear, if you wanted to repeat our exercises from the other night, you just needed to ask."

Amelia feeling the same sensation she felt when she took his hand a bit ago, pushed herself away from his embrace, but steadying herself by holding onto his forearms, wiggling her ankle to release her heel from the ruffle. As she worked it loose, she tried to explain what had happened.

"It's quite alright," Franklin also backtracked, "I was only teasing you. No need to fret."

Amelia realized she was still holding onto him even though she was now standing squarely on both feet. Feeling the blush rise in her neck she turned her head toward the fireplace to avoid his gaze.

A twinkle from the mantle caught her eye. She gasped, and released his arms, and crossed the few steps to the mantle. "Here it is!" she exclaimed.

Amelia looked back at him, holding up the watch. She couldn't be sure, but she thought she saw disappointment flash across his face. He so quickly changed it to a pleased look that she thought she might have imagined it.
"Should we head to the stairs to try again?"

"Yes," Amelia said, full of hope. "If you don't mind," she immediately asked, making sure that she had only imagined his sudden mood change upon finding the watch.

"Of course. We should. I'm sure you're ready to be where you belong. After you."

Amelia walked past him toward the door, but turned back and waited for him.

They went down the stairs, and Franklin positioned himself at the newel post so he could watch her.

Amelia reenacted coming down the stairs, putting on the watch, thinking about the future and stopping in the hall. Nothing happened. She tried a second time, putting on the watch and thinking of the past. She tried a third time going backwards. Exasperated, she started to try a fourth time. "I know I'm forgetting something," she said, as much to herself as to Franklin.

"I'm sure you're doing everything you can. Maybe the situation isn't right. Maybe it's not the right time of day."

His words churned in her head. As she arrived at the top of the stairs, a figurative lightning bolt surged into her brain. "I was *winding* the watch! It was on the wrong date, so I changed it to the right one, and then poof!"

"Well, then try that," Franklin answered her, with a tinge of exhaustion tempering his voice.

"You don't have to stay here with me, if you don't want to. If you have something more important, I don't mean to keep you," she said sincerely, tinged with a bit of guilt.

"No. Nothing is more important in this moment than helping you. Besides, I really am curious to see what will happen. I'm just," he paused searching for the right word, "frustrated... for you. But try again. Maybe this time it will work."

She came down the stairs again, winding the watch. The 3 was in the date window and it turned over to the 4. Nothing happened. She stood still and thought for a minute. "The dial was on the thirty-first and I changed it to the first. Maybe the specific day has something to do with it," she said as she wound the watch so the number 31 was sitting in the date spot.

"I've not seen that in a watch before," Franklin said, commenting on the flipping numbers on the watch over Amelia's shoulder.

"It really is quite handy to have the time and the day on your wrist. And it changes daily."

"What an interesting improvement. I wonder if I can have one made..." Franklin's thought drifted off when he saw Amelia charge up the stairs. She took a deep breath. He, unknowingly did the same. She started down the stairs.

"Wait."

"What?"

"Just in case this does work, and you get back to your own time, I just wanted to tell you that, I think..." his words fell to a quiet murmur as he turned his head down to look at his feet. She didn't hear the last few words he uttered. From this angle above him, Amelia thought he looked like a shy little boy. Very endearing. Her heart swelled.

"What did you say? I couldn't hear that last part."

His head flipped back up and his eyes met hers, slightly pleading, asking her with his eyes to not ask him to repeat himself. "I said, I think that you are a very lovely woman."

Amelia blushed. "I—"

They stared at each other in silence. She wanted to say something in return, but didn't know what. Amelia felt a pull on her heart from the direction of the future, and it shook her back into focus on her task. She didn't belong here. She didn't belong with this man, in this time, with these frustrating skirts. But those eyes that were looking up at her. They said so much, even though he was a little more than a stranger. A stranger who offered to shelter her and proposed. It wasn't a real proposal, she reminded herself. And Jack. Jack was real. She needed to get back to her time and Jack and her house. But this was a lovely vacation. She really could picture herself here in some moments. Enough, Amelia, she told herself. She snapped out of it.

"Thank you," she finally replied. "Both for the compliment and for being so astonishing in all you've done for me. I really don't deserve—"

"Well, you'd best get on with it," he said, cutting her off and putting a stop to the emotional goodbye they were having. "Travel safely, or whatever is appropriate to say to a time traveler. And please know, if you can return here, know that you're welcome any time."

She took a deep breath, gave him a nod of thanks, and started down the stairs. She wound the watch slowly and started walking down the steps. She hit the landing as the second hand passed the 9 on the last turn around the watch face. Franklin stayed at the newel post, not wanting to move. Amelia continued down the stairs and turned the corner to the hall, and the watch flipped from the 31 to the 1 and she pushed the pin back into the watch. She had taken a big breath and closed her eyes as the pressure of her fingers moved the pin back into place. She stood still holding her breath for a few moments not wanting to open her eyes. Amelia reasoned with herself that if she didn't know where she was, she had no reason to be upset for either leaving or staying. Even though it had only been two days, she did like it here in the past. She rebuked herself: a person cannot live with their eyes closed to everything. Opening up her eyes and facing whatever was in front of her was the best solution, she surmised. Amelia opened her eyes. She took a deep breath and a look around, and smiled.

Chapter Nineteen

Franklin felt his knees give when Amelia turned the corner away from him and disappeared into the hall. He ached to follow her. Instinct made him want to race after her, grab her, and stop her. But what right had he? He was not her *legal* husband. They were playacting, like children, and he barely knew the woman. But these feelings he had at the sight of her — he hadn't felt this happy in a long time, probably since his childhood. Already, his writing seemed better. He was inspired, and the ideas were clear and just kept flowing. He had told her he slept, but actually, he felt more rested having his ideas coming together and being able to commit them to paper. For the first time in a very long time, he could think clearly. Inspired ideas kept surfacing, even *with* constant interruptions of his thoughts of her in the middle of a brilliant thought.

Franklin's heart sank. He had done the right thing, hadn't he? She didn't belong here. She was... is... *was*... a beautiful spot of light that flickered through his life. He should be grateful. Maybe, if he was lucky, she might come back to visit. He sighed, feeling his melancholy filling him, the heaviness pulling him to sit on the first stair. Franklin should return to his study and work, but his heart wasn't in it, and his feet wouldn't move. He delayed walking down the hallway, confirming he was once again alone. Franklin sat for what seemed an hour in his self-inflicted purgatory. Finally, resigned to the truth, and his duty to his publisher, stood up and took a few steps towards the study. Before he even got to the hall, he was plowed over. He lost his balance and fell to the floor, taking his assailant down on top of him. There was an "oof" and an "ow" and a feminine voice cursed loudly. He took her by the arms and lifted her off him as he sat up.

"It didn't work," he exclaimed a bit too happily. "I mean, I'm so sorry that it didn't work. Are you going to attempt it again?" He looked into her eyes with concern.

Amelia sat back on her heels, somewhat unaware that she was sitting on top of Franklin who was lying on the floor, propping himself up with his elbows. Her brow wrinkled with frustration. "Yes. No. I mean—" she let out a large forced sigh. "I have to try again. But I think that if I was meant to go back just now, one of the numerous attempts I made would not have gone unanswered. I am done for today."

"But not for good, surely."

"No. Not for good. I have… responsibilities. I need to at least make the attempt."

"Yes. Understandable. Would you mind—"

Amelia's eyes snapped to Franklin's in a hopeful gaze. "Would I mind what?" she said, more flirtatiously than she had meant.

"Madam, would you mind removing your person from on top of me?" he asked meekly. "I don't think that the position we are currently in is good for our trying to remain," he cleared his throat, "on previously-agreed platonic grounds."

"Oh, yes, of course," Amelia replied. Her face filled with shame as she pushed herself up off him and moved out of his way as quickly as possible.

They stood awkwardly in front of each other.

"Yes, well. I'm sure you would like to get back to your writing," she blurted out.

"Yes. Must get more pages written today. And you have your appointment with the dressmaker," he stuttered. "Make sure you get whatever you might need and whatever you think you want. I'm sure that I can afford it. I, uh—"

"Yes, thank you." After their awkward exchange, they stared at each other again.

"Well…" With a nod and his hands clutched behind his back, Franklin walked off toward the study, leaving Amelia standing at the bottom of the stairs. She needed a drink. A tall, stiff drink. Looking at the watch again both in disdain that the thing didn't work and to check the time, she sighed at the defection and that it wasn't even mid afternoon. Taking a deep breath, she retreated.

She went to the ewer and basin, poured out water, and splashed it on her face a few times. She held her face with the towel holding on in frustration and walked to her bed. She flopped on the bed in resignation to her confused emotional state.

Amelia realized as soon as she had laid back it was a mistake. The corset was going to make it difficult and awkward to get up. Releasing a great, deep sigh, tears she didn't realize she was holding back rolled down her face. Tears rolled slowly at first, but thoughts triggered more fears, which created more tears. Amelia cried for the failed attempts to get home. She cried for missing Jack. She cried that she didn't miss Jack as much as a trapped woman should miss the man of her dreams. She cried that she might be stuck here. Forever. Then she cried, feeling awful that she might not mind if she stayed. The tightly laced corset denied deep sobs. However, the sadness she had within was not the large kind. It was deep and produced small, quiet rolling waves within her. Because she lay on her back, the tears rolling off her face slid down her neck and dripped onto the comforter.

Panic slithered through her chest, and it brought many unanswerable questions with it. What if this was to be her life? What if she could never return? What would happen to Jack, and her house? Spinning through these questions and trying to find answers, she stopped crying. Her head began to hurt. She didn't know if it was all the crying and the verge of dehydration, or if it was because of the lack of answers.

Never being one to let the unknown frighten her, Amelia tried sitting up and cursed as the boning in the corset not only stabbed her in her fleshier areas but it also pushed her back down flat. Corset boning did wonderful things for the décolleté, until it impaled one wearing it. She tried flopping her legs down to propel her torso up without success. Amelia thought about throwing her legs up and over her head to reverse somersault off the other side. Deterred as it might be a painful landing, that idea was a last resort. The one to follow the plan of loudly screaming for help. She then tried rolling side to side, like a child rolling down a hill, and after a few tries, made it onto her stomach. She was finally able to push herself up and off the bed.

This whole rigmarole was good for a few things. She had stopped crying and thinking about her fate. She got a little bit of a workout, something she hadn't done since arriving here. Oh, how she missed yoga pants. These last two things made her smile, and then she laughed at herself for having these silly thoughts in the midst of a catastrophe. Moments like this, the laughter amidst the pressures and insanity of life, make the world turn. Although this was a very bizarre circumstance, she decided to do her best to take it in stride. Amelia wasn't going to give up on getting home. But she wouldn't drive herself, or anyone else, crazy. It had happened, and she was here. Franklin's face floated across her mind, and she looked down at her left hand, the wedding ring blinked at her. This wasn't the worst of all possible situations.

As if this thought needed certification, she heard a loud, grinding ding. Sort of the sound her toaster oven   from college made when it was done. Amelia poked her head out of her bedroom door, curiously. The sound went again, coming from somewhere downstairs. Hearing no one else in the house, Amelia left her room and went down the stairs. She started toward the kitchen thinking it might just be a toaster oven, and as she hit the bottom stair, the sound went again. It was the front doorbell she realized. Emily must still be out, Amelia thought as she crossed the room to the front door. Amelia opened the door to find a tall, trim man stood with his back to her. Clean-shaven, with a button nose and a large smile that took up half of his friendly face, he was wearing a brown pinstripe suit with a brown bowler hat on his head. He was holding what looked like an old-fashioned doctor bag in one hand and a large briefcase in the other.

"How can I help you?" Amelia asked the man's back.

"Oh," he exclaimed and turned around. "Mrs. Dunne, I presume?"

"Yes?"

"Ah, I'm Mr. Caruthers. We had an appointment this afternoon." Confusion washed across Amelia's face. "I'm the dressmaker."

"Oh, yes. I'm so sorry. Emily did remind me of it this morning—do come in!"

As he entered the house, he wiped his feet several times on the rug at the same time he removed his hat and looked around the entryway.

"I've heard a lot about this place," he said to no one. "I've wanted to see inside. My father was the dressmaker for the author's aunt. I recently took over the business. But I assure you, I'm just as good as my father's reputation."

"I'm sure you'll suit my needs just fine," Amelia said, thinking to herself that she wasn't sure she would know the difference nor how long she was actually going to be here. "What do you need to work?"

"A little bit of space and a good bit of light. And a chaperone, *if* you don't trust me," he added, giving her a conspiratorial wink.

There was something so gentle about this man, she couldn't help but feel at ease around him. She was sure that the last part was a joke, and she decided to test him by teasing back. "Would I need a chaperone because of unwanted advances, or because you might talk me into buying much more than I should?"

"The latter, my dear lady. Unless you have a manly figure under those *ancient* robes, you have nothing to fear," he wiggled his eyebrows up and down at her this time.

They both broke out in a laugh.

"Why don't we head to the front room? Lots of room in there, and lots of light."

"Yes, Mrs. Dunne. That should be fine."

"This way, Mr. Caruthers" Amelia turned and walked off to the right of the stairway. "And please call me Amelia. Married life is so new to me, that I forget I'm now Mrs. Dunne." Amelia noticed how this rolled off her tongue. It was true, in a way. Maybe she would fit in better here than she thought.

"Well then, *Amelia*, I would be delighted if you called me by my Christian name: Jon."

Entering the room, she smiled at the feeling that a friendship was emerging.

***

Jon was efficient. Setting down his bags, he removed several items from the leather doctor's bag that looked like they might have been torture applications. He also took out a pencil and paper. Taking Amelia's measurements with the terrifying looking tools, she remained unharmed. After taking her measurements, Jon chatted with her about bustles and chemises, showed her some swatches, and made a few sketches. She took his advice on some of the colors, and stayed away from heavier fabrics like brocade and velvet, telling him that summer was coming and she didn't want to look like she was wearing the curtains. Amelia would have made a *Gone with the Wind* reference, but was pretty sure it wasn't even a twinkle in Margaret Mitchell's eye yet.

Jon started to pack up his bags, completing all he needed for her order. Amelia had paid no attention to how much time passed. The clock in the hall had chimed a few times, but it didn't seem necessary to keep up. She only noticed the room was dark when Emily knocked and started to scurry around the room, turning on lamps.

"Missus, I'm sent to ask you if you'll be having dinner with your husband tonight. I haven't been able to get an answer out of him, he must be in the middle of a grand idea. But cook would like to know." Amelia noted that this last part was said with a bit of a warning. Almost a mother's tone.

"Yes, please. Tell my husband that his presence is requested for dinner. And please ask Mrs. Finnegan if she would mind setting a third plate for our guest," Amelia pointed at Mr. Caruthers.

"Yes, missus. I'll do my best to rouse Mr. Dunne from his roost. And I'm sure cook won't mind adding a place at the table," Emily bobbed a quick curtsey and then left the room as quickly as she entered it.

As soon as the door closed, Amelia and Jon shared a laugh.

"My, my. She definitely runs this house. Do you think she knows it?"

"Oh, Jon. We all know that *Mrs. Finnegan* runs this house. The rest of us are just minions."

They both laughed again.

"No, but seriously," Amelia continued, feeling like herself for the first time in days, "My husband came with quite the dowry of help," she said. "I don't know what I would do without those two women," her voice moved to sincerity.

"Isn't it supposed to be the other way round, my dear? The dowry, I mean."

"Yes, I suppose you're right," she said and slightly blushed.

Just then a loud knock came at the door, before it swung open. Franklin walked in a whirl. He had several papers in his hand, and was absentmindedly walking into the library, "Amelia, Emily just informed me that we're having a guest for dinner and—" Franklin looked up just in time to stop directly beside the dressmaker. "Oh, hello."

"Franklin, *dear*, this is Mr. Caruthers. Jon." She nodded her head at her new friend. She then turned and said, "Jon, this is my husband, Franklin. " She turned her head back. "And yes, dear, if you don't mind, I'd like to have our guest stay for dinner. I would like to continue our lovely chat."

"Ah. I see. Well, I suppose I could take a breather. Smithers is trying to uncover the plot of the pirates while Michael, who is the unlikely hero, is stuck in the smugglers hold and—"

"I don't know if you've heard," Amelia said ,switching her attention from Franklin to Jon, "but my husband is a writer, and he pens gory adventure books," she said, matching Franklin's dramatic flair. "I can assure you he's really quite tame."

Franklin beamed at Amelia, as if sharing a private joke. "Well, I'll... just go wash up," he said, twisting his wrists, showing off the tattoos of ink the writing made on his fingers. "Smithers can remain confused until after our dinner has concluded," Franklin said, waiving the pages over his head on the way out the door.

Jon waited a few moments after Franklin's exit to speak, but then said in a hushed tone, "Well, my dear. You do know how to pick 'em handsome, don't you?"

Amelia laughed. "It's good to know we share similar tastes, Mr. Caruthers, since I'm putting my life, or at least my wardrobe, in your hands."

"Well, they *are* one and the same!"

Emily reappeared, and offered to show Jon where he could freshen up. Amelia went up to her room and washed her face and hands and tidied her hair. She decided to put on a little rouge. Her face didn't show signs of her earlier crying, but she still felt like brightening up her face. When she arrived at the dining room, both men were already seated, and in the middle of a conversation. When Amelia entered the room they stood, and sat when she did.

"You two seem to be getting along. What were you talking about?"

"Well, dear, Jon was just filling me in on the neighborhood gossip."

"Oh?"

"Yes, apparently we are in the thick of it," Franklin said conspiratorially, "Or at least we will be."

"Mrs. Harbinger, who lives one house to the south of you, was in my shop earlier today and heard that I was taking measurements for a young lady in this house," Jon's voice fell to a hushed tone. "She made the comment to Mrs. Price, who lives two houses to the north of you, that she was interested in finding out more about the mysterious woman who needed dresses in the Dunne house. Mrs. Price speculated that you were a niece. Mrs. Harbinger insisted that you must be a kept woman."

Amelia choked on the sip of wine she had just taken.

"What a surprise I must have been for you when I opened the door earlier," she said to Jon.

"In my line of work, you never know what to expect. When you opened the door I knew you would be delightful, whatever relationship you might share with Mr. Dunne," Jon flattered. "But, to be honest, I hoped it would be mildly scandalous," Jon said with a twinkle in his eye. "The women around here are awful gossips, and it would be fun to taunt them with information that they lack and are sure to grill me for,"

"Yes, well, although I'd love to perpetuate the gossip mill," Franklin said with contempt, "I think it's best you simply tell them that my new wife just arrived, and the train company lost her belongings."

"And that you forced me to wear your aunt's hand-me-downs, and I refused to go out of the house until I had my own clothes to wear," Amelia added.

"Well, you won't be able to say that for long,"Jon said. "I'm going to make you some of the prettiest dresses just perfect for you. Including correct hems. You're a bit taller than many of the ladies around here."

"That's funny. Where I'm from, I'm short," Amelia said.

"Where are you from? Minnesota, the Viking part of the country?" Jon asked.

Amelia, feeling like she had said too much, looked down at her plate and answered quietly, "Yes. Well, from near there."

"My wife's family is no longer with us and it saddens her to talk about them," Franklin jumped in and saved her. Of course he was good at creating fiction on the spot.

"I'm so sorry. We will speak no more about it," Jon said. "Instead we shall talk about the wonders that the new corset and the boned bodices I'm going to make for you will do to your figure."

"Well, even though I would love to hear about corsets, and how I would love to pass the evening with gossip and chintz," Franklin said with thick sarcasm, "I must return to manly swashbuckling and revenge."

"Oh, how will we ever get on without you?" Amelia said in a southern drawl throwing the back of her hand, which held her napkin, to her forehead. Both men laughed. "Go," she said, making a shooing gesture at him with the napkin, "leave us, husband, and go write, so I can buy *more* dresses."

He laughed, then kissed her cheek, and left the room.

Amelia turned a bright shade of pink.

"Ah. Young love," Jon said, sighing.

"Oh, I'm not in love," Amelia protested, but her gaze at the closed door that Franklin just left through told Jon something different.

"My dear, the old gossips might say it isn't en vogue to love one's husband, but that is only because they were married off by their annoyed fathers so they could live in another man's house and aggravate him instead. You might have married for convenience, but your husband loves you. Moreover, you love him. I have only spent a few hours with you, but it is obvious. There is no need to be ashamed and deny it."

Amelia, for fear she might reveal too much, changed the subject back to corsets and then to her dresses. Emily bustled to remove the plates, and asked if they would care to take coffee in the library. Jon declined, stating he needed to get home and start work for a very important new client with a wink at Amelia. She saw him to the door. He promised that she would have at least one new dress in a few days.

After Jon left, his observation of young love rang through her mind. Did Franklin love her? Did she love Franklin? Impossible. She loved Jack. And there was no possible way that Franklin could have fallen in love with her so quickly.

She climbed and readied for bed. It wasn't until she was pulling back the covers she realized she had forgotten to say goodnight to Franklin. She grabbed for her dressing gown so she could say goodnight, but second guessed it. Was saying good night an admission of having feelings? She shook it off. It would be fine if she didn't say it tonight, in fact, it might be better.

She turned out the light and climbed into bed trying not to overthink. As she fell asleep, she told herself that she would try the watch again tomorrow, and every day. She owed that to Jack. She wouldn't bother Franklin with it, as he seemed frustrated with the process. As she drifted off to sleep, the thought crossed her mind to remember to apologize to Franklin for not saying goodnight.

Chapter Twenty

After Amelia had formed a routine for Franklin only being here a few days, his moods evened out. They would greet the day together at breakfast, then he worked while she read in the library or worked with Emily or Mrs. Finnegan. Franklin met her for lunch in the dining room or his study. He knew she tried the watch in hopes she could return home every morning. But he didn't bring it up knowing if she was still here it hadn't worked.

Amelia liked exercise, and Franklin knew he should get outdoors more, so he suggested they take walks after lunch. It took away writing time, but afternoons for him tended to be work wastelands where he got little done, and her sadness lifted after their first outing, he was determined to continue daily as long as the weather was fine enough. After walking, he would return to his study to work until dinner with her, and then he would work into the evening.

At first Amelia didn't intrude on his workspace. After a while, she gained courage and a few times, she stood in the door to his study to ask a question or remind him that it was mealtime. One day, he was so distracted he didn't even hear her when she spoke to him, and only noticed her when she was gliding by the shelves that were near his desk poking the books on his shelves.

One afternoon during their walks, she asked to read one of his books. Returning home he burst into the study. After plucking a few from the shelf, then quickly returning them, he knew which one she should start with. He gave her one of his earlier works. Something that had a bit of his rudimentary style to it, but one he wasn't overly attached to just in case she didn't like it. If she hated it, he would be able to take it, and if she liked it, he could give her something better as a follow up. The next morning, she arrived in his study looking tired, but bright eyed. She had read *The Search for Count Demetrius* in less than a day.

"It was brilliant," Amelia said in response to his gruff greeting. She clutched the book to her chest, and flashed him a proud smile when his surprised gaze met hers.

"I'm glad you liked it," he said, standing hurriedly. Why did he seem to forget his manners around her, and feel like an idiot schoolboy? "Would you like to read—"

"Yes!" Amelia said a little too exuberant, she realized after the word came out of her mouth. "I mean, if you would like me to, I would love to read more of your work."

"You would?" he asked a little sheepishly.

She nodded. "Especially if the characters are as exciting. I couldn't believe that the Count disguised as the

133

servant the whole time. How did you come up with that idea?"

Franklin chuckled, and rubbed the back of his neck with his palm, a habit Amelia was beginning to learn he did when he felt modest or shy.

"I don't know. I was sitting here one day thinking about what it would be like one moment to have everything and then next to lose one's memory, and to wake up not knowing his identity, but to slowly have pieces return."

"It was brilliant," she said breathily. "Is it your best?"

"No, actually. I didn't know how I would receive it, and wasn't sure that I could take you disliking my best work yet. Therefore, I gave you the third book I ever wrote. I think it is probably the weakest next to my first published work."

"Oh. Well, I really liked it. And I'm not just saying that because I think I should. I really did like it." Their eyes met and she smiled again. Her smile was so beautiful, he thought.

Snapping himself back into the moment, he spun to the bookshelf. Franklin should not allow himself to fall farther for her or feel more than companionship, at least until she wanted more from him. He walked his fingers over the spines. These were familiar friends he had spent hours toiling over their creation. Which one to choose for her next?

"You don't have to give me the best one next. In fact, please don't tell me which one is your best until after I've read it. Less pressure on us both, that way."

Chuckling, he looked over his shoulder at her and smiled. He turned back to find his finger resting on *The Serendipitous Mask*. The story was about a man fighting for the woman he loved, as he hid under the guise of a swashbuckling rogue who fought an evil prince against injustice. He hesitated for a moment. It was one of his better ones. But did he trust her with it?

She watched his finger linger on a book. The suspense was challenging. Amelia felt her pulse surge as if she was a child waiting to open birthday presents. It was one thing to go to the public library, to choose a random book written by someone with no personal connections. Reading Franklin's book, Amelia felt like she was getting closer to him. She couldn't put it down. The book didn't give insight into Franklin's life, but it was his creation and showed a glimpse of the man. It was an intimate thing that he trusted her with his stories.

He crossed the room and handed her a dark green tome with a chocolate spine. All books were hard-cover in his library. She wondered if paperbacks existed yet. She exchanged the one she was clutching to her chest for the new book hesitantly.

"Thank you," *for trusting me again*, she wanted to say. "I'll try not to devour this one so quickly."

Franklin smiled. He was glad he had a book in his hands because the urge to reach out and caress her face was so tempting. He wanted to touch her, but didn't dare risk it. They were becoming comfortable around each other and he didn't want to risk it. She was good for him and he wanted her to stay. Breaking his train of thought, Franklin moved to replace the returned book to the shelf. Amelia's stomach growled loudly.

"Shall we go to breakfast?" Franklin laughed and returned to her side.

"Yes, please," she said, blushing. He took her free hand and placed it in the crook of his elbow and led her, holding his book to her chest, out of the study and into the dining room where they were greeted by Emily and a tray of sausages.

"I thought I was gonna have to eat these all me'self. I couldn't find either of you, and Mrs. Finnegan made so many," Emily said with a light scolding tone.

"Ah, Emily, I would hate to put you through that doom. I was just rewarding Amelia with another of my books as she has given up on *Wuthering Heights*."

"I have not!" Amelia said, removing her hand from his arm. "I just have decided to see with what fate I've saddled myself," she said, giving a playful nod in Franklin's direction. "That said, I'd rather never eat another one of Mrs. Finnegan's delicious sausages than deny myself *Wuthering Heights*." Contrarily, Amelia's stomach growled.

"Well, at least part of you agrees with me!" Franklin said, holding out the chair for her.

"*Husband,*" she gave him a coy look as he sat down at the head of the table, next to her, "I'm afraid we will never agree on Emily Brontë. But if that is the only woman to ever come between us, then I think we will have a happy union."

Emily tittered as she served the sausages and lifted the cover off eggs mixed with peppers and mushrooms, then left them alone.

The conversation returned to Franklin's books and his writing. He told Amelia that he first started writing in college while studying to take his mind off the laws he couldn't seem to memorize. He would make up stories and scenarios where his heroes avenged characters for breaking the specific laws he was trying to remember. His first attempt at a novel, he told her, was a lot of legal jargon with some sword fighting in the middle. It didn't work and wasn't published. His second attempt was his first published work, and although it sold well, it was about a lawyer trying to avenge the death of his uncle by breaking laws to get closer to the murderer, and then arguing his way out of them in court.

He came alive when talking about his writing. He seemed slightly ashamed of it, because he rebelled against his father's wishes. When she asked him if he was glad of his choice, he replied, "I am. But I still despair over it every day. I think the drive to write great stories is to prove to him that I made the right decision. That and to prove I'm a good man. I suffer greatly when I feel like I am not. I fall into deep caverns of frustration and sorrow."

With that admission, Franklin excused himself to go back to work, leaving Amelia to read. She had never been into books about fighting and swordplay. It wasn't a genre she liked in any form: books, movies, or plays. But for some reason, his work drew her in. She read through the next day. He didn't join her for lunch, so she read at the table. He did join her for dinner, but was withdrawn, eating quickly and left. She wondered if this was a sign of the "suffering" he alluded to earlier.

When she dropped into the study to say goodnight, he was not there, so she went upstairs and read more in bed.

Chapter Twenty-One

Emily's face was the vision Amelia awoke to. She was leaning over the bed carefully removing the book from underneath her crossed arms. Amelia must have fallen asleep reading it and had cuddled it close during the night.

As the day progressed she kept reading. Franklin didn't appear for breakfast or lunch, which was curious, but Amelia was so engrossed in the book, it didn't register. By mid-afternoon she had finished the book. It was amazing. She liked it even more than the first one he loaned her. The way that the man disguised his face and his love to protect the princess, and she gave up her future to be with him. It was lovely. Franklin was a gifted author. She loved the way he painted beautiful pictures with words. The moment Amelia finished the book, she closed it and sat back on the sofa in the library clutching the book to her chest, like a teenager with a love letter, and sighed. She sat unwilling to relinquish either the physical book or the story it held. Then she opened the book and read the last chapter again.

It was beautiful the way the masked man professed his love. No wonder Franklin hated *Wuthering Heights*. Heathcliff would *never* say anything like these beautiful words.

The moment she finished, she rushed to the study, knocked and entered without waiting for an answer.

"It is a brilliant book, and a magnificent ending," she proclaimed loudly to the entire room upon entering.

"I'm glad you liked it," came a halfhearted and almost mumbled answer from near the fireplace.

As she walked over, she found him slumped in a chair with a pile of papers in his lap. He was crumpling them one by one into balls and throwing them into the fire.

"Stop!" she cried as he threw another into the flames. "What are you doing? Please tell me those are nothing important."

"What is important? These pages are drivel. They are sentimental and overworked. They mean nothing."

"What are you talking about? Are you actually burning what you've been working on for the past month?" She crossed the room and snatched the papers out of his lap. He grabbed for them but only half-heartedly, and she got away with them before he could catch her unable to match her spirit. Amelia crossed the room with her back to the fireplace. She set the book she had brought to return on the chaise, and started reading the pages she plucked from him. Franklin watched her for a few minutes, but got up and started pacing when she became engrossed. She read for the better part of an hour.

"Well?" he asked as she set a page down.

Turning around slowly, Amelia shuffled the pages back into a neat stack. She then looked up at him, poised her face, and took a breath in.

"How much of this did you burn?"

"Probably more than half."

"And do you have copies?"

"That is a second draft. So technically I have another draft and notes in my desk."

"Good."

"Good. Why, good?"

"Because this is a very interesting book. I hate that I've read the middle first, but I want to read the rest of this and the beginning."

"I—"

"Franklin, you are a good writer. No. You are a great writer," she said looking at him with her eyebrows clenched. "You can't just throw away something because you feel sorry for yourself."

"I can write better."

"Then do."

He looked down into her face. Finally seeing her as a person, not just the roadblock that was stopping him from throwing the whole catastrophic manuscript into the flames. She held the papers out to him, offering the choice to take his manuscript and do with it as he pleased. Challenging him to keep them, or burn them. Franklin took the pages, looking at her for a moment. He turned away from her, walked over to the desk, and opened a drawer.

He drew out a large stack of papers almost three inches thick, held together with twine.

"Here. This is the whole thing. Maybe you should read it, so you can see…" *that I'm a fraud and I've lost my touch,* Franklin wanted to say.

She took the bundle from his hands, walked across the room, and sat on the sofa in front of the fireplace, untying the twine.

"You're going to read in *here?*" he asked, looking at her.

"Yup," was all she said as she flipped the cover page and started reading.

Again, he just stared at her. Watching her read, so many different feelings swelled up in him. He was terrified of her sitting in his presence reading—what if she didn't like it, what if she *did*? What if she asked him questions he didn't know how to answer? Why did she have to look so beautiful sitting in front of the fire, reading? Having her this close was amazing and incredibly frustrating at the same time. He had been purposefully not spending as much time with her recently, he now realized. He loved spending time with her, but she took time away from writing. More than that, he was developing feelings for her. She would leave him eventually. Even if she was from this time, his affliction would surely drive her away. He should not get more attached. She certainly wasn't showing attachment to him. Only friendship. He sighed to himself. She giggled, snapping him out of the reverie. He crossed to his desk and sat down. Not knowing what to do,

Franklin shuffled papers around at first. Opened a few letters, replied to a few. Picked up the newspaper, set it down again without knowing what he read.

After a while came a knock at the door. Franklin picked up his pen to make it look like he was writing, and over-enthusiastically said, "Come in."

"Sir, I can't find the missus," Emily said and then was quickly distracted by a giggle from the sofa. "Oh, there ya' are, missus." Amelia made no movement, she just kept reading. "Mrs. Finnegan wants to know when you'd like to have dinner."

"Please tell Mrs. Finnegan, that—"

Amelia interrupted Franklin before he could finish, "— that if it's not too much trouble, we will be dining informally in the study this evening," she said, without looking up from the manuscript.

Emily glanced at Franklin who was staring at Amelia with his mouth open. He looked back at Emily and nodded. She left the room, reappearing a few minutes later with a large tray covered with silver domes.

"Thank you, Emily. That will be all. You and Mrs. Finnegan may have the rest of the evening off. Franklin and I can fend for ourselves."

Emily and Franklin once again exchanged surprised looks, and again Franklin nodded. Emily gave a quick curtsey and left the room.

Amelia moved for the first time since she sat down on the sofa. She crossed to the food, took a plate and poured a glass of wine, and then crossed back to the sofa. All while continuing to read.

Franklin crossed first to the sofa to look over her progress, looking over her shoulder he saw two stacks of paper seemingly equal in size, so he got himself a plate and retreated back to his desk. A little while later, Amelia got up, replaced her plate, and poured more wine. Franklin got up under the guise of returning his plate, and looked again. The read pile looked to be twice as big as the unread pile. She must be about two-thirds through, he thought to himself. He picked up the tray and left the room, taking it to the kitchen needing some task to do. Getting out of the room seemed a good option. Especially since he knew Mrs. Finnegan would appreciate having her tray returned. Delaying his return, he even scraped and rinsed the plates.

Upon his eventual return to the study, Amelia was still reading. He added a log to the fire, then went to his desk and rustled papers around. Finally, he just sat back in his chair and closed his eyes.

"You can go on to bed, if you like. You don't have to stay up for me," he heard her say, his eyes still closed. He opened them and looked at her. She was *still* reading. Franklin didn't want to leave her here. Instinct made him need to stay to protect. But protect what? His bookshelves? His ink supply? His manuscript? She was obviously better at protecting his pages than he was. Letting out a large resigned sigh, he stood, crossed toward the sofa but stopped short, turned and left the room.

Amelia was glad he was gone.   She was so enthralled with the story that she didn't notice his presence except that his silence was so loud. When he left to take the tray out to the kitchen, it was like a prison sentence was lifted, but she wasn't sure which one of them received the pardon.   She didn't have much more to read when he left the room to retire for the evening. When he finally left, she sat back for a few minutes and relaxed her eyes. He was right. The story had major holes. But this was a first draft. No first draft is perfect.   Her thoughts wandered to how his publisher must deal with his moody and impulsive side regularly. How many stories had he thrown away like this? She cringed. How many stories had he tossed into the flames never to be enjoyed by others. This was worse than burning books. It was burning ideas.

Determined to finish, she picked up the next page. When she got to the last sentence on the last page, her eyes closed.   It wasn't as good as the published novel she finished earlier in the day, but it had potential.   She straightened the papers, retied the twine, and carried the bundle over to his desk. She grabbed a clean sheet of paper and picked up his pen.

Franklin—

You were right. This is definitely a first draft. It needs work, but it has great possibilities.

Why do you think that the pirate hides the proof of his royal birth in the treasure on the deserted island?

Who finds the treasure and brings it to the king?

Can you explore the relationship between his first mate and the maid more—I think that is an interesting subplot that would work in your favor to get the pirate closer to his King-father.

I have more ideas, but must sleep.

See you in the morning,

—Amelia

Franklin awoke the next morning from sleep so deep he felt like he had just fallen asleep. He didn't think he would sleep at all. He tossed and turned as soon as he got in bed. How could he leave her with the first draft of that manuscript?   Why did she catch him burning his manuscript? He should have pitched the whole thing in at one time and been done with it, instead of impetuously wallowing in his self pity by tossing in one page at a time. That woman was so… so… irritatingly… *beautiful* and he found himself wanting to do anything to please her, including making himself into a better writer. How could she like both books he had given her of his to read? Well, others had liked his books, why wouldn't Amelia?

He got dressed and went downstairs to the study. At the door, he knocked and waited for a moment, just in case. Not hearing anything, he crept in. The fire was now only smoldering coals and Amelia was no longer inside.

Arriving at his desk he saw her note and the bundle of papers. He picked up the note and crumpled it into a ball without reading it, and flopped into his chair. After a few moments of defiance, he smoothed out her note and read it. He read it twice. She made good observations, and didn't mention if she loved it or if she hated it.

His mind jumped to a question she had written. What was that part about finding the treasure? He untied the bundle and flipped through to find the section she was talking about. He read it a few times. His imagination flared. He could not pick up a pen fast enough. When he found one and a clean sheet of paper, he started to scribble furiously. His hand flew across the page, and soon he had a whole stack of new pages, making notes or notations in the first draft as he went.

***

Amelia woke up feeling upset, at both herself for intruding in on his writing process and at Franklin for giving up on himself. When Emily came in Amelia asked about Franklin.

"He's been in the study for the past hour. I went in to check the fire, and to bring firewood, and he was busy at his desk scribblin' away," she said, her concern was thick.

"Ah. Good. Emily, I want to wear my prettiest dress today. I believe Mr. Caruthers dropped off the rest of my new clothes yesterday?"

"Yes, missus. There was a very pretty green one. I think that would be loveliest on you."

"Very well. That one. Oh, and Emily, I'd like you to make my hair long and soft today."

"Yes, missus," Emily said conspiratorially.

Emily started to leave after Amelia's hair was finished and she was dressed, but Amelia called after her. "Will you ask Mrs. Finnegan to prepare a breakfast tray for Franklin? I'll be down in a few minutes and I'll take it into the study myself."

"Yes, missus," Emily said, smiling as she left.

Amelia admired herself in the mirror. Jon had done a lovely job with this one. It was mint green with wide Kelly green vertical stripes. They flared out from her waist and seemed to grow bigger, giving the illusion that her waist was smaller than it was. It also dipped low in the décolletage area, allowing her breasts to swell a bit at the top.

As she left the room, Amelia grabbed her watch and went down the stairs. She turned the dial as she did every morning, but her heart wasn't in it today. She slowed as she walked the last few steps into the hall and pushed the pin back in. Nothing. She was still in Franklin's time. Thank goodness, she thought, and released the breath she didn't realize she was holding. She had work to do here. She braced herself, drew back her shoulders, and went into the kitchen.

In a tone more chipper than she meant it to be, Amelia called out, "Good morning, Mrs. Finnegan. How are you this fine day?"

"Quite well, thank ya. I've prepared the tray ya asked for. There is enough coffee and food there for you both."

"Good woman. Thank you. Now, as for lunch—"

"I'll be preparin' somethin' light, how about sandwiches and a nice salad? Easy to eat while you're *readin' or writin'*."

"Did I say good woman? I should have said *brilliant* woman," and Amelia crossed the room and planted a kiss on Mrs. Finnegan's cheek. "Yes, sandwiches would be perfect. And if you make something cold for dinner and place it in the fridge, I think you and Emily can take the day off once you have everything done that you need to do today. I'm quite positive Franklin won't be emerging from his study much, if at all. And even if he does, I'm sure I can handle his needs."

"I'm sure you can missus. Especially in *that* dress," Mrs. Finnegan said, winking.

"Great minds, Mrs. Finnegan."

"Exactly!" Amelia heard as she carried the tray out of the kitchen and went to face Franklin. When she neared the study door, she heard a small voice behind her.

"Let me get that for you missus," Emily said, as she first knocked on the door and then opened it, and closed it behind Amelia.

Franklin didn't look up and didn't say anything upon her entrance.

Amelia poured a cup of coffee and took it to his desk.

She received something that sounded like "Frumuch," and then poured herself a cup. She sat on the sofa in front of the fire, sipping the coffee and occasionally glancing over at Franklin. When her stomach growled, he looked up, finally realizing someone was in the room.

"Oh. Good morning," he said and his face brightened. "I... got your notes, and have been... working." He stood up quickly and awkwardly.

"That I see," she said, standing up as well.

His eyes went up and down the length of her.

"Wow," he said under his breath.

Amelia took a moment to let him admire her. It was a pleasing and powerful feeling to have a man look over her when she knew she looked her best. "Thank you," she blushed slightly. Then in a businesslike tone, she directed their conversation. "Now. Shall we eat, or do you want to talk about the manuscript first?"

"I, well, we should eat," he said, as her stomach rumbled again.

She started serving the food, and they were just sitting down on the sofa when he started rattling animatedly off about the book.

"Your questions provoked so many new ideas. I'm using the first draft as a skeleton." He smiled and blushed as he looked away from her. "I'm trying to use the new pages, the ones I didn't burned, because you liked them." He stood. "I was upset when I went to bed, but," he turned to look at her, "I woke up and after finding your note, had extreme clarity."

He grabbed pages off his desk, bringing them over for her to read while she ate. He would let her read, and then ask a question, which he would solve himself before she even had a chance to respond. She only had time to respond with a quick yes, no, or nod of the head. Fascinated and pleased to be part of the process, she enjoyed being with him, even though she felt was not much help.

Eventually she finished eating, and he, not interested in food and going a mile a minute, bounced back to his desk and kept writing. Amelia removed the breakfast dishes, but not before pouring him a fresh cup of coffee. As she left the study, she smiled. He was a great writer, he just needed to be reminded of that.

She left him alone for much of the day. She took in sandwiches at lunchtime, and was given a few pages to read and to comment on. She gave her thoughts and left again.

He was so happy when he was busy. Franklin ended up writing the rest of the day and into part of the night. By the next afternoon, he had the manuscript finished, and he took it to the publisher, returning at dinnertime.

"You'll never guess," he said booming as he entered the house, "My publisher accepted the book after only reading the first two chapters! He's going to publish it!"

Chapter Twenty-Two

The next day Franklin awoke with the feeling that he wanted to do something special to surprise Amelia. They went out for walks every day, but they never went out on the town. He wanted to do something for her, to take her somewhere special. At breakfast, he mentioned he was writing a new story and asked her if she would mind if they went on their walk after dinner.

"I'm in a pivotal place in the outline of the story and I need to plow through it," he said. "And I won't be joining you for lunch."

Amelia tried to entertain herself throughout the morning, but failed at all attempts. Lunch was quiet. Unable to focus on the words on the page of the book she was reading, Amelia lectured herself for sulking in the afternoon. She went to the kitchen and offered to help Mrs. Finnegan prepare dinner. She had come to enjoy the slow pace and the regularity of the days, but she admitted to herself, a change in pattern was always good. Emily gave her some embroidery, but her stitches looked juvenile. In frustration she said aloud to no one, she didn't understand why anyone would actually enjoy making pictures out of fabric and thread. She put down the embroidery and stood. Accidentally, she moved the small sofa that she was sitting on. When going to move it back, she looked around and realized she didn't like the setup of the room. She suddenly got an idea for an adjustment she knew would help the room have a better feel.

***

Franklin came to collect Amelia just before dinner, and found her awkwardly loping across the room carrying a small armchair to the other side of the room. He ran to help her, only to stop in amazement as he looked around the room and saw the change. She had moved everything.

Amelia sat the chair down and looked at Franklin with a winded exuberance, placing her hands on her hips in triumph. His face had a stunned look on it, his mouth agape. She panicked realizing she hadn't thought to ask his permission.

Before, the room just felt wrong. And it felt better when she moved one piece of furniture. Then another, then another, and then the whole room needed reconfiguration. Before, it wasn't as inviting to readers as a library should be. It had felt like clustered furniture that someone had piled in the room, not knowing what to do with any of it. But now... it felt inviting. At least she thought it did.

Franklin hadn't moved from his frozen stance and he hadn't said anything. She waited for his anger to fly. She could feel it coming.

"I'm so sorry," she said as she started to lift the chair again. "I should have asked. The room just felt wrong to me. I shifted one chair by accident, and then one thing led to another, and, well... here you are." She took a step with the chair in her hands, "I will put it all back."

Franklin took Amelia in. Her hair, now disheveled, with pieces coming loose from her bun, gave her the appearance of a shocked lion tamer.

"Well, I guess I shouldn't leave you for long amounts of time. Or maybe I should." He scratched his head in thought. "You know, I rather like it."

"You do?" she asked, setting the chair down again.

"Yes. My aunt decorated this place, and I just left everything. I'm rarely in this room, rarely in any room except my study, until you arrived," he said, smiling at her. "Let's leave it. Although, beware of Emily. She won't be too happy that you've unearthed places she rarely dusts." He took another look around the room and said, "It really does look nice. More... inviting." He turned to look at her. "Anything else you would like to do in here?"

Amelia ran and hugged him. Franklin went stiff with surprise at her embrace and then cautiously wrapped his arms around her, returning the hug. "To what do I owe this honor?"

Still hugging him, she replied, "In my time, this is what I wanted to do for a living. To decorate rooms for other people. Professionally. But with no experience, no one would hire me and no one ever asked me for *my* ideas." She stood back from him with her arms still embracing him. "Thank you."

"You're welcome." He smiled with all the warmth of a blazing fire.

They remained in their embrace. Franklin knew he should remove himself from her arms, but he didn't want to.

Amelia's stomach growled. Franklin laughed, and stepped back. "Are you always hungry?"

"Only at meal times. And moving furniture is hard work and much more exciting than embroidery. Ever met a woman who gets a workout from embroidering pillow cases?"

"I can only imagine the strong man at a circus doing embroidery, it's intriguing and a bit disturbing!"

Amelia burst into laughter and Franklin joined in. They went into dinner laughing.

***

After dinner, as Franklin promised, they went for their walk. The evening was lovely. It was April, and the flowers were blooming and the air was warm, the chill of winter subsiding. They meandered through the park, through The Long Meadow, talking about Amelia's ideas for decorating the house. They walked through the Vale of Cashmere discussing the weather. Through the rose garden, still just a bunch of gray, thorny sticks this early in the year, talking about Franklin's book. He told Amelia how he woke up with a brilliant idea, and as he started to write, it developed into another idea. Which blossomed into a third idea. After capturing glimmers of each on paper, he just sat, not knowing what idea to follow. Frustrated, and having three ideas that he couldn't figure out how to finish, he came to find Amelia rearranging the room.

Amelia, caught up in his comical narrative, didn't realize that they had left the park and were walking down a street she didn't recognize. It was a lovely neighborhood full of budding trees. They passed a few other couples out for an evening stroll, and husbands rushing home from work. As they headed down Flatbush Avenue, Amelia could sense that Franklin was leading them somewhere. She wanted to ask, but loved that he was trying to surprise her, so she feigned ignorance and kept conversing.

Franklin stopped outside of a small storefront that had a pink and white striped awning with metal tables and chairs out front that looked like they were made of white lace. Through the large glass window, Amelia could see inside there were a few patrons, mostly teenagers talking and eating out of glass cups.

"Did you… take me out for ice cream?" Amelia asked.

"I thought… You might…" he sighed and rubbed the back of his neck with his hand, looking down at his shoes. "It's just that you enjoy food so much, I thought that you would enjoy ice cream."

She looked into his eyes for a moment and then reached out and took the hand that was still at his side and held it in hers. He looked up at her, and she smiled.

"I love ice cream," she said in a quiet confession.

A large smile spread across his face. He moved to the door and opened it for her. He followed her inside, and the sticky sweet smell of fresh baking waffle cones and creamed sugar greeted their noses. There was a stout man wiping down the tall and pristine white countertop. He was wearing an all-white coat and pants, with a pink apron around his waist, that matched the awning outside and the inside seat cushions. A few young couples were scattered around the establishment, most of their heads together in quiet conversations. A large giggle arose from the corner, where a teenage girl was licking at a cone while the boy across from her made silly faces.

"Whad'll it be, folks?" said the proprietor from behind the counter, pulling her focus back.

Amelia turned her head back to the counter. "What are you having?" she whispered to Franklin.

"Well," he whispered back, "they have three flavors; vanilla, chocolate, or butter pecan. You can get a cone, or in a tray with chocolate or caramel sauce. Or you can get a milkshake or a soda. I am getting vanilla in a cone."

"Hmm." Amelia put one finger up to her lips in thought. "May I get all three flavors with both chocolate and caramel sauce?"

"I don't know why I thought you would want anything less," he said, smiling. Franklin turned to the man at the counter and ordered all three flavors in a tray with both chocolate and caramel sauce on top. "And for me," he started and then glanced at Amelia who was looking around the ice cream shop again, her eyes hovering on the young giggling couple in the corner, "I'll have the same thing."

Amelia whipped her head around, having heard Franklin. "But I thought you wanted vanilla in a cone."

"You changed my mind," he said quietly, looking into her eyes. She looked back into his beautiful gray eyes for a moment before the intensity became too much for her.

"Here you are, sir. That will be twenty cents."

Franklin handed over the money and picked up the two dishes of ice cream. "Where would you like to sit, dear?" he offered his elbow to her. She took his arm and led them over to a table that was at the front window. They sat down, and Franklin noticed how her eyes sparkled as she looked hungrily at the ice cream. She lifted her spoon and hesitated, making eye contact with him. He had sat, but was leaning forward on his elbows with his chin resting on his fingers, watching her.

"Please, go ahead. I want to see if you attack the ice cream as voraciously as you did the living room."

She smirked at him and then took a spoonful of vanilla dripping with chocolate and caramel sauce. Chocolate dripped on her chin, so he leaned across and wiped it with his napkin. She blushed and then wiped the area again with her own napkin.

"This is amazing. Drippy, but amazing."

"I'm so glad you like it," he beamed back at her, lifting his spoon and taking a bite still looking at her. As the spoon left his mouth, his eyes looked down at the dish of ice cream before him. "Mmmmm! I can't believe all of these flavors actually work together, but it really is good."

"I can't believe you shoved some of each flavor in your mouth on the first spoonful! You're a wild man!"

They laughed together, tittering just like the two teens in the opposite corner. As they enjoyed their ice cream, they chatted about young love, marveling at the innocence of the couples surrounding them. Franklin and Amelia kept catching each other's glance and then coyly looking away, in embarrassment or denial, much like a young flirting couple themselves.

They finished their ice cream and Franklin returned the dishes to the counter, bidding the proprietor good evening. He opened the door for her as she exited. Outside, Franklin offered his arm, Amelia took it and shivered.

"Are you cold?"

"Probably from the ice cream," she lied. Trembling from the touch of him, she snuggled closer, taking advantage of the situation.

Chatter was sparse on the way home. When they arrived back at the house, a note on the front hall table from Mrs. Finnegan said that she and Emily had left for the evening and would be back in the morning.

Amelia, now feeling awkward and not knowing what to do, headed toward the stairs.

"I think I'll head on up to my room, if you don't mind. It's been a lovely evening, but I think I'd like to read a little."

"Yes, of course. I hope you enjoyed it?"

"Yes. Yes, I enjoyed it immensely. I..."

"Well, then," he said with a sudden rigidity, "I will leave you to your book. I should head back in and start work on the new manuscript. Good night," he said, giving her a tiny bow and walked off to the study without looking back. "Good night," she murmured softly after him. Confusion crossed her face. Amelia realized after they entered the house, he had not touched her.

She started up the stairs, wondering how he was attentive and flirtatious all evening, and then was suddenly cold. Her wonderment gave way to gratitude as she turned the knob for her door. Amelia realized when he had been standing next to her, all she had wanted was for him to kiss her.

***

Franklin closed the door to the study and turned to lean against it. He sighed deeply. *What* was he thinking? He liked spending time with Amelia. She was enchanting. And her thoughts on his manuscript helped him not only resurrect it, but inspired him to finish it. He had taken her out for ice cream to say thank you, but instead found himself longing to be with her. But he couldn't want that. She was bound to leave sooner or later. And he needed to live his life as he intended: as a bachelor writer who enriched the lives of others. He needed no one.

His brain, so inconstant, was not to be trusted. Melancholia, the doctors said. He was told there was no cure for it, and no way to treat it other than the pills that made him too groggy to get out of bed, let alone write. He refused to take them. He reminded himself that his horrid bouts of insomnia and melancholia were not things with which a decent man would saddle a beautiful woman.

Amelia made the world seem like someone had cleaned the mud off the windows. The sun shone whenever she was in the room. In his world of vanilla ice cream, she was chocolate and butter pecan and caramel all at the same time. What would he do if he lost her? She was not his to begin with, he reasoned. She would leave. They all do. He must protect himself and not get too close... but it was so hard to stay away from the light once one had seen it.

***

Amelia entered her room, marveling. Franklin seemed so happy tonight. His happiness was what made her want to kiss him. His smile was so beautiful. His aloofness just now was an odd turn. Amelia didn't understand. She thought over everything that happened this evening. Had she said something, made the incorrect response, or made a face at anything he had said? She couldn't put her finger on anything exactly. While they were at the ice cream shop he seemed even younger and more exuberant than she had ever seen him. Possibly because he had just had his book accepted, she reasoned. Sure, she had helped with that, but it was ultimately his book, his thoughts, his writing. She didn't do much, other than to keep him from burning it.

She thought of the way his eyes lit up after tasting all of the ice cream flavors at once. She laughed out loud, then covered her lips with her fingers, as if self-conscious that someone would hear her. He was so boyish and handsome at that moment. He was so excited when he rushed in to tell her that his book would be published. He didn't exactly thank her, but she would like to think that this entire evening was for that. Her heart swelled.

Amelia straightened up and pushed away from the door. This wasn't right. She couldn't feel for Franklin like this. Not that he wasn't a good man who deserved love, but she already had her heart reserved for Jack. Good, kind Jack who was off saving lives. She sighed. What was she to do? She needed to leave this place before she fell in deeper. Either that or she needed to be cautious about how she handled herself around Franklin. He was a friend, and nothing more. A handsome friend who took her out for ice cream and made her smile. Enough, Amelia! She scolded herself.

She moved away from the door and busied herself by getting ready for bed. As she pulled back the covers she was trying to think of Jack and not Franklin, but tonight kept creeping back into her thoughts. What a lovely evening it was. And it was such a lovely gesture. She lay down and stared up at the ceiling, *willing* herself to stop thinking of what joy it was to read Franklin's manuscript and to help him finish it.

Terror ripped through her mind. Had she changed history? Had she done something that might cause a ripple in time? Surely a book getting published wouldn't cause any major results. No wars would be started, or people killed, or lives ruined by a man putting his ideas to paper and having them published. Well, that is what they probably said about the *Declaration of Independence* and look what that did. Amelia sighed. What was done, was done. Or was it?

Chapter Twenty-Three

Deep longing for Jack continued, but it lessened with her daily routine. Although she had not figured out the logistics of her travel to the past, she was doing her best to enjoy being here.

Every morning, Emily would come in and help Amelia with the morning ablutions and preparations for the day. Emily would share the local gossip, whether she wanted to know it or not. After her morning visit with Emily, Amelia would attempt to return home, and would descend the stairs a few times winding the watch and would find herself still in Franklin's hallway. Failing to return to her time, she settled in the rearranged front room and would watch the foot traffic out the window. Mid-morning she would visit Franklin in his study if he hadn't surfaced before then. He would share his recent pages, they would discuss ideas, or she would just sit in one of his chairs and read one of the hundreds of books he had. Late morning, Amelia would excuse herself and meet up with Mrs. Finnegan to discuss menus, help with shopping, or just to hear stories about Franklin's past.

Amelia would have lunch with Franklin, often in the dining room, but sometimes in the breakfast nook. They would take a stroll in the park afterwards, discussing literature, the city, Franklin's writing, different things between 1912 and in Amelia's future that she missed, and other things. Returning to Franklin's, she would head to the library by herself, or would return to Franklin's study with him. Amelia loved just being near him.

One afternoon she looked around concerned if it was wrong that she loved it here? She loved this place, even though she felt guilty that she couldn't figure out how to get back home. Even though she did tried daily, some days she didn't yearn for her time at all. As days rolled by, fleeting moments of the future surfaced in odd moments like the earworm of a Ben Folds song, a craving for a caramel latte or wanting her mother's bracelet. She missed wearing it, because it made her feel close to her mother.

This recession of her need to return felt like a deep cut healing. The ache of the original wound pained her only in sporadic moments. When she was feeling safe and happy here in the past, then suddenly she would have a twinge of the present, reminding her that she didn't really belong here. No matter how much she liked it.

These moments reminded Amelia, she was only a visitor here, she would feel terrible. How could she feel comfortable here and forget about Jack? The man she loved and abandoned back in the future. She couldn't just give him up. She shouldn't. But the need to return to him seemed to diminish each day. Was it because time was making it easier to deal with? Because Jack was at a great distance before she came here? Or was it because she was falling in love with Franklin?

She didn't know what to do with that last thought, so she hid it in the back of her mind and changed "falling in love" to "felt deeply." Caring for Franklin was a Pandora's Box in itself—a thousand questions that all seemed to be answered with more questions. She wished she knew what to do. Or that she could find an answer in his books. For now, she would enjoy the time she spent with Franklin and the admiration he showered her with. She would push all other thoughts aside for now. Especially thoughts about Jack, as they only made her sad.

Chapter Twenty-Four

"Have I told you about Franklin and the first book he ever wrote?" Mrs. Finnegan said to Amelia as she skulked into the kitchen. "You look *just* like him when he was writin'. Only you seem to have less frustration and more sadness. Sit, child. Would you like some hot cocoa?"

Amelia shook her head but sat.

"How about some chocolate milk?"

Amelia thought for a moment, and then like a child making a great decision, she bobbed her head up and down.

Mrs. Finnegan made the milk and sat it along with a plate of cookies, freshly baked in front of Amelia.

"Now then. Tell me what's 'ailin' ya."

Amelia took a large gulp of milk and a bite of a cookie while she tried to figure out how to explain to Mrs. Finnegan without revealing the unbelievable parts.

"Well," Amelia sighed a deep sigh, "there is… was… is a man back home. His name is Jack. And I…"

"...can't stop thinkin' about him."   Mrs. Finnegan finished the sentence for Amelia. "Ya know, it's difficult to get rid of feelin's for someone you've cared so deeply about." Finnegan patted her hand in understanding.

"And it's not that I don't feel for Franklin, I do—" Amelia said, so Mrs. Finnegan wouldn't get the wrong idea.   But the moment they were out of her mouth, she knew she meant those words.   "—it's just that... when I was with Jack, I thought he was the only man for me. But things changed, here I am, and I'm conflicted. I miss Jack, I feel like I should go back, but I want to be here, too." Amelia put her head in her hands, and leaned forward on the counter on her elbows.

She felt the warm, calloused hands of the wise Mrs. Finnegan gently wrap around hers.

"Now, now, then."   Mrs. Finnegan whispered. "You love Franklin. Any blind person could see that. And I can tell you're awful sorry for the loss of your man back home. But ya made the decision ya did and now your duty is here. Rest your mind, child. No one ever said that you only had to love one person. They just said you can't go fraternizing with many people without creatin' jealousy and bein' called a lot of colorful names."

Amelia started to giggle through her hands and peeked from out behind them.   In her mind she heard Mrs. Finnegan saying things like "brazen hussy" or "slattern" in her accent and couldn't help but laugh. Amelia smiled at the wise woman before her, and took a deep breath.

"I do love him," she said, looking into Mrs. Finnegan's eyes.

"I know you do, dearie. And he loves ya back. He deserves to be well-loved and to love in return, just like you do. So let him do it. He can be a difficult man, but show me a man who isn't, who is worth anythin'!"

Giving Amelia's hands a pat, Mrs. Finnegan turned back to cutting the vegetables she was preparing.

After drinking half of the milk and two cookies, Amelia felt a little normal again.

"What's the story about Franklin's first book?"

"Ah," said Mrs. Finnegan smiling over her shoulder. "He was twelve. And he had to write a book on the pain and suffering of worms."

"What?"

"Yes. His father was redoing the garden, ripping out everything. Franklin was an only child, ya see and his father, always wanting to make Franklin's mother happy would entertain any of her whims. Well, Franklin wasn't happy that the worms in the garden were being uprooted from their homes, and so that little boy took it upon himself to write about the injustice. Only he didn't know where to begin. He knew his father's language was the law. It is what all his father's friends spoke. So, to get through to his father, that little boy wrote a story about a worm who had just made a nice cozy home in a peaceful backyard, only to be uprooted by a vicious, evil king out for revenge."

"Was it a picture book?"

"Oh, no. He was a serious writer even then. It had eleven chapters. Eighty pages long. He typed it up and had two or three drafts. One day he came in, with a long face, like the one you was wearin' when you walked in a bit ago. He sighed and sat down, fillin' up that kitchen with the hot air of his sighs."

"How adorable."

"Adorable, my foot. He had a temper, even then. After he spent a good ten minutes sighing, finally I coaxed it out of him why he was upset. He fussed about how his father said he refused to read a book unless it was published and bound."

"No."

"Yes. His father was hard on Franklin. And his mother ignored him, too busy with a social life and her whims, while she was livin'. Which wasn't much long after he wrote his first book. She went real peaceful, tryin' to give birth to Franklin's sister, who followed his mother shortly to the grave."

"Oh, I'm so sorry."

"Don't be troublin' yourself none. She was a pretty woman, and knew it, too. She and I tweren't close. I came over from his father's family. Anyway, I'm strayin' from the story. Little Franklin was determined to have his father read his book and save the worms in the backyard. So he went off to a publisher, with all the money he had in the world. Just over three dollars. He asked the man if he would publish one copy of the book for him."

Mrs. Finnegan stopped chopping vegetables and came closer to Amelia, still intently listening while munching another cookie.

"And what did that publishin' man do? He took Franklin's neatly typed papers, and sewed them together and put cardboard on the front and back with a leather spine. Franklin ran home in the middle of it and was lookin' for me frantically all over the house. 'Mrs. F,' he hollered out when he finally found me in the kitchen makin' dinner. 'What do I call my book? The man needs a title.' Well, I had no idea what to tell him, and I had no idea what was happenin' at that publishin' house. So I told him he should call it *A New Home for Displaced Worms*.

"Later he comes home, proud as a peacock, and struts into my kitchen and slaps down this bound book right next to the chicken I had just pulled out of the oven. 'There, Finney,' he said, 'That is my first published book.'"

"You must have been so proud of him," said Amelia.

"I was," Mrs. Finnegan returned from the memory and looked at Amelia. "He was so proud of that book. He showed it to his father during dinner. After, he dragged Franklin to his study and right in front of him tossed the thing into the fire. A maid who walked by the room said that Franklin stood there, his hands clasped behind his back, watching the thing go up in flames, and didn't shed a tear or protest. That was the moment that he decided he didn't want to follow in his father's footsteps, whether he knew it or not. I suppose he told you that he started out in college to be a lawyer, but it just didn't take?"

"Yes, he did mention that."

"He refused to study. At least that's what I'm believin' to this day. That little boy could remember all kinds of facts. He could recite whole radio shows after hearin' them once or twice. You can't tell me that kind of skill just disappears after you grow up. No, sirree. He wanted to prove a point to his father. Sadly, that point never took while his father was alive. He passed when Franklin was in his third year at the university. His father got real sick." Finnegan looked sad. "Franklin thought it was his fault for the longest time."

Amelia followed Finnegan's gaze toward the door expecting Franklin to be standing there. "How terrible," she said.

"Well, adversity brings out the traits we use most in life, strengthening us."

"I guess so. I just wish I knew what traits this particular adversity is strengthening." Amelia twisted the wedding ring on her finger.

"You'll make your way, dearie." Mrs. Finnegan said patting her hands. "Now, shoo. Out of my kitchen," she said, taking away the empty cup and plate.

Amelia smiled at her, and started to leave. She turned and walked back to the other woman, wrapped her arms around her, and Amelia gave Finnegan a huge bear hug.

"Thank you."

"'T'was nothin'."

Amelia let go and left the kitchen. Maybe it was the story, or the company, or the cookies, but she felt better.

She missed Jack. But Mrs. Finnegan was right, there was something she needed to learn about herself here. Amelia just hoped she could figure out what she was supposed to learn.

Chapter Twenty-Five

Returning from their walk one afternoon, they were greeted at the front door by an excited Emily.

"Sir, Missus, you have a visitor in the library."

"Who, Emily?" Amelia asked.

"Mister Caruthers."

"Did you order more dresses, my dear?" Franklin turning to Amelia.

"Oh, my, I don't think so."

"I don't think this is about dresses, missus.'

"Well, let's go see what he wants, shall we?" Franklin said, leading the way. "Thank you, Emily."

She had started to follow them down the hall, but stopped, bobbed a small curtsy and made herself scarce. Amelia thought to herself, Emily was probably going to a nook where she could observe everything going on in the room, unseen. That sneaky girl always knew the good gossip, and she had to have some way to listen in on conversations. Amelia smiled to herself. She was glad to have Emily around to be her informant. She was also glad that she had nothing to hide, because although Emily was trustworthy, one never knew another person completely. Or to whom they gossiped.

At the front room, Franklin opened the door, and allowed Amelia to enter first. She saw Jon looking about the room. When he heard Franklin shut the door, Jon turned, a smile blooming on his face. He crossed the room with both hands reaching toward Amelia's.

"How are my favorite newlyweds?" Jon asked, looking back and forth between the two, until he reached for Amelia taking her hands in his.

"We are well. Thank you." Amelia said, putting on an inquisitive smile. "And you?"

"Oh, the same. Lots of stitching. Lots of gossip."

"Maybe I should leave you two alone then," Franklin started to take a step back.

"Possibly. But before you go, I have some information that includes you," Jon said, still holding Amelia's hands, but looking Franklin in the eye.

"Yes?" Franklin said, in a morbidly curious voice.

"Well," Jon began, tucking Amelia's arm under his elbow and leading her to the settee. "Mrs. Windsor, you know who lives in the brown brick monstrosity on the corner of Eighth Avenue and Carroll—I was showing her the new fabrics for the season, and her terrible gossip of a friend, Mrs. Lafleur, who lives next door to her, came rushing in. She told her that she had actually seen you two eating ice cream and laughing together in public, like teenagers." Amelia and Franklin exchanged a look and both blushed. "Oh, so it's *true*! How *delightful!* Well, anyway. Mrs. Windsor couldn't believe that Mrs. Dunne actually exists. She thinks, my dear, that you are a figment of Mr. Dunne's writing habits to keep all of the eligible young ladies at bay. Until the gossip of you two actually being seen together started spreading, I guess many of the society ladies thought the same thing."

Amelia started to interrupt, but Jon just kept rolling with the information.

"The two old biddies went back and forth with different conjectures on how you, Amelia, must be nothing to look at, otherwise Mr. Dunne would have accepted more invitations and would have taken you out to meet other ladies in society, so they could properly invite you to their homes to greet you." Amelia turned to Franklin, her eyes squinted with confusion, tinged with anger.

"I'm sorry, my dear." He shrank back in the leather wingback chair in which he sat. "I ignore society's politics. I just assumed you wouldn't want to deal with the gossiping ninnies of this neighborhood. Truthfully, I didn't particularly want to spend an evening with any of their husbands," he mumbled the last part while sinking further in the chair.

Amelia had a confused look on her face and turned questioningly back to Jon.

"They asked me about you," Jon said picking up where he left off, "and I told them that I had only seen you briefly to be measured for dresses," Jon put a hand to his chest, "but you were lovely. Oh, and *how* they took *that*! They went into a tizzy, conjecturing what you must look like and trying to figure out what kind of woman would land a recluse writer. No offense, Franklin."

"None taken," Franklin sat up again. It was good to have a reputation as a writer. And he *liked* being seen as a recluse. Gave him the permission to remain aloof and out of the society that his mother always pushed him towards.

"Oh, no." Amelia wailed and put her head in her hands. Franklin stood and took a step toward her, a look of distress crossed his face.

"Not to worry! Mrs. Windsor threatened—excuse me, *proposed*—that Mrs. Lafleur throw you a party, since your wedding was out of town and your honeymoon travels were cut short due to Franklin's schedule. She was astounded to know you hadn't been out on the town at all because your clothing was lost along the way."

Amelia eyed Jon. "Who did she hear *that* from?"

"Well…" Jon stood up and looked away.

Franklin sat on her other side, taking her hands in his. She looked into his face and ran her fingers over his hair, smoothing out a few pieces that had gone rogue. Jon looked back at Amelia about to confess, but he was halted by the touching scene that was right in front of him. Jon sighed.

"I am sorry," Jon said, "I am a terrible gossip, and even worse about inciting more or enabling those women to do their worst. They always turn on each other and it is so fun to watch." Amelia turned her attention back to Jon, still holding onto Franklin's hand and thought Jon would be a fan of *The Real Housewives*. Actually, Jon might actually *be on* the New York one, if he were one hundred years older. Amelia smiled, and stifled a laugh at the thought. Jon took it as she was laughing at him.

"So... you're not mad at me?"

"Oh, Jon. No." Her chuckle rolled into a full storm of laughter. "Franklin, it looks like we have to make an appearance at a party. Now, when you get *that* invitation, you have to say yes. And as your punishment for not informing me of past invitations, you have to attend." He made a face and was about to say something but she cut him off. "And you have to be nice."

Franklin stood. "I think I can face anything, even Mrs. Windsor, and her bore of a husband, with you on my arm."

"Flattery looks good on you, Franklin. You should use it often. Especially to Mrs. Windsor." Jon winked. "You know her husband owns half of Brooklyn,"

"Just as long as I don't have to take Mrs. Windsor out for ice cream."

They all laughed.

"And to make amends," Jon said looking at Amelia, "I plan to make you a dress that will be the talk of the town."

"I'll accept your dress. But you can't fool me. I know I'll be a walking advertisement for you—and don't you try to deny it Mr. Caruthers!"

"Well, as I can tell that this conversation is quickly going to move into ruffles and chintz, so I'm going to excuse myself, and go do something manly, like write about sword fighting," Franklin said.

"Yes, yes. Go. Write another masterpiece while we discuss *important* things!" Amelia waved him out of the room while winking.

"Now," she said, turning back to Jon, "let's make a dress that will make jaws drop."

"But I thought you didn't want to be my walking calling card."

"Oh, no. I never said that. I just know *exactly* what you're doing. And I'm up to the task."

"Well… I was thinking something dramatic…"

They chatted about the dress for a long time. When Emily came in with refreshments, Amelia asked for her opinion. They were friends after all. Together the three came up with a great concept.

Emily suggested the dress have a square neckline to show off Amelia's neck. Jon suggested that he wanted to go a step further and give the dress high lapels that would stand up straight in the back, but fold over in the front. This would give the feel of a men's jacket and a Victorian collar. With the drama of the high neck, Jon decided he wanted to make a peephole on the upper back of the dress, but Emily rejected the idea stating that it would be too risqué for the first party—but for the next outing, it would be a fun surprise. Instead, Emily suggested that Jon needed to accentuate Amelia's other features. Amelia had a shapely body and had added a bit more padding to her curves recently since this society didn't allow her to take her regular jogs in the park. It just so happened that the places where Amelia's body naturally had filled out were the places that current society strove to accentuate. Her hips and bust were much curvier here, but it added to her silhouette in the popular way. Jon decided that he would divert attention to her tiny waist, which remained almost the same measure as when she arrived, no thanks to Mrs. Finnegan's cooking. The last thing they decided on was the color. Amelia suggested green, as Franklin liked her in green. Emily and Jon gave each other a look and a nod, and then said in almost perfect unison: sapphire. With that decision, the meeting adjourned.

***

The night of the party Amelia was nervous. What would it be like to meet these women? Would they be vicious? She had seen *Titanic* with Leo and Kate, and was a fan of *Downton Abbey*—were the women depicted accurately in these filmed versions of the time? Deep breaths. She would do her best, even though she didn't know much about the proper etiquette and how to behave. Emily kept bustling in and out helping Amelia get ready. Franklin had dined separately, so they hadn't seen each other since early in the day.

Amelia's dress had arrived yesterday, and she had tried it on for Jon in case of alterations. None were needed, of course. It fit like a glove. The uproarious approvals of Jon and Emily made her feel more confident. Mrs. Finnegan even stopped in to offer her appreciation of the dress as well. Amelia clung to those comments. She could certainly make it through the evening as long as she was wearing the beautiful dress.

Amelia had now eaten and bathed. Emily had left to take the tray down. Sitting by the fire, Amelia waited and tried to read. Her eyes wouldn't focus on the words. She had another of Franklin's novels and was about a hundred pages in, but couldn't comprehend any of it, she was too distracted. A fog of distraction that she was forgetting tapped at her brain all day. It had something to do with tonight, but she couldn't figure it out. Setting the book down in the seat she started pacing and tried to focus but was quickly jolted out of the thought by a knocking on the door. Lunging to her chair, she picked up the book while bidding entrance. She didn't want Emily to think she was nervous.

After hearing the door close, Amelia continued staring at the page but said, "Emily, how is Franklin doing? Is he dressed yet? I swear that man would rather cuddle up with his pen and paper than show off his wife."

"Well, you're partially right."

Amelia stood and turned quickly, horror filling her at the sound of a baritone voice that wasn't Emily's. Her heart flipped when she saw Franklin.

"Oh," she gasped, "I thought you were Emily." She covered her mouth in embarrassment and wrapped the other arm around her dressing gown-covered waist, hugging herself protectively. She tried to think of something to say, and couldn't bring herself to look at him.

"It's quite alright," he said taking a few hesitant steps toward her, "Finney mistakes me for Emily all the time," he said, joking to lighten the mood while ducking his head to meet her eyes.

Amelia laughed and looked up at him. Her breath caught. He was resplendent. In a full tuxedo, Franklin looked amazing. A bow tie and a vest with his crisp white shirt front and gleaming black shoes made him picture perfect. The way Amelia looked at him made Franklin warm and he looked down at his feet.

"You like it?" he asked hesitantly.

"Yes," and she crossed to him and circled around him, touching his shoulders, and then brushing her hands down his lapels. "You're dazzling." Looking Franklin over, Amelia became self-conscious remembering dressing gown was loose. She pulled it closed a little more.

"Well, thank you," he said, meeting her eyes. "I see... you're not yet dressed?"

"No. Emily didn't want me to wrinkle the dress, and she was supposed to come back and put up my hair. I am so embarrassed in the way I spoke about you."

"Ah, well that explains it. And you are right, I would much rather spend time with pen and paper this evening then go to the party. But I am delighted to step out with you."

Amelia's heart fluttered a little at his words. She didn't know how to reply. So many thoughts flowed through her mind. Finally, she couldn't stand the silence between them.

"I... Emily. I should find Emily," she said, starting for the door.

"Oh, I told her to wait until I came out."

"Oh?"

"Yes. You see I wanted to give you... ask you...this was my mother's," he said, drawing a velvet pouch out of his breast pocket. It was a much larger version of the one from which Amelia had recovered the watch. He stepped toward her offering it with both of his upturned hands.

She stepped forward and reached for it. "For me?"

"Yes. I mean, if you don't want to, if it doesn't go with your dress..."

Reaching out for the proffered pouch, Amelia met his eyes. She untied the strings that held the bag closed and reached in. As she pulled out the heavy object, he moved in even closer. Impatiently he removed it from her hand as she gasped at its beauty. He fastened the thing around her neck. "Go look."

Amelia went across the room to her vanity table and sat. She gasped again and met his eyes reflected in the mirror.

"This is... for me?"

"Do you like it," he asked, resting his hands gently on her shoulders. She placed a hand over his. He smiled down at her. "Father always bought my mother jewelry when he won a case in court. This case had been particularly lucrative and he knew mother wanted a very large sapphire. So, he found one and had the family jeweler— Mercer—made it into a necklace. I heard Emily say that your mysterious dress is sapphire, so I thought I would help gild the lily."

"It is simply stunning."

"As my wife, it is yours to keep. I certainly have no use for it. My mother would want my wife to have it, especially for her introduction to New York society." Then his face changed quickly. "I should let you get ready," and he turned and left the room quickly.

"Thank you," she barely said before he closed the door. He was so peculiar at times.

She turned back to the mirror to look at her reflection again. The sapphire was an inch large square. Set in white gold, little tiny daisy-like prongs held it in place. Skinny lines of metal ran outward in parallel lines, changing direction at the corners, and gave the impression of an art deco-style blue sun. The lines met a vine-like frame that was dotted with diamonds. It had a heavy link chain that was choker length, but made the pendant sit just below the notch in her throat.

Emily had come up behind her and gasped at the jewel. "That is a glorious necklace, missus. It will go perfectly with the dress. Mr. Dunne sure had a happy look when he left this room, I'll tell ya."

Still stunned at the gift, Amelia smiled at Emily's remark. As Emily twisted and pinned her hair, she just stared at the necklace around her neck in the mirror. Emily also applied her makeup and then helped her get into her dress. Before Amelia knew it, she was dressed and ready to go. Amelia's hair was up but it looked like it was cascading down the back of her head, soft and fluffy. The dress was a stunning shade of sapphire and it was the exact color of the stone. With its square neckline and lapel collar, the silk dress framed the necklace perfectly at her neck and then gave way to her pushed up décolletage. A diamond-shaped waistband hugged her front, and it wrapped around to her back in a straight line. The skirt dropped away from her waist making her hips look full, but her waist tiny. Several rows of ribbons and lace were at the bottom of the skirt. It was stunningly beautiful and the closer she looked at it, the more details could be seen. It was magnificent. Emily came up to her and put something up on her ears.

"Mr. Dunne said he forgot to give you these when he was in here before. They go with the necklace."

Amelia touched her earlobes and then dashed quickly to the mirror and gasped. The beautiful square sapphires dropped from her ears and twinkled.

"Now, you best be gettin' goin, missus. Don't want to keep 'em waitin' at your fancy party." Emily left the room smiling. She knew this was going to be an unforgettable night for Amelia, and she was happy for her.

Entranced with her own image and transformation, Amelia couldn't tear herself away from the mirror for a few minutes. She could feel that Franklin was downstairs waiting for her, and knew she should get moving. Amelia imagined the fairy tale that was about to happen: she would walk down the stairs in the stunning dress, and he would be at the bottom waiting for her, smiling up at her. With him looking at her, she would feel even more beautiful. They would go off to the party, and she would be admired by everyone and they would all want to get to know her. Amelia knew this was going to be a night to remember.

Pulling herself away from the mirror, Amelia started out of the room. She stopped, feeling something wasn't quite right. Even though she felt beautiful in this dress, she didn't feel like herself. Her glance brought her eyes to her nightstand and the watch. She knew she needed to wear it to feel more herself, and walked back to get it.

Closing her room door behind her, she relief with the watch in her hands. At the top of the stairs, she looked down, hoping to see him, but Franklin wasn't waiting for her. Well, she had probably taken too long, or he'd gotten a whiff of an idea and he went off to his study to work while she was primping. Sighing, she walked down the stairs in her lovely new dress.

Amelia started to put the watch on, and noticed that the date was wrong. She hadn't tried the watch this morning, or yesterday for that matter. It was now the first of the month, and she needed to change the date as yesterday was the thirtieth. Distractedly she turned the dial, and as the numbers changed from 31 to 1, the lights flickered and went dark.

Part Two
May — July

Chapter Twenty-Six

Standing in her hallway, she tried to convince herself that she had not gone back. But the electric lights confirmed it. Amelia closed her eyes like a child not wanting to wake up on the first day of school. She imagined herself at the party standing next to Franklin, who was being more courteous than he had ever been. His every look reminded Amelia just how beautiful she was.

But she knew. Days ago she had the feeling that the next time she touched the watch, it would take her back. She realized that she had been avoiding the watch the last few days. Oh, Franklin. Poor Franklin. Amelia didn't know what to do and was overcome. She had returned to her time just as easily as she had first traveled to Franklin's time. It was instant. She had wanted this for months. But now that it finally happened, she was shocked.

A sudden angry knocking made Amelia's eyes snap open. She waited to hear it again to make sure it was real.

Seconds passed. Amelia started to close her eyes to beg to jump through time again, but the banging jolted her out of her pleas. Jogging towards the front door to answer it, Amelia stopped herself in a panic. She couldn't answer the door dressed like this, she was in…She looked down—she was dressed in a pair of nice trousers and a lovely silk top, with an elegant blazer over it. Amelia was surprised that her clothing just changed from the period dress she was wearing automatically into something similarly appropriate for the current time. For a moment she mourned her beautiful dress that Jon had made for the party she was about to miss. But the outfit she was now wearing was a suit that was similar sapphire blue and a silky periwinkle blouse; something she would wear to a fancy dinner in this current time. But how…

The person at the front door hammered again. Whoever was there was very persistent. She walked toward the front door, her heels clicking on the newly-installed wooden floor. Knocking again, and a man's voice called out her name—it was a voice Amelia recognized. Could it be?

With energetic hope, she picked up speed for the last few steps to the door. It was odd to feel her legs without skirts wrapping all around them. She was excited. Had he actually traveled back with her? Or had he been able to follow her here? Her racing feelings made her dash to the door. She had seen him in what must only have been a few minutes ago, maybe half an hour, but the anxiety rose within her. How could she have not realized how she had grown to feel deeply for Franklin.

The wide smile she had as she threw open the door, sank. The face looking back at her was not the face she wanted to see, the one that lately made her feel like she was the most beautiful creature he had ever seen. The face she had left a moment ago, a century ago, of Franklin.

This face was familiar though—could it be? It was Jack.

"Well, you looked happy to see me for a second," he said. "Is it because I'm not dressed for the party I didn't know about, and you're mad at me?"

"Jack—I..." Amelia's breathless voice trailed off. "No, I was just... I just forgot what day it was and that you were supposed to arrive tonight," she improvised.

Amelia couldn't believe it. She had been gone for exactly two months.

Chapter Twenty-Seven

"W ell?" Jack asked her, "Are you going to let me in?"

"Oh!" She said as she jumped back out of the doorway. "Yes, of course. Come in. What can I help carry?"

"I've got it," he said as he waddled across the threshold with seven bags draped all over his body in different shapes and sizes, making him look like a large lumpy penguin. "Besides, you seem like you're dressed too well to be a bellhop."

"I, uh... have a dinner party that I was just heading out to," she spit out. Well, it was partially true. Tonight she was planning to attend a dinner party. Did it really matter that it was a hundred years ago? The thought of Franklin searching for her made her heart sink.

She needed to ignore that right now. Focus on Jack instead, she told herself. After all, hadn't she wanted to return to her own time? Focus on Jack. "Wow, if I didn't know better, I'd say from the looks of it that you've been traveling for two months," she said lightheartedly trying to distract from anything and everything she was thinking and feeling.

"Nah, I've only been gone for about sixty days. Give or take a day," he joked back and walked past her into the house. "Don't you treat yourself to this new invention called electric light?"

She looked past him into the dark house. "Oh, I was—" she thought quickly, what to say? "I was in my room getting dressed and it got dark. I ran to get the door and didn't think to turn any on. I'll help you to your room."

She quickly snapped on the light that was over the stairway. She grabbed one of his smaller bags and started up the stairs.

"So tell me about your trip," she said, trying to push away the fact that Franklin was probably scouring the house frantically looking for her.

Absent-mindedly, Amelia led him back to the room she had occupied in Franklin's house; the room Jack had kept his stuff in while he was here last time. While she led, he started to describe the rough first flight but how on his second flight he got bumped to first class. He talked about the chicken he was served for dinner, as he unloaded his body from all of his bags. He brought up the man he met in the airport who might be a good contact for purchasing tile for the kitchen and bathrooms while he started to unpack his immediately-needed toiletries, and hung up his sport coat in the closet. Amelia politely sat on his bed while he started unpacking but her mind drifted, half listening to

193

Jack, half trying to piece together her thoughts of what had just happened to her.

At some point she excused herself, saying that she needed to let the people know that she would be late for dinner, and she would let Jack settle in and unpack.

"Are you sure you don't mind if I stop by that party tonight, Jack? You just got home but I should at least make an appearance. I feel terrible that I confused the dates, and double-booked tonight," Amelia said. She needed to think, and she couldn't do that around him right now. She could leave the house. At least for a bit, to let her brain adjust, and so she could try to figure out her sudden time travel back here.

"Babe, of course not," Jack said, leaning in and giving her a kiss on the cheek. "You know how I was last time when I came home. I want to unpack, take a shower, and sleep."

"Good. Right, I mean," she said, catching herself. "I'll just go for a bit—"

"No. Please don't shorten your evening for me. I'll probably sleep until halfway through tomorrow with the jet lag and anti-circadian clock I've developed. I've been on a plane from Southern Chile for what feels like a week, and I was working such long hours these past few days. Please," he said as he walked over and took her face in his hands, "don't fuss over me." Jack looked into her eyes and gave her a light kiss on the forehead. "You fuss too much." Then he kissed her on the lips for a moment. Before she even gave the kiss a thought, it was over and he had turned his attention back to the suitcases. "Don't take this the wrong way, because it is great to see you, but get out of here!"

"Ok, if you're sure."

"I'm sure," he insisted.

"Do you want me to make you dinner or check in on you before I leave?"

"No," he said, "no need. I want a shower and then I want to make sweet love to that pillow."

"Well," she chuckled, "with a proposition like that, a gal can't help but want to get lost," she said in her best flapper drawl. "Good night," Amelia said, returning to her normal voice, "I'll see you tomorrow. Sometime?"

"Yes. I'll see you when I don't feel," he said, lifting his arm up and sniffing his armpit, "and smell, like a zombie."

She laughed and left the room, closing the door behind her. She let out a sigh, only realizing she'd been holding her breath since Jack walked into the house.

Chapter Twenty-Eight

Amelia walked away from Jack's door and headed down the stairs. She didn't actually have a dinner to attend or any place she needed to be, but she thought it best to keep up appearances and leave the house for a bit. She also just needed to get away from the house. She looked down at her watch. The party would be starting now—a century ago. She went to the front hall closet and grabbed a jacket and scarf. It was May first, she shouldn't need it. But she thought, if the night air didn't chill her, the thoughts of her predicament might.

What *was* she doing back here? How did she fall back? How must Franklin be feeling, and what would he be telling the other party guests?

Tears started pouring down her face as she grabbed her keys from the front table and walked out the front door, trying to make as little sound as possible. She was exhausted, and couldn't stop the tears from rolling down her cheeks. The pain in her heart started to flood the rest of her body.

Amelia found herself on a park bench, walking the nine blocks to Prospect Park without noticing. Amelia didn't know how long she sat there and sobbed. Luckily, it was a quiet spot on a bench just off a main path. It was the time of night between dog walking and late evening runners so foot traffic was almost non-existent. She was able to sob tragically without causing a scene. Not one single person passed by.

Hours seemed to pass. Finally feeling all cried out, walked back to her house. Jack would be asleep by now, and it was time to return to the house and face the ghosts—or actually, the hope that Franklin was haunting the house and he could give her solace, and help her figure out the answers she was seeking.

Amelia was in such a fog, she hadn't realized she was even back at her house until she had entered, locked the door behind her, hung up her coat, and was starting up the stairs. Out of habit, she started to call out for Mrs. Finnegan to let Franklin know she would be in her rooms, as she wasn't feeling well—but stopped herself before uttering a syllable. Amelia quietly walked up the steps, and went to her room.

Amelia sat on her bed with the light off. Somehow, things were easier for her mind to digest in darkness. What was she going to do? What *could* she do? Every question seemed to give way to another question, or it brought up two new questions. Was it *possible* to love two men at the same time, but in different years? Was it cheating if it was in a different time? What was the statute of limitations on the desert island scenario—"If trapped on a desert island with no hope of escape, blank is allowed..." and does it work with time travel? Should she tell Jack all that had happened to her? Would he believe her? Would it matter?

It seemed like only moments ago she sat on the edge of her bed, in Franklin's his time—funny that she had chosen this one to be hers, here. The thought hadn't registered with her through the last few months living in different time periods, until now. Strangely, it seemed to comfort her—as if he were here with her. She looked over at the digital clock. It glowed eerie electric blue. The time was 4:07. She should get some sleep.

Amelia stood up, clicked on the bedside lamp, and slowly undressed. It was an unfamiliar thing to remove these garments from her body. She went to unlace a corset and found bra clasps instead. She had to remind herself that her pants had no back ribbon to untie, but instead, a belt and a zipper in the front. Everything felt so foreign, but familiar at the same time. She knew she belonged here but knew it was completely wrong at the same time. Reaching up to her neck she went to remove the beautiful necklace and earrings Franklin had given her, only to find that they were not there. Looking at her ring finger she saw the wedding ring was not there either. For a moment she panicked and thought she had lost them in the park. Then she rationalized that she hadn't felt the weight of them, nor had Jack commented on them, so they must not have come through the transition with her. She quickly felt for the watch. It was there with her mother's bracelet back on her opposite wrist, the bracelet she hadn't seen in months. Odd, that. Her watch made it through time here and back, but other jewelry didn't and her clothing adapted. Well, it was easier the jewels hadn't returned with her, she thought. How would she explain a priceless necklace and a wedding band to Jack?

Not wanting to think about the past any more tonight, Amelia pulled on her pajama bottoms and a tank top and climbed into bed. However, they felt so wrong to her, so after a few moments of lying down, she rose back up and removed them, dropping them on the floor beside the bed. Crawling back under the soft sheets, she turned off the light. She couldn't get comfortable. Amelia had slept alone in the other time, but in the room Jack was now in. Her body anticipated Franklin's entrance at any moment, although she knew he would not come through the door. Amelia lay, willing herself to sleep and to quiet the questions that were in heavy circulation.

Finally, she fell into a fitful sleep. Amelia had a dream about both men meeting each other. Amelia sat off to the side while the two men heatedly discussed where, or rather when, Amelia was to live. Each argued she was more right in his time. She felt at any moment they would break out swords or dueling pistols. Eventually, with no conclusion reached, both men retreated to a room—which resembled Franklin's study, without walls, instead a hazy gray light formed the perimeter of the room. Amelia calmly sat on the settee, ignored by both men as if she wasn't there. She had been unable to speak, and could only watch Jack with his newspaper reading and rustling, and Franklin with his pen scratching feverishly at the paper on his desk, each waiting for some sort of movement from the other side. After what seemed like an agonizing eternity of watching the two men scowl in their own corners waiting for something to happen and feeling tension mounting—Amelia opened her mouth. When she did, only the sound of a faint car horn came out. Surprised, she closed her mouth, swallowed, and tried again to speak. She looked over at Franklin's desk, but he wasn't there. This time it was a fire engine's siren. She tried for a third time. A buzzing sound, which got louder and longer kept squeaking until Amelia in the dream suddenly gave way to her realization that it was the actual front door buzzer, and awoke suddenly, sitting straight up in bed.

Amelia jumped out of the sheets, and stumbled over the small pile lying on the floor beside the bed and ran out of the bedroom door. She thought to herself that it felt very chilly this morning for the beginning of May. She heard the sound again, and knew it had to be Franklin coming for her this time—she knew it. It had to be. She ran down the stairs and through the hallway over the creaky board. She looked down hoping her clothing had changed back and that last night was just an awful dream. When she did look down she was almost at the bottom of the stairs. She wasn't wearing anything at all. Her pajamas—she must have removed them in the night.

The buzzer impatiently rang again. She couldn't chance that the person at the front door, who she knew would be Franklin, would give up and disappear. She grabbed a canvas paint tarp from the sofa in the front living room to wrap around herself.

The buzzing had now elevated to knocking.

"Coming!" She shouted toward the door as she clumsily tried to fashion some sort of dress out of the shapeless tarp, tying two ends up around her neck, and trying to make some belting happen at her waist. She couldn't believe it, but she was *literally* wearing a tent.

Amelia threw open the front door to a man who was facing the street. The light gleamed off his hair just so. It was him. She *knew* it! It *was* Franklin!

"It's you!" she exclaimed.

The man turned around to face her.

"A *much* better reaction than last night," Jack replied.

He didn't notice her face drop again as he was fixated on her clothing—or lack thereof. As he stepped into the house, and closed the door behind him, she composed herself.

"Sorry! It took me so long to answer the door—I couldn't find anything to wear," Amelia joked, hoping he wouldn't notice her nervousness.

Obviously, he didn't because he wrapped his arms around her, and kissed her deeply on the lips.

"And I'm sorry to have woken you—must have been *some* party if you slept in this late! I went out this morning to get a paper and a coffee and forgot to take my keys! Habit of being in the jungle for months and living out of a tent—they don't really have front doors or locks, so no keys needed!"

Amelia then noticed he held a coffee in one hand and a newspaper in the other, as he stepped back away from her. He noticed her looking at them.

"I didn't know if you would want a coffee or a tea this morning, so I only got one for me. I feel like I've been gone so long I don't know what your morning ritual is these days."

"It's fine," she said, shaking it off as the thought that Franklin would have poured her a cup of coffee at the breakfast table, no matter what.

"Are you alright? You look perplexed," Jack noted.

"Oh no, dear," she said, feeling like he could see right through her. "You know me, always asleep in the morning. Especially when woken abruptly."

"Right. Right." Jack replied. "Always a lady of leisure. Well, I'll leave you to go back to bed. I'm going to catch up on all of the nation's gossip," he said holding up the paper. He kissed her on the nose and walked into the front room, and sat on the sofa that Amelia had just stripped of its protective covering and was now wearing.

For a few moments she stood alone in the foyer, watching as he settled himself and had a few sips of his coffee. Definitely two different men. Jack was so independent and unpredictable. These traits for a doctor always seemed both amazing and confusing to Amelia.

Her thoughts were interrupted when Jack, feeling her stare, shook the paper at her, and said, "Go back to bed, woman. You're sleeping standing up!"

She shook her head, pulling herself out of her thoughts.

"Right," She said, and covered her irritation with a forced chuckle. Odd. His abruptness never bothered her before.

"Go. I'm fine. Stop worrying about me. If I wanted someone to worry over me, I'd go to my mother's house!"

Amelia headed upstairs. Good. Jack thought her daze was concern for him. Halfway up she realized she was still wearing the tarp. She removed it, since she and Jack were the only two in the house, and once he had started into his paper, he would not move until he finished it—including giving the crossword puzzle a go. She easily had two hours, three if he fell asleep reading, all to herself.

She climbed the stairs feeling the overwhelming exhaustion and the circling questions creep back in. She reached the second floor of the house and an aching sadness filled her, making her heart feel as if it were disintegrating in her chest, making it difficult to breathe.

Amelia barely made it to her room—Franklin's room—before the sobbing seeped up from her stomach and took over her body. She fell to the floor and crawled to her discarded pajamas and rolled them up and placed her face in them to mute her sobbing. She might never see Franklin again.

Chapter Twenty-Nine

G roggy and perplexed, she awoke, unsure of the time. Amelia pushed herself up on her elbows and craned her neck to look. The clock on her bedside table said 4:07. The sun cleared through the windows to note she had slept away most of the day. Odd that it was exactly twelve hours later. Time itself is very odd, Amelia thought, pulling herself up off of the floor. She crossed to her dresser and dug until she found her most comfortable sweats, and her oversized Amherst sweatshirt acquired from the wardrobe of an ex-boyfriend. Wearing these was like a fitted security blanket.

In the bathroom, the face in the mirror stared back at her through puffy eyes with sadness and fear. She turned on the faucet—similar handles to the ones in Franklin's house, but shinier and stainless steel—and proceeded to splash water on her face.

Amelia decided she needed to be rational. She needed to attend to basic needs, which included interaction with the man who was physically here. She would think through all the time travel stuff later. Franklin didn't appear. Nor was she magically whisked back to him in the last twenty-four hours, so it wasn't happening any time soon. If at all. Her mind was blank as she dried off her face with a fluffy soft towel and luxuriated in it. Much better than the scratchy linen one she had been using the past few months. She wondered how many small details like this would be different.

Picking up the discarded clothes off the floor, she tidied the room and made her bed. The more physical activity she did, the less she would overthink and would be in the present. Putting on her running shoes, she went downstairs to look for Jack. He was exactly where he was the day before—dozing, sitting up holding a paper. She found a blank scrap of paper and scribbled a quick note, leaving the paper beside him.

Went for a jog. Be back soon. –A

She grabbed her keys from the table by the front door and walked outside into the sunshine.

***

The jog cleared her mind. Amelia had not figured anything out, nor had she actually thought about anything during her run. She had just enjoyed running. She had missed this. Amelia had forgotten what it felt like to work out, and not have any thoughts or feelings except the pounding of her heart and the gasping of her breath. Not to mention, feeling the freedom of wearing yoga pants and running shoes; to actually *run*. It felt so freeing. Although the sights of the park were familiar, as she got closer to home, she began noticing the subtle differences between the times she walked through the park with Franklin and now.

Each step closer to her front door, more and more thoughts of Franklin returned. The entire time she was in the past she thought relentlessly about Jack and how to return to this time. And now that she was here, Franklin kept popping into her mind. Amelia internally moaned.

It was then she made the decision to dive into her relationship with Jack. It made sense. He was here, in front of her, now. She would focus on him and figure out everything else later.

And the house, she had to return to the renovations. Thoughts of tile and contractors and paint ran through her mind and overtook everything else as she unlocked the front door. All the rest would work itself out. If she was meant to get back to Franklin, she would either fall back in time again, or figure out how she got there. Amelia distractedly contemplated tile color for the kitchen backsplash and as she started to set her keys down and she saw a note sitting there that said:

Went out for groceries. How do you have none? –J

She chuckled Practical Jack. Unlike Franklin, who was scatterbrained and needed others to do the chores. Amelia mulled this comparison as she climbed the stairs, headed to get cleaned up. A shower was just what she needed and so she started the water. She removed her sweats and dropped them carelessly to the floor, as if she knew the invisible Emily would come to retrieve them for her. As she was about to step into the shower, Amelia realized that she still had her watch on, and so she paused stepping into the shower, removed the watch and placed it on the counter by the sink. Then she stepped into the hot, steamy running water.

The warm water washed over her body soothing her muscles that groaned about how out of shape she had become. The differences between the past and her present were very interesting. Like this bathroom. One room in the house she wouldn't have to remodel. Previously a very modern renovation was done, with large mirrors veering the wall behind the sink. Huge gray marble counters filled one entire wall, and had three electrical outlets dispersed at different points down the counter to allow any possible needed electrical item a space to be plugged in. This shower with great water pressure, a huge shower head, and five different settings from "massage" to "waterfall" won, hands down, over the little tub that Emily had manually filled. These simple pleasures that she had come to expect, she missed when in the past. They were a gentle reminder this was the time she was born into. But, was this where she was supposed to be? This question would continually nag her over the coming weeks.

After a long, meditative shower, Amelia grabbed one of the fluffy towels hanging nearby and toweled herself dry. She combed her wet hair into manageable strings, and after realizing she was hiding from Jack, she went to get dressed.

Quickly she grabbed underwear, a bra, a pair of relaxed jeans that were on the top of the drawer, and a soft blue t-shirt and threw it over her head as she walked out her bedroom door. She would never curse bra hooks again after fighting with a corset daily.

She went downstairs and did a loop around the house. She looked for Jack first in the front room where she had left him earlier. Not finding him there, she then went into the study—although, she realized as she stood just in the doorway to that room, that was her ritual for Franklin. Not finding Jack there, she headed toward the kitchen after catching a whiff of something delicious floating down the hall.

The kitchen, still in a state of remodel, looked like a mix between a lumberyard and storage shed, with supplies and furniture piled all around. Amelia still needed to get in contact with the cabinetmaker that Toni's friend Abigail recommended. Pulled to the large pot sitting on the stove, she lifted the lid. Stew. Instinctively, Amelia looked behind her for Mrs. Finnegan to come scold her for sneaking a peek. The glance behind her, only offered her construction site of a kitchen with a note from Jack on the island.

Didn't want to disturb you.   Left the stew for you. Maybe we shall see each other tomorrow?   I need more rest, so I went to bed. Sorry my body clock is totally off! Thems the breaks!

Love, J

Amelia sighed. She felt bad that she was relieved he wasn't here. But until she could wrap her mind around her journey, she felt she couldn't face Jack.   She turned the burner of the stove on to reheat the pot.   Letting the contents of the pot warm, she cut a couple of slices of the crusty French bread sitting on the cutting board. When the stew was the perfect temperature, she spooned herself a helping and sat at the counter to eat.

On the nearby pad and pen she started to jot down the things she needed for work on the house.   Call cabinet contractor. Fix fireplace in study. Check for bricks that need replacing or fixing. Trip to hardware store.

If she was doing this out of need to regain a feeling of regularity, or was she was doing it to drown out the other things nagging at her brain, she didn't know.   Distracted, Amelia didn't realize that she had reached the bottom of the stew in her bowl until she lifted an empty spoon into her mouth for the third time.   Shaking her head to rattle some sense into it she stood placed the bowl in the sink, then looked down at her list.

After "trip the hardware store" her list read:

Sharpen quills in study

Have study chimney swept

Tell Mrs. Finnegan Franklin wanted boeuf bourguignon next week.

Shit. Amelia couldn't stop thinking of Franklin. The list was evidence. Crumpling the paper, she threw it in the trash with frustration. She *had* to focus. To pretend things were back to normal. Once she had a grasp on her life here, she would think about the time leap. She owed this to Jack. He was her boyfriend. Amelia refused to acknowledge the thought that Franklin was her acting husband. Her brain throbbed with these thoughts and she realized she couldn't keep them from overlapping.

Once she had cleaned up the kitchen and had put the stew in the refrigerator, she went upstairs and flopped onto her bed without turning down the covers. She lay on her stomach with her face in her pillows trying to make her brain stop thinking. After a few futile moments, she rolled out of bed, and sensibly changed into her pajamas. Turning down the bed, crawling in and turning off the light, she laid her head on her firm pillows. Thoughts of both men floated through her head, but soon Amelia drifted off to sleep.

Chapter Thirty

Days went by and she didn't see Jack. Maybe he was just on a different sleep pattern or maybe avoiding her. Most mornings she found him cuddled next to her but never heard him come in.

Amelia wasn't sure how she felt about any of it. After all, she was unfaithful. Was it cheating if you thought you were in a dream, but when you found out you were stuck in another time period and didn't know when—if ever—you were to return to your own time?   And it was only one time. What exactly was the statute of limitations on this sort of thing?

While stuck in the past, she had mourned for the loss of Jack, almost as if he were a dead lover. Although, technically she would be the dead one; living in the past, if she had never returned home she should have died before he was even born. Time travel was very confusing, as was the loss of one lover and the return of another. What was she to do? She didn't want to cheat on Franklin with Jack, but technically she had been in a relationship with Jack before she was "married" to Franklin. And really, she had to remind herself, the marriage to Franklin wasn't official. He had mentioned once, a week before she returned to her time, that if she wanted to they could sneak off and make it official. But *did* she want to? Oh, this is silly, she thought to herself. Who knew if she was even going to get back to Franklin?

Maybe thinking about all of this was pointless, anyway. She felt horrible for leaving Franklin so abruptly, but it wasn't as if she was keeping it a secret of trying to return home to her time. She needed to stop analyzing the things that happened and focus on the here and now.

Chapter Thirty-One

Life seemed to have more of a purpose after a few weeks back in 2012. The trip had opened her eyes in many ways. She was thrilled to have Jack, the house, and Toni and Alexia in her life. She was happy that things she was used to, felt the same, but brighter somehow. More than anything, she loved being able to wear pants out of the house. It was good to be back, to feel normal.

However, when she sank into the regularity of her routine Amelia had a continual feeling that she had forgotten something. At night after the workers left, she would walk around the house making sure that the burners were off on the stove, that the front door was locked, that her keys were by the front door, that the freezer door was closed. None of it was ever out of place, but Amelia still had the feeling that something was wrong.

Thoughts of Franklin drifted like a dream. When she first returned, anything could trigger a thought of Franklin, turning a corner in the house, looking at someone eating ice cream as she ran past them in the park, seeing someone read a book. As time passed it felt odd to remember him. When she did think about Franklin, it was difficult to hold onto. The details of his face or the moment she tried to remember seemed to slip away from her like an earring as it fell down the bathroom sink. The more she tried to reach for it the further it slipped away. Amelia would remember a moment with Franklin, and would question if it meant anything to him, or if it really happened at all.

One evening Jack went out to meet up with friends, and Amelia found herself reminiscing as she drank tea out of one of Franklin's mother's teacups, the ones she vehemently told him were hers the first time she met him. Her mind wandered back to that first day. She laughed aloud at some of their conversation. It was so irrational. She remembered him walking her upstairs, and she was in such a daze and had convinced herself that it was a dream.

She remembered the feel and taste of his lips on hers—something that even months later she could not forget. His hands on her skin. His body on top of hers. It really happened, but at that moment, just as now, it was all a dream to her. She wanted him to touch her again. She needed him to look in her eyes with that hunger and longing. Amelia realized in this moment that she ached for Franklin. She wanted and desired for him. Amelia now understood that she loved Franklin Dunne. Wait. No. That couldn't be right. She shook off the dreamy thought. Jack. She loved Jack.

As if on cue, Amelia heard Jack open and close the front door. Jumping up from her dreamy sitting position in the front room, she dashed to the front door, threw her arms around Jack's neck and kissed him passionately. He kissed her back, and then tried to push away to put down his things. Refusing to be denied, she hugged his body closer to hers, pressing her chest and hips into his body. Jack relented, and kissed her back, just as passionately. Amelia realized that although they had kissed since they both returned, they had not been physical. She needed the physical. Somehow, she knew she could clear Franklin out of her head if she had Jack, all of Jack all to herself. She leaned back a little, seductively looked him in the eye, and said, "Follow me." Amelia backed away, letting her arms drag across his shoulders, and then with one last look at him, she turned, flipped her hair, and bounded up the stairs, tossing off her clothing as she headed to her bedroom. She heard Jack chuckle behind her, and then heard his footsteps.

Standing facing her bed, but with her back to the door, she was completely naked by the time he came into the room. His large warm arms encompassed her and his lips traced a trail from the top of her spine up around her neck to her chin. She turned her face slightly to meet him, but he pulled her whole body around to him and pressed up against her. He still was completely clothed, and the printed letters on his sweatshirt pressed up against her nipples. It only made her need his body more. She pulled at his clothing, and then yanked him down on top of her.

They first made love very aggressively, fighting to be on top, and angling for position, until he finally won out. Amelia needed to be taken, to be possessed by this man. He lay on top of her panting after their completion. He started to roll away, but she wouldn't let him. It was as if she needed his body to make her stay here, body, mind, and soul. If Jack possessed her in all three ways, there was no way, she told herself, that she could feel that she needed to return to Franklin. She needed Jack to prove to her how much *he* needed her in the here and now. After a few minutes of just lying there, she started to kiss him again. He was very quickly aroused, and returned the affections. He moved within her more slowly this time, and almost trying to prove to her that he could please her and only her. It was slow, long, and insistent and all of her thoughts were on Jack and only Jack. Amelia understood his attentions, and knew it was exactly what she needed. She had officially returned.

Chapter Thirty-Two

Amelia threw herself back into fixing the house. It was as if traveling to the past and seeing this house in its glory had inspired her. She didn't want to recreate Franklin's house entirely, but she did know that she wanted to be true to it and its beauty. Many of the choices she had already made for the place worked with her new inspiration and view. There were a few things that needed to be rethought, and some things that weren't going to be changed, like her very modern bathroom that had been remodeled before she took ownership. It was very interesting that the bathroom was redone in depth, and places like the study weren't probably looked at for years. People temporarily living in spaces tend to not take pride in them as much. Which made sense, as they don't own the space, so why would they maintain its upkeep. Amelia shrugged this thought off as she looked at tile samples in the kitchen.

Jack came up from behind her and wrapped his arms around her waist, and placing his chin gently on her shoulder he said, "Go with the blueish-gray ones."

Covering his arms with hers, she leaned back saying, "You don't even know what these are for."

"Yes, I do. They're for the backsplash in here and possibly the floor."

"How did you—"

"I may have just arrived back and have been a little distant, but I have been paying attention to what you've been saying and to a little of what you haven't. I think the blue will look nice in here," he said, as he unwrapped himself and walked across the room to pour a cup of coffee.

Amelia's shoulders stiffened for a moment while Jack's back was turned. Did he know?

"I know that you've decided to focus all your attention on this house, because as a designer you need it to be the best it can possibly be," he turned to face her now, "but you don't have to make every detail perfect. And, I don't know if you remember, but you asked me to help you with this project."

Amelia looked across the room at him. She sighed with relief. He knew she was distracted because of the house. He just didn't know it was also partially because of her recent time travel. Maybe she was throwing herself more into this project now because she needed to immerse herself into this time. She needed to ignore feelings that still popped up of the man in the past. She was where she belonged, wasn't she? This man standing in front of her was amazing.

"You're right," she said, meeting his gaze and responding to more than his response to her. "Blue tiles here would be perfect." She crossed the room to him and wrapped her arms around his neck and kissed him. "And I think that the bigger version on this floor would be good too. I wasn't going to redo the floors, or at least, I didn't think I wanted to, but I think you're right. Why not? I'm redoing everything else."

After that, Amelia ran ideas by Jack because she needed to include him, and she liked the collaboration. It would be their house. Then, she would eventually blot out Franklin all together.

Chapter Thirty-Three

Jack got a phone call from his mother the final day the contractors were at the house. His parents lived two hours out of the city in Connecticut, so they had seen the house, and they had met Amelia. Jack's mother was mentioning that his father was having a big sixtieth birthday celebration and both parents really wanted Jack and Amelia to attend. They decided that it would be a lovely idea to get away for the weekend and stay with his parents.

"I promise if it's too chaotic at my parent's house there is a bed and breakfast just down the street where we can stay," Jack promised.

With all the chaos in the house, Amelia was ready to get away with Jack, even if it was at his parent's. So they packed their bags and headed up Sharon, Connecticut.

Jack's dad, Don, met them at the train station and as he loaded bags in the car, commented that even though it was summer, Amelia hadn't packed what seemed like an appropriate amount for a woman.

"Jack said it was a casual weekend, and your wife would probably insist on doing all of our laundry before we left, so I didn't see the need to pack for more than three days," Amelia quipped back.

Don was a semi-retired college professor who still taught two classes and wrote articles occasionally published in educational journals and books. He tended to dominate most conversations of which he was in hearing range. "Your mother," Don continued, "is still at the store, and should be home in time for dinner. I've whipped up a culinary masterpiece, although you city folk might not appreciate it."

"I'm sure we'll love it, Dad," Jack said from the back seat. "I didn't know Mom would be working at The Quilt Corner." Dot, Jack's mother, owned a quilting supply store. Although she intended for it to only sell quilting supplies, it had turned into a hangout for the local ladies to come and create. Then it grew to be a common tourist stomping ground, as the building was right next to a gas station. At first they got the overflow of bus tours visiting the wineries and seeing the foliage. Now it was a common stop for the tourists. The shop now offered a full tea service, a snack bar, and of course, they sold quilts and crafts created by locals. Actual supplies were still available, and the ladies still sat around while making new projects and conversing with the tourists, all while handing out business cards and taking orders for holiday gifts and baby blankets. Jack's mother first opened the shop when Jack was old enough to walk to school by himself, but then when he went away to college the business became huge, allowing Jack's father to go into an early semi-retirement.

Don took the long way to the house, pointing out changes to Jack. One house had a new hedgerow, the Martinez family had gotten a new car for their teenager, and the theater, an old converted barn, had a new annex and they were putting on *Annie Get Your Gun* this weekend. There were other things, but Amelia just was soaking in the quaintness of this little town while she sat in the front seat.

The house was a quintessential country colonnade in Connecticut. It had a white picket fence, a columned front with large windows on both stories, an expansive front porch with deck chairs, and the front lawn boasted a small rose garden, and had a prominent oak tree with a swing hanging from a massive branch.

Jack hopped out of the car and helped Amelia with her door, and then went around to the back of his father's station wagon and lifted out their bags. Don tried to take one of the weekender bags from his son, but Jack dutifully refused and slapped his father on the back. Amelia smiled at the scene. She missed the look and feel of a family. Jack's family reminded her a lot of her own. It was not often that she missed her mother and father, but in this moment, she did.

Amelia followed the men inside, and was greeted with a delicious meaty aroma that was warm and tantalizing. It made her think of Mrs. Finnegan. Amelia realized she hadn't thought of any of them, Emily, Mrs. Finnegan, or even Franklin in a while. She couldn't remember the last time she had. It had been weeks. It was an odd feeling to go from having everything remind you of someone, to having one random association many weeks later.

"We're up this way," Jack's voice from above her brought her attention back. Don had disappeared, Amelia assumed to check on dinner. Jack was up a few steps on the stairway. He began climbing again, carrying both her bag and his over his shoulders. She followed. The stairs were a lightly stained wood, and the walls were a lovely pale yellow. Picture frames were on every wall. There were a few pieces of art here and there, but most of the frames contained photos, a pictographic timeline of the family.

Jack led her into a blue room, and set their bags down. He took her into his arms and kissed her on the nose.

"I know it's a bit overwhelming, but it's my past, and you're my future. So I hope you're ok with it all," he said, enfolding her into his arms.

"It's not overwhelming. It reminds me of the home I grew up in. It's more nostalgia that you're seeing. It's been years since I've had my parents around, so I forget how much of this I miss out on. And how much I truly miss having a home to go home to. That reminds me, I should call my aunt and have her ship down some of those boxes of my parents' things to put up in our place, what do you think?"

"I think that is exactly what our place needs," he said, kissing her lightly on the lips and smiling.

"Dinner is almost ready," they heard Don shout up the stairs.

"Be right down," Jack yelled back. "Do you need to change or freshen up a bit?" he asked, turning his attention back to Amelia.

"I think I will freshen up a little, if you don't mind. You go have time with your dad. I'll be right down."

Jack kissed her quickly again. "Bathroom is just there, through that little door. Don't be too long," he said, and then he bounced out of the room.

He was so boy-like in his childhood home, and she liked it. She grabbed her makeup bag and headed to the bathroom.

***

Over dinner, Jack regaled Don and Dot with some of his field surgery stories. Amelia talked about the finished house, and how she wanted to market herself as an interior designer. Don and Dot gave more updates on locals Amelia didn't know, but apparently Jack did. They chatted until the food was eaten, and the leftovers were cold. After dinner Dot washed the dishes, while Amelia dried. The men went out back to look at the tree that Don couldn't decide if he wanted to cut down.

"He's so happy around you," Dot said to Amelia.

"He makes me happy, too." Amelia said back.

The two women shared a smile. They both watched out the window as the men wandered about the lawn, as dusk fell and lightning bugs started to blink on and off. It felt like a perfect evening.

Later that night, as Amelia was climbing into bed with Jack, she noted he looked so much like his father.

"I wanted to follow in the old man's footsteps. I wanted to teach," he said. "But then in college, I took an anatomy class because all of the biology classes were full, and I was hooked. I don't know what happened. It was as if something snapped into place, and I just knew I was going to be a doctor."

She smiled and snuggled closer to him in the darkness.

"I'm glad we're here. It's nice to see you outside of the city. To see who you really are."

"Agreed," he replied just before he dozed off to sleep.

***

Connecticut reminded Amelia of the slow life she had in the past, both of her own with her parents and of the time she spent with Franklin. Being here brought Franklin to the front of her mind. Although she didn't have much time to mull on it as they had a packed weekend. Don and Dot had a lot on the agenda and there was very little down time. They went to the pancake breakfast being put on by the volunteer firefighters. Then they went to visit Dot's shop for tea and then to Don's campus for lunch. At the clambake in the evening, Amelia wasn't quite sure if she was being introduced or shown off to the local community. When the evening was over, Amelia was sure she had met everyone in the town and their immediate families who had driven in from Connecticut, eastern New York, and a few from Massachusetts. People were in from all over for the clambake tonight and for Don's birthday tomorrow. The evening concluded with fireworks and then they headed back to the house. Amelia fell asleep on Jack's arm in the backseat of the station wagon. She let him help her up the stairs, undress, and get into bed.

Amelia awoke the early next morning and spent a while just looking at Jack. It had been a while since she had just looked at him. Studied sleeping his face. He was so peaceful right now. Amelia couldn't fall back asleep, and she thought she smelled coffee, so she carefully slipped out of bed and trod downstairs to get a cup.

Dot had left a note:

Jack and Amelia—

Left you coffee and some rolls. You'll have to make do for breakfast. We should be back by lunch. Be ready by 2pm for the party.

—Mom

Amelia smiled as she read the note. She looked over at the clock above the sink. It was just past 11am. Pouring herself a cup of coffee, she spied the rolls and grabbed one. With cup and roll in hand, she started back up the stairs and found herself drawn in by the photos. At the top of the landing she just stood back and looked at each one individually, as if she were in the Louvre. There were pictures of Jack on the swing out front, and pictures of baseball teams throughout the years. Pictures of the three of them at different town gatherings at different times of the year. A picture of Jack holding up a program for *Oliver!* with a huge toothy grin caught her attention and she had moved closer to really look into his eyes, to study them. Just then the door to their bedroom opened and the man, no longer the boy in the photo, stepped out. He smiled at her then he yawned. Maybe he wasn't too far away from the adorable boy in the picture.

"Whateryadoin?"

Amelia laughed at his sleepy, slurred question. "I'm checking out the family gallery. Did you have to give your teeth to Fagin to see *Oliver*?"

He laughed without sound, only an exhale, and shuffled over to her and leaned in for a sleepy kiss.

"Nope." Jack walked around to the back of Amelia and wrapped his arms around her waist and put his chin on one of her shoulders. "Believe it or not, I hated that show."

"No way! You look so happy in that picture," Amelia replied.

"It's true. Actually, this picture was taken just after I was told that I could have a double scoop of ice cream after the second half of the show. My mom was a volunteer at the theater for the longest time, so we saw almost every show. I was not a fan of musicals with orphans. Or single names for that matter. *Annie, Oliver, Mame, Othello, Anne of Green Gables*. However, *A Funny Thing That Happened on the Way to the Forum*, now that was theater," Jack said as he smiled into her throat.

Amelia leaned back into his arms. She loved the feeling of being held. Nothing expected and nothing to give. She was going to miss him when he left in two weeks. Amelia hoped he would want to settle down when he got back. It's not that she was in a hurry to have a husband and family, but looking at these photos made her long to be a unit, a pair, a couple. She wanted to have what all of those smiling people in the frames in front of her had. Moments with each other.

"Is there more coffee?" Jack asked, dipping his face into her neck.

"Nope. I drank it all. *And* I licked the tops of all of the buns your mother left."

"No you didn't, you stinker. I'm going to go get some," Jack said as he unlatched himself and smacked her playfully on the bottom as he headed off, and made a u-turn down the stairs.

Amelia watched him go then she turned back to the photos. She sighed to herself. Yes, she wanted a future filled with memories and pictures and smiles and she wanted to put them on her wall, just like this.

After she finished looking at the photos at Jack's house, she went downstairs with just enough time to enjoy a coffee refill and sit on the porch with Jack before they had to get ready.

***

Don's birthday party was fantastic. It was special and significant but low-key all at the same time. Many people they met at the clambake the night before were there. Don was very pleased that so many friends came to celebrate this milestone with him.

At the end of the afternoon, the party in the backyard seemed to be just getting started. Jack and Amelia were just leaving to catch their afternoon train as a few of the townspeople flowing in after the Sunday matinee brought instruments and started playing together in an impromptu concerto. Small towns were lovely that way. Jack and Amelia drove themselves to the station, leaving Don's station wagon in the parking lot to be picked up the next day.

When they were on the train back to the city, Amelia rested her head on Jack's shoulder. Although she seemed to have everything she wanted in this moment, and possibly her entire future, something was missing. She couldn't put her finger on it. A hollowness within Amelia left her with the nagging feeling something was wrong. She even got up out of bed to check the front door to make sure it was locked before she could let herself fall asleep. Amelia didn't know what it was, but just couldn't figure out the reason she felt this way. However, the next morning she had forgotten about it.

Chapter Thirty-Four

Life had become routine and Amelia liked it that way. She would wake up, drowsily throw on her running gear, and dash out to the park. Most mornings Jack would be up when she got back, ready with breakfast and coffee. They would sit and have breakfast together, holding hands and chatting. Jack was to leave the country again, so they both agreed to make the most of their time together. Sometimes after, or even during, breakfast they would dash up to her, now their bedroom and have a romantic interlude. There was always a good deal of lazing around, especially this past week since the contractor and his crew had finished work on the house. Jack and Amelia were acting like newlyweds, barely leaving the house, canoodling in any room, holding hands and kissing at every possible moment. They were in love.

One morning during breakfast, Jack told Amelia that he had gotten a text from his friend Brad, his old roommate in Manhattan. He and some buddies had an extra ticket to see the Mets game.

"Babe, I can totally buy a ticket for you, and we can go together."

"Jack, don't be silly. This sounds like it's a guy's night. You won't want me there. Besides, I think I would love to have an evening alone. Maybe I'll see if my friends want to hit the town. Since you came back, I've been neglecting them, and I have plenty of texts to prove it. I'll just go get my phone—"

As Amelia stood and started to walk out of the kitchen, Jack grabbed her by the arm and pulled her into him and placed a light kiss on her lips, and then moved his fingers up into her hair, removing the band that was keeping her hair in place, his kiss became deeper and more passionate.

"Well, then," he said huskily, "I guess, if you're going out with the girls tonight, I'll have to make sure that you won't have the need to look at any other man."

He took her hand and pulled her behind him, throwing a seductive look over his shoulder and stopped just in front of the study doors to kiss her again.

"I don't think I can make it upstairs," he said, putting his hand on the doorknob to the study and opening the door, and he started to lead her in.

"No." Amelia realized as soon as the words were out of his mouth that she didn't want to be intimate with Jack in the room that belonged to Franklin. It just felt wrong. They had made love multitudes of times in what was Franklin's bedroom, and other rooms in the house.

"No?" he questioned her. "Why not?"

"I…" she looked past him into the room. "It's just that this was the last room to be finished, and I… I am not quite sure that I want to…"

"… mess it up?" he said, finishing her sentence how he assumed she was going to finish it.

"Yes," she exhaled. "That and if you're going to threaten to wear me out," she rebounded with a quip, "I don't want to fall asleep on a rug or a sofa. I want my own bed," she said. "Besides, I want to try something that requires a headboard," she winked and then bounded down the hall without him. Jack shook his head, thinking to himself that he would never understand women and didn't know if he cared, then chased after her.

**

Several hours later they awoke tangled in a mess of bed clothes. Jack rolled so he was sitting on top of her, kissed her, and then leaned down to whisper in her ear.

"I'm going to," he said seductively, "shower first." This made Amelia giggle.

"Ugh! Of *course* you are! No fair seducing me into letting you shower first," she tried to wrestle him over, but he had her pinned to the bed.

"Victory is mine!" he said, kissing her on the nose and then hopping up off the bed, whistling all the way to the bathroom.

Amelia reached for her cell phone and tapped out messages to Toni and Alexia to see if they were available for the evening. It was already 4pm, so she wasn't counting on either being available. They both texted back they were unavailable right away but Alexia invited them all to dinner tomorrow night.

Amelia hopped out of bed and walked into the bathroom. "Babe, Alexia wants to have us over for dinner tomorrow," she bellowed loud enough to be heard through the shower glass and the water. "Neither she nor Toni can go out tonight—so all your exertion was for naught. You don't mind if we go, do you?" Amelia was now bent over the counter, leaning into the mirror, examining the pores on her face.

Jack poked his head out of the shower, "I don't mind at all. I'd love to see those screwy dames of yours. How else can I get the latest office gossip, or enjoy a good male bashing?" Amelia turned her head toward him, but still arched over the sink and stuck out her tongue. He replied to her, "Oh, and my exertions, as you call them, were not for naught. I am very proud of the mess we made of the bed and your hair."

Looking in the mirror, Amelia laughed at the mess on her head.

"I'm almost done," he said, closing the door. "Want me to leave the water on? I'd just invite you in, but I have to get going soon, or the boys will think I'm totally whipped."

"Yes, please. To both the water and the boys thinking you're whipped. I appreciate both."

She started toward the door of the shower, peeling off the robe she had thrown on to cross the room, but he was

233

already climbing out of the shower, and she was hit with a gust of steam, and a kiss from Jack. "Too late!" he said as he passed her and grabbed his towel.

As the water ran over her, she realized that Jack only had a few more days left.

"When do you leave again? The thirty-first?" Amelia yelled out of the shower.

"No, the thirtieth. June only has thirty days. You'll have to remember to change that vintage watch of yours that you like so much. I don't know why you wear that thing when you always have your cell phone…"

Jack continued to talk to her as he shaved, but Amelia didn't hear him. Changing the watch to the thirty-first? Why did an alarm go off in her brain just now? She fell through time to Franklin back in February. No, wait, it was March. March first. *That was it*. *The watch had to be wound on a day after a skipped day*. Time travel happened on the first of the month, when it did not follow the 31st.

Her brain whirred, exploding with thought. There were so many things snapped into place. And a thousand more questions surfaced. She had zoned out and didn't know how long she had been standing under the water when she heard Jack calling out to her.

"What?" she replied dumbly to whatever he had just said. "I had water in my ears," she recovered.

"I asked if you were almost done, so I could kiss you before I walked out the door."

"Just a second!"

While she scrubbed her hair and rubbed in conditioner her mind raced. Today was the…

"What day is today?" Amelia yelled out at Jack.

"The twentieth. I leave in ten days."

"Oh," she said as she finished rinsing and turned off the water. "Good to know," she opened the shower door, fogging up the bathroom. "Hand me my towel, please."

He teased her with it, pulling it back away from her when it was almost in her reach. She stepped out of the shower and onto the bathroom rug, and started toward him and made like she was going to capture him in her arms. "I will hug you and then you'll have to change again, and be late for your boyfriends," she threatened. He wrapped the towel around her, pinning her arms in, and kissed her gently as he laughed. She maneuvered her arms out and reached up around his neck. "I love you," she said more softly. "Have a good time and be safe."

"I will. And I love you, too," he said and started out of the bathroom to go. "What are you doing tonight since the girls aren't available?"

"I don't know," she replied earnestly. "I might do some design research, or I might just watch some TV. Oooh, I think I'm going to order in Thai."

"Oh, good," he said. "Order it while I'm not here. You know I'm not a fan. I'll see you later." And Jack left Amelia to finish toweling off. She heard the front door close as she was throwing on her sweats. She called the Thai restaurant to place her dinner order.

As she hung up her towel, remade the bed, and picked up all of their discarded clothes and placed them in the hamper, Amelia had pulsing thoughts about the watch. Would it work again? Would she want to go back? Would Franklin still be there? Could she go back to the same time and place?

She had no answers for any of these questions. She only knew that she *did* want to try it again.

Chapter Thirty-Five

The following week flew, as it always does when life seems perfect. Amelia and Jack had dinner with Toni and Alexia, and Toni's flavor of the week, a man named Chet who did something with motorcycles. No one was quite sure what.

One day, Amelia and Jack went out to Coney Island and rode every ride. They spent a day walking through Central Park, and they went to see a Broadway show that was about two musicians who met each other at the wrong time, had a beautiful relationship, but ended with one moving away as they weren't meant to be together.

With Jack's upcoming departure, Amelia felt she needed to tell him about her plans. Or as much as she could. As they were sitting on the sofa, she was reading a novel about a Victorian vampire huntress, and he was reading the New York Times, she blurted out, "I need to tell you that I'm taking a trip."

"Do you mean in your book?" he asked, rustling the paper to turn the page.

"No, I'm taking a… trip," she said guiltily.

"Oh?" He didn't move.

"Yes, I'm… going to see my aunt."

"Oh," he moved the paper to kiss her on the temple. "That will be nice. It's been a while since you've seen her."

"That's what I thought," said Amelia, continuing to lie, the words tumbling out of her mouth. "I don't know how long I'll be. I thought I'd take the train and just make it an open-ended trip. So in case you get back early, or even if you get back as planned, and I'm not around, I didn't want you to be worried."

"I'm sure it will be fine, babe," Jack looked at her lovingly and then buried his nose back in his paper.

Amelia stared at the newspaper he was holding for a minute. She lied. She *lied*. Jack, a sensible man who made fun of *Back to the Future* saying that time travel wasn't possible especially not in a Delorean, would not appreciate, nor believe that she had actually traveled through time. *And* she told herself, it was probably not the best idea to tell the man she loved that she was going to visit another man who she had slept with. Even if she wasn't crossing time, it probably wouldn't be the best of ideas.

She covered her bases with the story about visiting her aunt. Amelia would just have to hope that she could get back from visiting Franklin again before Jack got home.

***

After the first lie, the rest came easy. A few days later at lunch when she met up with the gals, she gave Toni and

Alexia keys, and told them both that with Jack gone, she was headed out of town for a few months, to travel. Well, it wasn't completely untrue. She told the gals that they were welcome to use the house while she was away, but for safety issues she had shut off the gas. The electricity would remain on, and all was paid for by her inheritance trust, she explained. She also asked if they could alternate popping over each week to grab the mail and make the place look a little lived in.

"Where exactly are you going?" Alexia, always after details, asked.

"I'm just traveling. I'm headed wherever life and time take me. I don't know if I'll be able to stay in contact too much, so here is the name and phone number of my attorney who is in charge of the trust. If you can't reach me, he can make decisions on my behalf," Amelia said as she handed them each Mr. Banks's business card.

She had met with Banks earlier that day, giving the same vague "traveling" story, and telling him that her friends had keys and access to the house, and would look after it. If Amelia was unreachable and there was an emergency, Toni or Alexia would call his office. Amelia insisted that if she didn't contact Banks within a year, to proceed with the liquidation and donation of the trust, as if he had never found her. Banks was hesitant, but promised he would do as she asked.

After putting all of the affairs she could think of in order, Amelia went back to spend the remaining time with Jack, knowing that everything was taken care of.

Part Three

July — October

Chapter Thirty-Six

J ack's departure was easier this time, possibly because of the excitement roaring through her: tomorrow was the day the watch would work. Or at least she thought it would. She kissed Jack goodbye, and watched him drive down the street. She didn't feel the pull that she had felt last time. Maybe she was getting better at watching him go.

They had spent the last night together wrapped in each other's arms. Amelia watched him pack, asking if there was anything she could do. When his bags were packed, zipped, and waiting by the front door, they climbed into bed. Maybe because they had spent so much of the last few weeks flinging themselves into passionate embraces, tonight they snuggled into each other, not rushing. They lay in bed and held each other. Amelia awoke to light kisses on her face. Opening her eyes, she looked into his. He became passionate and insistent with his kisses.

Later, Amelia lie awake, staring at the ceiling. She had gotten hot, both from their exertions and from his body heat. Lying so far away from him she felt guilty, so she moved one foot and one hand to keep contact since he was going away for twelve weeks this time. She did love this man lying next to her, very much, but her curiosity about Franklin and of her theory of how the watch worked just wouldn't stop circling around in her brain.

Now that she had it figured out, she had to try it— needed to try it. Tomorrow was the first day of July. The first of the month, which follows a month with less than thirty-one days. It was her chance.

It had to work. It must. She had thought over and over and over it, and it was the only thing that made sense. It was the only thing that was the same about both times she traveled. Her clothing, jewelry, time of day, walking pattern, thoughts, were all different. The only thing that was the same both times was the turning of the dial to change the date an extra day on the first of the month. It was just peculiar and detailed enough for her to miss, and eccentric enough to be the rift that could possibly make her jump through time. It was almost painful when the pieces snapped together in her head.

As she lay in bed next to Jack, all she could think of was the past. Beside her was this wonderful doctor who had such a passion for living, a man who wanted to fix today's problems, all she could think about was trying the watch and time travel—to see Franklin again. She was trying not to get lost in possibilities and the mechanics of time travel. It made her brain hurt. Instead she thought about what she had in her closet that might translate to something proper back in Franklin's time. She drifted back to sleep.

***

She had slept really late the next day, not waking up until close to noon. Out of habit she went for her run. While jogging through the park, she thought through things like making sure her cell phone bill was paid for the next few months, and calling her aunt, just in case she didn't make it back. She also had taken a luxurious shower, because it would be her last one for a while. By the time all of this was accomplished and she was ready to travel to Franklin, it was much later than she had intended. It was almost 6pm by the time she was ready to go.

Taking every precaution to not show up again in only undergarments, Amelia gave up her daily attire of a tank top and yoga pants. She was dressed in linen pants and a dressy tank top—she had other blouses, but none of them were short sleeved, and it was scorching hot outside today. After she was dressed, she took a few deep breaths, convinced herself that she really wanted to do this, grabbed the watch, and headed for the stairway.

Chapter Thirty-Seven

With her breath held, she turned the watch pin. She hoped this worked. The date turned from the thirty-first to the first, and waited.

She felt nothing. Nothing changed. Not the light, not the smell of the room, not the sounds outside. It didn't work. She closed her eyes in defeat.

Then, Amelia heard a horse clomping on the street. Her eyes flew open, and looked down at the watch in her hands.

Her pants had changed into a full-length skirt of soft muslin. She was back. Amelia breathed it all in. There was the faint smell of pipe tobacco hung in the house, the smell of horse manure wafted from the street, and the fragrant richness of stew floating from the kitchen.

Amelia headed toward the last smell, but her rush to find Mrs. Finnegan and the tantalizing food was quickly halted. She looked down over her entire body, to make sure that she was properly dressed. Her tank top had changed to a corset and chemise. She needed something to cover her torso. Dashing upstairs, Amelia walked to her room. Had he kept her things? She hoped so.

A horrible thought crossed her mind. She had spent so much time thinking of *how* to return, and that she wanted to come back. She didn't think of how he would react. What if he didn't want her here?

Ignoring the fear for now Amelia turned into her room and to her relief, things were as she left them. She opened the wardrobe and found her clothes. But wait, some things were missing. She moved things around a few times, before Amelia realized that her traveling clothes were gone. Odd, she thought. She paced to the vanity to figure out her plan, and saw a lump making the dust ruffle of the bed stick out. She tapped it with her foot. Heavy, it gave a thunk. Bending down, she saw it was a suitcase. She pulled it out, and opened it. Folded nicely, with sprigs of lavender sitting on top were all her traveling clothes, complete with toiletries. Clever man. He must have made it look to the staff like Amelia was traveling.

She went back to the closet to grab a blouse and a jacket that would match the skirt, but stopped before putting it on. Instead, Amelia crossed back to the open suitcase, removed the traveling clothes and replaced them with the skirt she arrived in, and the blouse and jacket that she just grabbed from the closet. She put on the traveling outfit, and added a coat and gloves. She took a deep sniff of the smoky lavender just before she replaced the sprig and closed the lid.

Amelia crept out of her room. She would probably be able to get down the stairs and out of the house at this time of day without being heard. Mrs. Finnegan was definitely in the kitchen, and Emily, she hoped, was out at market running errands. Franklin was either working in his study, or would be out doing business at this hour. Amelia wasn't sure which she wanted more: to "arrive home" through the front door, or for him to find her in her bedroom. Neither would be easy.

As she descended the stairs it hit her again that he might not want to see her again. He always said this was her home and she was welcome, but would he still mean it? At least if she was arriving with a suitcase packed, she could just turn around and leave easily if he didn't want her here. She should have thought about that upstairs, and grabbed an extra outfit. Amelia took a deep breath. It would all be ok. He put lavender in her suitcase. He had told her once, lavender was something travelers gave their sweethearts to remember them by. The sprig *must* mean something. And her room looked like it had been cleaned recently, so maybe he had figured out how the watch worked, too, and was hoping she would come back.

Amelia reached the front door without being seen. She quietly lifted the latch, peeked outside to see if anyone she knew was on the street. Seeing no one she crept out the door. Now that she was here, what was proper to do? Should she go away, and send a note ahead? Should she ring the bell? Should she just enter and call out? Would "honey, I'm home" work in this day and age? She was allegedly mistress of the house, and a mistress would...her mind flicked through every Henry James novel she knew, and also through a bit of *Anna Karenina*. Suddenly she knew. She should just walk straight in through the front door and ring the bell for the servants, and then start removing her gloves. The servant always came to whisk away the bags as the lady was removing her outer garments. Her stomach flipped with fear and excitement. She couldn't believe she was relying on literature to guide her. Another deep breath. She threw her shoulders back, swallowed hard, and walked through the door with as much poise and serenity as possible. She closed the door behind her, a bit loudly to punctuate her return, set her case down near the door just in case she needed to leave quickly, and walked to the bell pull just inside the door and pulled.

The clang of the bell called forth the explanation of her absence? Where would he say she would have gone? She thought quickly about places she had told him she would like to visit, and places that she might be familiar with. Maybe she should say that she was visiting her mother. No, he knew that she didn't have parents alive, and would probably not invent them for the staff, as it would lead to more questions. She had no idea and just as a thought started to form—

"Oh, missus! Lovely to see you again!" Mrs. Finnegan said as she helped Amelia take off her coat. "Franklin said he had a letter from you sayin' ya might be home today. He had us prepare your room for ya. I also have the brown stew a'bublin, because I know it's your favorite, and I thought it might be a lovely welcome home!"

Amelia tried to get a word in, but it might be best to let Mrs. Finnegan just continue on—maybe she would give details away about where Franklin said that she was.

"Oh, he was missing you somethin' terrible at the beginnin,' but then you newlyweds often do miss each other at first, even when you just go away for a visit. Although I think he should have gone with you. And you leavin' so quickly, too. But I guess that is understandable with someone who is ailin'," she continued. "But listen to me blatherin' on. He is in his study, I do believe, and I am sure he is waitin' for—" Before Mrs. Finnegan could continue, Franklin came around the corner from the study. He was casually dressed in a waistcoat and trousers, his normal dress when working from home. Amelia made a mental chuckle—this would be sweatpants and a t-shirt in her time. Oh, how she did love this look on Franklin. Her stomach flipped again, as if she were a girl going on a first date.

"Who is at the—" Franklin stopped abruptly, his eyes affixed on Amelia.

He rushed toward her, stopping a step in front of her out of decorum. He calmly reached his arms toward Amelia.

"Darling! I am so glad you're back." He leaned in and kissed her on both cheeks. "How was your trip to Philadelphia to see your aunt?"

Yes!—Amelia exclaimed in her head—Philadelphia! Of course! Brilliant man.

"As good as it could be," she replied, emotionless. She didn't want to reveal the wrong one and go against the story he had already told.

"Good to hear," Franklin replied. "You wrote that your aunt was ailing—did it affect the wedding?"

"Ah...no—the wedding was wonderful. And she did feel well enough to attend, but—"

Just then Finnegan intervened, the voice of reason in the rigid conversation, "You two needn't put on this show for me. Although, I do want to hear the details about the weddin'." She then crossed the room to grab Amelia's suitcase. "I'll just take this upstairs before headin' back to the kitchen to finish supper, and you two can say a proper hello. I'll have Emily unpack it when she gets back and I'll get back to my cookin'."

"Thank you, Mrs. Finnegan," Franklin said rigidly. Then a moment later a smile crept over his face as she passed and winked at him. Amelia was too busy looking at the house again to notice this exchange.

"Missus, dinner will be ready in half an hour—will that be suitable?"

"Yes. Thirty minutes should be just enough time to say hello to my husband," said Amelia as she blushed.

As Mrs. Finnegan started up the stairs, Franklin took Amelia by the hand. He led her toward his study, only fifty feet from the front hall, but in the silence in which he walked her forward, it seemed like miles. He opened the door and motioned for her to enter first. Amelia walked through then turned her head back to look at his face. His

251

eyes revealed nothing. Was he just putting on a show in the front hall and he really wasn't happy to see her? A thousand thoughts of fear, worry, and despair ran through her mind as she walked into the center of the room. It smelled like him—burning wood, leather, lemon for his tea, and a bit of pipe tobacco, all mixed together with another smell she couldn't quite put her finger on—they all mixed together and smelled of him. She relaxed as this smell was home to her. Amelia turned around as she heard him close and, to her surprise, locked the door.

"This way we won't be disturbed, though I think Mrs. Finnegan knows better, and Emily doesn't dare enter anyway. Neither will come looking for us. In fact, maybe I should give them both the night off..." he trailed off and started back towards the door.

"Wait. I need to know—" she heard herself call out, " are you happy to see me?"

He turned quickly to her and with only two strides was at her side.

"Oh my darling!" He exclaimed and took hold of her. "I don't think I could be happier to see anything even if I were a thirsty man crossing the desert with water in sight." He let go of her and stepped back, remembering himself. "Forgive me, I show too much informality. Please, make yourself comfortable," he said, as he ushered her to the sofa in front of the fireplace and they sat. He quickly jumped up again. "Yes, I'm going to give the ladies the night off, and then you can tell me everything." With that, he dashed out of the room. Amelia tried not to be put off by his running away.

Instead she turned her attention to the fireplace in front of her. There was so much damage to the actual mantle in her time, and she didn't pay as much attention to the details of it when she had been in this room with Franklin. Trying to recreate it had been quite a task. There were a few things that were different, tiny details that only she would notice, but overall she had done well. Amelia smiled. If she could take Franklin forward in time to see the place, she thought he would be proud.

The man of her thoughts burst back into the room, as if she had summoned him with her mind. She turned around toward the door. He juggled a tray of refreshments, and was out of breath. Amelia hopped up to help him.

"I... gave..."

"It's ok," she replied, taking the tray over to a small table between one of the chairs and the sofa. "Take a moment."

He took a deep breath and then closed the doors to the study.

"I gave the ladies the night off, so we won't be disturbed. Mrs. Finnegan insisted that I take a tray of her stew to feed you. Would you like a drink?" he asked, crossing over to a cabinet close to his desk. "I think under the circumstances, I need one."

"No. Well, maybe a small one. To take the edge off. I'm... well... You *are* glad to see me?" she asked him. "It's only that I figured out how to return and I just knew I had to get back here — to see if it worked — and I guess I assumed that you would, I mean, that it was possible, that you wouldn't mind, if..." Amelia let her voice trail, off not really wanting to finish her thought. She didn't know what to do if he didn't want her to stay. Where would she go if he didn't want her here? She pushed those thoughts aside, and looked up to find him just in front of her, a drink in each hand.

"Let's have a drink and a deep breath. And start at our own beginnings and then knit the story together in the middle?" he said, handing her a drink and guided her to the sofa. She sank comfortably and in one fluid movement, upended her glass and took the two fingers of scotch in one gulp, and then sighed contentedly and sat back on the sofa.

He chuckled at her actions and then tossed back his drink as well. "Yes, I am happy to see you." He stood, taking her glass and his and placing them on the other table, to be dealt with later. He returned to the sofa, sat on the arm next to her, and gently took her hand in his.

"Now, let me start at the beginning. Or, rather, the ending. I had left you in your room putting on jewels. I was suddenly struck with a bit of panic, which was overtaken by a story idea, and I dashed down here and started to write down some ideas. I remember the clock striking nine, and I thought it was odd you hadn't come down to collect me. I went upstairs, and all the lights were on in your room, your jewels were on the floor in a pile, and you were nowhere to be found. I was quite distraught, but I had my wits enough about me to call round to the party to say you had been stricken ill, and that we were staying in for the night. The next morning, I realized that your watch was gone, and that you must have ... returned.

"So how did you figure it all out?" Amelia asked.

He leaned back and started to stand up.

"No, no, no." she said, pulling his arm and gently insisting he stay seated. "I need to know. Please tell me."

Franklin looked at her and opened his mouth to start.

"No, wait, *when* did you figure it out—how long after I left?" She looked up at him.

Franklin sighed and stood up to face her. "I was very stricken to find you gone. We had spent so much time together and then you just... vanished. I knew that you probably left the way you arrived...and I might have been a bit presumptive, but I felt that you cared for me enough to tell me if you had made a plan to leave—so I deduced that you accidentally tripped back to your own time," Franklin explained.

"You didn't presume I ran off with the milkman or that I might have been kidnapped by a murderer?" she teased him.

"Well, I am an avid reader and understand that both of your scenarios could happen in a book," he chuckled, "but, my dear, I tend to observe facts first. I will grant you that I was a bit worried for the first twenty-four hours and then distraught for the next week. I missed you terribly and spent days trying to convince myself that you had a good reason for going—and that it wasn't that you didn't care, or couldn't be bothered to give me a hint that you were leaving." The last few words he spoke were tinged with deep sadness, they made her rise from her seated position on the sofa, stand in front of him, and look deeply into his eyes, letting her hand caress his cheek.

"I missed you so," Amelia said, with reassurance. "I don't want to get your hopes up, I will return to my time, if I can. I still have too many obligations there. However, I *had* to come back. I had to see you again."

Then she leaned back from him, putting her hands on his shoulders, "Wait, you only missed me for a week?!?"

"No, dearest. I missed you terribly the entire time. I counted days and hours until your possible return. I didn't sleep nights because at first you weren't here and then recently because you might be returning. Mrs. Finnegan does not jest when she tells you that I was ill with missing you."

Amelia looked into his eyes, and was entranced by them. Not able to look away from his face she started to reach out a hand to touch his cheek. Suddenly a thought crossed her mind, and she leaned back from him quite vehemently.

"It only took you a week to figure out how it all happened?"

"It took a bit longer than that to figure everything out. It took me a week to realize that your watch was the key and the calendar date was the door."

"Clever man. What made you connect those dots together?" she asked.

"Well," he said a bit sheepishly, "I was throwing books at the wall in frustration because nothing was distracting me from your absence nor relieving me from the agony of your sudden disappearance. I picked up the calendar to throw as well, and just before I drew back my arm, I looked down and noticed that I hadn't changed the week from when you disappeared. I'd been too distracted. So, I started to turn the page and wondered how long—exactly—you had been here. I remembered that it coincided with when I arrived home, which made it March the first. Then you disappeared on May first. I knew it couldn't be a total coincidence. I sat here for a long time thinking about it, until Finney came in to find me for dinner. I went up to dress—I don't know why—I had not since you left. I went to put my pocket watch on my dinner waistcoat and it hit me—your watch needed to be wound through a day on months that don't have thirty-one days."

"Brilliant man." Amelia replied and rewarded him with a smile. She looked at him and wondered if he had actually become more handsome while he was talking. She shook the thought away. She had come to see him, but she had to remember that she was not going to allow herself to feel more than friendship for him. "It took me a long time to figure it out," she said to divert her own attention back to the matter at hand.

"Oh, surely not."

"Oh, yes," she replied, a bit more dramatic than intended. She turned and crossed the room back to the sofa. Distance was probably a good thing, she thought to herself. "Well, when I first returned, I was in just as much shock as when I arrived here for the first time. I just didn't understand how it happened. My doorbell rang, and for a few fleeting seconds, I thought you might have actually followed me through time—"

If only I could have, he thought to himself.

"—But it was Jack returning home from his first round of his program. It was the oddest thing that he and I arrived home at the exact same time. Come to think of it, it is serendipitous that he left just yesterday. It's as if the universe has some sort of plan..." Amelia drifted off into a thousand thoughts that fizzled into nothing and her mind was stuck somewhere in the void. Franklin could see it, and he tried to bring her back.

"So Jack returned home..."

"Yes," Amelia snapped her head back to meet Franklin's gaze. "He and I got home the same night. It was the *weirdest thing*. My clothes changed back, but not to what I was wearing when I arrived, but instead some sort of translated garments... so I was in an outfit that would have been appropriate for an elegant evening out even then." Amelia looked questioningly at Franklin as if he might have the answer to the peculiarity of the situation.

"Ah, hmm," he replied, giving a confused response. "And what happened after you found yourself in that outfit?"

"Well, I went out for a walk."

Franklin looked at her questioningly. "A walk?"

"Well, yes. I told Jack I was going to a party, to explain why I was fancily dressed, which was the truth, sort of, so I... Well, that isn't important. Or maybe it is... let me give you the broad story first and then I can fill in the details later." Franklin stared at her and smiled. Warmth swelled in his chest. It was wonderful to have her back, even if it was only temporary. He crossed the room and sat in the chair next to where she sat on the sofa while she continued. "So, Jack came back and we were so happy to see each other, and I felt a little ashamed that I gallivanted into the past, and that I didn't want to tell him — not that he would understand...anyway, I threw myself into renovating the house, and then he and I spent a lot of time together. I remembered why I was so in love with him. We finished the house, and went to visit his parents in Connecticut, and then he left yesterday for three more months. Somewhere in all of that I think I pieced it all together, but it didn't quite all snap into place until a week ago when he went out to a baseball game and I found the watch and wound it to the right date. I had the same sort of thought process you did," she said looking up at him at last. "Without the calendar throwing," she said with a wink. "Since I figured it out, I felt a pull to return. After Jack left yesterday, without even questioning any of it, I had to try the watch. I put some things in order, just in case I don't make it back. And then turned the pin on the watch not knowing what would happen. But, here I am."

Yes, here she was, thought Franklin. He was so happy she was home. No, not home, he corrected his own thoughts. She doesn't live here. Well she doesn't live in this "when," but she had come back. That had to count for something. He had been hoping for her return, especially the last few days. But as this day had progressed, he had started to lose hope of her return. Thinking she didn't want to come back.

They talked over what happened in the months they were separated. He had worked on a manuscript that was almost finished, and he had started a second story. Things weren't clicking well in either one. "I would be happy to read them both for you," she said.

"I would appreciate that," he said and smiled.

Amelia filled him in on refinishing the house. She told him how she immersed herself in it, and how the study was her biggest project. She said that she had recreated it some, but gave it her own flare. "I totally understand that it is your study, and your place of work, but it is just too dark for my tastes, so in my time, I lightened it up. I gave it lighter blue paint. The stained glass windows weren't there when I moved in, but I did have some mottled, clear glass windows installed to give it the same feel, but to let in more light. And I put in a large chandelier. Nothing too fancy or gaudy. I knew you wouldn't like that." He noticed how she had included him, and the corner of his mouth lifted, but he kept intently listening, hoping she hadn't noticed. Amelia continued telling Franklin about the other rooms that she had worked on, and explained that she had completely redone the kitchen. Which reminded Franklin about the stew, and he jumped up.

"The stew! Finney will kill me if she knew I didn't feed you right away. My dear, please let me serve you some stew."

As if on cue, Amelia's stomach rumbled. They both laughed. "Apparently I would love some. And I promise *not* to tell Mrs. Finnegan that you were starving me out. Again." Amelia smiled at him coyly. She couldn't be sure, but she thought he blushed as he looked down and began to serve the food.

This seemed to make Amelia remember back to the night she left him.

"What did you do about the party?"

"Hmm? Oh, you mean the one we were supposed to attend that night? I sent round a card saying that you had to suddenly leave town." As if feeling her gaze, he turned quickly round to her and looked her in the eye. "Well, it was the truth. I didn't know what else to do at the moment, and we had the horse and carriage for the evening." Shrugging, he said, "To be honest, I was quite delighted that I didn't have to attend the party." He crossed over to her with the stew hoping it would clear the look of terror in her eyes. "I sent a card around the next morning — to say that your aunt had taken ill in Philadelphia and you had to rush off. I also mentioned that you were planning to attend a wedding back there and would be gone for some time, but that we would let our understanding hostess know when you arrived home and were willing to take visitors."

Amelia breathed out a sigh of relief. "It's a good thing you're a writer of fiction. You're pretty quick on your feet."

"Why, thank you. It was in the same instance that I thought to pack your bags and stow them under the bed, so that Emily and Mrs. Finnegan would think you gone as well," he said as he crossed to sit next to her and eat.

"Very smart. Very clever," she commended him. Pausing until he had a full mouth, she said, "You know, this means that we now have to contact Mrs. Harbinger and let her and society know that we are now once again able to accept social calls." He winced, and she smiled. "Don't worry, Mr. Dunne. Your wife won't make you attend too many. You are, after all, a very busy writer, and you need to have your time to pen your stories."

She started to laugh, and then after a moment of confusion, he joined in. He loved the sound of her voice, and her laughter. Franklin had missed this. It was a terrifying thought that there wasn't much he wouldn't do for this woman.

They sat up talking and eating and enjoying each other's company for a while. It was not until they heard the hall clock strike twelve that they realized how late it was.

"I suppose I should let you go up and rest."

"Well, we do have plenty of time," she replied. "I'll be here until October. Jack isn't due back until October fifteenth, and the first will be my first chance to go back."

"Yes," he replied, feeling the sadness creep in. Already she was thinking of her return, and this bothered him. "Let's get you to bed. I should try to get more writing done."

"I can show myself up. Do you want me to take the dishes out with me?"

"Yes, that would be appreciated. Thank you," he said as she lifted the tray and crossed the room. He trod after her to open the door. "Good night."

"Thank you. And you're sure you don't mind me staying? Not that I have anywhere else to go. But I wouldn't want to be an imposition—"

"My darling," he interrupted, "I wouldn't have it any other way."

She shivered at the warmth of his familiarity. "Well then," she said as she walked through the door, "I will see you in the morning for breakfast."

"Yes. I look forward to it."

"Good night," she tossed over her shoulder as she walked down the hall. He watched her go then closed the study door. He turned and leaned against it closing his eyes and taking a deep breath. She was *back*.

Suddenly ideas flooded his head. He dashed to his desk, and couldn't connect pen and paper fast enough.

***

In her room, Amelia found herself wondering about both being here and getting back to her own time. She had to return on October first to be with Jack, and Franklin looked so disappointed when she mentioned it.

Oh, but it was so wonderful to see Franklin again!

Amelia started the arduous process of undressing. She missed tank tops and yoga pants already. First thing tomorrow she would have Emily make an appointment with Jon. She was thrilled to be back here. These next few months were going to be lovely.

As Amelia was finally undressed, she noticed that Emily had unpacked her suitcase, and hung up everything. She had also set out the lotion Amelia liked. She smiled. It was nice to be taken care of. Pulling back the covers, she snuggled into the bed, and fell asleep smiling and thinking of all the days she had in front of her.

Chapter Thirty-Eight

A melia felt as if she had never left. Emily came in daily to help her dress, and sometimes to help her bathe. Baths didn't happen every day. It was just too much of a hassle with the water and the fold down bath. Amelia found she only liked them every third or fourth day. Showers were much easier.

Time with Franklin was easy. They breakfasted together most mornings unless he stayed up writing the night before. She read in his study while he wrote, occasionally helping him work through different story ideas and characters. Occasionally he let her read a page or two.

After a week of this rhythm, Amelia felt the need for information from outside their house. She was curious about the happenings of the neighborhood and Emily could only fill her in on so much gossip. She sent a card around to Jon under the guise of wanting to see some of the season's fabrics and styles. But knowing there would be a lot to catch up on, she told Mrs. Finnegan to set a third place at the table, just in case.

Jon arrived in a flourish of magnificence. Emily answered the door as Amelia rounded the corner after hearing the bell. Jon stepped inside with the elegance of a gentleman, offering Emily his hat, but upon seeing Amelia, dropped his briefcase, and wrapped Amelia in an embrace.

"It's so good to see you, my dear," Jon exclaimed.

"Jon, how are you? I thought of you so many times when I was home—" Amelia halted herself. She looked Jon in the eyes. She wanted to tell Jon the truth. However, she didn't know if everyone would be as understanding and accepting of her secret as Franklin. Maybe she would get Franklin's opinion on it. She realized Jon had said something to her, but she hadn't heard him.

"What?" Amelia asked.

Jon had started with the gossip about Mrs. Galley down the street having a funeral for her dog a few weeks ago, and how she had paid Jon to make matching black silk mourning dresses for her and the remaining dogs in the same style. Luckily the way Jon told his stories, he repeated himself, and he thought Amelia was agreeing with how ridiculous it all was. Amelia was caught up quickly. The neighborhood was split on their reviews of the event.

Retiring to the front room, Amelia and Jon chatted about all of the neighbors including the gossip following Amelia's sudden departure and mysterious aunt. Amelia repeated what Franklin told her he had spilled into the rumor mill. Might as well keep up appearances, she thought.

Their gossip was interspersed with talk of new fashions. Amelia ordered three new dresses, a hat and a pair of boots.

The boots she had were fine, but Amelia wanted ones without a heel. She didn't need the height, and her feet were usually covered by her skirts.

They were summoned to dinner, where Franklin regaled them with his current plot line.

Both Franklin and Amelia saw Jon off after dinner. Franklin wrapped his arms around Amelia and kissed the top of her head.

"I'm glad you're back. And I'm not the only one, my dear."

Amelia smiled. She was filled with happiness and warmth. Although something was nagging her at the back of her mind, but she didn't know exactly what it was. Resigned, she told herself it would surface eventually.

Chapter Thirty-Nine

Ten days back, Amelia was wandering around the house aimlessly. She had finished a book and had picked up another one, but her brain just didn't want to switch over to a new story. In a book hangover, she wasn't ready to let go of the characters and was still mulling over the ending. Nothing interested her, and was just meandering from room to room.

Mrs. Finnegan crossed her path and stopped when she saw Amelia. "And why, may I ask, are you just mopin' around the house when it is such a beautiful day out? Why aren't you out walkin', or deoratin', or doin' somethin'?"

"Oh, Mrs. Finnegan," Amelia was startled out of her trancelike state. "I... you know, I don't know," she puzzled.

"You were all happy to be back, and now, it's like you're a prisoner here." She patted Amelia's arm. "You know you don't hafta be."

"Oh, I know. I like being near Franklin as he writes. Somedays, I feel like I should be doing more. In my old life, I had so many other things I was doing and many different friends to visit. I just don't seem to have that here."

"Come with me," Mrs. Finnegan said authoritatively, and quickly turned and headed toward the kitchen.

Amelia hesitated.

"Hurry up, I have other things I have to take care of," Mrs. Finnegan said from a few steps down the hall.

Amelia followed her into the kitchen. She stood just inside the door, feeling a bit like a child awaiting punishment. Not that she expected punishment, but she was sure a lesson was about to commence.

Mrs. Finnegan set out bowls, jars, a jug of milk, and a bowl of eggs down on the large round table that sat in the center of the kitchen.

"Have you made bread before?"

"Pardon?" Amelia asked politely, not understanding the question.

"Bread, child. Have ya ever made it?"

"By hand?"

"Well, that right there answers the question. All right then, roll up them pretty sleeves of yours. Up to the elbow. No creatin' extra work for Emily, just because you'll be kneadin'. And here, put on this apron," Mrs. Finnegan said as she crossed the room holding out a roll of white fabric. Amelia put it over her head and found was pinafore-like and it covered most of her dress. Rolling up her sleeves, she watched Mrs. Finnegan out of the corner of her eye.

"Now," Finnegan continued while she started to arrange pots and the jars that she had put out. "This recipe was handed down through all the McAllen ladies—that's me mother's side. The Finnegans are my husband's kin. I've made this bread since I was a wee thing. So, I know it by memory. Try to keep up. And if you have questions, ask. Bread is a finicky thing and ya need ta do it just right, or it won't turn out."

Amelia nodded her head just once, like a child getting serious about a project.

"It's all right, darlin', step on over here, I'm not gonna' bite," Finnegan said in response to Amelia's hesitance.

"Are you sure I can do this? I'm not much of a cook. My mother never showed me how to do anything..." Amelia's thought trailed off as she remembered her mother, always frail. She didn't do much cooking, more warming things up, at least as Amelia could remember. They had family dinners, but nothing as delectable as Mrs. Finnegan made and certainly never freshly-baked bread.

She felt a light touch on her shoulder blade.

"Thinkin' of yer mother, are ya? Tell me what she was like while you crack six eggs inta this bowl," Finnegan said as she dragged a bowl across the counter and placed it in front of Amelia.

Reaching into the bowl filled with eggs, Amelia began cracking them one at a time, careful to watch for shells. Like each one of the eggs she cracked open, she opened up her soul a little bit to Finnegan, talking about her mother and how she died of a terrible cancer. How she had fought it for many years, for almost as long as Amelia could remember.

At first Amelia was told her mother just had a really bad cold, and that was why she stayed at home a lot, but when she started losing her hair, Amelia was very concerned. Her mother had fought and won the battle twice. But when Amelia was in college a third round of cancer came. Pancreatic cancer. It had spread to her spine quickly, and there was nothing to be done. It was one of the least studied and supported cancers, so it was a difficult battle.

Because Amelia's mother was bedridden, Amelia's father prepared a lot of pre-made frozen meals. What would Finnegan say to a microwave meal from a box, Amelia mused.

Finnegan listened to her intently, handing her measuring spoons and ingredients, only interrupting Amelia's story with instructions.

When Amelia seemed to be at the end, explaining that she was never really given a lesson in the kitchen, Finnegan halted her and said, "Well, anytime you want to learn, just pop your head in, dearie. I'll teach ya anythin' ya want to know." She smiled warmly.

"Do you have children, Mrs. Finnegan?"

"Good heavens, no! Me husband and that wee babe that you call yer husband have been enough to keep me busy. I think even if I could have children I would want for none."

"I'm so sorry." Amelia looked at the caring woman across from her with tenderness.

"Don't be, dearie. I've had a full life. And Franklin, with his life and needs, and his curious health, have been enough for me. I don't think I would have been able to watch over him as well, if I had me own children." She smiled fondly. "No, Franklin was enough for me." It was now the older woman's turn to drift off to the past, reminiscing.

Amelia would remember this moment later as she was putting herself to bed — everyone has the ability to time travel. Anyone can go to any place in their own past, at any time, and live there for a moment or a day.

Time travel was dangerous, though, only keeping the highs and lows. Hindsight is supposed to be twenty-twenty, but memories are clouded with our perceptions of how they should have been. Remembering the past every so often was important. Living in it is not.

Amelia wondered if she was actually living here, in the past— her current present. She thought she was.

How many times had Toni quoted that the ultimate goal to happiness is living for the present. Not living in the past or planning out the future, but living now, day to day, moment to moment. Maybe that is why Amelia hadn't researched Franklin even though she thought several times about doing an internet search. Maybe she knew that she would eventually come back here, and that she didn't want to know her own future by looking it up in the history books. Another reason she didn't want to go out and live so much out in the open. If she didn't make waves, change history, there would be nothing to report and nothing for people in the future to find.

Mrs. Finnegan came back from her mental time travel, smiling. "Now, where were we? We've mixed all the ingredients and we have the dough?"

"Yes," said Amelia smiling, catching the happiness that Finnegan felt.

"Good. Now, we must knead it and set it to risin'."

Finnegan started casting flour about the table like she was sprinkling magic fairy dust. Amelia started to giggle.

"What are ye sniggerin' about?" Mrs. Finnegan asked, putting her hands on her hips and giving Amelia—who towered over the older woman—her best authoritative stare.

"The way you're tossing the flour about, you make me think that you're a grown up Tinkerbell."

"A *who*?"

"Tinkerbell. From Peter Pan—"

"Ach, you mean the wee fairy from Mr. Barrie's new novel." Finnegan began to laugh and sprinkle more as she danced about the table, kicking up her heels as she did so. As she rounded the table, a big smile crossed her face as she came back to Amelia. "And for you, me wee lassie," she held out her palm which contained a little more flour, "maybe ye can fly with me magic dust," and with a pursed smile she blew the leftover flour into Amelia's face.

Both women doubled over with laughing.

"I think your fairy dust is fake, Mrs. Finnegan. I'm extremely cheery," Amelia said through her laughter, 'but I'm not flying."

"Ah, well. Maybe it's time I retire from the fairy business. Back to the bread it is."

Amelia stood and wiped flour from her face. She had started to cry from laughing so hard, and now had trail marks down her cheeks through the flour.

"Doncha worry, you'll get more on your face and hair before we're done. Now, plop that lump out on the table and we'll split it up."

The ladies tore the dough and each kneaded half. They split their own parts in half again and set it under towels by the window to rise. After cleaning up and putting away the ingredients, Finnegan poured them both some coffee and they continued to chat.

"Now, I wanted to discuss the menu with you for next week," Finnegan began with a clear agenda on her mind. "It's Franklin's birthday on Thursday, and I wanted to know if you had any big plans."

Amelia was taken aback. "I'm so sorry, Mrs. Finnegan. I didn't even know it was his birthday. He hadn't mentioned, and with my trip, I—"

"No need to worry, darlin', it's somethin' that usually a woman stumbles upon in her first year o' marriage. It's not like the menfolk telegraph it. Especially your husband.

"Birthdays were more of an excuse for his mother to have a social gatherin'. When she passed, his father didn't bother. Franklin pretends to want none of it, but when it's forgotten, his melancholia gets so much worse. So over the years, even when he was away, I made a point to make him a birthday dinner, no matter where I had to take it."

"I'm sure he appreciated it." Amelia gave a weak smile, and said "I appreciate it." Feeling bad that she didn't know it was his birthday. "Mrs. Finnegan, as you know him much better, may I defer to you for his birthday feast? I'm sure you know his favorites, and I would pale in comparison to your mastery."

"Now, now, dearie," Mrs. Finnegan reached out and took Amelia's hand in hers, "there are a great many things you've already surpassed me in doin.' Are you sure about the dinner? I'd be happy to share my ideas and collaborate."

"You're a wonderful woman to allow me to help. But truly, I believe in you completely. If you would like to share your thoughts on what you want to make, I would happily listen."

They shared a smile as Finnegan mentioned foods she would make, noting a seven layer chocolate cake. Amelia offered to stop and pick up ice cream from the ice cream parlor she visited with Franklin to go with the cake.

"I *love* that idea. What a lovely surprise!" Finnegan grinned. "Is there anyone we should invite for dinner?"

"I—I don't know. I haven't really met any of his friends. I know Jon—Mr. Caruthers—and I know they get along, but other than his publisher, I don't know anyone he spends time with."

"Well, why don't you invite them. I'm sure you could discreetly find out if he wanted anyone else here to celebrate. You can let me know by Wednesday so I can have Emily do the shoppin'."

"Sounds like a plan," Amelia said as she stood and crossed the room to look at the dough. After lifting the cheese cloth that lay over it, Amelia said, "My goodness, it's gigantic!"

"You've never seen dough rise before? Yes, it gets big. Then you have to punch it down and let it rise up again, and then you put it in to bake."

"I never realized what a process it is to make bread."

"When something is good, it takes work and care. The more love you give it, the better it turns out."

"True about so many things, Mrs. Finnegan."

The woman put a tender hand to Amelia's cheek and gave her a warm maternal look. Then with contented sigh said, "Alright, let's finish. I'm sure you have some quality mopin' still left to do."

"I think I'll leave that for another day, or just leave it to Franklin altogether," she said, winking at Finnegan. "I need to find projects around the house. And get out more," Amelia said more to herself.

"Me mother always used to say 'Busy hands make a happy mind'," Finnegan said, bringing the bowls of dough back to the table. "Now let's get started."

They finished kneading the dough, and floured the baking sheet for the bread.

"I'll let you know when it's cooled." Finnegan said.

"Thank you for the baking lesson," Amelia said. "I appreciate your insight and wisdom." And she left the kitchen, her mind full of ideas.

Chapter Forty

After Mrs. Finnegan revealed that his birthday was the following week, Amelia wanted to do something for Franklin. With the small budget Franklin had given for making improvements on the house, she had extra left he wouldn't miss. Amelia knew exactly what she wanted to get Franklin, and it would be a good excuse to follow up with something from her curious past —or was it her curious future?

That is how Amelia found herself, once again, in midtown Manhattan at the door of Lawson's Jewelers. It was much easier to find this time. The sign by the door noted the jeweler was on the second floor. With no buzzer, Amelia let herself in. At the top of the stairs, she saw the same glass door with the same lettering and frosted glass. She knocked gently on the glass, and almost as if déjà vu, she heard a similar voice tell her to, "Come in!"

After entering, she looked around. The place looked the same as before. Different pieces of jewelry were on display in the cases, but they still seemed emptier than they should be. The ancient cash register rested on the counter, looking shinier and newer than her last visit. It would look newer here than when she saw it. Although she had seen it in her past. Time really was a pretzel.

"How may I help you, dearie?"

Amelia's back was turned to the speaker, but she was certain now. It was the same exact voice. She turned around to find herself in the presence of the same hunched man with the wispy white comb over.

"Ah, it's you," he said, now seeing her face. "I was wondering when you would come."

"What do you mean? Do you know me?" Amelia asked, more out of piqued curiosity than from wariness.

"Well, in a manner of speaking, yes."

"Have I... been here before?"

"Well..." the old man winked. "I'm Mr. Mercer."

"I know. You won this shop from your brother-in-law, didn't you?"

"Ah, so you know about me, too."

"Yes. When I... I met you in the future...?"

"Ah, well, dearie, anything is possible." His enigmatic eyebrows raised, saying everything and nothing. "Now, how can I help you? Is it about your watch?"

"My watch?"

"Yes, that wristwatch," he said pointing to her wrist. "Uncommon among women these days. And most people visit here for watch repair."

"Oh, well no—"

"May I see it?"

"My watch?"

"Yes."

"Well, sure," said Amelia as she unfastened the watch and handed it over. As she did it flipped so the face was down, revealing the back. "That's funny. The inscription is gone."

"Inscription?"

"Yes. The back of the watch had this address with the name Lawson's Jewelers inscribed on it. That is how I found you in the first place."

"Well, well, well," said the little man as he turned the watch over to inspect it. "Fascinating." He inspected it more. Pulling out the pin and adjusting the date back and forth. "How interesting. A watch with a date that changes."

Amelia hesitated for a moment. She wasn't sure, but she felt he was being honest with her. She knew in the future she could trust him. So why not now? Her secret was already out, and something had drawn her back here. She looked over her shoulder, and then she made a decision.

"Mr. Mercer, I don't know what is going on here. I don't know if this shop is in some kind of time chasm or what is going on here, but I don't know that I care. I need to tell you something. I need to share it with *someone* and as you help me out, in the future, I have a feeling that this might be the way you find out." She took a deep breath. "I know this sounds unbelievable, but that watch helps me time travel."

Clocks ticking were the only sound to be heard as the older man stared at the watch, then looked up into Amelia's face. He lowered his glasses to see her more clearly, and then looked back at the watch.

"Don't worry, dearie. Your secret is safe." He patted her on the arm. "Now, that wasn't what you came here for. What can I help you with?"

"I'm looking for a gift for my… husband." Amelia said these words with an aged familiarity. It had been a while since she had called him that. "I need a birthday present. I was thinking of a watch, actually. My husband," there was that word again. She marveled at how nice it was to say, before continuing. "His birthday is this week, and I wanted to see what you had."

"Well, I do have a lovely selection of pocket watches."

"Do you think you could add a date component to one of them? You know, like mine has?"

"I… I don't know. It would take a whole different mechanism. I might have to take your watch apart to see how it works. I would have to build his watch from the bottom up."

"Oh, I… see. There is no way that you could do that without taking mine apart?"

"Not really, not precisely. I have never seen a watch like this before. I would have to see how it works. Would you mind?"

"Well, I…"

"I assure you that no harm will come to the watch. I will take very good care of it."

Although worry slithered into her brain about all the scenarios if something went awry, she handed the watch over anyway.

"All right."

"Good. I'll take a look at it and see what I can do. In the meantime, do you want to pick out a general body and style for the watch, and I'll design around that?"

Mr. Mercer showed Amelia different watches he had around the shop. Amelia decided on a brushed silver casing with a plain white face and Gothic script numerals.

As she left the building and headed out down the street to find the train back to Brooklyn, concern washed over her. What if something went wrong, and she couldn't return to the future?

Turning to go back to the jewelers, thinking that maybe it was not a good idea to leave the watch, she was distracted by a bookshop window a few doors down. In the front window several stacks of books sat. Center front was a smaller pile; a single copy was propped up to show the front cover. *Death to the Pirate King* proclaimed its title in bright green letters to window shoppers. Amelia beamed with pride and reached into her pocket for her cell phone to take a picture to send to Franklin. After a moment of panic of leaving her cell phone somewhere, she realized that the thing hadn't been invented yet. With the lack of technology, she stared at the window for a while, forgetting the watch. It was more important to take this in so she could describe the whole thing to Franklin over dinner.

Chapter Forty-One

Afew days later, Emily brought a wrapped brown paper package to Amelia who was reading in the library.

"A very old gentleman dropped this off for ya. 'E said you'd know what it is," Emily said offering the package to Amelia.

Standing to take the package, Amelia walked to the door and closed it with Emily inside.

"I got Franklin a surprise. Do you want to see it?"

"Mr. Dunne doesn't like surprises much." Emily's eyes changed from perplexed to excited. "But, yes! Is it for his birthday tomorrow?"

"Why, yes, Emily, it is. Oh, that reminds me about dinner, I need to tell Mrs. Finnegan—"

"Now don't you worry, Mrs. F has got Mr. Dunne covered in the food department. She says she has made him a birthday feast every year she has known him. Even those years he was off at university, and those years he couldn't afford a cook. She still showed up with his favorite dishes and made him eat."

"Oh, I would have *loved* to have seen that. Mrs. Finnegan lording over him with a pot of stew in one hand and a layer cake in the other, while he cowered in his college apartments."

Both women cackled loudly at the thought and then quickly covered their mouths and glared at each other with a mix of caution and propriety. They glanced at the door, hoping that no one heard their outburst and would come to spoil the secret. Amelia even poked her head out to make sure no one was in the hallway.

When the coast was clear, Amelia opened the package. There were two boxes inside the brown paper, and a note was in between them.

To Mrs. Dunne,

Here is your gift as discussed and the watch you entrusted me with. I hope you like the former, and I hope you don't mind that I amended the latter. If you have any questions or concerns in regards to either the work done or the discussion we had while you were in my shop, please do not hesitate to contact me.

Until we meet again,

—Horace Mercer

Amelia opened the first box. She found her watch within.

Upon inspection it was exactly the same. Amelia let out a sigh of relief. She flipped the watch over. It now had *Lawson's Jewelers* and the address inscribed on the back. Ah, so that is how that got there. Well, now she knew her future self would know how to find out information—or was it her past self in the future. Amelia smiled to acknowledge the pretzel of time.

Emily stared at Amelia holding her watch. "Do you want me to help you put it on, missus?" asked Emily in her brogue.

"No... I mean, yes, please." Amelia shook the time travel thoughts from her head. "I meant to say nothing is wrong. Sorry, Emily, I was just reminiscing, staring off into space."

"Quite all right, missus. I do it, too, from time to time."

Amelia smiled at Emily with thanks. Picking up the second box, Amelia felt her breath catch. As she lifted the lid, the watch winked.

"Ooh, it's lovely, that is," said Emily, carefully lifting it out of the box. "What is this little number where the three should be?"

"Ah, Emily. That is the calendar date. It's so Mr. Dunne can tell the day and time."

"That'll be very good for 'im. He tends to lose track of dates easily."

"I thought the very same thing. I have it on my watch. Apparently it's a newer invention. That is why Mercer was returning my watch with the new one. He needed to look at the workings of mine to see how to make it possible. The date changes itself after the hour hand has gone around the watch twice."

"Oooh, that is *lovely*, that is."

"Thank you, Emily. I hope he likes it."

"I'm sure he'll treasure anythin' from you, missus."

Amelia blushed. "I'm sure that's not true."

"I think he's more in love with you now than when we first met you. If you don't mind me sayin' so," she said, winking at Amelia. "I best be gettin' back. I have more things to do this afternoon."

"Thank you, Emily."

With that she left Amelia alone in the library with the weight of the pocket watch in her hands. She turned it over and over. He always remarked that he liked how she could tell the date from her wrist.

The pocket watch might be too fancy for his daily needs. Now that she thought it over, it seemed a little bit of a waste of money to spend on something Franklin would use so infrequently. Maybe this one he would use more. But she liked that he would now have something to remember her by. A lovely gift for this man who had done so much for her.

She also felt comforted that her watch was once again on her wrist. A terrible thought ran through her. What if Mercer, in his exploration of her watch, deactivated the ability to travel through time? Oh, no. Was she possibly stuck here? Again? Amelia felt panic rise up inside. She started to race for the door, but didn't know where or to whom she was running.   As her hand touched the cool knob, she stopped herself.

There were no guarantees that she would get back even if no one touched the watch. She had known that when she took the risk to travel back to this time. Going back was months away.   Who knew if it would work at any time? This is why she put things in motion in the future, with her conversations with Banks and her friends.

It would all be all right. Amelia would just have to trust.

Chapter Forty-Two

"I don't know many people," he replied when Amelia asked about inviting any of his friends to his birthday celebration.

"I know. I just... well, if you wanted people around to celebrate, I thought we could invite maybe Jon, and your publisher." She turned to him with a coy look. "If you wanted to make it a real talk of the town, we could invite the gossipy ladies from around the neighborhood."

"I just don't need—"

"I already know that you're not a big birthday person, and I know you're not much for social gatherings. Which, by the way, we should let people know that I'm back in town and we can accept invitations once again." She started to walk the perimeter of the room.

"But—"

"My dear, you can't hide your wife. *What would* people say?"

"I—wait, you're teasing me."

Pausing a moment, Amelia finally let the laughter bubble over. "Yes, I am, in a way. We do need to let people know that I'm back and make up for going missing from the last party we attended. Even if I have to make the social calls by myself." She turned back to him with a swish of skirts. "But back to your birthday. Would you like me to invite others?"

He hesitated a moment. "I suppose it wouldn't hurt to invite my publisher, and his wife. And I know you would like to spend an evening with Mr. Caruthers." A jovial smile graced his face. "Why not? Invite them all."

Amelia sent out cards to Carl and Ellen Stokes as well as to Jon Caruthers to invite them for a casual dinner to celebrate Franklin Dunne. Both parties accepted. Mrs. Finnegan was thrilled, she had guests to cook for.

***

The night of the party arrived. Franklin was recalcitrant to stop writing and get dressed for dinner.

"You never said that I would have to get dressed for dinner," he said, pouting like a child when Amelia rousted him from his study that afternoon. "Fine, don't dress for dinner, but your shirt sleeves are stained with ink, and you look just this side of a homeless man. If you don't want to dress, that is fine. Every birthday dinner needs a token hobo, if you ask me."

"You think you're so funny, don't you?" he scowled as he arose from his seat. "Wife, you are very lucky that I find you delightful." He walked around his desk to stand in front of her.

"Hmm... I don't think delightful is quite the word you're looking for, but I appreciate the substitution." Her head tilted to the side. "You don't have to dress in a tuxedo," she said, "but I would appreciate it if you put on a clean shirt, and ugh," she said as she leaned in to touch his shirt to make her point, but leaned quickly away, "take a bath. You smell like you work in the stables."

"Yes, *dear*. I'll go clean up so I don't offend our guests," he said as he started to walk out the door.

"Wait. You might want to take this with you," she said as she held out a small box with a bright red ribbon around it.

"What is that?"

"Happy Birthday, Franklin."

"Amelia," he said looking up from the gift in her hand to her eyes, "you shouldn't have."

"I wanted to. Here, open it."

Franklin carefully untied the ribbon and gently opened the box. "It's... it's magnificent."

"You like it?"

"Yes," he said, taking it out of the box and rolling the pocket watch over in his hands. "This is even nicer than the one my father gave me before I went to law school." Once again he looked up at her, his eyes tender. "*Thank* you," he said. He reached out and put his hand cradling her elbow and leaned in. He wanted to kiss her on the lips, but knew he shouldn't. They promised to keep their relationship platonic.

She was back, but he wasn't sure if it was to be with him. Amelia had plans to return to her own place and time. He wasn't sure how she felt about him. And she had mentioned her man in the future. He hesitated for a moment, but still needed to show his thanks. He did so with a light kiss on her cheek. His lips felt her skin warm with a blush. Maybe he was reading the situation correctly.

"You're welcome," Amelia said, finally able to look up at him. Her cheeks burned where his lips touched her cheek. Without thinking she moved her hand to where his lips had just been. This made her face burn more. He was still looking at her. She squared her shoulders, refusing to let this emotion overtake her.

"Well," he said, stepping back, "I should... go get ready," not being able to tear his eyes off of her.

"I should go check on the preparations with Mrs. Finnegan. I'll see you..." she let her sentence trail off as she walked out of the room, looking at him once more over her shoulder. Once out of the room, she hurried down the hall to a safe distance away then slammed her back against the wall, to hold her steady while she caught her breath. She had been holding it since he had kissed her. After a few minutes, Amelia, now composed, walked the rest of the way and into the kitchen to check with Mrs. Finnegan on the proceedings.

***

Amelia had changed for the party, and put on the earrings that Franklin had given her the night of her disappearance back to the future. She was wearing her hair down and soft tonight, so the earrings didn't seem as dressy. As she ascended the stairs, the doorbell rang. Franklin appeared from nowhere. As he passed the bottom of the stairs, he looked up and gasped.

"You look..." he said, grasping for words.

Amelia blushed again. "Thank you," she said. They stood staring at each other until the doorbell rang again, and Emily scuttled out.

"Well, are you two going to just stand there like statues or are ye gonna get the door?"

"Oh, Emily, yes. We both are going. Now." Amelia, whipped out of her stupor, made a shooing motion at Franklin and then continued down the stairs. "Thank you. You can go back and help Mrs. Finnegan."

"Thank ya, missus."

By the time Amelia got to the bottom of the staircase, Franklin was at the door.

"Welcome, Mr. Caruthers. What a delight to have you join us. My wife is just inside."

Caruthers stepped into the house, and saw Amelia.

"Oh, my! How lovely you look! If I didn't know better, I'd say you were the belle of the ball!" Jon reached for Amelia and spun her around.

As Amelia and Jon discussed her outfit, the bell rang again. Franklin joyfully dashed back to the door and let in the new arrivals. "Just this way," Franklin said and he led in a very distinguished looking older man with white hair, and lots of wrinkles around his eyes and forehead who was dressed in a soft navy suit. The woman that followed him was a petite woman who was very chesty, who was wearing a black satin dress, and had her hair loosely piled on her head, seemingly held up with diamonds.

"Mr. and Mrs. Stokes, may I present my wife, Amelia Dunne. Amelia, this is my publisher and his wife." He then turned to Jon. "And I'm sure you are already acquainted with this gentleman," Franklin said turning to his right, "is Jon Caruthers, tailor extraordinaire."

"Franklin, you are a flatterer." Jon said. Then with a slight bow said, "Mrs. Stokes, it is lovely to see you again. Mr. Stokes it is nice to meet you," Jon stepped forward to kiss Mrs. Stokes hand and to shake that of Mr. Stokes, and then he stepped back.

"Mrs. Dunne you are lovelier than your husband proclaimed you to be. He says you're quite the muse to his writing," said Mr. Stokes, coming forward to kiss her hand.

"My husband flatters me, Mr. Stokes. And I insist that you call me Amelia."

"Well then, you must call me Carl."

"And you must call me Ellen," Mrs. Stokes chimed in. "Amelia, it is lovely to meet one of the biggest mysteries in Brooklyn." Ellen gave Amelia a wink. "Thank you so much for inviting us tonight. Tomorrow we will be the talk of the town for having actually *seen* the Mrs. Dunne. Half of the town thinks that you don't really exist, that Franklin is fictionalizing a wife, just like his novels."

Amelia politely tittered. "Yes, well I was just telling my husband earlier that we need to start accepting invitations now that I'm back from my trip." Amelia felt she needed to solidify their story, "My aunt took quite sick, you know."

"No, I didn't," said Ellen.

"Yes, it was quite sudden." Amelia wanted to move the party along, so she said, "But let's not just all stand here in the front hall. Would you like to go into the library for a drink before dinner?"

"Yes, let's," Jon said cheerfully. "Lead the way, my dear."

Amelia led the guests to the front room. Franklin stood still, marveling at the woman that was portraying his wife. He didn't understand where she came from, or when, he corrected himself, but he did, truly, adore her. Looking at his new pocket watch he smiled as he saw the date that it displayed.

"Franklin, are you joining us?" Amelia's voice snapped him back into the moment.

"Coming, dearest."

***

The evening was quite a success. Franklin and Stokes chatted off in a corner about politics while the ladies chatted with Jon about the latest Parisian fashions.

When Emily came in to announce dinner, they all adjourned into the dining room, where Mrs. Finnegan had laid out a feast. There was roast turkey, green beans, sautéed spinach, pickled beets, roasted potatoes, cranberry jelly, and of course, freshly made bread. Amelia helped some with the food preparation, and she boasted to the guests about Mrs. Finnegan.

The dinner was delicious. They returned to the front room where Mrs. Finnegan had laid out cake, coffee, and brandies. Mrs. Finnegan and Emily stayed to join in singing *Happy Birthday* to Franklin who insisted that she and Emily stay for a slice of the cake.

Mrs. Finnegan then launched into stories of Franklin that delighted the entire room. One about Franklin's first published book that Amelia already knew. One about Franklin's fifth birthday, where he wanted a toy train that was half his size, but didn't receive one. He protested by sitting in the middle of the stairs an entire day making it difficult for anyone to get up or down. He even slept on the stairs. Mrs. Finnegan had scooped him up to put him to bed, and the next day his father showed up with the toy noting that because his son, who would be a lawyer one day, stood his ground.

A few other stories were told about Franklin, his stubbornness, and his goodwill. After a few helpings of cake, and the coffee had turned cold, Mrs. Finnegan excused herself. She had Emily remove the remaining coffee and cake. Their departure was a cue for Jon, Ellen and Carl to all make their goodbyes.

After seeing their guests out, Amelia and Franklin were alone in the front hallway.

"Well, darling, that was a lovely party."

"Oh, so you did like it. I was happy to throw a party for you, Franklin."

"Yes, I'm glad that you did."

They stood in silence.

"Well—," Amelia began to turn for the stairs.

"Amelia, would you—"

"Yes?" She said as she quickly turned back toward Franklin.

"Would you care to join me for just one more drink?"

Smiling, she said, "Yes, I would like that very much."

They returned to the front room, and lowered the lights a little. He poured them both a glass of wine and joined her on the sofa that was angled perfectly to people watch out the big bay window on the front of the house.

"When did you renovate this room? I hate to say it but I hadn't noticed that you changed it until tonight," he said sheepishly as he relaxed on the sofa.

"Of course you didn't, Franklin," she said, smiling and patting his knee. "You barely leave your study. I could probably even rearrange *that* room and you wouldn't notice until you went to sit down on a chair and it was no longer there."

"True," he said and chuckled. She joined in.

A moment of quiet hung in the air as their laughter receded.

"I rearranged it last week. I like watching the people on the street. This beautiful window is a perfect level, and unless this room is lit, the people outside can't really see in. I tested it. It's not the best arrangement for the furniture as the room doesn't flow with the sofa like this, but I figured we wouldn't really entertain large groups. And if we would, we could just turn this sofa back around to the room and move these chairs," she said as she nodded to the chairs that were positioned just off the arms of the sofa, "just to the other side. The furniture isn't that heavy. Emily and I can do it by ourselves."

He smiled at her use of we. To cover why he was smiling he replied, "You really are a talent at this. I didn't realize there was such an art to furniture arrangement."

"Thank you," she smiled with a warming pride. She glanced at him but quickly looked away and took a drink. She could still feel his eyes on her.

Moments of silence went by before she heard him shift a little and his head turned back out to the street.

"Not many people out tonight," he observed.

"No."

They sat in silence. Both staring out at the street and both feeling relaxed but on alert to every movement, every breath the other was taking. Nervous tension started to swell in the room creating the need for one or both to speak. Neither knew what to say. Amelia and Franklin both rested one hand on the sofa at the same time, and touched pinky fingers. Both drew away their hands quickly as if touching fire, and apologizing at the same time. They both nervously laughed at the occurrence.

As they sat in silence, Amelia thought about a first date from her past. Sitting next to Franklin she was experiencing first date feelings. Nervousness started to bubble up — the fears had been there as soon as she sat down, but ignored them until now when they started to take over. Waving them away, she told herself to stop being silly. She had spent a lot of time alone with Franklin. But why did she think about every gesture now?

Franklin took in Amelia's scent. She smelled like vanilla honeysuckle, flour, and something warm and appetizing. He wanted to move closer. They hadn't spoken about their...relationship upon her return. He had assumed that their plutonic agreement still stood, but her gift, and the way she looked at him... No. He wouldn't let himself think too much about it, to hope. The last week had been blissful and painful for him. Franklin had missed Amelia. The light that she had awoken in him, flickered and threatened to go out. The hope she would return kept it a mere glimmer and when she returned it was like the torch flared and he wanted to light the whole world with it, but kept it hidden. Restricting himself to stay on his side of the sofa, he sat on his free hand. He wanted to take her face in his hands and kiss her over and over, and never stop.

All night he thought about how she made his life better. The world was light and more worthwhile when she was around. She wanted to wake up each day, wanted to talk to people and to celebrate life's milestones. He hadn't wanted any of that for a long time. He just wanted to escape into the worlds he created and stay there. It was safe in his stories. It was easy in his stories.

Her present, that magnificent watch, made him hope there was more there than just a friendship between them. A lovely gift, and a huge gesture on her part, she had it designed after her own watch, she told everyone at dinner. The watchmaker had to deconstruct her watch to figure out how to make it. Franklin knew the sacrifice this was to her. Allowing a jeweler to possess the ticket back to her own time. She took so many chances in doing that. What if her watch wasn't returned? She would have been stuck here. The sacrifice was made on his behalf, to give him a gift and make him happy. It gave him hope. Franklin reached out to take her hand in his.

Amelia sat still. She had so many questions. Life that included Jack waited for her in the future. She couldn't just toss all of that aside to have a fling in the past. It wouldn't be right to any of them. In fact, because she and Franklin were intimate once, she already felt a wedge between her and Jack. Amelia didn't know what drew her back to this time, or why she felt she needed to return. She didn't know why she needed to get Franklin such an elaborate gift and celebrate his birthday. All she knew is that she had the want to, the desire to, the need to. Feelings swelled and surfaced. Was it possible? Was she really in love with Franklin? Was it possible to be in love with two people?

No. She shouldn't. Jack had a budding career as a doctor and he was her future, wasn't he? Franklin wasn't a famous novelist, but he was a successful one. Amelia puzzled through her thoughts none leading her to why she had come back. Perhaps she already knew that answer and didn't want to admit it.

She felt his hand take hers. Turning she looked toward him the sparkle of his eyes glinting the light from outside the only thing visible. They hadn't lit any lights, the room only lit from outside. In the shadows she saw his blank face, giving away nothing. His hand covered hers. Did she want to be holding his hand? She should take her hand away from his; she didn't want to invite more attention. Or did she? That first night was so lovely, although it was so long¹ ago, maybe she was remembering it incorrectly. Maybe… maybe it was just nice to do things for someone, to have someone to do things for and then be rewarded with some chemical, romantic electricity, and hand holding.

She felt his lips on hers before saw him move in the darkness. A soft kiss, not demanding. A touch, as simple and as lovely as his hand reaching out to take hers. Amelia knew she should lean away or at least not kiss him back. But she did neither. Her lips melted into his. She reached her free hand up to his cheek, accepting the kiss, asking for more.

Franklin wrapped his arms around her, pulling her in to kiss her deeper. He had wanted to kiss her in the front hall a few days ago when she had returned, but he restrained. He had been feeling confusion, fear, and lust all mixed together these last few days. None of which he wanted to admit. He wanted Amelia to want him back, to love him back. Did she? Was she kissing him now out of pity or did she really feel the same way? Suddenly his questions flooded his mind with wild intensity. He pushed away from her.

"No," he shouted.

She was alarmed and shaken both by his shouting and his sudden retreat. He scrambled up from the sofa away putting the furniture in between them.

"I'm... sorry. I... don't know what came over me. Must be the liquor. I've had so much tonight, and I... shouldn't have...indulged... I'm... sorry." And with that he rushed out of the room, leaving her alone in the dark.

What just happened. Amelia felt even more befuddled. That kiss. Raising her fingers to her lips Amelia admitted to herself, she was in love with Franklin.

Chapter Forty-Three

When Emily came in the next morning, Amelia quickly shooed her out. Saying that she was over-tired from entertaining the previous night. Amelia took breakfast in her bedroom and asked that she have lunch in here, too. She read all day long, staying in her nightgown and robe and not leaving her room. Well, she *tried* to read. As she was reading she found her mind wandering back to the events last night, specifically the moment when Franklin kissed her in the front room. Her mind meandered, analyzing everything leading up to the kiss and the moments after. She thought different scenarios. What if she were the one to push him away or pull away first? What if neither of them had? Anguish flooded her mind. She knows what she should feel. Or what she wanted to feel. Had she enabled this? Was it a bad thing to like what happened between them? What was going to happen next?

If she never left her room, or at least didn't come out for a few days, maybe he would forget about it. They could go back to normal.   No, she told herself, that was silly, he wouldn't forget about kissing her.   But maybe he would pretend like he forgot, and then... oh... but she didn't want him to forget.   She didn't know what she *wanted* him to do, but she didn't want him to forget. She was so confused.

Emily dutifully brought in the lunch tray, and took away the breakfast remains when she left.   It was curious that Emily wasn't trying to rouse her or even to talk to her.   She always seemed to know exactly what was going on.   There was no way that Emily could know what happened.   She and Mrs. Finnegan left shortly after the guests.   It *was* very curious.

After her lunch, Amelia became restless.   She had taken to pacing the room, walking a few steps back and forth, frustrated with her lack of calm. She would throw herself into a chair or on the bed, only to be up and pacing again minutes later.

A knock came on the door, but it didn't open.   Emily had taken it upon herself to knock and let herself in these days, and would only halt if she heard Amelia holler out "stop."   Which Amelia did one day, just to see what would happen—Emily paused a moment, knocked again and peeked her head in with eyes closed asking if it was "now alright to enter."   Smiling to herself, remembering the moment, Amelia waited for the door to open.   It didn't. There was another knock.

"Come in," she said authoritatively.

"Pardon me, missus, but neither you nor Franklin have come out of your room's all day," Mrs. Finnegan said as she entered. "I know it's the day after a party, and what with the festivities, and celebratin' until all hours, you's taken to a bit of a layabout. But Franklin canna be roused. And with you staying in your room, and Emily sayin' you're short with her, I just wanted to check that you're well?"

"Am I well? What do you mean Mrs. Finnegan?" Amelia asked puzzled.

"I... well, I wanted to make sure you were feelin' fine, healthy-like. That the food dinna make you... sick."

"Oh, no! Mrs. Finnegan, I'm so sorry to worry you this way. I feel just fine." Amelia motioned to her body as if to prove it. "We stayed up too late and I had too much to drink, so I'm just relaxing today." Amelia saw the concern on Finnegan's face was beginning to fade away. "You said neither of us. Franklin hasn't been out either?"

"No, and he won't accept a tray. Emily left both a breakfast and a lunch, but he won't open the door, and he didn't touch anything."

"I know sometimes when he is working he forgets to eat, is it possible—"

"He hasna been writin' today. Sometimes he gets like this—moody and quiet, and he locks 'imself in. I havena seen it in a bit, ya know. He was like this a bit when ye went to visit your aunt. But he whipped himself up into a project, and was back in his study bein' his broodin' authorin' self soon enough."

303

"Well, give him the day. Probably too much to drink and has just been sleeping it off." Amelia said, trying to convince herself as much as Finnegan.

"Ah. Yes, that must be it," Finnegan said. Then her tone changed to be a bit conspiratorial, she said "We'll leave 'im be til tomorrow, then we'll rouse him."

"Yes, if he doesn't come out, I'll go in and wrestle him out," Amelia said jokingly.

"That might not be the best idea, but you're on the right track. I'll let you go back to restin'." Finnegan started to walk out of Amelia's bedroom, "Oh, what are you wantin' to do about dinner tonight?"

"If Franklin hasn't been eating, he probably won't want much. And I'm going to continue to rest." Amelia wrapped her arms around herself. "Would just leave a plate of something in the kitchen, and I'll go help myself if I'm hungry? And maybe leave a note for Franklin that you're leaving something, if he storms the kitchen for food. And Emily want to take the rest of the day, please do so."

"Thank ye, missus. With all of the work yesterday, and the preparation the day before, I'm a bit tired. I think I will head out early."

"Alright, Mrs. Finnegan. And thank you again for all of your help with the festivities yesterday. He did enjoy himself immensely."

"Good, good. Twas nothin' dearie. I'm jest glad you got him to celebrate! I'll see ya tomorrow, then." And with that, Mrs. Finnegan left Amelia.

A few minutes later Emily popped up, Amelia had gone back to sitting and reading by the window, letting the breeze from outside caress her face.

"Missus, Mrs. Finnegan and I are leavin' now. I just wanted to check in to make sure you don't need anythin' before we go."

Amelia turned around to the doorway, where Emily stood in the frame. "I'm fine, Emily. Thank you for checking," Amelia turned back to her book. "Have a lovely evening."

She heard her bedroom door click, and then a few more minutes later, she heard the front door close. Amelia read with more focus now. Entranced in the story, she didn't notice that it grew late until the words on the page were difficult to read. Amelia got up to turn on the lights, but as she started to cross the room, she felt weariness wash through her, and crawled to her bed. She sunk into the mattress, pulled the covers around her, and was asleep before she knew it.

In the middle of the night, Amelia awoke to the sound of her door clicking shut. For fear that someone was in her room she didn't want to move and alert the person to her state of awareness, so she continued to breathe deeply. After laying still for what seemed like half an hour, she popped her head up out of the covers like a gopher out of the ground. There was no one there, and her bedroom door was closed. She must have imagined it, she told herself, and went back to sleep.

The next day when Emily came in, Amelia willed herself to get up and dressed. One day in bed was luxurious, more than that was just pathetic. She couldn't hide from Franklin. And the kiss they shared. The mixture of liquor with celebration and frivolity, a birthday, and residual feelings she told herself it was nothing. As Emily helped her with her hair, Amelia thought through what she was going to say to Franklin. After all, she had plans to return to her own time in October. This was just a visit. Nothing permanent. Plus there was Jack to think about. Therefore, the kiss was just imprudent, and it was just a good reminder that they needed to observe their original plutonic pact. She did care for Franklin, but it was not passion. It couldn't be. No matter how she thought about him.

As this last thought rounded the front of her brain, a question echoed through the back. Was it only friendship, Amelia? She shook off the question with her head, which Emily took to mean that Amelia didn't want her hair up. Which was fine with Amelia, she missed wearing her hair down all the time. Deep in thought, Amelia didn't hear Emily leave the room. Darn! She thought to herself, she wanted to ask if Franklin had emerged. Oh well, she should probably see Mrs. Finnegan about breakfast. Amelia told Emily that she didn't need a breakfast tray this morning.

Downstairs, she took a deep breath before entering the dining room. With the doors open, her entrance wasn't dramatic. Keeping her eyes down until she was squarely in the door, she stood there for a moment, waiting for something to happen. She waited. And waited. Finally, after what seemed like plenty of time to have been acknowledged, she looked up. Amelia found she was the only one in the room. Feeling sheepish, she quickly shepherded herself to her seat. As if she had just sat in time, Emily sashayed in and set down the coffee.

"'Ow would ya like your eggs this mornin'?"

Amelia paused for a moment and stared at Emily. Had she seen Amelia standing in the doorway, stupidly?

"Ah... um... scrambled? With cheese and tomatoes and peppers?

"Very good, missus," Emily said as she returned the way she came.

"Will Franklin be in?" Amelia said, stopping Emily with her voice.

"I 'avena heard hide nor hair from him. I doubt it," and she turned and left the room.

Amelia felt all kinds of emotions. She didn't even know how to begin dealing with them. Wanting some mental clarity, or at least an abstraction of her morning fog, she reached out and poured herself a coffee. After a few sips she still felt so many things, they were just sharper now, in focus. She felt angry at Franklin for not being here at breakfast; she felt worry that something was wrong with him; she felt humiliation standing in the doorway waiting for Franklin to acknowledge her and it was made worse knowing Emily saw her there. Amelia didn't want to admit she felt any type of affection for him. This was only a visit. Temporary.

After that kiss the other night, and his lack of being around, she was completely confused as to how she should act and feel. Amelia had neatly filed away their first escapade, back behind her college flings and the terrible boyfriends. She didn't want to open it back up. It was much safer this way. They were *friends,* she had her own life and he had his. She was happy to share in his when she could.

Emily was setting a plate in front of her before Amelia realized she had reentered.

"Will there be anythin' else?"

"No, Emily. Thank you." Amelia was left alone with her steaming eggs, her now cooled coffee, and her thoughts.

This was how she spent most of the day. Brooding with thoughts of Franklin. Her mind clearly wanted to define what they were to each other. To quiet these voices, she tried to concern herself with his lack of reappearance. She could not get an answer from Mrs. Finnegan or from Emily as to what was happening up in his room and why his trays were returned untouched. Emily helped Amelia ready for bed that evening, reassuring her that the most he ever stayed locked up in his room was three days.

Another day passed and no sign from Franklin. And another. On the fourth day, after her breakfast, Amelia was through with waiting for him to emerge. Her emotions were raw. She had felt them all, over and over again, trying to find answers, or resolve in any of these feelings. But finding none, went to seek out the only person that could give it to her.

She knocked lightly. No response. She knocked a little harder. No response. "Franklin," Amelia called through the door while knocking louder. No response. "I'm coming in," she said, almost asking a question when she said it. Amelia waited for protestation, or the door knob to suddenly jiggle in her hand. No response. She turned the knob and pushed.

It was dark and the pungent smell of unwashed, sour perspiration was so thick she could taste it. The mix of dirty laundry, fried onions, and burnt metal hung in the air.

Blinded by darkness, she couldn't move until her eyes adjusted even though she knew the room's layout. Squinting, she looked around trying to find Franklin. A gap in the curtains allowed a tiny seepage of sun. She carefully made her way to the windows, cautiously stepping over piles of who-knew-what. She threw back the curtains, and tossed open the window, beckoning fresh air. The early autumnal morning breeze blew in spicy, and warm, splicing through the stench in the room. Amelia took a deep breath of the air outside and closed her eyes as if fresh air would cure everything. She turned back to the room, opened her eyes, and surveyed the sight before her.

Piles of clothes were everywhere. Books were strewn all over the floor, opened to random pages as if a mad man were trying to solve a puzzle. A chair laid pathetically on its side. And on the bed, a heap of bedding that moved up and down.

Not knowing where to start, Amelia looked around the room a few times to process. She came in here to recover the man, she reminded herself. The only one who could help her sort her feelings, the voice in her brain echoed the reminder.

Squaring her shoulders, she started over to the bed. "Franklin," she called quietly. "I've come to wake you up," *oh that sounds stupid*, she thought. "Franklin. Franklin?" Amelia was now standing by the pile. He moved a little. "Franklin?"

Having gotten no more response she just stood there. Minutes ticked by, and she felt so awkward. He wasn't responding, so she assumed he was asleep. Probably just as well, as frustrating as it was that he wouldn't answer her questions now. Amelia sat on the bed softly. She sighed heavily.

"Oh, Franklin," she said halfheartedly to the lump, twisting her hands, specifically twisting her wedding ring around on her ring finger. "Why have you been hiding? That is a ridiculous question. You're hiding for the same reason I was. And I don't know why I'm talking to you in this state. You probably won't hear me. But I have to say my mind is a mess. I don't know how I feel about it all, either…"

She sat, twisting her wedding ring. Minutes dragged by. She was just about to leave and then from under the covers she heard a muffled voice.

"What do you mean, you 'don't know how you feel about it all either'?" he asked, barely stirring from his position, and startling Amelia who had become drawn into the act of moving the ring around on her finger that she had mentally left the room.

"I..." she turned to look, seeing he was still a lump. "I refuse to talk to you when you're like this. I need to talk to a person, not a lump of covers."

There was movement, and he started to sit up.

"Don't look at me."

"Fine, I won't, but we need to sort this out and go back to living," she huffed as she turned away from him, still sitting on the bed.

"No, I mean, I'm not quite in the best state of dress."

"Oh, Franklin, don't be silly, I've seen you completely naked, remember?" she said, springing up and sitting back down, now facing him with one leg folded in front of her on the bed, the other toe still touching the floor.

Franklin started a low rumble of a chuckle. "Oh, *do* I remember...." he said wistfully as he squinted over her shoulder at the bright light coming in through the window. "I have tried to forget, but it plagues me almost every night, and sometimes during the day. I've started to write you so many times. I've torn up and burnt the pages over and over where I write you into books. I just can't..."

"... think of it?" she asked, looking away.

"No! I can't *share* you with the world. Sometimes I think if I put you on paper, I can keep you forever. Here. With me. But then I think better of it and discard it, because you cannot, should not, be shared with judgmental readers, and limited to a page."

"I don't quite understand—"

"No, of course you wouldn't. You travel here as if a vacation and you play at this life. When you go, what happens to the rest of us?" His voice rose, and his bare chest heaved with mild hysteria. His blood shot eyes darted around the room, finally settling on her face. Looking like a character out of a pirate novel, his face was unshaven and his hair was ruffled and windblown.

She reached out toward him with her left hand, her entire body stretched over the bed between them to smooth down his hair. He grabbed her wrist before it reached him. Shaking her wrist to point out her ring, he asked, "Why do you wear this?"

She looked at him, puzzled for a moment. "Because we agreed—"

"No, why do *you* wear it? You don't need to wear it around the house when it's only us, but you still choose to." He dropped her hand and stood up and crossed the room with his back to her. He was wearing the same rumpled linen pants from the night of his party. He took a deep breath and tilted his head up to the ceiling putting his hands on his hips. "Don't you understand? Every time I see my ring on your hand, you give me hope," he turned around to face her again, "only to send me down the rollercoaster dip of emotions, and launch me into this deep depression that plagues me." A small sob sounded. "Because no matter how this feels," he motioned between the two of them, "you are going to leave me." He turned his back to her again. "And I am so in love…"

Amelia sat stunned on the bed. She was afraid to move because she didn't want to scare him from revealing more.

He sighed deeply and said, with his back still to her, "I'm sorry… but I need to know, do you love… do you... feel *anything* for me?"

Looking down at the ring on her hand, which she had once again been twirling with her opposite hand, Amelia said, "I… "

She felt him turn back towards her, but she couldn't look up. He took one step toward her, but stopped before taking any more. Now he was the one who didn't want to move for fear of scaring her from saying what she really felt, or possibly saying nothing at all.

"I *do* feel something for you. I… always have. It's just —"

"Your man in the future," he said finishing her sentence and running his hand through his messy hair a couple of times, and then dragging it down his ragged face.

"No! I mean, yes. There is that. Jack does exist, and he is always in the back of my mind. But being here, with you," she looked up across the room at him, "it makes me feel things for you. I find myself wanting to be near you," she looked back down at her hand again. "I felt that way from the moment I left back to my own time, and for every day since." She looked up at him with pleading eyes, "but I don't know what to do about it."

Franklin, frozen in place, stared back at her. It was if they stared at each other long enough the answer would come. Amelia's face started to contort; she was trying to prevent the tears from rolling down her cheeks. Having no luck, one drop spilled over from each eye. It was as if they were magical tears in a fairy tale, and they released Franklin from the spot to which he had frozen. He ran to her and knelt down beside her. She placed a hand on his cheek.

"I can't stop what I feel for you," he said looking up at her. "I've tried. I promise you I've tried. I feel terrible. I shouldn't have kissed you. I've tried to stay away from you for days. My heart and my head have been dark with anger at myself for having kissed you."

Amelia couldn't speak. All the questions she had been wanting to ask wouldn't come. Maybe they didn't need to.

They sat like this for a while, neither knowing what to say. Amelia sniffed, and looked away.

"I came into your room."

"What?" she said, and she whipped her head back around to him.

"I knew I shouldn't have, and I'm so very sorry," he said backing away from her quickly, as if he was avoiding her slap. "I needed to be near you, to see your face. My melancholia flared, and I felt like I was the lowliest person alive, not even worthy to breathe the same air as you. But I needed to see you. So I dragged myself down the hall to your door. I walked back and forth to your door several times in the middle of the night. I finally opened it, and crossed the room to your bed. You looked so peaceful, and I knew it had *nothing* to do with me. I could never make you that serene. I just had to feel some of that serenity, and before I knew it, I was reaching out and stroking your hair, like some sort of perverted lech," he crawled away from her now, almost sobbing as he spoke. "I touched your hair and felt a peace come over me. And then you moved, and the peace was shattered. I felt like there were a thousand shards of glass within my body just floating around, stabbing me enough to make me ache and bleed. It was painful but not enough to kill me."

Amelia remained emotionless as he spoke. He had distanced himself far from her at this point both mentally and physically. She wanted to reach out and touch him, but was afraid to move. He sat gasping on the floor, folded over himself.

"I came back to my room," he started speaking again his voice raspy and broken, "and I told myself that I wasn't worth anything you had to give, and I started ripping apart this room, unable to stop myself, thinking that if I tore this room down, I would feel better inside. Drunk on my own anger, I tried to rid all the feelings from myself and hide from the light. I felt so undeserving of things like food or you." He looked up at her now. His eyes pleaded. "I only came in once."

She hesitated before speaking, "I forgive you—"

"No!" he said with defiance, sitting up a bit straighter, "I don't deserve your forgiveness. I don't deserve anything you have to give. So I ask you again, why do you wear my ring?"

She looked at him trying to understand.

"Franklin, you're a wonderful man. You're a brilliant writer. I wish—"

"Don't say it."

"Say what?" she asked, confused. "Say that I wish I didn't have feelings for you, that this was only a friendship, or even better, just a 'vacation' as you called it. But it's *not*. I don't know what I feel, because I'm afraid to feel it. I'm afraid that it makes me a terrible person because I feel deeply for two different men. I wish I could just tell you freely how I feel, but honestly, *I don't know* how I feel. Kissing you was…"

"Terrible? Horrible? Grotesque?"

"No," she said, her voice said as if it were holding something precious. "It was beautiful."

Silence rang through the room. A breeze blew in from the window, caressing Amelia's face as if it were a gentle hand wiping away anguish.

"Is this… is this how love feels?" Franklin quietly asked from the corner that he had absconded himself.

Her voice cracked a little as she found it again, "What do you mean?"

"Like my heart is being squeezed within my chest with someone's hand — your hand possibly — one moment.

316

And the next it is floating, as if on that breeze coming in the window."

Amelia looked at Franklin as if she had never seen him.

"Have you never been in love?" she asked.

"No. As a matter of fact, after my experiences with you, I don't think I truly ever have."

Silence befell the room again.

"Yes."

"Yes, what?" he asked.

"I have really only been in love, or what I thought was love twice, and yes, that is *how* my heart has felt each of those times."

"Oh. Does it feel that way now?"

She sat for a few more moments feeling mute—the words stuck in her throat. She rose. Amelia walked to the door, and stopped when she was inside the frame. She turned her head slightly, wrapped her arms around herself, and looked back. "Yes," she replied and walked out the door.

Chapter Forty-Four

Emily entered Amelia's room the next morning to help her dress. Noting Amelia's morose mood, Emily suggested a nice warm bath scented with lavender. Amelia acquiesced knowing water has a curative effect. She bathed, dressed, and went down to breakfast feeling better, but not having expunged her upset.

Amelia was sitting in the dining room when she heard a whistled tune. Following the sound into the room came Franklin. In the time since she had seen him yesterday morning he had bathed, shaved, and changed into clean clothes. And apparently had changed into a different man than the pathetic Dumas prisoner persona he was wearing when she last saw him. This man was chipper, happy and upbeat. He was even smiling. Amelia stared in confusion.

She looked up and blinked at him repeatedly as she realized he had spoken, and she didn't know what he had said because of the massive confusion flooding her mind.

"Do you want me to pour the coffee?"

"Oh, yes." She shook her head to clear the fog. "Please," she said, adding on the last word. This new Franklin made her completely forget manners.

"I've been up since about four, writing. I must say, it is rather good. I can't wait for you to read it."

"Four yesterday afternoon?" she asked in a hazy disbelief, still not actually active in the conversation.

"No, this morning. After our conversation yesterday, I slept and then got up last night, and bathed, shaved, and cleaned up my... mess of a room. I came downstairs, and ate a bit, and then went back up to sleep. Had a couple of hours, and then was awakened by a brainwave for a story, and have been writing ever since. Emily just halted progress by telling me that you were ready for breakfast."

Amelia gaped at him not knowing what to say, like a fish with her mouth open.

"It is alright that we dine together, I assume?"

"Yes... of course," Amelia said, closing her mouth looking down at her plate to stop from staring incredulously at Franklin. "What... changed? You were... adrift, and now you're back."

"Ah, well that is the disease, isn't it? I know I've told you about it. I would assume it still exists in your day and age, unless by some miracle they've come up with a way to shock the mind into being happy. Or at least content." Franklin chuckled at his joke. He looked up to see Amelia blankly staring at him, and he cleared his throat and looked back down at his food. "Yes, well. I get these terrible bouts from time to time. Anything can set it off, especially

319

when I have an emotional high or low. I guess our..." he paused, cleared his throat and looked back up at her, "... interlude after the guests had gone... Well, it had me hoping, and then I realized it was a hope far greater than I could or should have. You have been very clear that this is just a visit, and nothing more, and I should respect those wishes. I couldn't control myself from spiraling into a vortex of negative emotion. I just wanted to sit in the dark and hope that the world was just passing by." Franklin stared off past Amelia. He was no longer looking at her, and seemed to be talking to the room in general. He took in a deep breath and sighed. "And then you came in. You literally gave me a breath of fresh air. You opened the windows and showed me that life had gone on. Whether I was living in it or not. I realized that I actually didn't mind that time had moved on.

"Something was nagging at me, in the back of my head. Something about this spiraling emotional vortex. Like I said, I went back to sleep but was awakened by this story and I just started writing it."

"So you snapped out of your bad mood, just like that?" Amelia said, finally able to find the words.

"It's not a *mood*. Unfortunately, it's an inability to be happy. It's chemical. According to my doctor, it's incurable. But because it's in the brain, but it is adjustable. I try to control it, but I cannot. That is why most of the time, I spend my days just writing or living moderately. Too much excitement on either side of the spectrum can be detrimental. This round of it was actually a mild case.

When I was studying at university, I would dive into it and stay in the dark place for days. Finnegan would find me in the most dreadful states. I wouldn't know what day it was and my apartment would be a shambles."

"I don't understand. You can't reason with yourself and snap out of it? Oh, that sounds terrible." Amelia shook her head. "I don't mean it that way. I guess I mean—I'm trying to understand what you're going through, not belittle you," she said seeing anger cross his features. "I just want to understand a little more what happens. Like when my mother died, I knew it was coming, but I just was sad for months." She went to a distant place in her mind. "It was like the world had become a perpetual rainy, cloudy, gloomy day in winter. I just couldn't kick it."

"Yes, it is like that," Franklin said excited to have someone understand, "but it's much worse than just a gloomy day for me.

"I have a continual gnawing feeling of worthlessness that worms its way through my brain gnawing at my happiness and will to live. It continually tells me that I don't deserve anything—friends, family, love, ideas, success, living. Nothing is off limits. It gets louder and louder. The darkness seems to blanket it, so I hear less.

"The medicine that the doctor gives me helps, but it makes my thinking fuzzy most of the time, and I don't like the lethargy I fall into. I lose my train of thought, and ideas are harder to harvest. I've found I can control the disease most of the time.

"I should have known better about last night and taken a pill then. The night of the party—the night that you returned to your own time—I had the wherewithal to take one that night, and so I could think clearly enough to continually take them, or at least not reject them. I believe the pills were being set on my dinner trays left at my door, but I refused to take them. It is a terrible drunkenness of moroseness."

"I think I understand. It's a vicious cycle of hating yourself and not caring enough to take something or do whatever to pull yourself out of that pit that you've crawled into." Amelia looked at him with her brow crinkled.

"Yes. Sort of."

Her contemplation and his embarrassment lead to silence while they ate.

"Well. That was the worst breakfast topic I've ever introduced. I'm sorry, my dear." He sat his silverware down on the plate and folded his napkin. "I wanted to come and enjoy your presence, not taint the air with mine."

"You didn't. I mean, I always enjoy your company. I just... I've experienced depression, just not at your level." She set her fork and knife down. "I empathize with it, and it's reasonable that you can pull yourself up out of it... but I guess I don't really understand, because I've never lived it like you do."

"Yes. True." He scooted his chair back from the table, crossed his legs and put his hands together, only fingertips touching. "Which is actually a great segue back to my new book."

"Yes, you said you wanted me to read it?" Amelia asked, folding her napkin and looking at him with expectation.

"Well, when its ready." Franklin stood changing his mind and walked behind Amelia's chair. "Or maybe now, if you want. I mean, why not?" He pulled out her chair and put his hand out for her to take while she stood. "If it's a terrible start, maybe you can help me fix it," he said smiling and he led them to the study.

***

As Amelia flipped through pages, from time to time she snuck a look at Franklin. She was perplexed that less than a day before, this man was a completely different person. It was mind-boggling how docile he was now compared to the wretch he was only hours ago.

She knew depression existed. She knew it completely changed people. Experiencing it herself on a small level, it was disconcerting and worrisome. She knew deep down that he would never intentionally hurt her. But at the same time, could she really be sure of anything?

The morning wore on with the two of them discussing his new work in the study. He was either pretending he was fine, or he was back to being the Franklin she knew. After lunch and a stroll, she let him have the afternoon to himself.

Retiring to the front room, Amelia was mesmerized once again watching people pass. Amelia's mind wandered back to their kiss. She had thought about it many times over the past few days. It really affected her, but it affected him so much more. What did that mean? Amelia felt there was a connection she wasn't seeing. Something that would make sense of it. She hoped if she sat here long enough staring blankly out at the street something might register. But nothing did.

Emily came to fetch her for dinner, and Amelia gave up looking for an answer wouldn't come. She sighed deeply, and followed Emily towards the dining room, hoping for a more festive, and less contemplative evening.

Chapter Forty-Five

Days slowly returned to normal following Franklin's escapade into the doldrums of his mind. But Amelia felt uneasy around him. She realized had never seen him this way before. The time she found him depressed, burning manuscript pages was one thing. But this was entirely different. Terrified of the depths he was capable of falling, Amelia felt conflicted. She wanted to be near him but not knowing his behavior swings and she might be the cause. Returning to their old routines of dining together, he seemed fine at meals. And he seemed normal as they went for daily walks. He delighted in having her help with his work. But Amelia thought it too good to be true. How long would it last?

Amelia seemed to be the only one on edge. Mrs. Finnegan and Emily went on with their routines as if nothing had ever happened. Amelia wanted to ask them both about how often something like this occurred with Franklin, but never seemed to find the right time or moment. Mrs. Finnegan would probably know, after all she had known Franklin most of his life.

During another round of baking bread two weeks later Amelia was helping in the kitchen and finally got her chance to ask Finnegan about it. Neighborhood gossip turned into talking about Finnegan's sister who was in Atlanta and was having a grandchild. They talked about the price of vegetables and books they had enjoyed. Amelia took it as a signal to segue about Franklin.

"I've read his new manuscript," Amelia started. "It seems inspired."

"Mmm?" Finnegan gave a noncommittal sound.

Amelia wasn't sure how to proceed. She didn't want to just jump right in. "Both Franklin and I are enjoying the menu changes."

"Good, good," Finnegan said as she wiped her brow.

"And I'm really settling in here." Amelia took a deep, but silent, breath and said what was on her mind. "How often does he go into his fits and rages?"

Finnegan was silent for a long time.

Maybe she shouldn't have asked, she thought to herself. Then she questioned if she had actually said it out loud, as Finnegan continued on as if she hadn't. Just as Amelia inhaled to ask again, Finnegan spoke.

"It is a hard thing to answer."

They met eyes across the table where they were kneading separate lumps of dough. Amelia's were full of questions, and Finnegan's were full of secrets she swore to keep. Shaking her head, Finnegan looked away, returning her attentions to the dough. Thinking it was the end of the conversation, Amelia just kneaded in silence trying not to take out her frustrations at the non-answer on the soft lump. She then placed her dough in a bread pan, and grabbed more dough and started to knead. All while trying to think of another way to get Finnegan talking again. About anything. She didn't want to turn the woman against her. It felt as if they were friends—no, family. She didn't want to create a rift.

"He was a gentle boy," Finnegan continued cautiously after a very long silence, her voice wavering. "I don't know if it was the death of his mother, or the stringent way he was raised by his father, that cracked him. He so wanted to be loved and cared for. His mother never showed him much attention when she was alive, but yet he yearned so for it. He would sit on a chair outside o' her door for hours…" Finnegan turned away to wipe her face on her sleeve. Amelia was sure she was wiping away a tear. Finnegan heaved her shoulders in a deep, calming breath, and turned back to the table, taking up her kneading, but not making eye contact with Amelia. "I told ya about the first book he published?" She continued again after a moment of kneading bread in silence. "That day, after his father threw the book in the fire, he punished Franklin fiercely. He yelled at him nonstop all day, and then he wouldn't talk to the child at all for weeks. Franklin was afraid to come out of his room, and then he started developing a terrible need for human touch. He would sneak up on me and just touch my hand or my arm. I, not knowin' he was there, would jump and scream at 'im."

The more she talked, the sadder and more upset Finnegan got, and the thicker her accent became. "He would hide in his room after that. His father would yell somethin' fierce for Franklin to show up at dinner, and then would sit in silence, ignorin' the boy. Sometimes, his father wouldn't even show up for dinner, but would insist Franklin eat by 'imself in the large dinin' room."

Sighing deeply, Finnegan crossed the kitchen, wringing her hands in her apron to remove the flour. She grabbed for a brown glass bottle that was hidden behind the canisters, and removed a glass from the cabinet above. With her back to Amelia, Mrs. Finnegan poured herself a glass of the dark brown colored liquid. She raised the glass to her lips, and in a swift tilt of her head, threw back the liquid in one swallow. Shaking her head, either to relieve herself of the feeling of the liquor burning her throat, or to relieve her mind of the terrible visions she was reliving, Mrs. Finnegan braced herself on the counter holding herself up.

Quietly, her voice rose from the other side of the room, "He was just a boy. Just a boy, an' I pushed him into the way he is…"

Feeling the need to comfort, Amelia crossed the room in only a few large steps over to Mrs. Finnegan, "How were you to know what would happen?" she said, wanting to embrace the caring woman in the hopes to release her pain, but instead opting to lightly place her hand on Finnegan's. "Besides, Franklin has told me, as well as I have learned on my own, that this feeling he has, this uncontrollable sadness, is not just something that comes from how he was raised. It partially comes from his blood." She paused again. "You said his mother was often unhappy, maybe she was also depressed, and she passed it onto Franklin. You mustn't feel that you are to blame." Amelia was making no strides in comforting Mrs. Finnegan. "Besides, if it weren't for you, Franklin wouldn't have had as much love and support all these years. He wouldn't be the man he is today without you. The good parts of him are because you took care of him."

Mrs. Finnegan sighed a hefty sigh and her shoulders relaxed. Her tear filled eyes turned to look at Amelia.

"You're a dear, sweet girl," she said as she reached up and patted Amelia's cheek. "He's lucky he stumbled into you."

"I'm sorry I asked about his condition. I didn't realize it was difficult for you. I won't ask again." Amelia gave the woman a squeeze then went back to the table to finish kneading her dough.

"You're worried about his behavior, and wonderin' if that is how you'll be livin' for the rest of your life. I understand, love." She walked over to Amelia. "Let me tell ya this: he's been happier than I've seen him in a long time, since he was a boy. These... fits... that he has, used to be longer and more frequent. Usually the doctor has to roust him out with medicines. I canna promise he won't do it again, but I do know that when you're around, it's easier on him."

Amelia looked up and met Finnegan's smiling gaze, "That's comforting to know." And she shared a smile.

An hour later with the bread in the oven, and the kitchen cleaned up, Amelia headed to the front room. The new knowledge of Franklin rolling around in her head. She she was ill at ease with what Mrs. Finnegan said: Amelia, made Franklin better.

People change because they want to change, not because another person makes them better. Amelia sat and watched the people pass by, and the night sky grow dim. She just didn't know how to feel about anything anymore. However, her heart was telling her it longed to stay near him.

Chapter Forty-Six

One afternoon, Franklin returned to his study after lunch to write out a plot searing through his mind. Amelia felt an itch to get out into the beautiful day and walk about the park, even if it was alone.

She strolled along caught up in her own thoughts, until she heard her name. She looked behind her to see Jon jogging lightly toward her. As always, he was dressed in finery to go somewhere formal.

"And where are you coming from, Jon?" Amelia asked as he caught up to her.

"Ah, well, nowhere important. Just was meeting a friend for lunch, and now headed back to the office to finish up a few things. But I'm not in a hurry."

"Would you like to walk a bit," asked Amelia.

"If I'm not disturbing you—you seemed to be in quite a trance. I had been waving at you and calling your name, for a few minutes."

"Oh?"

"Yes, very deep in thought.   Anything you wish to discuss? I promise you, I have always kept your secrets!"

"Oh, Jon, I never worry about you. Well, I *would* like to talk about something that is weighing heavily on my mind. You know what little family I have is in Philadelphia," Amelia began her story as she led them to a park bench. "It is really just my aunt, but I do miss her and the pull to be with her is great. I don't know if I can bear to live so far from her." And just like the other times she discussed it with anyone but Franklin, she said, "And, well you see there was a man back home that I still have feelings for. I do love Franklin, but I always wonder about him as this marriage was quite sudden." Jon nodded in contemplation.

Amelia stopped not knowing how to phrase it, but then continued. "I know it sounds terrible, but I still think of my other beau. My heart aches for him sometimes, no matter how happy I am with Franklin.   Marriage is a vow, but sometimes I wonder if I made the wrong choice." Amelia turned to Jon with questioning eyes.

"Well, then, I think you need to go back home. I think once you have a dose of what you're missing here, you'll see what you really want and need," Jon said, clasping his hand over hers. "If we withhold things from our lives they only become a greater pull. However, if we give in to them, walk towards them, look at them from the inside instead of a far distance, we can understand them much better. Go. You need to. You'll find where your heart really lies."

Amelia looked up into his caring eyes, "Thank you. I want to go, I know I need to. I guess I just needed the permission to look into my feelings was the right thing. I care for my old beau. I really do. This marriage just happened so fast and when I went back—," Amelia caught herself right before she said something she shouldn't. She dabbed at her eye with a handkerchief while she corrected her thought, "—to pack up my things and see my aunt, I missed Franklin..." she looked down at her lap. "I guess I don't understand where I'm meant to be. I don't know where I belong."

"Well, maybe that is because you fit so well in both places. Which is a blessing and a curse. It means you're the one who gets to decide."

They talked for a bit more. Jon turning the conversation to tidbits of gossip to lighten the mood. He mentioned the new fabrics that just arrived, a few from France. Then standing to go, he wished her luck in her decision.

"And know that whatever decision you make, I support. I will always be your friend, no matter how far away you may travel."

"Thank you, Jon," Amelia said standing. "I will take your thoughts to heart. I feel much better having had this talk with you." She leaned in to hug him. "Thank you my friend. I hope to see you again soon."

"I wish the same. Goodbye, Amelia."

"Goodbye, Jon."

As he walked away her eyes fondly trailed him. She was glad to have friends like Jon, Emily and Mrs. Finnegan. If only she could take her friends with her through time.

**

The end of the month was nearing. Amelia was torn. She didn't know what to do. Feeling like she needed some sort of sign to tell her what to do, Amelia kept searching for one. She had responsibilities back in her time, but her heart requested she stay with Franklin. This conversation kept repeating itself over and over in her head; the pros and cons of both options ran on a loop in her thoughts. Her feelings were very strong for Franklin, but it seemed that her first responsibility was to Jack and her life. The fought her feelings for Franklin, the greater the pull became. Still she waited for some sort of sign she should stay. None came. The night of the thirtieth, Franklin asked her at dinner, "Tonight is your night to travel, is it not? Have you made a decision?"

"Franklin, there is something about you that keeps drawing me in. I don't know what it is. I want to be with you, to stay here with you, but I have a *life* there. I have my own future. If I stay here, I don't know what I have. More of this? Or would it be different? I know that no one can tell what lies ahead, and no one can make promises for the future, only vows—but I need more than that to give everything up."

"What is that? What do you need?"

334

"I... I don't know. A bigger, stronger feeling that this is the right choice? I can't stay. Not now. I have to go back and at least give that part of me one more try. Maybe I'll be back, or maybe that life is the one I'm meant to live. We both will just have to trust."

Franklin pushed his chair back and stepped out of it angrily. He roamed the room like a caged tiger. "But, I... you..." He whipped around, slamming his hands onto the table and leaning toward her. "I don't want you to leave." His eyes pleaded, his arms shook with tension. "I know that this is sudden, but Amelia, I am in love with you. I want you—no I *need* you to stay with me."

Suddenly she knew. It all snapped together. Amelia was terrified to say the things she needed to say, but if she didn't say them now, she might never get to say them. She looked down at her hands, trying to focus on something in the room. The pounding in her heart grew faster and harder.

She looked up and into Franklin's eyes. "I cannot stay. I love you. I realize that now. I am so in love with you. But I would never feel right about choosing you if I just abandoned Jack. I know I would always wonder what happened to him, and think daily about breaking his heart. That isn't something I want to live with." She stood up to face him. "And before you say anything, I know it's a gamble to move back and forth through time. I know I could be stranded. But, I need to know the direction, the path that is right for me. The one I'm destined to take. I was brought here for a reason—whether it was to enhance your life or to grow stronger in mine, it was a reason." She walked away from him, shaking her head. "I'm being drawn back for a reason. I can't just disappear from my own life. It would be a terrible thing to do to the people I care about. I would never be happy here knowing that I left all of that mystery of my whereabouts behind." She walked over to him taking his hands and trying to make him look at her. "I have to go back. I have to try things out and set them right. If it doesn't work, and isn't the right choice, I'll be back."

He leaned forward touching his forehead to hers. "I want to give you all the love I have, but it is not enough to make you stay at this moment." Franklin sighed. "There is nothing more I can do or say. Remember this moment, Amelia," he said as drew back and looked directly into her eyes. "Remember I fought for you. And remember, you chose."

Amelia wrapped her arms around his neck and hugged him as hard as she could. With her head on his shoulder she whispered, "I know. You might not believe me, but this choice, I have to make." She pulled back from the embrace, but still held on to him. "I know I will always wonder if I don't go now." She leaned back and smiled at him. "At least I know if I go forward, I can search history to find out what happens to you." Her eyes turned sad and dropped to the floor. "But I don't have the luxury of seeing into the future to make sure that my friends and Jack aren't devastated by my disappearance." She backed away and started to take off the watch and plucked out the pin. Amelia looked up into his eyes once again, and smiled.

Tears welled blurring her vision. "Thank you for fighting for me. I wish I didn't have to do this to you."

He nodded at her and gave her a halfhearted smile. "I'll tell everyone you were headed for your aunt's again in Philadelphia. I have a feeling she is dying for good this time, and you might stay there indefinitely."

"Right," she smirked and gave half a laugh and looked down at the watch. She started to turn the dial. Amelia wanted to tell Franklin one more time that she loved him, that she *would* be back to him, but she just didn't know. The pull was so great.

Amelia paused a moment in the winding, she knew there was time before the close of the time travel window. She looked up again at him, he had turned half away, so she was only in his periphery. "Franklin," she said, and he looked back at her. She smiled and lifted her hand, "I hope we meet again in this lifetime."

He smiled and started to take a step toward her, to embrace her one last time. Amelia, with her eyes on him, resumed winding before he could reach her. In a blink she was gone.

Part Four

October — December

Chapter Forty-Seven

It was a brisk feeling to fall through time. She wondered if everyone felt as if they had been drenched by icy water. Then she laughed to herself about other people traveling through time. Was she the only one? Or were there more?

Amelia took a deep breath and looked around the room. It was just now turning to dusk. She could have spent more time with Franklin today, but why put off the inevitable. Her return to the present was imminent. There were so many things to be settled. She didn't realize how quickly and how easily she had deep feelings for Franklin—she didn't want to admit to herself that she could love two completely different men. At the same time, feelings for Franklin was an odd sensation. It was as if her hand had been in boiling water for a while, but she hadn't realized the water was making her uncomfortable, until she remembered she still had a hand. Life had been so diverting, that she just didn't notice the change.

Amelia refused to feel sad. Even though she was second-guessing herself. She started to wonder if she could travel twice in a day… Maybe it wasn't too late to return.

Shaking the thought out of her head, Amelia went into her bedroom. Her travel outfit turned into a formal suit, something she might have worn at her old desk job, but this one had lots of ruffles down the front of the shirt. Not an outfit to match her current life. She sighed in frustration, and then laughed at herself. It wasn't like she came home naked, or in the awkward style of the time with a petticoat and corset.

In no time she was redressed in yoga pants, a tank top and a big comfy sweater. The house was cold, so she had also put on some sheepskin boots. October was always a guessing game on what to wear as the air got crisper. It was definitely a bit warmer in Franklin's time, or maybe it just seemed so because she was wearing more layers of clothing. Amelia went into the basement and lit the pilot light and turned on the heat at the boiler. The familiar rumble of the radiator hummed.   When she returned upstairs she saw copious amounts of mail that piled up on the floor by the front door. Scooping as much of it as possible in her arms, which was all but a flyer and a pre-approved credit card application that fell out of her hands at the last minute, she walked to the kitchen.

Knowing the room by feel, Amelia crossed to the island in the dark, plopped down the mail, turned back to the door to turn on the light, and then went to the stove and put a tea kettle on to boil. Maybe her love for Franklin was more like a teakettle; she hadn't realized the heat was even on until it was bubbling over... again she shook the thought from her head. Instead of thinking, she turned to the pile of mail on the island counter. Putting her hands on her hips, she sighed at the sight. Grabbing the recycling bin, she started on the pile. Obvious things went in first, sales circulars, menus, and junk mail all got tossed in. The pile reduced down to very few things. There were three months of design and fashion magazines that she had stacked up together. Those would be a good distraction later. The tea whistled and she got herself a cup. There were a few invoices from the last of the home improvements.

Underneath it all was a well-beaten legal sized envelope with familiar handwriting with her name and address on the front. There were a good amount of colorful stamps gracing the upper right hand corner of the envelope. She was entranced by the thing for a minute. Almost mystified, she turned it over and ran her hand over the back of the envelope. The corner had been ripped open a tiny bit, probably by being shuffled around through so many countries to get to her door. She ripped open the envelope, and pulled out a yellow lined piece of paper that was folded in three. Unfolding the sheet, her heart leapt as she saw Jack's signature at the bottom. Unable to comprehend the letter the first time, Amelia read it again to make sure that she understood it. Jack was coming home. If all went well, he would be arriving within the week.

Chapter Forty-Eight

Amelia was excited to see Jack. But Franklin would just pop into her brain at any time. As she was brushing her teeth. While waiting for coffee to brew. On her morning jog through the park. And a million other irritating times. It was confusing and excruciating. She hadn't felt this cut off and unable to shut out the thoughts in a long time. It was one thing when she was young before cell phones or the internet didn't exist. In other words, before she had the ability to randomly check in via text or social media post. Franklin was of a completely different time, and there was no way to reach him even if she wanted to. Even if she knew what she wanted to say to him.

Trying to ignore all thoughts was her first instinct. She had made this choice. He had asked her to stay but it didn't feel right. Her life was here. With Jack. Who was coming back soon. This was her life and she couldn't keep escaping into the past. This is where she was born. This is where she belonged. There was no need to try to hold onto these thoughts.

Ignoring the thoughts only made it worse. So, she started to indulge them. Most were short memories, things they did together, moments they shared.

At night, as her head hit the pillow she would envision the way she wished things would be, future moments they would share or even Franklin showing up on her doorstep instead of her finding her way back to him.

But they were all just dreams. They were lovely moments she would have forever. His slow mutinous smile when she tried to make him laugh. Amelia awkward conversations they had at first that gave way to sharing any idea and accepting her thought. Although she thought she felt this with Jack, the feeling was more all encompassing with Franklin. It was almost if he was the human form of a down duvet that she was snuggled in.

Indulgence in these thoughts only seemed to make them grow and flourish. Her heart ached from these memories.

Now. She had to live now. There was no going back. He had his own life to live—or, he had already lived it—either way she looked at it, she needed to continue forward in hers. Amelia told herself if they were meant to be together, they would be. But with the gap of a century between them, it was near to impossible.

Amelia, needing reinforcement, met up with Toni for drinks—Alexia couldn't make it that night—and they discussed Amelia's predicament. With an adjusted story placing both men in this time, Amelia made it more of a

Jack versus random man she recently met, had a great conversation with and then they randomly met a second time. Amelia said it felt innocent at first because the man lived in a different place and was to stay in his home. She didn't even know how deeply she felt about him until after. Even though she was the flighty, flirty one of the three friends, Toni had good advice.

"Well," Toni said after hearing the story, "the way I see it, you have two options. One: give up everything you have and go after him, with the tiniest of hope that he is all he says he is *and* he felt something, too—which is possible, but highly unlikely." She paused for a moment to allow that to sink in, and took her friend's hand. "Or the second," she smiled, "is: entertain thoughts of him, give them a moment of your time. Know that you had the experience of a lovely shared moment in time but it will never have a future, and let it go."

Amelia sighed. Toni was right. It was a fleeting moment. A dalliance. She had to let Franklin go. He was a good man; she was sure of it. She knew he felt deeply about her, too. But, sometimes life delivers moments that are only that: moments. Amelia was given the gift of a moment with Franklin, and that was all. She had to just accept it for what it was.

Chapter Forty-Nine

The next morning Amelia awoke to find a warm human nestled up to her. Drowsily, she rolled over and placed a kiss between his shoulder blades. His gentle humming noise made her happy, so she did it again. Then, she nuzzled her cheek in the same spot and wrapped her arms around him. His back tilted toward her and his neck turned to her so his lips could meet hers. It had only been a few days, Amelia had missed his lips. It was dark outside but sunrise was not far off, and twilight caressed the outline of his body. After a few tame kisses, he could no longer hold back from her. She couldn't remember why she was mad at him this time... so with the heat of passion aimed at her, Amelia gave in as he moved on top of her and adjusted her hips to where he wanted them, and nudged her legs open with his knee. Like a starving animal she drank him in, taking his tongue in her mouth, and taking him inside her, slowly at first, and then all the way home. She answered his hip thrusts into hers by thrusting in return while arching her back. For a moment, something seemed... off, but it was probably that she just didn't remember why she was angry and she didn't remember having gone to bed.

Their lovemaking was sweet and as passionate as two lost lovers reconnecting. When they had both come to a blissful end, he shifted to lay next to her and she flopped over him, her head on his shoulder as he wrapped his arms around her.

As Amelia drifted back to sleep, she noticed his scent was different. But the thought long with all the cares and worries fell away as consciousness dissolved.

***

Amelia awoke alone in her bed to the sound of a rushing river. No it was the shower. She sighed contentedly and started to drift back to sleep. Just as her mind gave way to sleep, Amelia's consciousness made her sit straight up in bed, wide-awake. She clutched the sheets to her naked chest, like an embarrassed and terrified teenager after her first time having sex, wondering what she had just done. She looked around the room in confusion.

The shower water stopped. A chill ran through her as she pieced everything together. Moments later, clad in only a towel, Jack walked into the room.

Chapter Fifty

"Why do you look horrified to see me?" Jack asked stifling a laugh.

Amelia quickly composed herself, and let out an awkward laugh. Relaxing her hands she loosened her grip on the sheet around her.

"Oh I'm not," she said, forcing herself to smile warmly. "It's just that... I thought that I ... I mean I *dreamt* that I slept with another man—after we were finished, and it seemed to be so real. So when I saw you I was surprised... it was you," she explained as the words tumbled out of her mouth. It was the truth. Just not exactly the truth. "And... and when I heard the shower running I thought...it was him," a nervous laugh escaped her. "And so when you came out, I wanted to be... protected."

"Was this 'dream man' as good as me?" Jack teased as he crossed the room to her side of the bed. The towel was too small and showed off his upper thigh as he crossed to her. Her eyes couldn't help but to be drawn to that slightly seductive sight.

"Well...he was different..." she said, her nervousness drifting away, her voice relaxing into a playful tone, as she moved her eyes first to the center of his legs and then slowly up to his face, taking in his torso as they moved upward. "But I'd have to gain a little more evidence, you know, do a little more research to offer you a complete analysis. She smiled and moved her hands off the sheet allowing it to fall away slightly, revealing her naked breasts, and nipples that were starting to get hard. What was she doing, she thought to herself? No time to change her mind, or think it over. With this attraction to Jack searing through her, she was unsure that she wanted to change her mind.

Jack reached for her chin and tilted her face to his as he bent over and kissed her on the lips, softly at first and then he deepened it. She reached for his towel and tugged it away from his body. Amelia wrapped both arms around his neck, while lifting herself up onto her knees, making him stand, and pressed herself up to his clean naked body. He leaned back from their kissing, still wrapped in her arms.

"Maybe later." He gave her a peck on the nose. "Not to sound callus darling, but right now I need coffee and my paper." Reaching up, he unlocked himself from her arms around her neck and took a step back to grab his towel. "I can promise you that it was me in your arms, and my utter exhaustion can prove that. I got in late last night and didn't want to be away from you a moment longer." With that, he started back to the bathroom, not bothering to rewrap the towel, giving her a delicious view of his naked bottom.

Just before he reached the door, he turned and asked, "Are you going for a run this morning, or should I make coffee for you, too?"

She sighed a little dejectedly to herself and said, "I should," she sighed, "especially since I won't get any more of a workout in here." She sat down on her heels facing him, and faked a pout. "But if you're not going to satisfy me, a coffee would be great."

He flashed a cheeky smile at her. Jack looked as if he was trying to find just the right compliment to give her, but couldn't find it and so he looked slightly defeated. Instead he said, "Alright, see you in about an hour," as he walked out of the room and he started whistling.

Amelia smiled a confused smile. She wanted to say something more to him. To tell him *something*, an explanation for her odd behaviors and quirky mood. But, Jack never needed details. This was her need to keep things honest and open. Being a doctor made Jack distance himself from emotional details, Amelia told herself. Or maybe he was just so happy to be with her again, he simply hadn't noticed that she was keeping anything from him.

Amelia dropped back into the welcoming pillows. She shut her eyes hoping transportation to another time, if only in her mind.

After an exasperating five minutes of both men dancing around her mind, she pulled herself out of bed. She threw on running clothes and headed down the stairs, double-checking her laces at the front door, and walked into the sunny morning.

Chapter Fifty-One

As soon as she reached the running trail, Amelia felt she was being chased by something and took off running as if it would save her life. Not wanting to confirm she was being followed, she refused to look back over her shoulder, just in case something was actually following her.

She knew it wasn't true. Nevertheless, she still ran harder and faster. Amelia tried to ignore things rising up in her brain letting her pulse drum out the thoughts. No matter how hard and fast she ran, no matter how loud her pulse beat, the thoughts were winning, and were only escalating in volume.

When she got a cramp in her left thigh, she limped off to the side of the track to stretch. As she did so, tears streamed down her face. There was no way to outrun what was bothering her. Amelia had no idea how to get what she really wanted. She didn't even know *what* she really wanted, other than to feel at home and loved.

Thoughts of both Franklin and Jack flooded her mind. Franklin the studious gentlemanly scholar with his glasses perched on his nose, reading sitting next to her in front of the fireplace in his study. Jack the rugged doctor with the strong arms, decadently passionate in bed, but was not indulgent in emotions.

Amelia was so confused. Two men, neither perfect, but both wonderful individuals. Like a schoolgirl trying to figure out which boy to date, Amelia felt muddled and ridiculous with these thoughts. And in actuality it didn't matter. She was here, now. In Jack's time, going back to Franklin was off the table. Jack was a good man. She was attracted to him, it was almost impossible not to be, but it was more than that. She admired how he worked long hours and was passionate about saving people. She loved that he seemed like a superhero, but was human, too. There was something so mountain man/Davy Crockett-esque placed in modern day about him. Amelia laughed out loud picturing him in a coon-skin cap in the ER during surgery. She loved these things about him. She loved *him*. Didn't she?

Jack rarely shared intimate things with her. She didn't know if this was a doctor's code kind of thing or a Jack thing. He would tell her if she asked, but he didn't just offer anything, and he didn't tell stories.

Franklin, on the other hand, was happy to talk about his writing and on occasion would have her read what he was working on. He asked her opinion on his work, and oftentimes used her suggestions. He would share stories of his youth and life.

Odd that in this life she loved a man who specialized in physically fixing brains, and in that life she loved a man who wanted to form and change men's thoughts, as his fiction was fun, but also had a message. One used a scalpel as his main tool, and the other a pencil. One wanted to cure physical issues while the other wanted to feed the soul. So different, but both had the desire and the ability to heal. This was her attraction to both. Jack. Amelia cautioned herself, she must focus on Jack.

When Jack came home from long stints out of the city, she didn't know what to expect. Some days he was the Jack she knew, but sometimes he was quiet, introspective, and stayed holed up for days. She wondered what he was subject to in the field. Conditions and lack of supplies probably lowered his success rate with third world patients. This return he didn't seem so beaten down, but there were days he seemed less than alive.

He was a very good man, and good to her, no matter what his mood was. It was good to see him. She had missed him.

Last night, well this morning actually, was so unexpected. Last time, they reacquainted more slowly. He would join her in her bed at an unannounced interval after a few days of being home. Snuggling in, he would just hold her and they would make pillow talk, or just look and touch each other again. Sometimes this would be all that would happen. Or sometimes this would only last hours before he made love to her. At all of these times, he seemed to be asking forgiveness. For leaving her, for not curing everyone, for being a man, and for a thousand other sins that were not of major consequence for her. But, last night, he seemed to be seeking proof that she was only his and demanded it through their lovemaking.

As she sat in the park, she wondered why this seemed so odd. Before she could draw a conclusion, the shadow of another runner passed over her. The trail was getting crowded, and she needed to get home. Her ankle, longer throbbing, could take weight. She could walk on it without feeling much pain. Amelia took a deep breath and asked to be shown answers, and headed back towards her brownstone.

Another note awaited her, and she found it as she tossed her keys on the front hall table. It was from Jack and it said:

Dinner. 8pm. Dress up. Pick you up right here.

The note made her chuckle. It seemed he was coming back to reality, too. She was glad that she wasn't the only one. Maybe Jack is everything she needed. As she headed to the kitchen for coffee, Amelia smiled to herself excited about her date with Jack tonight.

Chapter Fifty-Two

At exactly 7:57pm, Amelia exited her bedroom and bounced down the stairs. Wearing a sleeveless emerald green dress with her hair piled high on her head with a few tendrils strategically escaping, Amelia realized she styled herself in a contemporary version of her style in 1912.

Jack was waiting—peering up the stairs waiting for his date to appear. He smiled and looked down at his feet and started to blush which made Amelia blush.

"You look stunning," he said when she reached the bottom step.

A smile lit up her face. Then jumping, like a teenager suddenly remembering his manners, Jack dashed toward the front hall closet.

"I'll get your coat," he said as she nervously smoothed out the skirt of her dress which was her fifth choice. She had pulled it out to try on first, but it didn't seem perfect. It seemed too fancy. Then after trying on a strappy red dress, a light blue dress with a ruffled neck, a silk sapphire blouse and charcoal skirt, and then a purple empire waist dress. Finally, she returned to the emerald. Once she tried it on, she knew it was perfect. With a high collar that fastened at the neck it blossomed into lace that covered to the top of her chest and covered her back down to the waist. In the front, the lace covered a sweetheart neckline of green silk. Flaring into a matte emerald, the skirt caressed her legs a few inches above her knees. She wore black patent heels, and the emerald stud earrings Jack gave her for Christmas last year.

Jack returned, breathless. As he wrapped her coat around her gently, Amelia felt Jack's admiration. After she fastened her coat, he placed his hands on her cheeks and kissed her. Then he offered her his arm—beaming at her. She took it, and off they went into the night.

***

Their reservation was at a French restaurant a few blocks away so they walked. When they arrived, the Maitre D' took their coats and ushered them through a room lined with burgundy tapestries that made Amelia feel like she had just entered the famed restaurant Harmonia Gardens, from *Hello, Dolly!* They were ushered to a quiet table in the back that viewed the entire restaurant, but curtains encircling the booth allowed for their complete privacy. Amelia didn't think that restaurants existed like this anymore, she marveled.

As the Maitre D' walked away, a waiter arrived at the table with champagne and an hors d'oeuvre that looked like fancy mozzarella sticks.

"I hope you don't mind, I ordered ahead," Jack said.

"Sure, I love it," Amelia said. She noticed Jack seemed a bit jumpy. But she pushed it away thinking it was because he only arrived home yesterday and their first day back together always was a bit of a warm up.

She had forgotten how easy it felt to be with Jack. How made her smile or laugh at things that happened to him, or his musings on life. A little voice kept nagging that something wasn't right about this evening. But like Jack's nervousness this evening, she dismissed it, chalking it up to their time apart.

After their dinner plates were cleared, Jack got very serious.

"So the program has a contract with me for another year of service in other regions of South America, and I have to go back in a week." Amelia nodded. She knew that the program would keep him traveling. "I'll be gone for three to four months this time." He stopped and swallowed hard. She nodded for him to continue. "And I'm thinking of offering to do an extra year … they need people. Good people." He paused and then he looked up at her. "What do you think?"

Feeling so many different things, wanting him to stay, wanting him to be fulfilled, she stammered out, "I want you to be happy, of course. But if I'm honest, distance and timing is hard on a relationship."

Her response resonated within. She wondered about which relationship she was talking about and what "distance and timing" she actually meant. As Jack picked through the pros and cons, it was Franklin's face she saw in her mind. In her future.

Then all of a sudden a solo violin burst through her memory just as a plate of something chocolate was placed in front of her. Amelia was jerked back into this current moment and she felt a bit faint. She was just about to excuse herself to the bathroom and was putting the napkin on the table when she noticed the plate. It wasn't a mess of chocolate. A tiny cake sat in the center of the plate with "Marry me?" written out in chocolate sauce.

Puzzled, she thought the plate had to have been brought to the wrong table. She started to laugh and she raised her head to look at Jack across the booth to point out someone had given her the wrong desert when the violin music swelled again. But Jack was now kneeling on one knee next to her holding an open ring box, its contents winking back at her.

It was the perfect moment. It was beautiful, thoughtful and so lovely. It was just like a romantic movie, and what every woman hopes will happen.

But here inside this perfect moment Amelia realized, she did not want any of it.

Chapter Fifty-Three

"Think about it. *Think* about it." Jack repeated over and over the phrase she offered him when he proposed. To ruin this beautiful evening made Amelia feel awful, but she wasn't sure she had feelings for him anymore, and the once clear future with him was foggy and possibly not what she wanted.

Unfortunately, she realized these things the moment he was kneeling before her. Much to her chagrin, the thought that she was married to Franklin kept popping up in her mind. Ok, well, not legally married. But—UGH! She could not deal with both of them at the same time. Franklin would have to wait. Especially with Jack's repetitious, "Think about it," mocking her. Questioning her. Badgering her.

Unrelenting, he followed her home, repeating that stupid phrase reminding her of both the geeky stalker she had in 4th grade and a parrot who only knows one phrase. Down the blocks, up the steps, into the front hall as she put away her coat—his chivalry from earlier was obviously *not* unconditional. As they walked up the stairs, and into her room he kept repeating "think about it." He sat on her bed like a sad puppy, and had stopped repeating her words over and over. His eyes continued to watch her as she removed the gorgeous dress and hung it in the closet. He said nothing while she put away her earrings and shoes. He just stared at her as she took off her underwear and put on her pajamas. He sighed deeply when she walked into her bathroom to brush her hair, her teeth, and wash her face. When she returned to the room, he was gone. She sighed audibly and crossed to close her door.

She lay down in her bed and turned off the lamp. In the dark, thoughts of Franklin flooded her mind. She thought of their first meeting in the hall. How he suggested they should tell the house staff they were married and she— although surprised and a bit in wonderment, still thinking she was dreaming—completely acquiesced. Without hesitation. But, here she was, in reality, in her *own* time, with the man she should be with, and he had proposed to her perfectly. And all she could think of was Franklin.

At first sight, she thought he was so attractive. She hasn't realized until now how much she wanted to kiss Franklin in that first moment. When he had suggested they be "married" to explain her sudden appearance she was stunned. It was so easy. She smiled thinking back that an instant marriage proposal was fine, but a kiss was scandalous. Kissing only happened after courting and the legal documents. How times have changed. Refusing to think of Jack's proposal, Amelia drifted off to sleep and could almost feel Franklin kissing her.

***

She felt him crawl into bed beside her. He was naked and ready for her. Her pajamas were off in an instant. He kissed her. It was familiar but didn't seem quite right, but her body moved in perfect correspondence to his. Wanting. Needing. Knowing exactly how to behave. If only her heart and mind would follow suit.

"Marry me."

At her moment of climax she breathlessly whimpered a quiet, "yes." Then exhausted, he rolled off of her, turned her and sidled up his body behind hers. He wrapped his arms around her and contentedly they both fell asleep.

***

Part of her knew, as the morning light drifted in, which man was in her bed. It didn't mean that Amelia couldn't hope, in the few seconds as she flopped her body over to face him, that it would be the one she really wanted.

Jack was dead asleep. She never understood how he achieved this state. Her movement hadn't phased him except for the apathetic snort or two as he readjusted.

Like the morning before, thoughts of both men flooded her mind. Was that right? Was that wrong? How could she marry the man in bed with her if she loved another? Why should she refuse Jack if the man she loved wasn't her this time?

The questions became too much for Amelia, making her restless so she crept out of bed and into the bathroom. She had only been home for a few days but the questions were still the same and the answers seemed right in front of her, but unattainable. Frustrated, she turned on the water and stepped into the shower.

Chapter Fifty-Four

After hiding out in the shower long enough, she decided to face the music. She expected to see Jack laying in her bed, but he wasn't there. The bed was made, with the ring box sitting on her pillow. She sank onto the bed, picked up the box and opened it to look at the ring. Nothing. It didn't make her heart sing, or her life seem complete, or touch her with infinite happiness. Amelia knew that a girl was supposed to have these soaring joyful feelings. At least for a few weeks or months after first getting asked. Amelia felt none of it.

They had been drifting for a while, but neither of them acknowledged it. He was away so much, she had this house. They were good on paper, but she had known better than a relationship that only looked perfect. She had known love and passion. Even if she could never have Franklin again, he imprinted on her that she deserved to feel these feelings and have them returned.

As she walked down the stairs she heard his cheerful whistling of something sounding like Paul McCartney's "Amazed" coming from the kitchen. She walked in to find him cooking up a storm in a college t-shirt and pajama pants. He was making some sort of egg dish with three different pans on the stove, lots of cut up vegetables on the island, and coffee waited in the pot, freshly brewed. He turned to smile at her as Amelia poured herself a cup, praying it would give her strength. She stood and watched him cook for a few moments, and he turned and smiled at her. She weakly returned the smile.

"What's wrong, hun," he asked as he grinned like he had just won the biggest prize at the county fair and sidled over to her to give her a big, wet, sloppy kiss. She didn't kiss him back.

He stepped back and looked her up and down, assessing her like the doctor he was.

"I..." Amelia started.

"Well," he cut off the thick silence she couldn't finish, "eggs will be ready soon, my bride, and we shall feast this morning!"

"This isn't going to work."

"Well, you'll just have to wait—I can't make the eggs cook any—what?"

"I don't think I can marry you, Jack."

He stopped scraping the pan with the spatula in his hand and just stared at her. With pleading in her eyes, waited for him to answer. He didn't. She took the ring box out of her pocket, and set it on the island next to the bell pepper. He looked like his eyes were about to tear up, but instead he turned back to the stove, turned off the burner, scooped the eggs onto two plates, and placed one on the island. He stared her down, grabbed a fork, and walked out of the room.

Clueless, Amelia stood in the kitchen. Picking up a plate she went to follow him. She looked in two other rooms before finding him in the study, eating at the large desk.

"Jack—"

"I thought you loved me," his forehead crinkled in confusion as he paused, shoveling his eggs in his mouth. He had consumed half of what was on his plate already, and judging by the amount that was on her plate, he had eaten a lot.

"At the time, I'm sure I did. I still do. Just not in a romantic way." She took a deep breath and shook her head. "I'm terrible, I know. I don't know how to say this without it sounding awful…" she started to step back and retreat.

"Is it another man—"

Without hesitation, she said, "Yes."

"Who?" he looked up at her, perplexed. "There are no signs of another man around this house, and you don't seem like a woman hiding an affair. I do suppose it is possible since I am gone so much, but—"

"You wouldn't believe me if I told you."

Jack looked directly into her eyes with stone cold seriousness. "Try me."

Well, she thought, why not? The actual truth was as ridiculous as a woman refusing a man she loved for no reason. "I fell through time." Amelia blurted out. "One hundred years. In this very house. The man who lived there, lives there...he... I thought I'd never get back here again. When it first happened, I cried and cried over losing you when it first happened. I mourned you and you hadn't even been born yet. You didn't even know I was gone. I suffered the loss of you for days and weeks. Because, back then, life for a woman was decorative. So he, Franklin, helped me... establish that I was his ... wife."

Jack growled like a wounded animal about to lash out and looked away.

Amelia pleaded, needing him to know the truth, "You have to understand that he offered marriage to protect me. It was for my safety. At least to begin with. And then I was there for so long, that feelings started to ...I've never had that before, just someone—a complete stranger—have so much chemistry with me that after only a few moments he was willing to save me from my problems.

"I love you, Jack. I truly do. I wanted us to have a future together. Months ago I wanted it more than anything I've ever known...but the truth is, I feel I've left my heart with him. I came back to be with you but my soul is still in the past. Every day I think of him. I've tried to stop but all I want is to go back. But, I feel that I was yours first. I've promised myself to you first—even before you proposed." She looked down. "You both hold my heart. It's completely ridiculous. I know that." She looked into his eyes. "But it is the truth."

He stormed out of the kitchen and she followed him into the study where he went to the desk and made a guttural sound as if he were summoning Franklin for a fight slamming both fists down onto the surface. A disrupted paperweight rolled next to his hand. Jack stood for a moment, stalwart. He began to fiddle with the paperweight that was on the desk. Then he picked it up and crossed the room looking at the glass orb with curiosity, stroking the smooth, cool surface with his thumb. He stopped a few feet in front of her. Drawing his arm back suddenly, with a violent pitch, he hurled the paperweight at the unfinished fireplace. It shattered, no match for solid brick. A laugh started in his belly and rose up.

"You know," he said calmly, finally looking back at Amelia, "I actually believe you."

Chapter Fifty-Five

"You can stay as long as you need to. Until you leave next week, or longer if you need. There's plenty of space here," Amelia said, and left him in the study. This confession had made her stomach turn and she no longer had the desire to eat had left her. Needing something to do she started to clean up the detritus from breakfast and as she started to scoop up the remaining bell pepper, she saw the ring box. Panic rose up in her so, Amelia left the mess and instead changed to go for a run.

She entered the park at Grand Army Plaza. She ran down through the park all the way down West Drive, and to the end of the park. She walked back up Prospect Park West. Returning home, she first went to the kitchen and found it clean. The ring and its box were also gone. Probably for the best.

At first she hid in her room, but realized that was ridiculous. Might as well face him. First she checked in the front room where he had read his paper, but Jack was not there. Amelia went upstairs and stopped by his room. She gently knocked on the door. Not hearing a response, she gently turned the knob as not disturb him just to see if he might be sleeping. No Jack. And his suitcases and clothes were gone.

Returning to her room, she saw her phone on her bedside table blinked. A message from him. She wasn't sure she wanted to hear it. After a few deep breaths and some courage, she rolled her shoulders back and hit play.

"Amelia," his voice made her skin into gooseflesh. Jack sighed. "I had to leave," Jack sounded deflated. "I had to. I love you too much to relive your rejection every day. Even if it is only for a few days more. I hope... ah...I don't know what I hope for. I hope you find... what you're looking for... happiness.... " There was the vacant sound of someone trying to figure out how to say goodbye. And then the message clicked to an end. Pulling a pillow close to her, Amelia tucked herself into a ball waiting to cry. But no tears came. Only dusk.

Chapter Fifty-Six

Amelia didn't know what to do. She awoke several times the next day, but didn't want to get up. She just wanted to sleep. Sleeping meant ignoring reality and the anguish of the partnership she refused.

As she went in and out of a numb sleep, she thought of the path that brought her here. She had chosen Jack, hadn't she? She returned from the past to be with Jack. To live a future with *Jack*. So why, when given that option, did she refuse?

Franklin was a moody brute whose life was already solidified. It was literally in the history books, or at least documented somewhere, somehow. An internet or library search would prove his life happened. As in the past. But Jack... she could form whatever life she wanted to with him. The future was theirs to make.

There was no telling what kind of life she would have had with Franklin. Why was she thinking of him? Franklin wasn't an option. Now neither was Jack.

The same choices, the same mistakes could be made with either man. With any man, for that matter. Life seems to give the same choices over and over in different forms. A person makes one choice and if it isn't the right one, another set of choices is presented; different but similar. If a bad choice is made, life circles back around to offer another. Life is circular. Why can't time be, as well? Man-made time *is* circular. Every day starts and ends the same and starts all over again. A circle.

These nonsensical thoughts seeping with insight cycled through her head. It was night again by the time Amelia decided to get up.

An ache that was coming up from inside of her, she needed something to fill the hole. Food? No, she was sure she couldn't eat. Water? Probably. Hydration was always good. She padded barefoot to the kitchen for water. The smooth wood of the stairs gave way to the cold tile of the kitchen, and the large difference in temperatures on the floor jerked Amelia out of her stupor. After downing a glass of water, she remembered she hadn't showered from her run yesterday, and was stiff and stinky. Plodding up the steps again, she decided to run a nice bath.

The water flowing into the tub was meditative. Lighting candles she breathed in the floral loveliness as she removed the sticky workout clothes. Amelia eased her body down into the warm water, tension and sorrow eased out of her skin and dissolved into the water.

As she soaked, Amelia pulled at the strings of her thoughts. She had loved Jack so much, but at some point she had fallen *out* of love with him. It was a fine line between the two, but there was a difference. She would always love him. He was a wonderful man but because of her love for him that she needed to let him go. It isn't right staying in a relationship when someone feels trapped. Splashing water over herself as if to rinse off her guilt, one tear fell down her cheek. She wiped it away with a deep sigh. Amelia refused to let herself cry more.

Emptying the water from the tub felt like she was letting it all go, the pain, the anguish, the longing. The emptiness was still there. She knew it would be for a while. Maybe she deserved it. Being alone was something she needed now, to figure out her life. But Franklin's face kept floating across her mind. No. She couldn't think about Franklin right now. When his face refused to stay out of her mind, she gave up and got out of the bath. She toweled herself off and put on clean pajamas, and climbed back into bed. The act of getting a glass of water and taking a bath had convinced Amelia's body that she wanted more sleep, and soon she drifted off into a dreamless rest.

Sun streaming through her curtains across her face woke Amelia. It came back. She had made a choice. She needed to get out of bed and live with that choice no matter how much it hurt.

Amelia just didn't know where to begin. Getting dressed was always a good start. Talking with friends was another. Amelia called Alexia. It was early enough that Amelia could get dressed and make it into the city to meet for lunch. Alexia conference called Toni, and both agreed, with excited squeals, to meet. Living in paint clothes these past weeks made Amelia love that she had an excuse to dress up, so she dug out a cerulean silk blouse, a black blazer rolled up to the elbows, and dark blue jeans. She put on heels and did her hair and makeup. Grabbing her purse she left the house.

Lunch was at their favorite place, a little restaurant that none of them ever could remember the name of, only the location. It was bright and had outdoor seating in the summer and in the fall and winter, it was nice and cozy inside. The menu was filled with various sandwiches and salads, and the place seemed to be modeled like the TV show *Friends* with sofas and mismatched chairs and tables. It was very bohemian, especially for downtown Manhattan. They ate and caught up. Alexia was currently dating a high profile banker, Toni was going out on her third date tonight with a chef who won a reality TV show. Amelia broke the news about her engagement, and brought up Franklin, not as a reason to refuse Jack, but as a separate topic. Amelia mentioned how attracted to him she was and she liked spending time with him, but didn't know if it could go anywhere. She told them that he was a writer.

Toni, always paranoid, said, "We should Google him. Find his picture. Maybe his books are online!"

Amelia shied away, playing it off as a new relationship, and didn't want to reveal his last name just in case it went nowhere. She did promise she would look him up when she got home and fill them in on any dirt that came from the search.

Lunch ended with hugs and Amelia promising she would call again soon.

On the subway home, the idea of looking him up turned into a great idea. She got off the 2 train at The Brooklyn Library and entered the building that looked to her like an Egyptian Palace relocated in the middle of a busy roundabout.

Amelia always felt an excitement run through her body when she walked through the doors of a library. Maybe it was her love of books. Maybe it was a memory of her weekly visit to the library with her mother when she was little. Maybe it was the promise of adventures hidden in the pages within the building. As she walked past the card catalogs that were just for show, all books were digitally cataloged now, she smiled at happy memories of digging through those drawers to find just the right book and its location. Memories of being just tall enough to reach the drawers to flip through the cards seeking the secret location of a beloved tome. There was the feeling of a treasure hunt to the card catalog. Clicks on the computer to find out which location a book weren't as satisfying. However the online catalog, and the ability to have any book in the system delivered to a location of her choosing was tremendous. The New York Public Library was a truly magnificent beast.

Even though it was a weekday, the library was packed. And people say no one reads anymore! Amelia walked over to the computer bank and typed in "Franklin Dunne" and then hesitated with her finger over the Enter key...

What if he wasn't there? What if this was all just a dream? Worse. What if he was there—and she found out he was married and happy without her?

Don't be silly, Amelia, she told herself. Just look. It's not like if you don't look then it didn't happen. You would just be avoiding it. And you'll eventually want to find out, and today is as good as any day.

She hit enter, and waited. The cursor turned into the hourglass of death endlessly spinning to remind the user it was still thinking. Time stopped as the system scanned. Five titles popped up on the screen. Amelia clicked on the first one, it was not available. Lost and out of print, the note said. On the second one, a copy was available in the special collections at the main branch on 42nd Street. She would have to view it in the branch. She looked at the time on the computer, it was 5:15pm. She wouldn't be able to get there in time to see it today. Amelia made a mental note and checked to see if the three remaining titles were available.

The third title was missing. The last two titles were part of this branch's special collection. She wrote down titles and call numbers and walked over to the desk and waited for assistance. The librarian, the antithesis of the clichéd librarian, walked over to her. He was a tall Italian looking man who had a very warm smile.

"Can I help you?" asked the gorgeous librarian.

Amelia had so many responses, some appropriate, but most of them not. She handed over her paper, and choked out a simple, "yes." He smiled as he took the paper.

Apparently this wasn't the first time a woman tripped all over herself in his general direction.

Watching the clock, Amelia impatiently waited for the man to return. She knew very well that just because the card catalog said that the books were here, didn't mean they were. They could be on loan or could have disappeared as well. Franklin Dunne wasn't a name that was familiar to Amelia before she had fallen into his life and seeing in the card catalog notes on all his books, that they were out of print, wasn't very encouraging, especially as the minutes ticked by.

The Adonis returned smiling his beaming smile. "Sorry it took me so long, they were really buried. You have to look at these over in the research section, and I'll need a picture ID and your library card to let you have them.

As Amelia dug for her wallet she joked, "You don't need my first born as well?"

"I would but we don't really have room for the children, at least not on this floor," and he winked at her. "And of course you'll need to return them to this desk at least ten minutes before we close," and he winced as he looked at his watch, "which is in about twenty minutes."

Putting her cards down on the counter, she took the books, "I guess I'll see you in a few minutes, then. Thanks," Amelia said as she took the books from his hands and turned away. She took a giddy hop toward the seating area.

The leathery covers in her hand reminded her of her real task here. On top was the first book Franklin gave her to read, and as she cracked the cover, she felt transported back to his study when he handed the book to her. She read the first few lines on the first page and was sucked back into the book and being with Franklin. The second book she hadn't seen, and she ran her fingers over the lettering. She opened the book and started running her fingers over the pages as she read.

Enthralled by the book, Amelia didn't hear anyone approach. She jumped when the handsome librarian put his hand on the table and leaned into her. She asked him to repeat himself—as she knew he said something, but didn't hear it because she was so deep in thoughts of Franklin.

He laughed, "I said, it's closing time. I need to return your books. We open at ten tomorrow."

Smiling a perfunctory smile, Amelia closed both books and slid them towards him.

"Here, I brought your ID and card back for you."

"Thanks," she said as she stood up and looked into his eyes. There was something there that he seemed to want to communicate. She tilted her head in a question, and he opened his mouth and drew a breath. But instead of saying anything, he nodded and turned, taking the books back to the desk.

In a haze, Amelia started walking. It wasn't until she was out of the main doors that she realized that her driver's license and her library card were still in her hand. She felt a piece of paper with them, and assumed it was the call numbers of her books. Looking at the slip, she saw that "Jerry" and a phone number were written on the paper. She looked back at the library and laughed—he had literally slipped her his number. The handsome librarian, a dream guy, was interested in her.

But the warm feeling of being wanted left her quickly. Her thoughts turned to Franklin and she felt as if she were looking in his eyes. He was all she wanted. Amelia knew she had to go back.

Chapter Fifty-Seven

O nce the choice was made, Amelia didn't want to back down even though she second guessed herself. But nothing else was right. The preparation to leave here forever was her biggest hurdle. The decision to keep or get rid of everything she owned was one that she kept vacillating over. But if she didn't return, the lawyer could just take care of any of it. Her last conversation with Banks assured that.

A few months ago, she told the lawyer that she wished her benefactor's wishes to remain intact if anything happened to her. She told Banks if she didn't check in or if she hadn't accessed her bank account in twelve months it was safe to proceed as if Amelia never claimed the money.

Her friends were another thing altogether. She didn't know how to handle things with Toni, Alexia, and her aunt. She ended up writing them all letters about following her passions and how she met someone and was leaving to be with him. It was vague enough, but it would serve as a goodbye. Entrusting the letters to Banks with instructions to say Amelia was once again traveling, if anyone asked, and told him to mail out the letters December 2, 2013, a year from tomorrow, if he hadn't heard from her by that date. This seemed to make it all final. She was ready. Amelia was going to give up her life and be with Franklin.

December first arrived. The warmth made the day feel more like October. Only two weeks prior it had snowed lightly. Amelia took one last stroll around her block, stopping at the deli for her favorite chips and one last diet soda. Walking around the house she looked at everything as if to say goodbye. Which was silly. It wasn't like she was moving out. She would be in this house. Scrolling through pictures on her phone, she tried to commit all to memory. Then she turned it off and set it down.

She walked up to the fifth step - it was sort of tradition now to come down the stairs as she adjusted the watch. Taking a deep breath, Amelia looked around and smiled. "Goodbye," she whispered as she turned the dial past the twelve, making the date turn to the first.

Chapter Fifty-Eight

Breathing in the scent of the past, Amelia finally felt like she was home. Turing to dash upstairs, Amelia started toward the hope of another pre-packed suitcase prepared by Franklin—assuming he did the same as last time. Then she would quietly scurry down to the front door, walk in, shout hello, then drop the suitcase and march into the study.

Two steps up, all of that went out the window. All she wanted was to see Franklin. Amelia ran down the stairs and the moment she reached the study, threw open the heavy study doors. Her breath left her. At his desk, deep in thought—Amelia knew that look, he wouldn't move unless she really got his attention. A peevish thought crept into her head, and she smiled to herself. Creeping slowly across the room, just out of his periphery she snuck up behind him. When she was standing directly behind his chair she put her hands over his eyes.

Franklin grabbed her by the hands, then jumped up, spun her, and pinned Amelia's arms behind her. In less than three seconds he had her backed up to a bookcase, and had somehow a letter opener and now poised at her throat. His moves were so quick and out of character; Amelia was terrified. Nose to nose, they stared at each other, both out of breath, his wild eyes glaring into hers.

Silence filled the room as he put together what was happening. When it all registered, the letter opener clattered to the floor. In exasperation he threw his hands in the air and turned away from her, rubbing his hands in his hair. Sighing a deep sigh, his hands dropped to his sides. "I'm.... I could have...." Franklin turned around and looked at Amelia sheepishly. "When did you..."

Amelia took a deep breath. "Just now. Although if I thought you would kill me, I would have waited until dinnertime, when my appearance wouldn't have been as much of a shock. I—"

Franklin began to laugh. "You know, you are quite funny. It's a dry wit. I hope Jack appreciates it."

Amelia winced.

"Well he...I...we aren't together—"

Apparently, that was all he needed to hear. Franklin was back in front of her almost as quickly as before, and pulled her in so close, not even air could pass between them. Her hands instinctively moved up around his neck and their lips met—first softly and tenderly, and after a few moments of light reignited passion overtook them both. Kisses became fiery and passionate. His arms encircled, pulling her to him in the hope that she would never disappear from him again.

His arms grip on her relaxed a little but his lips did not. Reaching between them he started to unbutton her jacket, and then traveled up her chest to her shoulders where he peeled the garment from her. For a few seconds he held her captive, using the sleeves as manacles and kissed her roughly. She responded by smiling, and then pressing her body against him. After a few deep passionate kisses like this, he released her by removing the jacket from her wrists and tossing it aside.

Her hands moved quickly and deftly to the buttons of his waistcoat, unbuttoning and then unhooking his watch chain—making sure it was safely in his pocket. After all, it was precious. It was the watch she gave him. As he helped her remove the waistcoat by struggling out of it, she started on the buttons on his shirt. After his waistcoat was on the floor, his hands went to work unbuttoning her blouse while his lips went back to hers, stealing a few kisses. They both pulled away from each other—he, throwing his suspenders off his shoulders followed by the removal of his shirt, as she shrugged out of her blouse. While her hands went behind her waist to start work unfastening her skirts, his hands went to her breasts, bubbling over her corset. He touched them lightly at first, as a sculptor admiring another's work. Then his hands enveloped the tops allowing his sense memory of her to return. He then replaced his hands with his lips, gently kissing each, before moving up her neck and over her chin while he popped open all the hooks on the front of her corset. Amelia was enjoying the attention to her chest and moaned while her hands were still untying her underskirt. It fell to the floor revealing her legs, just as her corset hit the floor releasing the rest of her. Franklin, now in a rush, removed his own trousers, shoes and socks all the while trying to keep a hand on her body. Sensing the same need and desire, she threw her camisole and bloomers to the floor and kicked off her shoes.

The late afternoon sun streamed in from the windows, and the fire burning behind her gave her an angel-like glow. He looked at her entire body, stopping at her eyes. Amelia blushed and lowered her chin to the floor in embarrassment.

He took her chin in his hands and drew her eyes up to meet his. "You are so beautiful. Have you missed me as much as I have pined for you?"

One small tear rolled down her cheek as she nodded yes. Their bodies mashed together and tears started to roll down her cheeks. Gently, he picked her up, one arm under her knees and the other cradling her back. Amelia wrapped her arms around his neck as he carried her over to the fireplace and lowered her onto the bear rug in front of the hearth. Plush and prickly against her skin, she lay back on the fur. Franklin knelt down beside her, his hands moving over her, touching every inch of her skin. One hand went into her hair, gathering it all up and angling her mouth to kiss him. The other caressed her hip and slid up to her breast.

As the afternoon sun moved up the wall, reflecting the sun setting outside, his knees spread her legs and he settled into her. They returned to each other completely, as if time had never separated them.

Chapter Fifty-Nine

Her temple rested on his chest as she listened to his heart thrum, reminding her he was real. His hand rested atop hers as his chest rose and fell in a contented rhythm. One arm wrapped around her, keeping her close and safe from anything else that might come between them. His palm rested on her hip, and his fingertips caressed her buttocks. A blissful sigh escaped him. Questions burned through her and though she felt guilty breaking this spell, the constant thrum in her brain wouldn't let her relax. These questions, and the smell of the stew had crept into the study making her stomach quietly rumble, stirred her focus.

She stroked his chest with her fingertips in hopes of stirring him. He only clasped her hand in response.

"Franklin…" she said almost in a whisper, quietly and sweetly.

His response was the sigh of a sleeping child.

"Franklin…" she said a little louder and sing-song.

His fingertips moved slightly over her buttocks, and lightly squeezed.

"Franklin."

His right hand moved from on top of hers on his chest, wrapped around her lower back, and rolled them over so that he now lay on top of her and he languidly kissed her on the lips and then started moving southward on her body.

She stopped his migration by placing her hands on his face and angling his chin up so she could look him in the eyes.

"My darling," she said matronly, "I would love for you to do that, but there are matters we need to discuss."

And, on cue, her stomach rumbled in agreement. Franklin chortled returned to eye level with Amelia, lifted just above her, his legs intertwined with hers. A precaution to make sure she wasn't leaving him any time soon, for food or for any other reason.

"So, I can guess from that," she cleared her throat, "display of affection, you are happy to see me. I can't imagine what you would have done if it were your publisher," she said grinning. "However, I need to know how you Mrs. Finnegan knew I might be coming back today? As she knows that stew is my favorite. Where is she, by the way? And Emily? And I would like to be caught up on everything that has happened over the last two months."

He groaned playfully as he buried his head in her bosom.

"Just like a woman to need to know every single detail in the middle of love making," he let out a muffled moan from in between her breasts.

She playfully whacked him on the back and replied defiantly, "It wasn't in the *middle*."

"Yes, my darling," he said as he raised his head from her breast, "You are right—it was just the beginning," he said with a seductive smile and grabbed a handful of her backside. "You must tell me, what *weren't* they feeding you in the future? I swear there used to be more to hold onto back here."

She slapped him a bit harder than before now across his bicep.

"Hey—"

But before she could finish her protest, he kissed her deeply on the lips. She liked how much he loved her body.

"Do you need to sit across the room from me to make you behave?" she asked in her best stern schoolmarm tone.

"Alright! Alright. I give in. I'll behave. He chuckled as he leaned up on his elbow. "For a few minutes, anyway. But to quote Mrs. Finnegan 'we newlyweds can't go for that long without each other.'" He said, mimicking her voice. Then he lifted a hand and caressed Amelia's cheek. "And, my dear, two months is a lot of time that we need to make up for," he said with a devilish smile.

She looked at him sternly, as she gently rolled up onto her elbow to face him. He kissed her nose, and she gave him a glare.

"Oh, darling, I have missed you—even that dreaded look of disdain you throw at me," he said coyly.

She laughed, breaking the seriousness again.

After her laughter settled down she said, "You must explain—"

He interrupted, "Are you planning on disappearing tomorrow, my love?"

"No."

"Well then, the day after?" he asked earnestly.

"No."

"Two weeks from Thursday?"

"No," she replied, "but, I am curious—"

"Well then," he said matter-of-factly as he pulled her back beneath him, "plenty of time to explain in the coming days. I don't plan to leave your side much."

She started to speak, but he put his pointer finger over her lips and continued, "I have been awaiting your return for what seems like an eternity—although the calendar tells me it has been a couple of months," he said as he stroked her cheek with his thumb and looked into her eyes. "I would love to answer all of your questions in due time. But right now, I need you to assist me in other matters."

The questions that were incessantly bothering her only minutes before seemed to fade, and she acquiesced by placing her lips on his and instead she now only heard the crackle of the fire, and the rising rate of her own heart beat as he fervently kissed her back. They made love more slowly this time, enjoying each other completely.

Chapter Sixty

Amelia had dozed off and was only roused sometime later by Franklin's caress. It was now completely dark in the room except for the embers in the fire. When she felt him move somewhat suddenly, she awoke, and lifted her head.

"What is the matter? Is everything alright?" she asked.

"I don't know. I heard something at the door."

He got up and crossed the room. She remained on the floor and grinned to herself like a teenager as she enjoyed the view of his bare backside. He bent and picked up a piece of paper. He was quiet for a few moments, and then chuckled, and opened the study door. Even though Amelia was out of view of anyone standing outside of the doorway, she ducked down and tried to make herself invisible. She heard the door shut, and he was back at her side carrying a tray. He knelt down, and set the tray beside her.

"Mrs. Finnegan was worried about you, so she left this. In her note she also took it upon herself to give herself and

Emily the night off," he said as he sat back down on the rug.

They both laughed, and once again her stomach rumbled.

"At least someone is worried about my stomach!" Amelia said.

"I would be worried about your stomach, but you have other parts of your body that are so much more desirable."

She cuffed his arm playfully.

He laughed. Then removed the metal dome from the tray revealing two bowls of steaming stew. It smelled heavenly. Slices of freshly baked bread sat beside the urn welcoming them to help themselves. He stood and started to walk away.

"Where are you going?" she asked.

"We need some wine to go with this to celebrate!"

She thought about protesting, but wine sounded good. Amelia grabbed a slice of the bread, squishing it, listening to the lovely crackle of the crust and feeling the springy resilience she loved. Without ceremony, she dipped it into one of the large bowls of steaming stew, and then shoved the whole thing in her mouth.

He returned with two glasses and with a freshly uncorked bottle, and started laughing the moment he saw her chewing with her cheeks stuffed.

"I guess I should feed you more often," he said.

"Yes, you should take better care of me," she retorted.

"I thought I had. Three times," he teased back.

She blushed before locking eyes with him. He poured a glass of wine and smiled at her as he handed it to her. Amelia took the glass and clinked his wine glass. They drank to each other and devoured the food. After she wiped the last of the stew from the side of the bowl, and he had finished the bottle of wine, they snuggled together against the sofa facing the fire and collectively sighed.

"I am glad to be back," she said. "It is such an odd thing. It's the same exact house that I live in, but it doesn't feel the same without you. And although I could leave the copious amounts of clothing worn in this time, I would give just about anything to come back here for any of Mrs. Finnegan's cooking."

She nuzzled Franklin's neck and closed her eyes, his head resting on hers in response. Enjoying the warmth of the fire and the food in their bellies, they just enjoyed the moment. An urge to taste her again, encouraged him to kiss her again. Slowly at first and then with more fervor. She kissed him back before a thought crossed her mind. Her brow furrowed.

"How ... was it this time—"

"Darling, it was lovely, I enjoyed myself immensely. All three times in fact."

She smacked him playfully on the shoulder, "That's not what I'm getting at, you ass!"

"Starting with the new pet names already? I'm not sure that—"

"Stop teasing, Franklin. I'm trying to be serious." She tried to stop giggling before she continued. "How was… how was the time without me? Were you… ok?"

"Well, the same darkness fell over me when you first left. That first day that I told myself I would survive, that you would be back. But days drifted by and I began to doubt. Then, I got the glimmer of an idea that rippled through my brain. I couldn't catch it for the first few days. Then it wouldn't stop. I think I might have written my best work yet. The odd thing was that I wanted to keep editing it —which for me is odd. I usually want to write everything down and give it to my editor. But I kept reading this one. Tweaking little things. I kept enjoying it, and then thinking… what if…?"

Amelia looked at Franklin who was now looking up at the ceiling. She smiled at him admiringly—he had never been this passionate about anything.

"Every time I read it, it was like I was reading someone else's work. I was laughing at things I wrote. There would be something that needed explanation in the plot and I would make a note to insert it, and then a page later, I would answer my own question. It was a beautiful tapestry of words that I had put together. When I took it to Stokes to read, he was mesmerized." Franklin turned back his head to Amelia, who was still beaming at him, and he kissed her forehead. "I did it. I even thought to myself, if I never saw you again and died that night, I would die a happy man."

"Franklin, I'm so proud of you."

"Thank you, darling. I'm quite proud. I'm also glad to report I haven't swung into a bout of sadness since then. I've been riding the wave of happiness, continuing to write. Honestly it was just, these last few days, I started to hope for your return again. How were your last few months?"

"They were... interesting," she said, turning her face away from his curious eyes. "I had to understand what I felt for Jack...even though I could not stop thinking about you."

"And how were things?"

"Yes, well, he proposed...." She turned down her eyes not wanting to relive that evening. Looking directly at Franklin was difficult.

The crackle of the fire was the only sound breaking the silence that seemed to drag on.

Franklin, unable to stand the tension said, "I've never had to compete with a man from a different time for a woman. I'm not sure I know the protocol. And how does one challenge another to a duel to a man who has not been born yet?" His brow was furrowed as he stared at her.

"You don't mean it," she said still unable to look at him.

He looked back at her and a smile crept over his face. "Oh, my dear," he said brightly, "Do you not know how much I love you? How I would travel to the ends of the earth—or time, if it were possible for me—to make you mine?"

Turning her body completely towards him, but still unable to look him in the eyes, "I came back to be with you. I choose you. I choose this life and I don't want to leave you again."

He grabbed her around the waist, and pulled her close enough that their eyes couldn't focus on anything but each other. "Good. Because I have no intention of letting you go."

Falling asleep, she murmured, "It's supposed to snow tomorrow. I love snow."

After he had pleasured her once more pulled a blanket over them. He kissed the top of her head, and fell asleep.

Chapter Sixty-One

Emily's light knock at Amelia's bedroom door woke Franklin. The maid scurried in and politely acknowledged him, he left in his robe. Franklin headed to his room to dress with new found vigor, knowing he needed to answer correspondence from yesterday, then he would whip his current novel's manuscript into shape. A dream last night gave him inspiration.

When Franklin entered his room crossed to the bright light coming from his windows. Curtains, still drawn back from yesterday, allowed his view of the street. Pillowy snowflakes were suspended in a dance. He stood mesmerized. It felt as if he were a miniature in a snow globe shaken.

Childlike innocence overtook him and he ran back to Amelia's room. Hadn't she murmured her adoration for snow last night? He wrapped as politely as he could on the door, his excitement bubbling up even more. Emily saw the huge grin on his face as she opened the door.

"I was just leavin' sir. You can go on in."

Franklin re-entered Amelia's room, and Emily closed the door behind her and walked down the hall. He had been distracted trying to keep his composure during Emily's departure, so he hadn't noticed Amelia just rising from the bed. He looked up and saw her standing naked across the room. She turned and their eyes met.

"I, uh, um… I'm sorry to disturb you…" he trailed off and looked down at his feet. He was suddenly self-conscious. Was it because of the innocent need to tell her about the snow? Was it because she was absolutely beautiful naked? He looked up again to see that she had reached for her robe, and just modestly held it in front of herself, "… but," he started to find words again, "it's snowing outside." These last words, he found the courage to look her in the eye. She was beautiful. He couldn't believe that the creature that he was staring at was not only in his house, in the same room, and he had held her only recently in his arms.

"Really?" Amelia said, as excitedly as he felt when he first saw the snow. His enthusiasm was shared between them and the tension broke. She walked to her windows and threw back the curtains, the bright white morning proclaiming the magical world outside. He admired her naked backside, which she didn't bother to cover up in her excitement over the snow.

Amelia was ecstatic. Snow was a marvel that never ceased to amaze and fill her with wonder. Especially the large fluffy flakes that floated like feathers slowly cascading with no care in the world. Self-consciousness came over her a few moments after she had been standing at the window. Her unclothed back was to Franklin. She hoped he didn't think that she was taunting him on purpose. Amelia grabbed for a robe. For some reason she felt like she shouldn't just stand there naked, even though she was just about to step into her bath. She had never felt this truly naked. As two warm arms wrapped around her all of this was forgotten. She tilted her head back to rest on his shoulder.

"It's beautiful," she murmured and sighed, still mesmerized by the snowfall. "Thank you," she said as if he were the one giving the precious gift. She turned her head to look him, and sighed with contentment before turning back to watch the fluttering white ballet.

They stood there, embracing and watching for a while. He kissed her temple, and she turned into it. A perfect moment. Then Franklin, feeling his novel calling, unwrapped himself from around her. Kissing her between the shoulder blades he then backed toward the door. Taking a final glance at her as she stood at the window, her arms still wrapped about her as if he was still there, enchanted by the gentle motion of the falling flakes. He soaked up the moment; Amelia staring out the window, filled with wonder. Her curves, caressed by the morning light reflecting off the snow, made her look like a Renoir painting. He smiled as he shut the door and walked back to his rooms. It was a moment he would return to for the rest of his life. He hoped he would do it justice when he wrote this scene in one or more of his novels.

***

For the first time in her life Amelia knew she was truly in love with someone. This man spoke to her heart so deftly. She had only known him for a short while, but it felt like they had known each other for an eternity, even though they just met a few months ago.

Amelia felt this decision was right more than she had ever felt anything. She didn't understand her connection to Franklin. Maybe this is what love at first sight feels like, she thought to herself. Her heart was fuller than it had ever been. She had finally found home. She wasn't sure who said home isn't a place, but a person, but she felt it whenever she looked at her husband. Amelia hadn't even known she was searching for it, but here it was, in the shape of Franklin.

It really didn't matter how they found each other, but they had. Amelia was truly happy for the first time in a long time, if ever. Jack was a good man, but he wasn't what she wanted, and needed. He didn't feel the same in her arms as Franklin did.

Living in the past had its complications. Amelia was well aware of that. She also knew that there would be trouble and complications as she adjusted to both this time and being a wife. She was willing to risk everything for him. She hoped he felt the same.

Chapter Sixty-Two

Four weeks after her arrival Amelia started to question her decision. The honeymoon phase was over.

After he had declined both lunch and their regular walk today Amelia went to find Franklin in his study. After politely knocking and receiving not response, she entered softly not wanting to distract him or wake him up—she had walked in on him dozing a few times. After closing the door she was not two steps in the room when bellowed a deep, "Go AWAY!" from somewhere near the fireplace.

"But I…"

"Did you not hear me? Go. Away."

"Franklin, it's me. You didn't have lunch today, so I wanted to see if you wanted—"

"GET. OUT!"

Confused and stunned, Amelia retreated from the room, and closed the door behind her. Not understanding what just happened, she went to her room and stared out the window.

Amelia knew he was having a hard time finishing this book. He was much more distracted lately than he had been at first, and she had seen less and less of him. However, she didn't know Franklin well enough to know if his barking response to entering the study was momentary frustration or real anger. Would this be a long-term mood?

Amelia sat and watched the day turn to dusk without registering it. She knew she should go downstairs for dinner, but her pride didn't appreciate the tongue-lashing earlier. Between pride and hunger, her pride won out.

At the window, she remained, staring at nothing until the lamplighters started down the street. She thought the heard Mrs. Finnegan and Emily leave for the evening so she undressed and put herself to bed. She picked up the book from the bedside table that she was reading each night, but kept finding herself at the bottom of the page, not knowing what she read. She gave up and turned out her light.

Amelia awoke sometime later. She opened her eyes, not knowing what woke her, as her room was quiet and it would be hours before the sun would rise. She lifted her head slightly off the pillow and scanned the part of the room that her eyes could see. Franklin was sitting in a chair that he had pulled next to the bed. He was slumped in it, and staring at her, glazed and stupefied.

"What are—"

"I'm sorry," he pathetically whispered.

She propped herself up and gave him a confused look.

"I am an abominable person to have treated you so coldly," he continued.

The memory of the afternoon and her hurt pride made her take a deep breath. One look into Franklin's eyes and it diminished into the need to soothe the pain his voice yielded. But her head was still foggy from sleep and she could not think of a fitting response. Instead she started to reach a hand out toward him. He stopped her with his words, and she pulled her hand back.

"As you know, I am onto used to having people around that aren't under my employ," he paused and cleared his throat before continuing. "I suffer from this overwhelming melancholy. Many days I suffer with hate for myself, feeling sad and worthless, and overwhelmed with fear that others believe me to be worthless as well. I become enraged with anger over having these thoughts. Or I grovel in submission to my own fears and weaknesses."

Amelia shifted in the bed to make herself able to see him better.

"I hate myself," he continued in a helpless tone, staring at her with an unfocused gaze. "I war with myself—which is detrimental to my character and relationships with others, but it allows me to dive into my characters and really find deep stories, and write them. This disease makes me a terrible man, but it makes me a damn good writer." He leaned forward with his elbows on his knees, and rubbed his face with his hands.

She slowly reached her hand out to take his, but at the first touch from her, he winced and sat back in the chair refusing to look at her.

"I want to be a better man. I *need* to be a better man. And I am when I'm around you. But my writing seems to suffer. This latest manuscript, the ending is plaguing me.

"People have always treated me the way they treat me, as if I'm an anomaly, a freak. And I do what I have to do to get by. If I hurt myself or push others away in the process, then so be it. As long as the work doesn't suffer…"

As his thoughts rambled and drifted, taking Amelia on a roller coaster of pity, frustration, and the need to smack this man across the head for the idiotic thoughts he just shared. Overriding this was the need to love and protect him. Knowing that anything spoken would not get through to him in this moment, she removed the covers, and got out of bed. Crossing to him, she took his face in her hands and lifted it up, angling it toward hers. After placing a gentle kiss on his lips, she knelt on the floor, put her head in his lap and wrapped her arms around his waist. Franklin sighed and then in one swift movement, removed himself on the chair and was kneeling in front of Amelia on the floor. He placed his hands on her cheeks, carefully. His watery eyes stared pleading and searching into hers. Amelia needed to say something, but found no words.

She stared back into his searching eyes, feeling her pity swell and turn toward frustration. "You really—" she started to scold, but he flinched, so she stopped.

Instead of continuing, she threw her arms up around his neck and drew his body to hers. "Don't do that again," she whispered into his neck. "If we are going to fight, then we will fight. But, don't yell at me for no reason. Put a sock on the door or a flag out in front if you want to be alone."

Franklin chuckled at that, "Not that you'd pay attention to a sock or flag." He pulled back to look at her. His fingers traced her face. "I don't deserve you."

"True. You probably don't," she said, her mouth turning up into a beautiful smile.

He pulled her back into him and buried his head in her neck and hair. They stayed like that for a few minutes, then he drew them both up to standing. He stared into her eyes, marveling at her beauty, and kissed her deeply. He gently lifted her night shift over her head and cast it aside. He then gently lifted her to the bed, and showed her just how thankful he was that she had forgiven him.

***

Amelia awoke to Franklin's gaze from across the pillow.

"Have you ever been truly loved?" he asked earnestly.

"I think so. But I don't think I've ever loved someone else," she said.

"That *is* a great tragedy."

She laughed. "Like what the Greeks wrote?" She lowered her voice in mock seriousness as she scrunched her eyebrows together.

"Yes," he said in all sincerity. "Exactly as tragic as the Greeks, it's as if Sophocles himself wrote you. Have you seen yourself? How beautiful you are? Especially naked." He waggled his eyebrows at her.

She laughed and then rolled onto her back. "I guess I only paraded for my few girlfriends and the gays."

"What is parading? And girlfriends and gays? What an expression. For ladies that practice ill repute and anyone who is in high spirits..."

"Ha." She thought for a moment. "No I guess that does sound odd. How would you say it? Um...to my close lady companions who know my confidence," she said with a bit of a British accent, "and to...I think they might be called The Wilde Type?"

"Oh. Well yes, that is a very different meaning. Although, I'm not sure if it's better. And when you said that just now that you, 'parade for' those types of people, you were demonstrating self-loathing. Why?"

"I don't think it is self-loathing. It's not that drastic or dramatic. It's simply that I have never expected extraordinary or fantastic things for my life. I have always wanted love and family, to use the talents I was given to make living spaces beautiful and comfortable, and to generally enjoy life. It is not self-deprecation, but simply joking about my low expectations for my life."

"And here I thought I was the one suffering from melancholia."

"I don't mean that I'm sad about my life," Amelia said, but felt that statement was incorrect the moment it left her mouth. "I'm smart and educated and have a dream, but I've felt for a while that something greater was planned for me. Maybe you are it," she flipped onto her back and stared up at the ceiling.

"I think you were meant for a great many things." He propped himself up so he could look into her eyes. "I take one look at you and am enchanted. I want to spend every possible moment with you, looking in your eyes, wondering what I can do or say that will please you. I want to earn that beautiful smile." She awarded him with a shy smile but quickly looked away. His hand reached out to her chin and turned her face back to him. In a whisper he said, "I fear you will disappear from my life again. But I want you to be mine forever. I want you to stay, my behavior from yesterday in the study to the contrary. I have fallen in love with you, and if I can follow anywhere, I will. You are an amazing woman, Amelia, and I will build my life around you from here on out, if you will let me."

Amelia felt like she stopped breathing. Franklin said that he *loved* her. Her mind spun in a thousand different directions. She turned her head to look at him, "I love you too, and I'm not going anywhere," and she leaned in to prove it to him with a kiss.

Chapter Sixty-Three

This third trip was still an adjustment. This time she came back with no regrets, no concerns about her other life. With no questions to be answered she settled in a lot more quickly.

They received invitations regularly, it seemed like this time of year was heavy with social engagements. It made sense, the holiday season was big in any time too for getting together with friends. They had been out to a few dinners, but nothing like a ball or large dinner. Franklin didn't care for the pomp and circumstance of it all, as his mother always made him play the part as a boy. Amelia liked the idea of being more social, but didn't feel right going out into large crowds until she immersed herself in this time a bit more. She wasn't sure about how to behave, and until she didn't worry about how to act in proper society, she too balked at major social engagements.

This changed only when Carl and Ellen Stokes, Franklin's publisher and his wife, were throwing their annual holiday party. Ellen stopped by to deliver the invitation herself, and convinced Amelia that they had to attend.

"You just have to come to my party," Ellen said as they took tea in the front room. "Mr. Caruthers has made you many elegant dresses and you must show them off!"

"Ellen, you flatter, and I won't promise anything, but I'll do my best to get my husband there."

During the tea, Amelia skirted the subject, but afterwards, Amelia started to think, why shouldn't they go? It was a casual gathering, and Amelia thought that both she and Franklin could handle it.

"Darling," she said as she entered his study an hour after Ellen had departed, "Mrs. Stokes just stopped in, and she has invited us to her party. Well, it's not a party, it's just a holiday get together, and before you say anything, I think it would be good for me to get out. And I think it would do you some good to get out and meet up with your fellow authors, I know that you won't want to—"

"Amelia, do you want to go?" he asked, halting her pitch to go.

"Well... yes," she started hesitantly, and then resolute. "I think it would be a nice outing."

Looking up at her smiling, Franklin gave in, "Of course we will go. When is it?"

"Friday."

"As in two days from today? That is short notice."

"She says we should have had an invitation delivered a few weeks ago, but since she was in the neighborhood and hadn't heard back either way to her RSVP, she decided to stop in."

"Well, now that you mention it, there have been many invitations this year. I haven't had a chance to look at them, I've been so busy with my book. Here," he reached under a pile of papers. "Maybe you should be in charge of these, it would be your job anyway as my wife to reply," he said as he handed her a stack of sealed papers.

"Franklin! There must be twenty invitations here. I can't believe you just held onto them. I'll reply to them all. And you'll be ready to leave at 7pm on Friday night?"

"I know, I'm terrible. I told you, I have a major disdain for society. Yes, for you I'll be ready at 7pm. As long as you promise not to disappear on me."

"I won't. I'll let you get back to your work."

Kissing his cheek, Amelia left the room, and winced at his mention of her accidental first trip back to the future. She knew it was just a joke, but it stung.

Friday night arrived, and Franklin was ready at seven. He had even ordered a hansom cab to take them to the party. It was a blustery night. It had already snowed twice this week, and it was coming lightly down now. Since the Stokes lived about a mile away, it was a good idea to be driven.

When they pulled up to the house, it was all lit up. With the snow falling, it felt like a beautiful holiday card. The party inside was very festive. Amelia was overwhelmed. She knew that she would be out of her element, but this was really terrifying.   Never good in large groups, Amelia preferred more intimate meetings.

"Look who made it out in the snow," exclaimed Carl Stokes as he crossed the hall to Franklin and Amelia. "It's great to see you, old man!" He shook hands with Franklin while slapping him on the shoulder. "People are always asking if you really exist! Amelia," he said, kissing her on both cheeks, "do you mind if I whisk him away?"

And before she knew it she was standing alone in the front hallway. Well, alone with fifteen other strangers. Like vultures to a fresh slab of meat, the women ascended on her. Amelia felt like she was suffocating. She answered so many questions as obtusely as possible. Yes, she was from Philadelphia, yes, she and Franklin were married. Yes, she was not a figment of Franklin's imagination. Within half an hour she was exhausted.

"Ladies, ladies! Please," a familiar voice seemed like an angel come to avenge her, put a glass of wine in her hand and kissed her on both cheeks. "Now," Jon said, taking his place next to Amelia, "who can catch me up on the gossip that you lovely ladies are talking about?" He turned to Amelia and said, "this terrible weather, my cab took forever to get here."

Amelia smiled thankfully up at this friendly face. He smiled and winked back at her. Then to distract and engage his audience, "Now Mrs. Wilson, how is your next door neighbor's yippy dog?" And the conversation flew from there.

Jon shepherded Amelia all around the party. She was introduced to so many writers published by Stokes and others from the neighborhood. Amelia channeled her best Jennifer Ehle in *Pride and Prejudice*. She was polite, would answer questions when directed to her. Otherwise she would listen very intently. Trying to absorb and observe everything that was going on, Amelia's head was spinning by the two hour mark.

Jon had left her for a moment to get a refill on drinks. Amelia looked around for Franklin, who seemed to disappear entirely. She wasn't all too sure that he hadn't called a cab and gone home without her.

"You're Mrs. Dunne, aren't you," said a flowery alto voice to her left.

Amelia looked over her shoulder to see a silver haired woman, with a very fluffy lavender high necked dress with a ghastly amount of ribbons. A big bosomed woman, her corset was straining to hold her flesh in. "Yes, and you are?" Amelia tried to keep her attention only on the other woman's face.

"Mrs. Jackson. Marie Jackson. I'm a fan of your husband's. Or at least I was."

"I'm sure I don't know what you mean, Mrs. Jackson. How were you a fan of my husbands? You're not one of the women who tried to marry him off to your daughter are you?"

The woman cackled with laughter, "Oh, dear me, no. I have sons. Six strapping young boys. I used to love your husband's work when it was action and adventure stories.

Now he seems to be much too touchy feely. You should tell him to leave the emotions out of his stories, and go back to the devilish swordplay."

"Well madam," Amelia felt somewhat infuriated by this battle-ax of a woman, "my husband is a fantastic writer, and I'm sure he appreciates your patronage. I'll pass along the word to him about your preferences, however, he rarely listens to my suggestions, so you might be stuck with the, how did you call it, 'the touchy feely stuff'."

"Well, my dear," said Mrs. Jackson, taking a step closer to Amelia and taking a conspiratorial tone, "are you sure that you're not using your womanly ways to have him write stories that you would prefer? Hmm?"

"Mrs. Jackson, my husband is a versatile writer, and I doubt he thinks about what anyone thinks of his work while writing," Amelia's voice was rose bit, and people started to stare, but she didn't really care. To have this woman infer that she was changing Franklin's writing style by sleeping with him. The nerve! "I think he is more talented and has more depth than only writing the silly swashbuckling adventure stories you love so much. He is capable of writing much, much more."

"Well, I—why, Mr. Dunne," Mrs. Jackson was now looking over Amelia's shoulder. Amelia tensed up. This woman was goading her and she let her temper, which rarely got out, flare. The awful woman continued, oozing with flirtation towards Franklin, "I was just talking to your, ahem, lovely wife here about your writing style."

"So I heard. From the other room." He looked into Amelia's eyes. She couldn't quite tell what he was saying to her with his look. "My wife is quite complimentary, and quite adamant about her feelings for my writing." His hand was now cradling Amelia's elbow. You must excuse us, I've got an early day tomorrow, and we must be going." With that, Franklin somehow whisked Amelia out the door, and into a waiting cab.

As soon as the door was closed, Amelia started to speak again, "Thank you Franklin. That woman was a terror and a bully, she—"

"Amelia," he had never said her name so sternly before. She was stopped more by his tone than her name coming out of her mouth.

"But I—oh dear, I didn't get to say goodbye to Jon, oh that woman was so –"

"Amelia," he said again with an even more unyielding tone than the first time. He faced straight ahead, and the cab was so poorly lit, that she didn't know what kind of face he was making.

She knew by his tone something was wrong. Silence filled the car like smoke after a candle has blown out. Amelia wanted to say something but didn't know what. She didn't know what just happened or what was wrong.

"Did something happen," she timidly asked, "while you were away from the rest of the party?"

"No, you know what happened," he said, shutting her down.

She waited a few moments, her brain trying to reform how to handle the situation.

"Do you want to talk about—"

"No, Amelia, I don't."

"Franklin, I didn't mean to—"

"Amelia," he said, shifting his head towards her just a little, but still not looking at her, "you have no idea what you've just done."

"Was that woman important, I'm happy to find her and apologize—"

"No," he said trying to stamp out this conversation and he turned his head to look forward again.

A heavy pause happened again. Maybe a change of subject would help. Oftentimes when he was cross she could lighten the mood and then later double back to the situation that made him upset and he would acquiesce and actually discuss the problem.

"I was thinking of having Jon over for dinner this week it was lovely to see him—"

"Amelia," he said, his voice rising.

"Franklin, I'm so sorry if I offended your patron. I really didn't mean to cost you anything. I—"

"It wasn't that. It was what you said about me writing things better than swashbuckling stories." He paused and clasped his hands together. "That hurt me."

"Franklin, I can't believe that is what you're getting from all of this, but it wasn't what I meant. I just meant that I think you're so talented, and that you're capable of writing well in many genres—"

"Well, maybe I'm just not as well read as you, coming from the future and all."

"Franklin, what does that have to do with anything? You're so talented, I—"

"Amelia, just leave it." As soon as the cab pulled up in front of the house, he jumped out and dashed into the house, as if to avoid a downpour. Amelia sat stunned in the cab for a few moments. She started to get out, and then realized that maybe they both needed a moment.

"Driver, would you mind driving around the park?" Amelia shut the door and the cab rolled away.

***

Something was off for a week and it festered. She didn't know what it was and it took her a few days to work through it. At first she was upset at herself that she had said the wrong thing and offended him. Then she was incredibly upset that he had made her feel terrible about stating her opinion. Why did it hurt so much, this seemingly insignificant infraction? She was supporting him, and he took it as an insult. Why? Why did it matter? Why did it hurt? What was the real reason?

Amelia was once again asking her reflection when it came to her. Could she really ask him for it? She would have to put everything she was on the line. She would have to open up and lay everything she was on the table, open up her heart and lay it all out—which was terrifying—what if she couldn't handle him throwing it back in her face? What if he said no. What if he took back everything, including that he loved her? She had turned her back on her past and future, because she loved him so deeply. What if he wouldn't do the same for her. Where would that leave her? There was a lack of trust between them. She sat in a stunned silence, staring at herself in the mirror. She jumped when she felt his hand on her shoulder.

"My dear, are you alright?"

She looked into the mirror and up into his concerned eyes. Shaking it off, and forcing a smile, she replied, "Yes, just deep in thought."

"I can see that. Emily was worried and sent me up to get you. She said you weren't moving. She said she had been talking to you for fifteen minutes trying to get you to come down for dinner."

"I didn't even hear her. I—" Amelia abruptly turned in her chair to face him. A frown crossed her brow; "You do love me, right?"

Franklin chuckled and knelt down beside her, putting a reassuring hand on her cheek. "Of course darling. I love you. I love you so much."

She sighed and leaned into his palm as she closed her eyes. Maybe everything would be alright... she just had to have the courage to tell him.

***

Although Franklin tried to make conversation, Amelia was so distracted, and failed to join in. She didn't realize dinner was over until she heard the scrape of his chair as he stood up.

"My love, you're so far away." He crossed to her. "Why don't we go take a walk? The night is lovely, and with the fresh snow, it will be a brisk breath of fresh air. It will help clear your head."

"Yes…" Amelia replied distractedly.

They were bundled up and walking together, arm in arm. The paths had been shoveled by someone earlier in the day, but the pavement was dewy with the moisture from the snow. Strolling in silence, Franklin was worried about Amelia. She was never this quiet, but he didn't say anything. They had been walking like this for half an hour when Amelia abruptly stopped.

"I wish…" she paused, feeling overwhelmingly self-conscious. She looked up into her eyes and felt the terror of completely revealing herself, and not knowing if he would catch her. "Never mind. It's… selfish."

As she started to walk away, he stopped her with his voice, "What is it? Tell me."

Amelia stopped in her tracks. It felt like her breath stopped in her chest, too. Even though she was deathly afraid, she turned back to him and willed herself to look into his eyes. "I wish… I wish you would trust me."

"I—"

"I can feel that you don't. Just because you've let me in further than you've let a lot of other people, doesn't mean you trust me. There is a lot you have locked away that you don't share, because you don't trust me. I don't know what to do with that—because from the first day we met, you demanded I trust you. I was scared, and I was confused. I was afraid to trust you, but you convinced me that it would be ok."

"I know—"

"Please, let me finish," she demanded. She took a deep breath to help regain strength, and tried to will the tears that were forming at the corners of her eyes to stay put. If they gave her away, she had no chance at getting out what she needed to say—and she needed to say this more than she needed to breathe at this moment. "I need you to trust me because… I need to know I can be trusted by someone I love deeply. I need to know that I have the ability to take care of you as much as you've taken care of me. I've convinced myself I am broken and undeserving, and I don't know if, given the chance, if I can handle being trusted by someone I love so deeply. I really don't know if I deserve to be trusted, because you tell me you won't. You love me. I know you do. You have told me, and I believe you. I love you and I will fight for you, but if you don't let me in, I feel helpless and continue to feel like I deserve nothing you're giving me. It is incredibly selfish. But if you can't trust me, what am I doing here?"

"I—"

Silence fell between them. They were only a few feet apart, but it was a rift that seemed to get wider and deeper every second that passed. She looked down at her feet, but could feel him looking at her, trying to figure out what to say. His loss for words, and his inability to give her what

419

she wanted pulled her farther and farther away, until the force was so great, that it made her body need to move — so she started walking in the opposite direction. She didn't care if he followed her. In fact, she hoped he wouldn't. This was one of those moments where both people threw their hearts out on the table, and tried to figure which is more important: self-preservation, or sacrifice. Which is better for their souls in the long run: to give up their individual pains for the other to see, even though the dark, disgusting, and even horrific secrets we all hold in the bottom of our hearts might scare the other away for good?

Amelia let herself in the front door. She trudged up the steps, feeling so heavy that she didn't even know how she reached her room. Closing the door behind her, she flipped the lock, something she'd never done. Her back to the door, she slid down to the floor.

The most frightening thing of all was that she knew exactly how Franklin felt in these lowest of the low moments. Amelia was there now. She had not locked the door to keep anyone out. No. She did it to protect everyone else from herself.

Chapter Sixty-Four

Silence between Amelia and Franklin pulsed for days. Both would show up for meals, but neither spoke. There was nothing to say. Neither knew how to move forward.

Before, there was always the lingering knowledge that Amelia would have to return. Now that she was here permanently, they both felt stuck.

Daily, Franklin sat in his study trying to capture his thoughts. But he would start to write, thoughts of her distracted him. There was much he kept from her. And not because he didn't trust her. He didn't trust himself.

Surviving on his own before this woman burst into his life out of nowhere. And now this made all of the decisions for him. Franklin wasn't sure he liked feeling out of control. His own brain defied him, throwing him into bouts of sadness. True they were lessened when she was around, and even better now that she had come to stay. However, he couldn't promise either of them that this lessened state of depression would be permanent. It had only been a few months since he even met the woman. He wanted to tell her everything. He wanted to be closer to her. But so many people close to him in his past showed that they couldn't be trusted. His mother, god rest her soul, was so focused on outward appearances that she kept her son who often had tantrums, hidden away. His father hated him for what seemed like the death of his mother, even though he had nothing to do with it. Mrs. Finnegan had said more than once that his father was reminded of his mother when he looked at Franklin. Whether or not this was true didn't matter to Franklin, as his father and he shared an equal level of stubbornness. Even if his father was still living, Franklin would probably do everything in his power to defy the man who needed his son to follow in his footsteps, all the while doubting every step. It's hard to believe in yourself when it seems as if no one else does.

***

Amelia felt right about her decisions to end the relationship with Jack and to return to Franklin. Amelia loved Franklin; she would give her life for him—in a way, she had. She didn't understand why he wouldn't just open up to her. Everyone she had ever come close with opened up and shared almost too much. And Franklin had, at first. But looking back she saw it wasn't trust, but instead she was a crutch to get him through a rough patch in his life. If they were really going to be something together, he had to give her something. She had to have his reassurance that all of this wasn't for naught.

Even though she was convinced she was never returning to her time, she still wore the watch every day. The days were cooler now than it was when she first arrived, and the long sleeves she wore daily now hid her wrists. However, when she would reach something it would wink at her from just above her hand. It was a reminder that she could change her fate, if she wanted.

***

The days marched on. Both hoped the other would speak first. Hoping that the other would come up with a solution or a salve to heal this rift between them. It didn't come. It seemed like the words Amelia spoke in the park all those nights ago froze both of them in time and space. Time is supposed to heal all wounds, but this one wasn't healing. The first night Franklin didn't show up for dinner didn't unnerve Amelia. After two weeks of silence between them, she gave a sigh of relief when he didn't dine with her. She had sat for a few minutes, and then got up and paced for a few while waiting for him to show up. It wasn't like him to be more than a few minutes late for dinner, but when the clock in the hall chimed the half hour, Amelia was resigned. Emily scuttled in as if on cue, and asked, "Missus, would you like me to go ahead and serve."

As if driven into a trance by her own pacing Amelia replied like a robot, "Yes, that would be just fine Emily. It appears as if Franklin isn't joining me tonight."

At the end of the meal she stood to leave before dessert and without waiting for Emily to check on her. Feeling exhausted, she retired to her room, and readied for bed by herself. Although she couldn't sleep, she dozed feeling the obnoxious sensation of being awake, while not really awake. Aware of her surroundings, but knowing that time is ticking away at a snail's pace. It was because of this state that she heard her door open, and saw the light, even though she was faced away from the door. It wasn't meant to be audible, but she heard Franklin sigh, and then a few moments later the door closed, dousing light from the room.

The next night, Franklin failed to appear at dinner again. Nor the night after. Amelia had dined by herself for a week straight. On the eighth night, she came down to the dining room to find nothing set. She called for Emily, and waited. No one came. Amelia smelled dinner, so people were here. She looked at her wrist, thinking she might have been off and checked the time—no, it was 7pm. Amelia walked to the kitchen and carefully poked her head in. Lovely smelling steam filled the air. The kitchen was somewhat clean, as Mrs. Finnegan always tidied up the kitchen before plating the food. Clean plates were set on the counter, awaiting food to be put on them and Mrs. Finnegan and Emily were at the kitchen table. Mrs.

Finnegan was absorbed in a book and Emily was playing some version of solitaire.

"Good evening, ladies," Amelia said with authority. "Is there some delay with dinner?"

Emily froze in her game, and looked from Amelia back to Mrs. Finnegan with a terrified look on her face. Mrs. Finnegan gave a very small, but very stern look across the top of her book at Emily, who sighed and went back to her cards.

"No, no delay with dinner. Just a problem of where to serve it. Ya see, I think that you and Franklin need to work out your differences before you deserve dinner."

"Deserve dinner? Why I—"

"Don't be raisin' your voice to me, missus. You might be the lady of the house, but we all know I'm in charge," Mrs. Finnegan looked up over her book at Amelia as to put a very distinct period at the end of that sentence.

Taking a deep breath, Amelia braced herself for a tongue lashing.

"And what would I need to do to... deserve my dinner?"

"You canna have a marriage if you both walk like ghosts through this house. Bumpin' into each other and wantin' the other to admit they're wrong. What is that book you love so much that the two love each other, but they keep makin' all t' wrong mistakes and condemn each other to a prison of their love—"

"*Wuthering Heights*," Emily chirped up helpfully, looking up from her cards, but quickly regaining her pretend interest in the ten of hearts as both Amelia and Mrs. Finnegan darted her a look.

"But Heathcliff and Catherine lived under different circumstances, they—"

"Oh and did they now? I only read the book once. Thought it was complete shite." She stood up and slammed her book down on the table, scattering Emily's cards. "If two people love each other, they need to say it to each other. Every day." Mrs. Finnegan crossed the room to the door, and took her coat off the hook and started to put it on. "They need to shake each other out of the idiocy and the pride and pain of their pasts." She crossed the room toward Amelia with the vehemence of a hurricane wind. "You two have sacrificed a lot for each other. You need to stand up, admit it, swallow your pain, and move on together." Mrs. Finnegan, anger rising, moved back toward the door, "A relationship takes work—"

"But I—"

Mrs. Finnegan turned back toward Amelia's interruption, "No, ya haven't." She stood stoically in the center of the kitchen, facing Amelia. "Ya might have started the first battle, but this is a long war. You need to think about that. You chose this life, but did you consider all of the casualties? Did you consider that you'll have to keep fighting? You've run home twice, which I won't call cowardice, but I wouldn't call it brave, either. You cut a man who has known little love, off from the love he feels for you. Twice. Of course he isn't going to be forthcoming. He is a man, which makes him stubborn. He is sick, which makes it even harder. You are the woman. You figure it out."

Mrs. Finnegan grabbed another coat from the hook and handed it over to Emily, who had successfully willed herself to disappear while she was standing in the room. Amelia only noticed her again as she took a few timid steps toward her outstretched coat.

Amelia, entranced by Mrs. Finnegan's scolding, stirred slightly when she felt the light pressure of two hands on her inner elbows and a light kiss on her cheek.

"She means it, missus. We won't be back for a few days, partially because of Christmas, and partially because you two need to work things out. I wish you the best of luck."

Amelia heard the sharp closing of the door and felt a gust of cold, signaling that she and Franklin were the only ones in the house.

Searching for other means of action, the only one that made sense was to make herself a plate of food. Amelia set her plate down on the kitchen table, on top of Emily's unfinished card game. She stared at the food for a while and then back into the empty kitchen. Amelia didn't know what to do. Mrs. Finnegan's book caught her eye, she reached over her food that was now cold, and picked up the book *Alice's Adventures in Wonderland*.

Amelia sat there and thought about the rabbit hole she had fallen through, and how it felt like she had just been sentenced to beheading by the Red Queen's sister, Mrs. Finnegan.

***

After nibbling on the crackers and cheese she found, Amelia cleaned up the kitchen and went to bed. Cleaning made her feel slightly in control. It was a nice feeling, as it seemed, like Alice, she had been falling endlessly. Amelia floated in and out of sleep. Lewis Carroll images filled her head. Mostly the dreams were Alice following the White Rabbit, who kept looking at his watch, that looked a lot like the one Amelia had, and shaking his head at how late he was. As the morning sunlight pushed its way through her curtains, Amelia lay in bed pondering the significance of the White Rabbit, and his concern with time. Her thoughts moved on to Alice. A girl seemingly courageous in every situation that presented itself to her. Alice didn't take no for an answer.

Feeling inspired by that fictional girl, Amelia got up and put on a light blue dress. She wouldn't stand for this silence anymore. If she were going to live here, she would fight for it. Even if Franklin and she would disagree, and probably argue, she wasn't going to just sit by and wait. After all, an argument is better than unending silence. No solutions can come from silence.

She went down to the kitchen and poked through the icebox. She created breakfast: some eggs, a pot of coffee, and toast. After setting all of these things, and two cups on a tray, Amelia walked into Franklin's study, emboldened with all the courage she could muster, keeping Alice in the back of her mind. Franklin was not here. Setting down the tray, she wandered over to the bookshelf by his desk. With a cautious look back at the doorway, she turned to his desk. Papers laid in three neat piles. A set of two piles laid on the blotter, one a smaller stack of blank sheets, and next to it a pile of what looked to be written on sheets sat upside down, but revealing ink through the back. She picked up this pile, looking back up at the doorway to double check he wasn't around. She paused to listen, but heard nothing. Afraid to move far, as Amelia didn't want to be caught, she turned the pages, skimming this latest work.

It was a lot of scattered thoughts, and was more like a rambling than anything that could be thought of as work. She sighed. Hearing a creak outside the room, she scurried away from the desk, after replacing the pages she had touched. Amelia took her place beside the table holding the breakfast tray. After a few moments, she picked up the coffee pot, so as if to look like she was nonchalantly pouring coffee for herself, like it was something she did every morning.

Rubbing his face with one hand, and pulling a suspender up over his shoulder with the other, Franklin galumphed through the study door, expecting it to be empty. He stopped when he saw her and his hands dropped to his sides. His heart flipped to see her, as it always did. His face sank as he looked into her eyes then proceeded to walk to his desk. "What are you doing in here," he said more gruffly than he intended as he picked up his last written page from its pile.

"I…" she started timidly, and then corrected her level of courage, "I came to bring you breakfast. It seems our help has left us for the holiday."

"Oh?

Amelia stood with the coffee pot in hand while silence filled the room. Waiting for him to say something. Franklin, not knowing what to say, shuffled papers around on his desk.

She squeezed her eyes together and took a deep breath that sent shivers all over her body. "Franklin, you need to talk to me. Even if it is just fake pleasantries. We need to get back to talking to each other," she looked at him pleadingly.

Looking up to meet her eyes, Franklin sighed, "You're right, of course. Besides, it is Christmas."

"I never cared for the holiday much, actually," she said and set the coffee pot down. She crossed the room and gave him the cup of coffee and sat on the sofa in front of the fireplace. "With my parents gone, there wasn't really anyone to celebrate it with. I hadn't known Jack long enough to celebrate one with him. I had hoped…" her voice trailed off. She hadn't heard him cross the room, but looked up to see him offering her a cup of coffee while holding his own cup in the other hand. She stared at the cup for a moment. Something as simple as being offered a cup of coffee seemed rife with meaning and significance that she couldn't quite comprehend. As he sat next to her on the sofa, she took the cup. They sat, sipping in silence.

"It has never been my favorite holiday either. I don't think I need to mention why. Mrs. Finnegan stopped decorating years ago, because it would throw me into an even bigger dip of melancholia to think about it. I try to glaze over the day, as if it is any other."

"We are a pair, aren't we?" Amelia said, turning her head toward Franklin. "Both desperate to love and trust, but lacking the courage to do so." She stood up. "I'm sorry, I thought I could do this, but I can't." She started to walk out of the room.

"What are you going to do? You can't return for another two months."

Amelia looked back at him with a glare, "I mean I can't talk about Christmas with you while I'm the walking wounded. I'm terrified you'll hurt me again, or worse, you'll leave me to hurt on my own."

"How did I hurt you? You were the one who decided to put yourself into this life. You were the one who came back knowing who and what I am, and you demand me to be more than that—"

"Yes, Franklin," she said as her eyes turned to him. She demanded her tears stay where they were, so they wouldn't give her away. "That is what love *is*. Demanding each other to be better together than we ever were separately." Amelia wanted to say more, but the words wouldn't come. So she walked out the door.

***

431

Sitting on her bed a bit later, she heard a light knock on the door. Even though the tears had dried hours ago, she wiped her cheeks clear of them. "Come in," she said.

"I don't want to keep apologizing to you—"

"Then don't," her voice was filled with contempt.

"How do we move on from this, then?"

"I don't know. I'm here Franklin. I chose to be here, now. With you. We both need to show up each day, do the best we can and then talk things out when we can't. I don't understand what brought me into your life, but I'm meant to be here. I wish I could change all that I am in order to understand you better, or to make you trust me. I wish I could make you realize I'm here to stay."

"You say that, but I can't be sure of that. You've left me twice."

"Because I had to. If the situation was reversed, you would have done the same. I had to be responsible for my own life. Just as you now have to be responsible for yours."

"I don't think I understand your definition of responsible," he said in a confused and sheepish way.

"Why are you so infuriating?" she said as she stood up and started to pace the room. "I need you to just be you. Not what you think I want to see or be. Just you. We need to figure out how to live beyond just our attraction to each other. We need to survive through your bouts of depression and tumultuous creativity; we need to figure out these highs and lows and how we can fit me into them. There is no way for you to be better if you don't let me in."

432

"But what if you go away again?"

"How can I prove to you that I don't intend to leave you? Ever."

"Stop wearing the watch," he blurted. "Why do you wear it everyday?"

"The watch? I—" she stopped. She was going to lie to both of them and say that it was just a comfort or so she could tell the time. But they both knew it reminded her that she always had a choice.

"You see, you've not truly decided that you're staying. How can I trust you if you can't even commit to yourself that you're here for good?"

"Will it make it better, Franklin? If I take off the watch, will you be more comfortable?"

"Yes," he said, without a moment of hesitation.

"Fine. I won't wear it. But my telling you that I'm not going should be enough. Here." She held out the watch to him. "Do you want to keep it with you so you'll know I'm not going anywhere? Lock it up or hide it away so you can prove to yourself I won't leave?"

"I—"

"Make the decision Franklin. You can hold onto it. But I'm not going anywhere."

Her hand that held the watch was still extended to him. They stared across the room at each other. His face gave away nothing. He wanted to trust her. He really did. The love he felt for her was so great, but he was terrified. Not knowing what to say, he backed out of the room.

Watching his retreat, Amelia felt anger and sadness. She wanted to throw the watch after him. She wanted to run after him and shake this nonsense out of him. But more than anything she wanted him to be strong and to say to her that he needed her and couldn't live without her. Amelia knew he had said that to her once, but she wasn't sure if he would ever say it again. She hated how much she needed to hear it.

***

The next day, she opened her bedroom door and found a small wrapped dark blue package that was tied with a black satin bow sitting on the floor. Amelia looked down the hall to see if Franklin was there. Not seeing him she held the package to her chest and went downstairs. She walked into the dining room to see him sitting there, with a cold breakfast set out. Franklin must have set it all up as there were still no signs of Emily. He hadn't started eating but was instead deep in reading handwritten pages he brought to the table. Silently she slipped into her chair and reached for the coffee pot, placing his gift on the corner of the table, between them.

Setting the pages down, he looked at the box and then to her, "Good morning and Merry Christmas, darling. Are you not going to open your Christmas present?"

"Is that what it is? Are you sure its not an 'I'm sorry' present?"

"Well, it might be that as well," his eyes crinkled as he grinned. Leaning forward, he continued, "but either way, you're not the least bit curious?"

Smiling, she turned to meet his eyes. "I am, actually. But this doesn't mean that everything is smoothed over."

"Fine. Instead, think of it as that I'm trying to get back on track."

Nodding, she reached for the box, and tugged on the ribbon. She opened the top and revealed a beautiful set of ruby earrings. They twinkled with passion. She immediately put them on.

"I take it that you like them?"

"Yes, they are stunning," and in one motion she stood up and was behind him, hugging his neck and kissing his lips. "Your mother had exquisite taste."

"Oh, these weren't my mothers. I bought these for you a while ago."

"They're stunning," Amelia said breathlessly as she sat back down. She looked at Franklin. Maybe this could work between them, she thought. Her heart was tethered to his now. This was the life she had chosen to live. She would wake up every day and fight for him. Amelia was once again happy, but in the back of her mind she wondered how long it would last.

Chapter Sixty-Five

January, a bleak month, passed without much excitement. They celebrated the New Year together with a glass of wine at midnight, and he spent the night in her room. They talked about plans for the future, as new couples do at the turn of the New Year. He talked about book plots he was contemplating. She talked about redecorating rooms in the house. They talked of children and as they stared into each other's eyes, this terrified couple from two very different upbringings, swore silently to each other that it would be an amazing adventure to raise children.

Amelia ordered new spring dresses from Jon in the second week of the month. Neither Amelia nor Franklin really cared to go to any social gatherings after the last debacle, so they never accepted invitations. With the snowfall being higher than normal this winter, they weren't able to get out much, anyway.

Occasionally, Jon and sometimes The Stokes' would join them for dinner. But they liked their quiet life.

It didn't last. In mid January, Franklin fell into terrible bouts of melancholia. He would disappear for days in his room. At first she could snap him out of it, and he would have a few good days. Amelia would stomp in and haul him out followed by beastly arguments. Sometimes he would lash out viciously at her while she stood there and listened, walking out when he was done. Sometimes she would list all the reasons he had to live. Luckily, it seemed to only plagued his days, and during the nights he would return to sanity. By February it was only bad days. They called the doctor February 8th, who after thorough analysis gave Franklin new prescriptions. Switching the medication made Franklin even more unbearable for a week, and they called the doctor again. After a few days of an even newer medication, Franklin went into a tantrum of epic proportions. He continued to be angry for two days, screaming and yelling, nonstop. Writing had ceased. He was a crazed man, and it seemed like there was nothing that anyone could do, not even Amelia.

"I don't understand why you're even trying, I'm not worth it. We're all going to die, and it won't matter anyway," Franklin wailed at her in the foyer, as she had just come in from a walk, to escape his last bout of anger.

"Franklin, what are you—"

"I DON'T KNOW WHY YOU EVEN TRY!" He stood there as if willing a fight to start up again between them.

Starting to brush past him to put away her coat, she sighed a deep sigh and he grabbed her arm. "Ow, Franklin, you're hurting me. Let go. Let me take my coat off at least."

"Is it that I'm not worth trying for? Am I too much to handle? Is my work not good enough?" She had shaken him off and hung up her coat. He continued to shout irrationally. "Do you just stay here because you have to? Because you pity me? Is Jack a better man?"

This was the first time in months that either of them had spoken his name. Amelia stopped.

"Why would you bring up Jack? I chose you. I'm here. I have *been* here. I chose you. I said goodbye to Jack months before I came back. Even if I did go back—I'm not saying I am—even if I did, Jack wouldn't be a part of my life."

"Maybe he should be," Franklin said and walked off.

Amelia leaned back on the solid wall and put her fists to her forehead, rubbing the pain of the ongoing headache she had for a month.

She didn't know what to do and was at her wits end. Amelia didn't know if she wanted to scream or cry or hit something. She felt stuck, hopeless. Not one to back down from a fight, Amelia stomped into Franklin' office.

The next few hours they yelled and screamed with no resolution. Amelia was exhausted. Neither of them had been sleeping. Neither of them was fighting fair.

Finally, in the middle of one of Franklin's endless self-deprecating rants, she mumbled, "Maybe I should go home."

He stopped a few words later, "What did you say?"

She looked up at him. She thought her words were inaudible.

"I—"

"No. Say it."

"Franklin, it was—"

"Say IT."

"Franklin—"

"SAY IT. *SAY IT,*"

Looking him straight in the eyes, she took a deep audible breath and repeated, "Maybe I should go home."

"I *knew it!* I knew you would leave me. At the first moment things got difficult—"

"At the first *moment*?!? Franklin, you've been intolerable for a month. You said you would try to get better, but I've not seen it. I've been more than reasonable, continually trying to seek out the good in you and bring you back to the living, only to be berated again, and more, and bigger. I love you so much, but there is only so much I can take."

For the first time in what seemed like days, Franklin was at a loss for words. The silence roared in her ears to torment her, provoking her to say everything she had been holding back.

"If you're just going to sit there bemoaning your fate and dragging me into your negativity, then one of us is a

439

fool. I refuse to let it be me," interjected Amelia into the silence that had filled Franklin's study. She stood up and started to leave. At the doorway she turned back hoping he would stand, race over to her, or say something to stop her from leaving the room, but instead he just stared at her empty chair. She left the room, feeling everything inside of her break. She loved him so much, but if he didn't love himself, how was she to continue to love him for the both of them? It wasn't possible. She now knew where she belonged and it was not here. She felt like she couldn't breathe and she needed to leave as soon as possible. But where was she to go? She stopped dead in her tracks in the hall. What day was today?

Her thoughts cleared from the interaction that had just occurred the more steps she took away from the door. Today was the 28th. As early as 12:01 she could leave, and the clock in the hall had struck 9 pm just moments ago. Maybe she should just collect her things and get out of the house—but would the watch work anywhere? Amelia wasn't sure. She would just stay in her room for the next three hours.

All she wanted was Franklin to fight for her, to come after her, but she knew he wouldn't now. But would he ever? How long would she have to wait? Tears started to fall down her cheeks—men have crossed oceans and deserts and war torn countries to gain what Franklin could have had by taking only a few steps toward her. Though she had *crossed time* for him, *he* was not willing to cross a room. She kept hoping that something would free him from the mental cage he stayed in. But he could not, would not. He did not understand or comprehend the torment he insisted on putting on them both through.

Amelia walked through her bedroom door and slammed it behind her.

***

Emily had already drawn the curtains and the fire and had turned down the bed. Good. Amelia would not be disturbed. The need to breathe fell heavy on her chest. Amelia knew she would only be able to breathe deeply back in her own time.

After removing her jacket, she locked her door, and sat down at her desk to the underscoring of her rustling petticoats. On a blank sheet of paper she wrote the words:

Dear Franklin,

Those words were written with ink that felt like it poured from her broken heart. To write more would be infinitely painful.

A quarter of an hour went by as she stared at the fresh white rectangle laying before her. Amelia had many things to say, but her hand stood motionless. Perhaps it was because the sensible limb knew it was futile. Perhaps it was because she changed history already and didn't want to leave another mark. Perhaps it was because she lacked the courage to actually say good-bye to the man who possessed her soul, and thereby closing the door to him forever.

The clock in the hall struck eleven o'clock. Writing a few short sentences, all that she felt she could, Amelia signed the note with –A and sighed a deep breath that ended in a choked sob. She folded it once, and wrote his name on the front. No need to seal it, everyone would know soon enough.

As the clock struck the half hour, she walked to the fireplace, letter in hand, and watched the red and yellow flames dance around their blackened home. Amelia set the note on the mantle. Emily would be sure to see it there when she came in the morning. She would make sure Franklin would receive it first thing. Amelia felt a chill pour over her even though the blaze should have been more than enough to keep her warm, but she did not move to get her jacket.

The quarter hour chimed.

It was amazing to Amelia how much these past few months were spent maneuvering her way around time, falling through it, or trying to stop it. And here she was now, actually willing time to speed up.

Just as Amelia felt an amused chuckle rising up, the clock in the hall struck midnight. The first of March. She second guessed her choice. Did she really want to leave this all behind? To leave Franklin and her heart? Amelia berated herself for giving her heart and her life away because she had succumbed to thinking that Franklin *actually* loved her.

"Well, time to get on with it," Amelia thought out loud. "Time, tide, and trolley wait for no one. But time waited for me," she mused.

Amelia banished the jovial thought. She had to focus and be precise if she was really going to do this. Otherwise, she would continually wonder and seek answers. Amelia would be like Alice down her rabbit hole, with only more confusion at every turn. From a man like Franklin, there are no answers, only more questions.

With a deep breath, and the thought of Alice's crazed Wonderland in her mind, Amelia started to wind the watch. She wound quickly through the first twenty hours—this had become such the habit, that Amelia now knew the feel of the watch and could actually start to feel the gentle pull around hour twenty-two. She slowed her winding and unclasped the watch from her wrist.

As Amelia wound the watch through the twenty-third hour, she thought she heard footsteps, but knew it was only her imagination. She continued winding. Amelia paused for a moment as she thought she heard her name and a gentle knock on her door. A jiggling of the doorknob followed, and jangling keys started actually sounding real to her—but Amelia knew it wasn't real. Franklin was resolute earlier, and if he didn't budge then, he wouldn't now.

Winding past the number 9 on the dial for the last time, Amelia moved her hand to make the final turn of the pin. The key in the lock clicked. She made a twist of her wrist giving the final move to the little hand.   The date on the watch changed.

Her door flew open and Franklin threw himself through. Amelia looked up and her eyes met his.   He had come to her.   Amelia's eyes welled with tears and she opened her mouth to speak.   In the same moment, she dropped the watch from her fingers and vanished.

Chapter Sixty-Six

What had he done? Franklin stood helpless in Amelia's room watching her disappear. His heart felt as if it had been ripped from his chest and disappeared with her. Unmoving, he contemplated how he could have been such an ass. Why had he waited? He had just sat in his study for hours after she walked out, feeling rejected by the one woman — no, the one *person* who understood him completely. More than he understood himself.

Amelia always asked thoughtful questions. She would smile and chuckle when he bemoaned something serious, *always* an irritation in the moment but it was a deeper knowing. Later when he replayed those conversations, he knew she was trying to lighten his mood, to make him better

Tonight was different. Franklin didn't understand what she meant by "only one of them was going to be a fool…" He had pondered that sentiment, that phrase, for what seemed moments, but was hours he sat in his study.   It echoed over and over in his mind.

"Only one of us is going to be a fool and I no longer allow it to be me," she had remarked.

What could she—no. She was in love with him, this he knew. "One can never tell with women, especially me," he said aloud to the empty room.

A clock chimed in the study, ripping him from his thoughts. Amelia had chosen Franklin, and he rewarded her choice by discarding her like an unwanted blanket.   *Oh, God.* The clock chimed again. It was midnight. February 28th. She was going back.

He had to stop her.   He had to tell her he failed her. Franklin shot out of his seat like a racehorse out of the gate, unable to move fast enough. The house suddenly felt like it was at least waist deep in water and his legs could not make their way through. Damn! Why was Amelia's room so far off in the house? Up the stairs he flew. Past his room and down the long corridor to her hallway.

Amelia was a sensible girl, he thought while running. No. She was a sensible woman, with her hair as it fell in pieces out of its chignon, a piece on her neck always naturally curled when the rest of her hair was straight. The curve of her breast, how it fit into his hand so perfectly. And the crinkle in her eyes and bridge of her nose just after she tormented him. She was a breath of fresh air, reminding him life was worth living.   Franklin vowed he would try harder if he could only see her face one last time.

As he reached her door he yelled out, "Amelia!" She was a sensible woman. She would not be so impetuous as to leave on the stroke of midnight, he tried to reassure himself. He *knew* he had a chance. He knocked before trying the knob—he could just enter—she had told him that he was allowed—but she was most likely cross, and more likely to throw something at his head. Franklin attempted civility first. When he got no answer he tried the knob. It didn't move. Locked. Crying with terror through the door, "Amelia!" He received no answer. Franklin started to feel the panic rise, it overtook his reasoning. He pulled out a key and thrust it into the lock. As he opened the door he saw her in front of the fireplace, looking at her hands. Franklin called out her name one more time. Amelia looked up at him with equal parts surprise and regret. With her gaze still boring into him, she dropped the thing in her hands and vanished.

Terrified, Franklin leapt across the room in what felt like one gigantic step. Feeling around for her, like a man in the dark, he tried to find her as if she was invisible and not gone. He watched her do this other times. Franklin knew Amelia was gone.

As he stopped trying to grasp she was no longer there, Franklin stepped back and felt something under his shoe. He started to kick it out of his way when he saw the glimmer of silver on the floor. Bending to pick it up, half way down he stopped. The watch. His heart broke knowing she was never coming back to him.

Franklin left the thing where it lay, and backed away as if it were tainted with contagious disease. He turned to the fireplace and saw a folded paper sitting like a tent on the mantle with his name on it. He gently picked it up and rubbed his left index finger over his name written in her delicate handwriting, as if he could feel her fingers in his one more time by doing so. He unfolded it gently.

Dear Franklin,

Although I love you with all of my heart, I fear its not enough love to make you a whole person. The only solution for either of us to survive is for me to go. I leave two things here tonight: my heart because from the first moment I met you, it belonged to you; and the watch, so I cannot return to reclaim it.

—A

The letters were smudged from her tears. Franklin crumpled the paper and raised his arm to toss it into the fire. He stopped just before letting go. No, he thought, keep it as a reminder of her. With determination he stared into the fire. He wanted answers but he knew he wouldn't get them and he didn't deserve them. With an angry sigh Franklin left her room, with the intention to never return to it.

Part Five

March first and beyond

Chapter Sixty-Seven

As Amelia vanished from a fire lit room, with Franklin rushing toward her, she hadn't realized that she had closed her eyes.

Upon opening them, she found herself in a dark, cold room. In her time. Alone. Unable to bear her own weight any longer, she sank to her knees, just as tears she had been holding back, unrelentingly burst from her eyes.

She cried herself to sleep and woke up the next morning on the floor, sore and stiff all over. Amelia thought over and over, "I made the choice to return here. Crying won't turn back the clock."

Purposely, she had dropped the watch so she would not second-guess her choice and run back in a few months time. Peeling herself up off the floor she went to her wardrobe, grabbed clothes, and went to shower and rinse off the dirt, tears, and the past. The hot running water didn't replace the emptiness, which seemed to spread around her chest like a black hole.

Afterwards, Amelia wandered the house in a daze. She walked downstairs, and found herself on the sofa in the front room, but didn't remember sitting. Overwhelmed with grief she crawled into a tiny ball and wrapped herself in a blanket. Tears couldn't be halted. She lay on the sofa feeling every explosion of her sorrow.

The tears and sobs finally stopped, but she could not move from the sofa. She felt if she moved, everything would fall apart and Amelia did not have the strength to witness nor try to piece together a broken world.

Amelia lay there trying to push the thoughts and questions from her mind. All of the feelings she had were so overwhelming. She lay there trying to tune them out. Ignoring them, because she didn't want to think. They were thoughts and questions that she didn't have answers to. Feelings never had answers—they only begat more feelings.

Instead, she tried reasoning with herself although she felt at the moment she was insane to do so, but tried it anyway, failingly. Amelia tried comforting herself with the thought that all along she knew it probably was going to fail. They were too different, she was the one trying to adapt herself to him, but he was not receptive to her changes. Voices of matronly figures crossed through her brain at this moment saying nuggets of unwanted information like: never change yourself for a man, it won't work. "*I know*," Amelia thought out loud in hopes those voices would dissipate, or at least not judge her so harshly.

She tried to piece together all the good things if they were good moments or if she just projected goodness onto them? There were moments when Franklin looked at her that she could swear that he felt something. Moments where he wouldn't stop looking or touching her and she felt like she would burn up with passion for him in return. Were those moments just in her imagination? It all felt like one big dream at the moment, but she knew she hadn't dreamt it all. Some of it was real. Wasn't it?

Trying hard to think in the other direction, Amelia recalled all of the negative or bad moments, or even just the mundane. Yes, it was great to sit and read all day long, but life had so much more in store for her. And those moments that seemed like days when he wouldn't speak to her— because he was so locked in his head by his demons–were agony. She might have stumbled onto his world, but once she knew her true feelings, she threw herself into his life. As much as he would allow, anyway. Franklin was always so guarded, so she never knew how much feeling was actually there or how deep she was falling for him.

And then there was the sex. It was passionate and fulfilling, but the last few times, he would leave her bed right after. He did this to punish himself as well as punish her. She would relinquish the sex for just a touch from him. His touches became less and less as if he had some contagious disease which she could contract through his touch. She would see it in his eyes, he would go to touch her and stop suddenly. He wanted to but he was just not capable. Amelia truly did not understand the man, she admitted to herself.

These thoughts went round and round in her head. She watched the light outside, signifying this awful day was passing. After a while, her thoughts quieted to almost nothing. There were only so many memories, and only so many times she could rake through them. Her brain was tired. The house was silent. Her body started to relax and unclench and she allowed her muscles to stretch as if trusting that they wouldn't leave her in the moment that she needed them most, when everything seemed to be failing her. In this moment where she needed solace and strength her body could give her for her unfixable actions.

Quietly it crept up, as if it had been waiting for the exact perfect moment to arrive. The thought was very matter of fact and although it was a little emotional in a good and bad way. *She would never see him again.* By leaving the watch she had cut off all means of communication and travel. She was horrified by the thought but quickly comforted by this next thought: she had made the right choice. Amelia would never again look in his eyes, or feel his lips on hers—both things she would treasure and remember forever—but in leaving the watch, she clipped the only tie that would have allowed more. She had done the right thing, she told herself. She had done the right thing. This thought drifted through her mind, and she drifted off to sleep on the sofa, as she didn't have the energy to remove herself back to her bedroom. Amelia kept forcing herself to repeat over and over in her mind: I have done the right thing

***

The first few days in 2013 were challenging for Amelia. She threw herself into trying to boost her interior design business by taking meetings, and networking to make the memory of Franklin disappear. To her chagrin, she would walk into a room, the light would hit a wall just so, or she heard a floorboard creak and thought it might be Franklin coming down the hallway.

There were so many wonderful things about Franklin—she wondered if she had done the right thing. *That* is why she had decided to leave the watch, she reminded herself, so this inevitable post-mortem questioning would not lead her back to a future in the past.

It was hard enough being in a relationship in one's own time where she knew the rules and protocols. It was even more difficult to live in a different time—a time where women had completely different rules then men, and equality was observed differently in each individual home. With Franklin and his emotional instability, his feelings on the subject of equality and women's rights seemed to waver. In those final weeks it seemed as though his views might be shifting to a typical Victorian man that viewed her more as a possession than a person. No matter how progressive he had seemed to be, and how much freedom he had originally offered, Franklin didn't see her as an equal. Yes, Amelia thought, keep these memories coming. They would help her from receding into the thoughts of only the good times, and keep her from crying.

However, just as soon as she would acknowledge a negative, Amelia would rebut herself with a happy memory; a moment—just a glimmer—of Franklin's true nature. A moment that would prove to her that he was a wonderful man. The way he always found her when walking into a room and showed his appreciation that she was occupying space close to him, no matter if they were with or without company; by embracing her with all of himself, or pecking her on the cheek, or as had become a more common occurrence taking her in his strong arms and kissing her fully on the lips with passion.

Amelia had entered the study, his study, today to check the fireplace for loose bricks that might need to be replaced or re-mortared. As she neared the fireplace, she heard Franklin's voice:

"Have you ever been loved?" he asked her, as she remembered a night, not so long ago.

"I..." she hesitated as she hugged herself, giving Franklin the feeling that she hadn't.

"What a tragedy," she heard him reply in what seemed like a teasing and pitying tone.

"Like the Greeks," she replied aloud to the fading memory, returning to the present. She started to chuckle lightly, but then burst into tears, and she ran off to her room and threw herself into the comfort of her bed.

***

After that day, Amelia did her best to stay out of the study. The strongest and most emotional memories seemed to haunt her there. She couldn't bear to have them rear their heads at any time, which would usually result in an outpouring of emotion, generally sadness accompanied by tears.

As each day passed, and the year sojourned on, the days got easier to live, and crying became less of a regular occurrence for Amelia. Each day, it was easier to wake up next to no one. Each night it was less painful to fall asleep on her own, although, mornings she seemed to rebound faster. Amelia found that she could enter more rooms without relating them directly to Franklin, and she stopped hoping she would hear him turn the corner, saying her name.

There were other things, too. Tennis shoes and yoga pants were once again a staple, and it was nice not to have five layers of clothing to climb into daily. Amelia really appreciated not having to climb into a corset each day, although she did miss the comforting feeling of a full torso hug, and the beautiful lines it gave her at fleeting moments in front of a mirror.

The thing was not that she had left him. Not that she was alone. Again. But that he had given her something; taught her something. He told her that she was beautiful and taught her how to make herself feel that about herself. She walked differently. She moved with a loveliness that she didn't even really notice, but others did.

And then he was gone. And so was the feeling. Without him there to remind her that she *was* beautiful, how could she keep it up on her own? Like happiness, the idea of beauty is easier to keep up with a partner or a buddy or just someone else to constantly encourage that feeling. The rug that she felt had been pulled out from under her was, in fact, a description and reminder of her own loveliness.

When she finally realized this she was angry again: angry with him for taking away something which rightfully belonged to her, and angry at herself for relying on him and only him to deliver this needed feeling. She made herself an addict of description of her own beauty. And why? She could tell herself. She had many friends who told her constantly and bolstered her confidence in her looks and her general adeptness at being a woman. She continued the flow of anger and disappointment in the direction of his absence. It was a space shaped in his silhouette; as if someone had taken scissors and just cut him out of the paper of life and moved him somewhere else. She realized, in this moment, that she was not angry at him but, instead constantly angry at herself for not giving herself what she seemed to rely on men for. But it was a lingering thought, a solid one, one that was hard to digest. So she went back to being mad at him, or mad at the space that he used to occupy.

Chapter Sixty-Eight

Her cell rang. Alexia was calling about meeting up for a drink. Amelia didn't want to leave the house because then she would admit she was back in the future. After an hour, Amelia felt guilty and returned the call, saying that she would meet them.

As she showered and dressed, she thought about what story to cover why she had disappeared.

At the wardrobe, she noticed how the pants that were once too tight were now a little big. Stopping at the table in the foyer, she grabbed her purse and heard the familiar jingle of the keys in her bag. She left her house, locked the door, then turned to flag a cab. Amelia didn't realize until much later, she didn't have a single thought about Franklin.

Amelia awoke the next morning, in her bed, no memory of how she got there. What a night. She remembered meeting up with the girls, having a drink or two, and dancing like a rebellious catholic school girl at her first night club. She remembered getting in a cab when she felt tired, but not drunk. She leaned up on one elbow and rubbed her face. Amelia had a thought last night that was evading her, but couldn't recognize it even now. She felt horrible. How was she this hungover.

Suddenly she sat up on the bed, a river of emotions running through her brain, full as the Hudson River after a heavy rain. Thoughts like trash and beautiful sailboats rushed downstream. They were going faster and faster, rushing past. Franklin. The watch. Never to return. And the sex… she didn't understand why she thought of sex with him at this very moment.

Suddenly Amelia felt dizzy and overwrought. She ran to the nearest bathroom and made it to the toilet before throwing up.

No. Amelia picked herself up after dry heaving for a few moments. No. She thought as she looked in the mirror while brushing the disgusting taste out of her mouth. No no no. She pulled the calendar on her phone. This couldn't be right. It couldn't… she had missed her period. She was two weeks late. Amelia was never late. She rushed to the drug store around the corner.

Fifteen minutes later, she was back in her bathroom with four pregnancy tests, all newly used, watching time on her cell. It passed slowly.

Her alarm finally went off.

She looked at the first test. Positive. The second test. Positive. She paused a moment before looking at the third test. Positive. She didn't bother looking at the fourth. Amelia was pregnant. With Franklin's baby.

Chapter Sixty-Nine

Pregnant. Amelia couldn't believe it. She stood stunned staring at her reflection in the bathroom mirror. A million thoughts ran through Amelia's head—the main thought of "this just can't be" seemed to be on continual loop.

As she did her best to block out the terrifying thoughts of diapers and crying and disgusting baby things, Amelia stared her reflection down.

Pieces started to snap together in her head. She had been feeling queasy these past few days, but thought it was the heavy need to leave Franklin. Picking him had been the wrong choice. That she needed to choose herself. What was the quote from his book? She must have read the passage at least twenty times.

"When forced to make the choice between two opposing forces, good or evil, black or white, turn away from either opposing choice given, and instead, choose yourself." When she read it she wondered what made him write it.

Now, Amelia knew that he had written it because of her. But, when?

Amelia shook the thought of Franklin reaching out to her from the past. She needed to move forward. She knew she would thrive better in her future than in his.

She looked up at her own face in the mirror again. How did this happen? "Well, Amelia, she told herself, you know how babies are made." This made her remember the ridiculous conversation her mother tried to have with her in the eighth grade. Throwing out every clichéd phrase to try to start the awkward conversation.

Finally, Amelia, looking up from *Gone With The Wind*, just as Scarlet was about to give birth, as fate would have it, gently said to her mother, "I know what sex is mother. I had health class in sixth grade. I know about condoms and birth control and I have been warned about the things boys will try to do. If you want me to tell you about the anatomy of men's and women's reproductive organs, I can do that, too."

Giving her daughter a look of shock, which turned stern, she sighed and smiled as she crossed the room. Amelia's memory of anything after that was cloudy, but she thought mom sighed and said a quiet "Thank you," into Amelia's hair as she hugged her.

Refocusing back to her reflection, "You were such a little shit," she scolded herself. Her knowing smirk then fell back into a look of terror. *How* would she be able to raise a child by herself? Her mother wasn't here to help to turn a mewling baby into a functioning human being. How would she manage?

She was overcome with tears. She realized how alone she was. W*hy* did she leave the watch in the past? Franklin had abandoned her emotionally but he wouldn't have financially, baby or no. He would have helped her raise the child. *Their* child. NO. She stopped the thought. It wasn't an option to return to the past, so why question it. She had made the choice and now had to focus on the future.

After Amelia pulled herself out of the never ending spiral of thoughts she threw the four pregnancy tests in the trash with a forceful resolution. She walked away then walked back to the can, staring down the evil sticks. She narrowed her eyes then snatched sheets of toilet paper and tossed a few covering the sticks as if to make them disappear.

A week later Amelia returned from her doctor's office with different pamphlets and a confirmation that she was in fact pregnant. Topics of the brochures ranged from the advantages of natural birth, to adoption. She had absently grabbed them. Smiling babies and uteruses kept her company on the train the whole way home. Walking into the kitchen, she sat on one of the barstools beside the island and stared at the one on top. Adoption. She sighed a redolent sigh, stood up, and dropped the adoption brochure in the trash can. She *would* keep this baby. She didn't know how she was going to manage, and this *certainly* was not the way she pictured having a family, but then again she didn't imagine anything of past year to ever have happened.

Traveling to the past. Breaking up with Jack, the perfect man. Inheriting this house.

With thoughts of the inheritance she realized that she needed to call Mr. Banks. She tapped the screen to find his number. The nasal voice of the receptionist who answered brought memories of Amelia's first visit to the law firm. She remembered the woman's sharply bobbed black hair, and her glaring look.

"Amelia Dunne—I mean Epoch—for Mr. Banks, please."

"Yes. He has been expecting your call."

Before Amelia could ask the receptionist why Mr. Banks was expecting to hear from her, the line clicked, and Amelia was expelled into the purgatory of muzak. Mr. Banks broke up the mellow jazz with his warm crackly voice.

"Ah, Ms. Epoch. You have returned from your... trip?"

Amelia sensed that he knew something, but she pushed the thought aside. She needed to discuss her monetary holdings and thereby her future and her baby with Banks, and wasn't going to let the oddness of both the receptionist and the feeling she was getting from Banks and his greeting derail her.

"Yes. Yes, I have."

"Good," Banks jumped in as Amelia was taking the breath to continue with her task. "I need to meet with you about some matters of your inheritance."

"Oh?" Amelia said with a slightly concerned tone.

"Yes. No need to fret dear. Just paperwork. But the sooner you can make it in—"

"I can head to your office now. I should be able to make it there by 3:30."

"Well, it's not that urgent, but let me see... Yes. I have an open afternoon. So today will be fine. I'll have the receptionist add you to my appointments for 3:30."

"Thank you."

"Oh, and Ms. Epoch—"

"No need to fret."

Amelia was taken aback by this from the man with the wispy white hair. She didn't know how to reply, so she ended the call with, "I'll see you soon."

"Good. See you soon."

Amelia grabbed her purse and keys and headed out. Near the subway, her friends popped into her thoughts. She dialed Alexia's office.

"Alexia? I'm home. We need to meet for drinks tonight. Great. See you and Toni at Macaleers at seven."

She tossed the phone into her purse descending the stairs into the subway.

Thirty minutes later, she emerged from underground. She was early, so she stopped at a deli in the building next door to Mr. Banks' office. She ordered a turkey Panini and French fries. Amelia picked at them even though she hadn't eaten all day. She thought of the pamphlets sitting on the kitchen counter, suggesting abstaining from processed foods while pregnant. So many changes to make. It's a good thing she wasn't addicted to lunch meat. Coffee was going to be another thing altogether.

Her mind wandered to Mr. Banks. What did he need to discuss with her? Paperwork he had said. What kind of paperwork? She started to feel panic rise in her stomach. Maybe the money was running out? Maybe it was gone. It wasn't possible. Was it?

Maybe history was altered and Amelia never inherited the money. But then why would her key still work and why would Banks know how he was? Maybe her final actions made Franklin angry and he changed the stipulations. Fear petrified her. He wouldn't do that. Even as livid as he had been he wouldn't have been that vindictive.

A text message from Toni broke her concentration and brought her out of her trance.

Can't wait to see you tonight.—T

Amelia noticed the time stamp on Toni's text was 3:29. She was supposed to be at Banks' office. Throwing away her sandwich she dashed out of the deli.

The line at the security desk was long. The elevator, slow. It was 3:45 before the doors opened to reveal the stern receptionist who watched over the Law Firm of Albert, Smith, Banks, and Banks. The same helmet headed bob greeted her today with a smile. Amelia was ushered into the conference room. After waiting fifteen minutes, the receptionist came back in saying Banks was on a call and asked if Amelia would care for a drink. She disappeared again, only to make Amelia jump again when she returned with her coffee.

What *if* Franklin had canceled her inheritance? She didn't know when he had drafted the inheritance in his timeline. They never talked about it. She only had ever mentioned the law firm when she saw correspondence on Franklin's desk. If he had drawn up the paperwork before she returned this last time, surely he could have amended it or rescinded the paperwork. The question that lurked in Amelia's mind was, did he hate her so much as to hurt her this way?

A clearing throat snapped her out of speculation. Amelia looked up and saw Mr. Banks staring at her across the table.

"What did you say?" Amelia assumed she missed what he said.

Banks chuckled and said, "I said, you're looking well my dear. You have a lovely glow about you. And that is interesting, considering..."

Amelia snapped her head so she was now facing him straight on. She looked at him with a questioning stare. What did he know? He unpacked the same cardboard box as before. There were several envelopes that he had set out on the table. The three large manila envelopes and the small, lumpy standard sized letter stared up at her from their resting places.

"Now, my dear. Shall we begin?"

"I... I guess so. Must close this chapter eventually." Amelia let out a forced laugh as she clasped her hands in front of her and set them on the cold, smooth surface of the conference table. She squared her shoulders. She could certainly survive whatever was about to happen.

Mr. Banks consulted a paper to his right.

"Ah ha," he said, as he glanced from the paper to the table and back again. "Yes," he said, reaching for the small envelope and slid it across the table.

"Mine?" Amelia asked, not moving. Her knuckles had begun to turn white.

"Yes. Nothing to be afraid of dear. Are you feeling ill? Oh dear." Banks rose out of his chair, worried, but stayed on his side of the table. "Should I call Ms. Jones? It's been a long time since I've been around a woman who was with…"

Amelia snapped up her eyes to meet his. What wasn't he saying? A woman who was with—out means? "Who, what?" She said laying her palms flat on the table to calm herself.

She didn't realize that she had set them down on top of the small envelope that he had pushed over to her.

"I… just… it's that you… don't look so well, my dear," Banks sputtered.

Amelia slumped in her chair and let out a great sigh. Absent-mindedly, she picked up the envelope and tore open the corner. Upending the envelope she let its contents fall into her hand. Toying with it for a few moments she looked down into her hand. Blithely, she thought, "Oh, it's just my wedding ring," and slipped it on her finger thinking she must have left it somewhere while washing or helping Mrs. Finnegan or Emily—

Amelia bolted up and looked at her hand. Then she looked at an equally startled Mr. Banks. His shock was more for her health and well-being, but she didn't know that yet. Nor was she concerned with Mr. Banks at all at this moment.

"My ring! He left me my ring?"

"Yes, and with explicit instructions that you weren't to receive it until after the first of March, this year.

"But…how?"

"Well, from what I understand from the very specific instructions that were left, and the paperwork that was drawn up by my grandfather for your… husband…," Banks paused to look at Amelia. She blinked once but didn't deny it so he continued. "The late Mr. Dunne, or should we now call him Frank? As that was his legal name. Anyway, your late husband had amended this paperwork three times. The last time," Banks picked up the single sheet of paper and confirmed it again, lowering his glasses down his nose to see the paper better. After a moment of self-conference, and a few positive hums he continued, "Yes, the last time he had split the inheritance and left this ring," Banks gestured to Amelia's hand, "and this box…." His voice drifted as he dove into the cardboard box on the table. "Ah. Here."

Banks produced a velvet box large enough to hold a small plate. She could see the box was heavy as Banks walked around the table. He sat down in the chair next to hers and held out the box for her. She lifted the lid and gasped. It was the necklace and earrings Franklin had given her. She had not seen them since that night of that dreadful party. As Amelia sat dumbfounded, Banks eased the jewels into her hands. Balancing the box she gently touched the necklace with her finger. None of this felt real, but the stones, the ring, the earrings, they were here, proving the last year happened.

Banks started talking again. She set the box on the table and closed the lid. Banks had set three stacks of paper in front of her and looked expectantly at her.

"I'm sorry, Mr. Banks," Amelia blinked up at him, now on the other side of the table. "Could you please start over?"

"Certainly. This," he pointed to the document that was nearest her left hand, "is the first copy of the will that you saw at our original meeting. This," he motioned to the center page in front of her, "is the addendum he made just before he died."

Amelia felt her breath halt in her chest. "What—," her voice squeaked. She reached out and picked up the cup of coffee, now room temperature, and took a sip. She choked on it, but it wet her dry mouth. She cleared her throat and tried again. "What were the... um... changes from the first copy?"

"Let me explain this third document and then we will come back to the revision. This," Banks leaned forward and placed his fingertips on the table, spread like tree roots, near the third document, "outlines the regulations for the funds dedicated to the education and welfare needs."

"But… I don't intend to go back to school. I've already finished. He knew that. Why would he—?"

"It's not for you."

"Oh?" Amelia's head snapped up to meet Bank's eyes. "Then… who?"

"I do not know how to say this… it is for the unborn child."

Amelia shot up out of her chair with such vehemence the heavy chair rocked, threatening to fall over. Her right thumb absently twirling the recently reclaimed wedding ring. "But how…?!!" She started to feel her legs get wobbly, and Amelia started to sink back in her chair. She repeated Bank's words, "*My* unborn child. How…how did Frank know?"

"That, unfortunately my dear, was not mentioned in any of the paperwork. What is mentioned is that your child will be taken care of. Your husband has seen to that. There is a trust fund for his welfare and schooling for his first twenty-one years. There is an additional college fund, and a trust for him after he graduates college. There is a stipulation that if he doesn't complete college with at least a bachelor's degree that the final trust will be willed to the Brooklyn Public Library."

"But… I…"

"My dear, I realize it is too much to take in. Just know that the child will be taken care of. Oh, and you are legally required by this document to let me know what happens with the child."

Confused, Amelia looked up at him. "What do you mean?"

"I know this day and age women can and do decide if they want to raise the child, give it up for adoption, or... other alternatives. Just so you know, the money will follow the child, whatever your decision. If you so choose to... abort... the money will go directly to the library. All of it. If you choose adoption, the money will be distributed to the adoptive parents. But, of course, if you choose to keep the child, you will oversee the funds."

Standing up just as quickly as before, Amelia said in protest, "I would NOT. Give up. Franklin's child." As she gripped her hands together, her statement sunk in. She wanted the child growing in her stomach. Obviously, so did Franklin. But how *did* he know? This question ruminated in her mind. Maybe this was one of Franklin's odd sixth sense things. Amelia was so overcome by her outburst and the realization of her choice. Banks sat down across the table, and smiled at her as a proud parent would. His arms were crossed over his chest and he sat back in his chair, looking totally at his leisure in this moment.

Feeling like an idiot, Amelia composed herself, pursed her lips, and sat down slowly, hearing her mother's voice in the back of her head to "always remain a lady, even in difficult times." She took a breath. "Alright, so how does the trust for the child change the second document?"

472

"Oh, it doesn't affect it. Neither document affects the other. This new version of the will stipulates that you, Amelia Epoch, received all rights and royalties to the Dunne estate. It is, in fact, more money that you previously thought you had inherited. Technically, the document you first saw was a sort of dummy will, as this version is the latest update, and negates all within that document. But, we were required by the stipulations set out by Mr. Dunne to show you that one, but act by this one.

"Now, to the legalities. Mr. Dunne employed this firm to oversee the estate for the next seventy-five years, which includes both your part of the trust as well as the child's trust. We will help manage the trust for the child until he turns twenty-one. However, if you wish to terminate our services, I can draw up the needed documents—"

"No."

"—and—What was that?"

"No need, Mr. Banks. I think you have a better grasp on my life than I do at this moment. And I think I need you to remain a constant for me." Amelia smiled warmly at him, conveying her need for his legal services and his friendship. "That is, if you don't mind?" her eyes questioned.

"By all means, my dear. We have served your family for years, and we will be happy to assist you as long as you need us."

"Wonderful." Letting out a sigh Amelia continued, "So, what does that mean? The last part about inheriting all of the Dunne estate. Do my payments change? And what about the welfare trust for the baby? How do I make sure the purchases I make are only for the baby? How am I going to do all of this?"

"Well, dear. I will help you as much as I can. There are details that will be up to you, of course, but I can help somewhat. I have been overseeing the home improvement trust and I can tell you that because you are continually under budget on your projects, you are good at managing money. As the overseer for the child's trust, I can tell you that if you choose to keep the child—"

"Like I said, I am keeping the baby," Amelia said matter-of-factly, this time, with very little emotion. Almost as if she were simply stating her own name.

"Yes. Well you will practically have full use of the money. I will come in and audit your bank records from time to time, but as you have your own trust, I'm sure you will use the child's money wisely and well."

The whole day was an out of body experience. Was this all really happening? For the first time in her life Amelia knew exactly what she wanted: to raise Franklin's baby. It was a bizarre realization to know that she wanted, no, that she needed to keep this baby. Thinking back, she knew the first moment she saw the pregnancy stick change.

"…And as you know, he died shortly after."

Amelia snapped out of her thoughts. "What? Who died?"

"Mr. Dunne. Shortly after this last draft of his will his doctor diagnosed him with pneumonia. He was ill for several weeks, and during that time he was told to rest and

474

not write. His depression, or what did they call it, melancholia, flared. Newspapers reported with the mysterious disappearance of his wife," Banks gave Amelia a conspiratorial look, "he went into a fast decline."

"When? How long after I—um, I mean how long after he signed the new will did he pass?"

"Not long. A little under two months."

"Oh." Emotion, once again, overtook Amelia. Her heart raced in her chest. It was hard to breathe. Franklin was dead. She reasoned he must be by this present time. Even if he had lived a full life, they would have never met in Amelia's time.

It was not possible for him to live to a hundred and twenty years old, and Franklin couldn't time travel. They had tried it once. One "leap day" as they referred to the last day of the shorter months, Franklin wore the watch to travel into the future with Amelia. It didn't work with him wearing it, or with the watch she had made for him.

Even if she *had* changed her mind, brought the watch with her and tried to return after her frustration died down and her heart healed, he would be gone. No matter what time she chose to live in, she would have to raise this baby by herself. It would be a whole lot easier to raise the baby in this time, she thought. Modern medicine in itself was enough of an inducement. Absently, her hand moved to rest on her stomach, as if to protect the small part of Franklin that still lived.

Once again, Banks' voice brought her back into the room.

"I'm afraid I have one more item to discuss with you, but in your delicate state, I'm afraid you might not be able to take it."

"What would that be, Mr. Banks? My delicate state is on an edge, but if you don't tell me everything, especially after all of this, and I leave here wondering, I don't know if I'll ever sleep. Again."

"Now, now Mrs.—"

"Don't, Mr. Banks, just—"

"I've had to lie to you." He sputtered then wrung his hands. "Your husband was your benefactor. Alexander Frank was a pseudonym... or a reversal of his name. You were, well are, the widow of Franklin Alexander Dunne."

Amelia sat in silence. She looked up at Mr. Banks. "Is that the end of it?"

"Yes."

"No more surprises?"

"Not that I know of." He chuckled then looked at her and saw the uneasy and almost crazed look in her eyes. "No. I was just making a little joke. Absolutely no more surprises." He sighed. "I feel better now that everything's out in the open."

Amelia twiddled her wedding ring.

They sat in silence. Eventually Mr. Banks shifted uneasily before saying, "Do you need more time to think about all of this or do you have questions?"

"I don't have any more questions at this time that you can answer. I'm sure I'll have many in the future, though. I will keep you and your firm on as my council and I will sign whatever documents necessary. Also could you send copies to my address to have on file so I can look them over and hope to…" *reconnect with Franklin* is what she wanted to say, "…to answer any questions that may arise? Unless there are any more hidden surprises I'm not yet to be privy to."

"No my dear, you now know all we know. And of course, we will send over copies. You may call on me at any time with questions. As such a long time client to the firm, you and your family are of high priority and we are willing to assist you at any time as immediately as possible," and he winked at Amelia.

He passed Amelia a pen and pointed to where she needed to sign. With two scribbles, the legalities were squared away. Amelia placed the large box containing her necklace and earrings in her purse. She shook Banks' hand again, and in a fog and walked to the elevator.

The time on her phone read 5:48. She would just make it in time to meet her friends if she flagged a cab.

What an extraordinary day. Franklin was the one looking out for her all along. She sighed and wiped at her eyes. Tears would have to wait. The car was pulling up to the pub, and she didn't want to greet her friends with tear stained cheeks.

***

Amelia couldn't believe how much she had missed Toni and Alexia. This evening made her thankful for friends. Mrs. Finnegan, Emily, and Jon were great friends, too.

Amelia wondered what a dinner party with all her close friends together would be like. Amelia was pretty certain they would all get along well. Jon and Toni, especially with their love of fashion and gossip. Alexia and Mrs. Finnegan would talk about running a business, and Emily would enthrall them all with her stories. Supportive friends found her in whatever life she was living, and she was grateful for that blessing.

Amelia wasn't sure how much to reveal of all of the things that had happened in the past year to her two closest friends. They chatted for fifteen minutes, and she realized that it would be more difficult to steer around the truth than to actually reveal what had happened, irrational and unbelievable as it might be. It was a risk. They might not want anything to do with her. The story was so far-fetched, but Amelia didn't know what else to do.

In the end, Amelia decided to tell them the story of the past year. She told them about finding the watch and the mysterious jeweler. The first time to the past, and how she was sure she was stranded intrigued Toni, and even more so when Amelia revealed the embarrassment of having slept with Franklin the first night there because she thought the sex was a dream. At first her friends laughed and interjected. Then it turned to humming sounds, and then they both fell silent. Amelia didn't didn't know if they believed her or not. Amelia was just about to finish the story. She was at the part where she and Franklin had just gotten into their last big fight and had dropped the watch to return to the future only to find she was pregnant, when the waitress returned to take their dinner orders.

Although she was caught unawares with the appearance of the waitress, Amelia ordered immediately, wanting to finish the story. The other two seemed to take forever to make dinner selections, Amelia sat back with as much patience as she could muster. She tried to remain calm and not anticipate their reactions. Neither had said anything or made any sort of sound for a while.

The waitress left, and Amelia looked both of her friends in the eyes. She finished the story and revealed she was pregnant. Alexia and Toni then turned to give each other a look, and then Toni shrugged. They both looked back at Amelia.

"I can't believe I'm saying this," said Alexia, looking back and forth between Toni and Amelia, "but I totally believe every word."

"Me too," chimed Toni almost immediately. "What was it like? The clothes? The city? Was it a lot like *Kate and Leopold*? I love Hugh Jackman in that movie—was your guy, um what was his name, Frank—was he like Hugh Jackman?" Toni asked earnestly.

"Hush, Toni, you're making her cry!" said Alexia.

Amelia reached a hand up to her cheek. She didn't even feel the tears start to form, let alone fall.

"Wow. I never realized how much courage you had, Meel," said Toni as she gave comforting strokes to Amelia's head, now cradled into her.

Amelia let out a half cry, half laugh.

"You know, I have no idea where it came from."

"I can't believe you just got up and walked away like that. Not many women can slam the door shut on a man that they are in love with," said Alexia still holding Amelia's hand.

"That is also surprising. I was so angry at him. He refused to choose me, and he wouldn't fight for himself. I loved him—no, I love him still, so very much. But it didn't matter. And even if I had chosen to go back, he would have been dead before I could get back to him. I don't know what would have happened if I stayed." She shrugged, the realization sinking in. "There is no way of knowing," Amelia said, more to herself than to her two friends. "And, if he hadn't died—." Amelia took the tissue and blew her nose. She straightened her shoulders. She looked back and forth between her friends. "I'm not crazy for wanting to keep my baby, am I?" she asked.

"No!" they both chorused together in a wave of comfort.

Amelia laughed with relief. She knew with her friends beside her, she would be able to get through all of this.

Conversation moved to Alexia. Dinner arrived while they were discussing her new promotion at the office. Then they talked about Toni's upcoming wedding.

"I will have to rethink the bridesmaid dresses now. In five months you shouldn't be showing that much, but I still want the dress to be flattering on you. Pictures are forever," Toni said looking at Amelia who returned the look with a smile.

"And of course she's picking a color that will look perfect on us all and a style we will be able to wear again," chirped Alexia sarcastically.

"Shut up," Toni playfully bantered back.

"Oh my god! The dress is *gold*, Amelia. GOLD. I'm gonna look like a girl version of Elvis," said Alexia.

"I wanted you to look like a Bond girl," Toni said back with a tiny trace of a whine.

"Well, it is her wedding," Amelia intervened, "but, Toni, please don't put a fat, pregnant woman in a gold lamé dress in August. It's just not right. Could we do a nice mellowed copper or a non-shiny, darker gold?"

"Ugh. You guys have no fashion sense. But fine," Toni said as they were all hugging goodbye. "I'll rethink the color."

***

As she walked up the steps to her brownstone, Amelia looked up at the sky as a single tear fell. She summoned courage. Amelia experienced this past year, but she had the feeling that it was her life to come that was going to be the greater adventure. She took another deep breath as a breeze whipped up. She closed her eyes and felt the wind on her cheek.

Amelia thrilled at the wonder of her life. She had great supportive friends who knew all of her secrets and believed her. Most importantly, she was going to be a mother. Amelia took another deep breath and put the key into the lock of the house that would shelter her for the rest of her life.

Epilogue

For the first few weeks of her pregnancy, Amelia threw herself into anything she did. She ran every day. She read obsessively about being an expectant mother. The contractor was assigned a firm deadline, the house had to be completed in four months. It would cost more, but she wanted to have serenity before the baby came, and she didn't want this project looming into winter.

Amelia realized how much she missed things like her cell phone, hot showers, and the Internet. She spent many hours luxuriously abusing these amenities. However, her need for technology waned. She would leave her cell on her nightstand only checking it twice a day. She had to renew the landline phone service because the contractor complained about not being able to reach her on her cell phone. There were only so many hours a day she could troll the Internet. Social media lost its appeal once she had caught up on news from friends and colleagues. Showers, however, with all the running water she wanted was a love she wouldn't give up, and she took at least one a day.

As the house was nearing completion, Amelia found she had less to do. Boredom and thoughts of Franklin led her to search for all of his works. Through her searching, she found a collection of leather bound copies before she was able to track down all of the first editions. She found a third complete set at a rare book shop in Park Slope. They were well loved, and not in the best of shape, but after sending them to a bookbinder, they were just what she needed to use to read. While the set of first editions and the rare leather bound set lived in the library, this used set lived in Amelia's bedroom, and it became her habit to read every night before bed.

The remodel of the house went at a faster pace than estimated. Amelia kept the fireplace exactly as it was. Maybe it was the memory of her other life, or maybe because it just seemed to make the room work. She had the mantle replaced as well as the moldering bricks. She made sure that the one brick stayed loose. It was silly, hanging onto the past, but it seemed cruel to cement that final brick.

Hoping to find something upon her return, she had looked behind the brick weeks ago. There was nothing there. Absently she thought about it from time to time, but Amelia never looked behind the brick again. Maybe she didn't want to find it empty or if something was there she didn't know what to do with whatever she might find. Most likely, she never looked because she knew her future lay in front of her.

Three and a half months after her return, the house was finished. Amelia hired a photographer to take professional pictures of the remodel. Luckily, she had taken some amateur photos of the mess it was when she and her friends made their initial visit after she inherited. With the before and after photos of her house, she created a website and applied for a business license for an interior design company called Dunne Designs. Her contractor suggested her to two of his clients and she began work on rooms for both of them. From there word of mouth spread, and Amelia's career launched.

Dinners and lunches with the girls became a regular thing. After the house was finished, sometimes the ladies would even have sleepovers at Amelia's, because Toni and Alexia loved having their own bed and breakfast in Brooklyn.

Amelia turned her room from Franklin's time into a beautiful guest room. She made the smaller room that was across from hers, into a nursery.

Busy with the remodel, her new business, reconnection with friends, and planning for Toni's wedding; Amelia's uncomplicated pregnancy went by in a flash.

In the eighth month after returning, on September 30, 2013, it was recorded that Alexander Franklin Dunne was born to a widowed Amelia Dunne in Brooklyn Hospital. Amelia had legally changed her name with the help of Mr. Banks. The day she signed the paperwork, Franklin's voice rang in her ear. "Come along, Mrs. Dunne," he had said, and it had always seemed to fit, as if the name had always belonged to her.

***

After the baby was born, Amelia worked from home. There was plenty of room in the huge house, and she could take care of Alexander while she continued to work. She had never been happier. Word of mouth spread quickly. Amelia was a popular designer because she gave people what they wanted and was good at finding cost effective ways to make their dreams come true. She never pushed her own design agenda on her clients; she didn't need to. Her clients trusted her and she was reliable. Before long she was booked two years in advance.

Her friends thrived, too. Toni's wedding was beautiful and Amelia stood at her side in a simple black bridesmaid dress with gold accents. Alexia got promoted again and again, and eventually started her own company. Missing her other friends, Amelia did research through ancestry companies and found Mrs. Finnegan passed away a few years after Franklin. When Amelia found this out she thought that since Finnegan had raised Franklin, her days of service were over when he was gone. Emily was difficult to trace, as not many people made mention of servants in household documentation. It wasn't until research on Jon that she found Emily.

Jon hired Emily to help with sewing and basic needs after serving the Dunne house. Eventually she was made a head designer in the 1940s for Caruthers Couture House.

Jon passed away in 1952 and Emily in 1953. It was very satisfying to find her friends, but it was unsettling to know that people who had touched her life in great ways had passed away before she was even born.

***

Alexander Franklin Dunne grew up to be a strong, healthy, and very imaginative young man. Yearly, Amelia would take him for a ride out to Far Rockaway to visit a gravestone. Alex, as he was called, made no connection of his relationship to the stone other than he would regularly say, "Mommy, that man had two of my names."

To which Amelia replied, "Yes, darling. You were named for that man."

She knew one day she would have to explain who the headstone actually belonged.

When Alex was in high school, a writer for The New York Magazine did a series of pieces on influential New York writers, and Franklin was the subject of one. The reporter found Amelia and asked to interview her because of her last name, and what he assumed was a distant relation to the writer. Amelia simply confirmed he was a relation and had heard he was a brilliant but depressed man. Creative and driven to a fault.

The author of the magazine article wrote in the published article, "Mrs. Dunne, unsure of her relation to author Franklin Dunne, as it was her dead husband's relation, seemed wistful when speaking about the author. It was almost as if she wished to meet the author himself."

The article also uncovered the incredible coincidence that both his interviewee and the wife of Franklin Dunne, were both named Amelia.

Upon its publication, Amelia was worried someone would uncover the truth, inconceivable as it might be. But no reader derived a conclusion and no stranger asked about Franklin again.

***

Alex was a happy baby and a great kid. Amelia had a very easy time raising him. Early on, he showed potential as a writer. He also was fascinated with science fiction, science, and time travel. He loved *Star Trek* and *Doctor Who*. At first he had some difficulties in school, but his 4th grade English teacher, Mrs. Mee, encouraged him to write. From then his creativity flourished. He wrote in any spare minute on anything resembling paper. Amelia was not surprised when in high school he showed interest in Franklin's books and he even asked if he could read one. He read all of his fathers books in a month after that. It was not a surprise when Alex declared himself a creative writing major in college.

He would come home from semesters in college having written so much. Alex wrote and wrote about anything and everything and in any form he could. He was always in the middle of a book or novella; he wrote articles for the school newspaper; he even had written a few screenplays after encouragement from a   film major friend. At first, he wouldn't let Amelia read them.   Saying they weren't finished or it wasn't his best work. She had, of course, snuck a peek when he wasn't nearby.

Then his sophomore year he mailed home a thick package of work for her to read. Next she heard college was publishing him in a book of short stories. When he came home for Christmas, he had news that the friend in the theater department had made two of his works into films. The following summer, Alex had an internship with a film company in Los Angeles.

Alex finished college with rising success. The summer after he graduated, he came home to the house on Polhemus Place and took over the study. Amelia had remodeled it so it was still masculine, but had a contemporary airiness. However, even after she had put her own touches on it, she couldn't escape the loss of Franklin. It seemed like every time she entered the room, one of their fiery conversations, most times the last conversation they ever had, would fill her mind. Therefore, she converted the front room, which was formerly the library and used that as the office for Dunne Designs. It was also more convenient to entertain customers there as it was just off the front hallway, and it had great views of the street.

Amelia was not bothered when Alex took over the study. Her son's reign in the room was much like that of his father. Alex never showed much moodiness before, but became sullen and anxious at times if he was spending too many hours alone in the study. Amelia did her best to draw him out of the room at times like these. He never fell into the great depths of depression like Franklin would, but

Amelia was going to work diligently to ensure that Alex would not go the way of his father.

***

Alex thrived when he worked in the study. Something about the feel of the space that made creativity flow through him. There were moments he couldn't type fast enough to keep up with his flow of ideas. Occasionally he scribbled notes on papers beside his computer. But the papers scattered or built up or the notes were illegible. It was unnerving.

Amazing thoughts shoving at each other like teenage football players through a doorway around his brain. If he didn't get them out onto his computer or on a piece of paper, he *knew* he would lose them.

At times, he would lose control tearing up sheets of paper in anger, throwing things across the room, while yelling and screaming. His mind was offering these beautiful, amazing thoughts and ideas and his body was infallible and couldn't keep up.

One of the days he felt blocked, Alex threw himself up from the desk knocking the desk chair over. What he wanted to say just hadn't translated to the page. He picked up the entire manuscript and flung it with a growl of frustration. Like fall leaves in a light breeze, they fluttered all over the room. After the papers settled, he relaxed his clenched fists and laughed at his ridiculous outburst. Resigned, he picked up every scattered sheet. Moaning inwardly after collecting them all, he now had to reorganize it. Maybe it would just be better to chuck them all into the fire and start over, he thought. Why didn't he write page numbers, he scolded himself? He flopped the pile down on the desk, and righted the chair and sighed as he sat. After a few moments of rubbing his temples trying to find inspiration or momentum, he sat up squaring his shoulders. A bit of white caught his eye. One of the papers had somehow landed on the fireplace mantle. Perplexed at the far distance the sheet made, Alex tilted his head to make sure he wasn't just imagining it. It was easily ten feet away from where he had stood to toss the pages out at the room.

Alex stood and cautiously stalked the resting piece of paper, as if doing his best not to frighten it. As he neared the page, he realized it was the one he scribbled an idea down about time travel. It was a plot that just wouldn't work. Snatching the paper, he started to crumple the page. Alex looked up at the mantle. His mother had redone almost everything in this house the year he was born. The brick wall looked seamless from a distance, however, a slightly protruding brick caught his eye.

As if by reflex, Alex reached out to the brick, placed his fingers around it, and gave it a tug. His fingers slipped off of it, but it moved, so he wiggled it back and forth. His crumpled notes fell from his hand as he raised his other hand to the brick and levered it out of it's hidden spot. Feeling a bit of surprise when came out of the wall, Alex looked around feeling he wasn't alone. After confirming he was still alone in the room he placed the brick on the floor. His mother would kill him if he scratched anything with a

brick.   He stood on his tiptoes—his 5'9" was not tall
enough to see directly into the recesses of where the brick
was. At first glance he saw nothing, but squinting he saw
something inside at the very back. Alex reached in and felt
a folded paper and a small and soft thing. He pulled both
out. He set the soft, velvet jewelry pouch aside and opened
the paper.

Alex could tell the paper was old, but its creases and
pristine appearance told Alex that he was the first person to
find it. He wondered why his mother put it here—it *had* to
be his mother, with the way she oversaw all design projects
and details, she had to know about the loose brick.

Intrigued, Alex paced to his desk and looked around the
room again once more, as he felt he was being watched.
Once again he acknowledged he was completely alone. So,
he opened the paper and found a letter.

My Dear Amelia,

*I am at a loss. It has been a month since you left us, left
me. I don't know what to do without you. I can't write, eat,
sleep. It is as if you took the very breath from my life when
you traveled back to your own time. My heart feels as if it
has left my chest. That my very soul left with you.*

*Apologies are necessary and mostly from me.   "I'm
sorry" in a letter seems formal and cowardly. Those words
don't even begin to repair what occurred between us.
Please come home to me so I can begin to make amends. I
will dedicate the rest of my life to make it up to you for all
the idiotic things I did and said.*

I am not the only one who misses you. Your Mr. Caruthers asks about you and has sent around several cards. Emily and Mrs. Finnegan are distraught. I told them you had gone back to Philadelphia to be with your aunt. Mrs. Finnegan told me, scolded me actually, for letting a pregnant woman travel (if she only knew to where you actually traveled.) Amelia, is it true? Are you pregnant? If you are, I was an idiot to not realize it. I was so consumed in myself that I just couldn't see anything. All the more reason for you to return. Please come home so we can raise our child together, so I can take care of you as I promised. I'll get the help. I'll try harder. I'll do anything. Please just come back.

I hope this reaches you. You mentioned that you were thinking about rebuilding this fireplace in your time. I hope to God you didn't seal up this brick. Hopefully, the watch will make it to you as well. You know how to use it. I hope to see you on the first of May. Please turn the pin and come back to me.

You must know how I felt about you, how I feel about you still. Amelia, you are the most beautiful creature I have ever seen, ever shared breath with. I am lost without you. From the very first moment I saw you scolding me in the hallway in nothing but your knickers and skirts, I knew I was in love with you. I am as in love with you now. I will forever be in love with you. Please Amelia, I beg of you, use the watch and return to me.

Your loving husband,
Franklin

Alex set the letter on top of the mess on the desk. He opened the small pouch and tipped it to pour out it's contents. A delicate watch glinted in his hand. He sat back in the chair. The watch hands weren't moving. Twiddling with the pin, he pulled it out and started to twist it. It was the first of May, so he might as well set the date right. The lights flickered.

***

Amelia knocked on the study door, looking for Alex for dinner. A distant memory danced across her brain of this same action in the past. After Alex didn't answer, she let herself in, but didn't see him. Noticing the mess on the desk, she crossed the room and sighed. He would have to clean it up himself. She refused to give in during these tantrums. Amelia noticed the papers sitting on top that were creased. It was signed by Franklin. Amelia rounded the desk as she picked up the letter and fell into the chair as she read. When she was finished reading it and tears were streaming down her face she noticed the velvet pouch from her watch sat on the desk. And it was empty.

She reached for Alex's pen and a blank sheet of paper.

***

Dear Franklin,

I miss you. I don't know why I'm writing this because you will never see it. The chances of me ever seeing you

494

again are almost non-existent, but then, our original meeting should never have happened, so there is always a chance.

I dream of walking along the street and seeing you walk toward me. Sometimes I'm angry at you. Sometimes I'm stunned. Sometimes you take my face in your hands and kiss me and the world stops. Sometimes I tell you exactly what I feel. The only consistent thing is that we don't walk off together.

There are times when I go for days without thinking of you and then I walk into the room and your memory is sitting there, waiting.

I'm reading a book where everyone is in love with the wrong person and no one ends up happy. As I read thoughts of you seep in. I am continually perplexed by this. We didn't have much time together. I am now, and was before meeting you, an independent woman.

Why do you repeatedly haunt me? There are so many things left unanswered. The way I left. The way things were between us when…

Maybe it's lack of answers that leave me wanting, needing you. Maybe it's because I didn't say good-bye. I think of our time together, and I wonder of things I wanted to say but didn't; moments I didn't kiss you when I wanted to; seeing your face that last time and wanting to call out to you, to hold you.

My heart is broken, and after all these years, refuses to heal. Something about this pain is different. I'm healing, but I will never heal completely. I think my heart wants to hold a place for you.

I again think about why I'm actually writing this letter. I know it is for me and not for you. I cannot make you understand or feel the things I do, through this letter or through time.

I love you, Franklin. I always will in some way. I know that I will never understand anything that happened. I can only know how deeply I felt and hope you felt the same.

I need you to go. I need you to leave my mind. I need your memory to cease being so important. I need to stop hurting at your memory. My dearest Franklin, I hate to write this, I need you to disappear—which I realize is ironic, because I was the one who disappeared. This haunting needs to stop. We were not good for each other. We had a moment in time. That is all we were supposed to have. Wanting more is irrational, selfish, and detrimental. Please let me go.

~~Yours,~~
~~Love,~~
~~Sincerely,~~
Goodbye,
Amelia

***

Dear Amelia,

I received your letter today. Your son, our son, brought it. He looks so much like you. I am thrilled to have met

496

him. You raised a wonderful young man. I wish I had helped in raising him, but I will see to it his well-being will be taken care of. He says he is a writer, too. Something he calls screenplays, he tells me that in the future they are very important, and can be fantastical. In fact, the more fantastical, the better.

He doesn't tell me much about you. This is his second time to see me; although the first time here he told me he was a student and wanted to study the technique of writing I use. Deep down I thought I recognized something in him during his first visit, but was enchanted by his youth and vigor, that I myself felt excited about writing again, and was distracted by it all until our two month internship ended with his disappearance.

I have written you many letters, one a day. I'm sure you now know that I wrote to you. I wrote your story, our story, and of time travel. It has had a thrilling response in the first printing and my publisher wrote that the second reprint would be double. I did it, Amelia. I became something because of you. The time I had with you made me a better writer. A better man.

There is no easy way to say this, but I am dying. This isn't great news as where you are I'm already dead. I know that is how you got the house and the watch. My love, I am not scared. I have written a brilliant story and I have loved truly and deeply. What can a man such as me ask for else?

I love you, my darling, although I didn't show it enough. I thought you would be around forever. I thought we had all the time in the world. But even if you had stayed, we wouldn't have had much time. I was two minutes too late to stop you—although I suspect you would have left that night even if I had been there an hour sooner.

I am sorry for the pain I cause you.

You are an amazing woman. Much stronger and smarter than I. Our son tells me that you continue to wear the ring I gave you. Please continue to wear it. Our son tells me that you never married, and that there were men that came around, but you never chose one. And that if asked, you tell people that you were widowed. I guess it is the truth, although not on the timeline that most would agree on.

As your dying husband should vow, I will love you until the end of my days, which, with every cough, I am reminded comes sooner than expected. Although our son has told me what was recorded of my death that I died of an incurable disease. But I know that it is my regret and shame I have carried from the day I let you go that actually killed me.

I want to write more, as you deserve explanations, apologies, overtures of love. But the writer has run out of words, and I fear I have only three left. So, my darling, my dear: I love you. Watch over our son, and make sure when it is time he inherits the house. Our house. It is nowhere near enough, but it is all that I have. I will love you. Forever.

Your husband,
Franklin

Amelia dashed to the study with the absently crushing the letter in her hand. A flicker in her brain drove her to the bookshelf.

"Mom, what's wrong?" Alex called after her.

Amelia barely heard him, her brain pounded. She knew she had seen it when it first arrived and she remembered being puzzled at its appearance. It had to be here. It *had* to be. She ran her fingers over the spines of her collection of first editions. Franklin title's had been her foray into collecting, but after a while she had started to collect more than just his work. Her collection, nearly one hundred and fifty antique books, including a beautiful *Moby Dick*, a complete Jane Austen collection, and of course, to spite Franklin, *Wuthering Heights*. They were in no particular order, except with books from general time periods grouped together.

Finally, her finger touched the spine she was looking for. As if it were an electric socket, she felt a bodily shock from the book. Amelia pulled the book from the shelf and gently caressed its cover. She turned it over in her hands to open it. The spine cracked as the cover gave way to the blotter page. Gently she turned it to reveal the dedication page. It said: to my lovely wife Amelia and our son Alexander. She sighed and turned to the title page. Amelia smiled and read the title aloud *"The Time Turner."*

The End

Acknowledgements

To you the reader, thank you for picking up this book, and either flipping to this page, or reading all the way to the end. A labor of love, this book was born from working through a broken heart and doing Daily Pages from *The Artists Way*. I found myself journaling daily and got tired of complaining about a recent breakup. So, I started to write him letters, which evolved into writing chapters. I found myself addicted to forming this story. I wrote on the subway on the way to work, on my way home, until I passed out at night. I wrote in any waking moment that the muse struck. Although this book is not autobiographical, the heartache is true. So, wherever you are, guy-who-hurt-me, thank you for the inspiration.

First I want to thank those people who always told me to "just keep going" or "when is it going to be done so we can read it?" or "I'm so proud of you." Susan Edyburn, Jon Sparks, Kevin Graham, Angie Atkinson, Grace Bennett, Joshua Jordan, Renee Tatum, Lecinda Bennett, Jessie Larson, Nicole Anderson, Melissa Mendoza, MaryKate Licul, Shanna Ossi, Jess Hendricks, Chrissy Sheehan, Derrick Diazoni, Alexandra Roth, Michelle Bruner, and Michael Keeney--there is a little nod to each of you in these pages. And to Erin Vivero, TiMothy Belliveau, Jessica Nevins and the rest of my cozy Connecticut family, thank you for being my sanity.

A big thanks to my two life cheerleaders: Leslie Farinacci and Lesley Logan-Crowell both who helped with the first edition art.

A HUGE smooch and thank you to all who contributed to the crowd funding project that helped to foot the bill for this book: Jamie Damaso, Kristin Vredevoogd, Paula Rossman, Jessica Clements, Sandy McKnight, Mandy Decker, Joshua Jordan, Eweleen Good, Maggie Howell, Jenny Hoofnagle, Diane Southworth, Gaye Berger, Brad Siroky, Pierre dePerez, Nakisa Aschtiani, Tatum Kenney, Christina Sagnimeni, Garrett Deagon, Edward Chamberlain, Wendy Larson, Emily Gallagher, AmberRose Dische, Justin Waggle, Jon Sparks, Judith Bradshaw, Erin Nelsen, Jill Kolodzieski, James Vaughn, Tammy DeLeon, Faith Bowen, Susan Hallman, Abby T, Greer Lawson, Melissa Fite Johnson, Kobus Nolte, Jill Kasner, and Melisa Cole.

Thank you to my social media goddess, Rebecca Woodman Taylor.

Thank you to anyone who called, texted, emailed, or sat down with me over the past few years who asked me anything about this project, and listened with encouragement: you kept me going!

And to my Momma—here is your first grandchild.

If you enjoyed this book, please encourage your friends to read it! Review it on the website you purchased it, and on Goodreads! Connect with me by joining The Time Turner Facebook page at https://www.facebook.com/timeturnernovel/

Thank you!

Second Edition Note

When hard things are in process, we're always saying "this is the hardest thing I've ever had to do"…and I don't know if editing this book for this second edition was that hard, but it was like looking at video of myself ten years ago and watching in slow motion the stupid things I did. Also editing yourself is just plum hard. If I could write without editing, that would be a lotto I would sign up for.

That said, I'm republishing this book because it is my first baby and it took a lot, then and now to get her out into the world. Is she perfect? Not even close, but then nothing really is. It is a dream of mine for someone to come along and option the bones of this story and give it another life, because the story is so good, but I don't know that I did it enough justice, and there is only so much a one-woman-team can fix.

Also, I've had so many people over the years tell me that their dream is to write a book. If I give out one piece of advice more than anything, it's "go write your book. Just do it, even if you think it's a story we have all heard, it's your version of the story, and there is a reader (or a million of them, fingers crossed) who want to read it. People will always want stories to read.

That said, I echo what I said in the first thank you, as it is the most important thanks of all, thank you dear reader for picking up this book, flaws and all. Thank you from the bottom of my heart (both from now and ten years ago when I needed a life line to pull myself out of the Franklin-esque depression I found myself in.)

Xoxo, *Clare*

More About Clare Solly

Clare Solly is a modern day Renaissance woman living in New York City. She is an actress, a writer, and by day an executive assistant among many other things. Clare has a Masters Degree in Psychology with a focus on nonprofit management.

Many crowns live in her apartment including the one that accompanies the title of America's National Elite Natural Queen 2022. At the date of this publication, Clare has published another book *Christmas and Cleats* but more are to come. Clare loves to do anything creative and crafty, and can get lost in a puzzle or a book. She loves to cook and bake and is a bit of a seltzer addict. A believer that a cup of coffee makes morning better, she also thinks that bacon is better when it's crispy, and pineapple does belong on pizza.

In addition to writing, Clare runs two different theatre companies in NYC: The Bechdel Group and Company of Fools Theatre where she loves to foster and challenge new writers.

Feel free to find her on Instagram @actinglikeclare or email at claresollyauthor@gmail.com.

Made in the USA
Middletown, DE
04 December 2025